ROBIN CHAPM...

The
SECRET
of the
WORLD

D0101588

SINCLAIR-STEVENSON

First published in Great Britain in 1997
by Sinclair-Stevenson
an imprint of Reed International Books Ltd
Michelin House, 81 Fulham Road, London SW3 6RB
and Auckland, Melbourne, Singapore and Toronto

Copyright © 1997 by Robin Chapman

The right of Robin Chapman to be identified as author of
this work has been asserted by him in accordance with
the Copyright, Designs and Patents Act 1988.

A CIP catalogue record for this book
is available at the British Library
ISBN 1 85619 262 8

Typeset in 11.5 on 12.6 point Baskerville
by Deltatype, Birkenhead, Merseyside
Printed and bound in Great Britain
by Clays Ltd, St Ives plc

For Boo and Harry

'If his dream last he'll turn the age to gold.'
Ben Jonson

'The highest comes from the lowest
and the lowest from the highest.'
Hermes Trismegistos

'The world loves to be deceived.'
Isaac Newton

☿

For this while I am at an inferior conjunction as I pass between the sun and the earth. But soon I shall be seen for what I am: a morning object gloriously visible to mortal eyes. None other than Mercury himself.

At a mundane level, however, things are different. There I'm little more than a sparkling vapour a-drift among the orchards of Manhattan or the backwoods of the Bronx. Some have reported glimpsing me as Will o' the Wisp; others claim, equally erroneously, that I'm the ghost of that old terror, Governor Stuyvesant. I've even been rumoured to haunt the Broadway trail but this is not so – that path is overtrod by too many restless spirits. But I do – when love moves me – slip beneath the doors of the hospital called Jerusalem to visit Sally. There she lies quite lost to the world.

The Algonquin have come to accept me. They smile, and all the children laugh, when, emanating among them I tease the women while wreathing their warriors in a silvery fume not unlike their own tobacco smoke. In their primordial wisdom they call me correctly the messenger without a message.

The citizens of the town (all now rich beyond even a Hollander's dream of avarice) maintain that I frequent the Gentlemen's Canal. Again not so. Though when corporeal I used to piss in it. No, I'm more likely to be seen beside the windmill, or among the graves set about St Nicholas's Church or floating along Pearl Street on my way to comb the beach beyond. Whenever there's a decent moon I snuffle there, hoping to uncover some evidence of Rusty: one of his teeth perhaps, or even his whole skull.

Sometimes I'm tempted to blame Rusty. At others to bless him. Yet neither inclination is appropriate. Some events are ordered by fate. Our simultaneous combustion was. Of that I have no doubt at all. Every constituent was in place – in the heavens above and upon the earth below. Rusty's violent intervention, although purely instinctive to him, and quite unlooked-for by me, but not by Sally, was nevertheless perfectly preordinate.

1

I admit Sally and I deceived him. But there again we were not at liberty to act out of our characters any more than he was: gods are constrained to be themselves quite as much as people, quite as much as elements. After all, it is the quality of quicksilver to slip and slide, for copper to be easily worked and iron to be hard. The same goes for Mercury, Venus, Mars. If we, of all creation, cannot be mercurial, venereal, martial, who can?

My searches on the shoreline for some relic of Rusty are of a conciliatory nature. I wish to make my peace with him or, at least, assuage his angry spirit by giving his bones – if any there be – some decent place of rest. For it was he who took the brunt of the explosion which blasted Pearl Street, vapourised me and seared Sally beyond recognition. But this mission is, I fear, in vain. Rusty must be ashes at least, cinders at best, fit only to bed down the footings of the future. For, thanks to him, it has become the practice here to extend the shoreline by close-packing the waterfront with garbage enclosed in wooden cribs as a site for new building. Already the citizens boast they are grown tall out of their own ordure.

Since our eruption the town burgeons. New York is rebuilding even faster than Old London did after the great fire of '66 – a catastrophe I observed in the company of no less a natural philosopher than Mr Isaac Newton. Already streets and houses are spreading beyond the Wall into the Boweries. And Pearl Street where we prospered so famously has become a highway at one remove from the East River.

The enterprises we established there are no more. The three houses that contained them were razed to the ground. In their place stands a brand-new banking house built of stone. It is plain, solid, and of a truly grim proportion. Its vaults are stacked with gold. The gold we made: Rusty, Sally and I, not forgetting Mr Newton.

The gold held there is known as the nation's reserve and it is believed to be the foundation of the New World's economic order. But be that as it may, my greatest satisfaction resides in the thought that owing to my experiments in my laboratory (below Sally's whorehouse) I have proved my mentor, Mr Newton, right. Since it was he who – oh, forgive me, here's Great Sol rising in majesty again. I must evaporate anew.

♂

Stuck out in the cold, that's me. Way, way out. And am I still seeing red? You bet your sweet life I am. My bones may be deep in shit on

West Side – why evil Enoch keeps looking for 'em below Pearl Street I do not know – do not ask me, squire! – but like he's got it wrong again. That slimy two-faced son of a bitch was never so much your crafty cunning man, more a right cunny. But be that as it may the fact is your essence of Ironside – *me* – the Cockney captain you can trust, Rusty to some but not to all, oh, no, is way out here, back in his old orbit among the other frigging cast-off spheres. Another victim of the big bang. And he does not care for it at all. No, sir! God's light, it's fucking freezing!

Every so often, like when we coincide, I sneak a glance across to Earth. Just a quick gander, a sharp butcher's, a swift dekko for old times' sake. The place looks much the same – you know, lumpsa cloud, loadsa sea, a nice spread of *terra firma*. A most welcome sight really. A pleasing eyeful. God's truth, what I'd give to be back there – down and around, alive and kicking, sorta human, in dear old London Town. Or even New York. Though that was a real hell-hole when we was first there. Like it was the fundament of the known world, right? Jesus Christ, it was horrible. Your original tight-fisted, tight-arsed Dutch burgh. Well, ex-Dutch actually. 'Cos like we'd just conquered it again, hadn't we? Still, Sally, me and Enoch, we soon got the joint loosened up and dancing to our tune. And made our fortunes all over again. Talk about history repeating itself – it went ape-shit!

Our recipe for success was much the same as it been back in '69 at London on dear old Pudding Wharf except for one thing. Like there, in them days, Enoch, the Alchemical Genius, had his laboratory next door to our pussy palace, whereas at New York on Pearl Street it was bang underneath. Yer what, mac? You don't know what I mean by *pussy palace*? Where you bin, matey? Right. In common or garden New World-ese I am referring to Sally's bordello or sporting house. Or in plain old English – knocking shop. Yeah, Sal ran it while I pulled in the flesh for her to flog. Like sell, right?

Of course at that time New York wasn't much more than a one-pot entrepot. But it did have pretensions. Oh, yeah. Places, like people, all want to better themselves, don't they? After all, even the cullies I used to take for their last frigging dollar was as much after advancement as me. How else came they to get chiselled? Mind you, they operated on trust while me, I've never done nothing except on must.

Sally's house at London was nice. Run on naughty convent lines – know what I mean? But at New York we went up-market. Was we hoity-toity! Jeez! We was the most exclusive establishment in town what wiv our dancing virgins, our discreet boudoirs for the more discerning pillars of society, not to mention cards and dice or my bank next door known as The Golden Fleece.

Nor was that all neither. No, sir. Like I was big in waste disposal, hog-racing and even rent-boys. Furthermore I was on the town council. How about that? I'll tell yer – I was so on the up I was up for mayor. Me. Rusty Ironside! Mayor of New York! In fact I'd just been elected by a landslide when Enoch – but words ever fail me when I think what that bastard did. And Sally. Oh, yeah, she was in on it, too. Whatta carve up, nay, double cross. God's cods, I'm seeing red again. Like my choler keeps recurring.

Anyway suffice it to say the moolah was flowing in and we was seemingly in clover, right? We couldn't put a foot wrong not on Pearl Street, not nowhere. Money had smelt cunny and cunny money and money power and power yet more power wiv yet more cunny attached. What's more, I was about to become a father. Like my French lady-friend was on the point of producing 'Ercule, wouldya believe?

But in the event – if I had eyes tears would spring to 'em – when it came to the crunch that poor little bastard got blasted heavenwards wiv the rest of us. Know why? Because I went critical. Oh, yeah. Bellicose. Like I bust up Enoch's frigging alchemical machine – his triple glass – wiv a dirty great . . . Oh, Christ, here they come again wiv another loada garbage. Horse manure this time. From my racing stables as was. So like by rights it's all mine, really. But what can I do about that now? Now my earthly parts are just old bones? Well, I dare say I better shut my fleshless gob for a start. Or else. Know what I mean? 'Course you do. Be good, box clever, see ya!

They tell me I've become a star. 'Dear Sally,' they say, 'you're reborn.' I wish I could believe them. I'd like to. I'd love to see myself – me, Sally Greensmith, late of the Old World and the New – riding the heavens in the company of the moon like they say I do.

According to them, my two fellas, I mean, the one known as Enoch Powys, the other as Rusty Ironside, I'm the goddess Venus herself. They say I rise before dawn out of Long Island's surf and there I am shining in glory beside the setting moon. The pair of us shed our light upon the brave homesteads of New England. Our beams, together with those of the rising sun, turn thatch into gold, ploughshares to silver, earthenware to pewter.

But that's only their talk. They say it to comfort me. Enoch drifts in here like a ghost just to be near. Yet all he can see is a lump of human clay swaddled from head to foot in muslin bands. The nurses say there isn't one bit of me that wasn't scorched. When they remove these cloths my scars will blaze like beaten copper. God alone knows what sort of fright I'll look once I'm healed at last and can walk abroad. I expect I'll dismay people. Sour milk in the breast. Scare the turkeys. And I'm sure the natives will vanish at my approach.

When I dream of him Rusty disagrees with me. But then he was always argumentative. He says, or rather the loose teeth in his skull chatter while every bone rattles – Rusty never seems to have any flesh on him now, not since he blew us all up – he says I'm going to be as gorgeous as ever I was. The ideal bedmate once again. The warrior's fancy. Cupid's mum.

Enoch says much the same except he puts it more poetically. He insists – oh, that insidious Welsh whisper of his! – I shall once again walk on earth as Love's perfection, Beauty's self, Pleasure's proof.

But that's enough of now. What about then? Since to understand the present we must ever recall the past. Another saying of Enoch. Still we may as well start with him. With my meeting him, I mean, back in the Old World, back in '69. He says our conjunction was figured in the stars and that we were fated to tread Life's road together.

First off I took him for a bare-arsed tinker. Or else just another scapegrace divine. Or was he some poor scholar thrust out of his college? The city of Oxford was but a step away. From the look of the old pack at his back, his mildewed gown torn to dancing ribbons and his worn-down clogs he could have been any of these.

He had kept ahead of me for a good hour. Was he, I wondered, making like me, for the Whispering Men? Some twelve paces later I got my answer, for of a sudden he broke his stride, turned to the stile and, coming to it, gazed intently upon the stones.

It's a pretty circle out of ancient times. Hell's teeth the preachers tell us they are, thumping their tubs. They say they're wicked. Pagan. But I don't. And folks roundabout don't. In these parts we know a fey place when we see one and trust to the old magic. To me these stones are like family. A ring of grandads. Grey, fond, not so upright as they were nor so tall yet glad to do a day's turn. As a green girl I reckoned the smaller stones among them to be the old boys' sheep or nanny goats. And one I made sure was their dog. It has a sharp-eyed, crouching air. From all of which you may rightly guess I was born and bred close by. And fled here when my family irked me. Which was often. But that's no matter now – not any more – save to show I am a country girl at heart however cityfied I have got since, God help me.

The westering sun caused the stranger's shadow to reach towards me. It slid along the road like a snake. Next thing I knew he had turned from the stones to gaze directly at me. Placed thus I could not make him out as anything except a blackness against the burning of the sun. But I knew he could see me, looking, I hoped, for all the world like the runaway apprentice I wasn't.

He said, 'You've dogged my heels for three miles now, boy.'

'Maybe we follow the same road, sir?' I answered, keeping my voice low and manful.

'Where are you headed for?'

I strode forward to stand beside him at the stile.

'Here,' I said nodding at the circle. 'I aim to lay up here. The sun'll soon be down. It's a good place. There's no harm here. Leastways I've never found none.'

'Has it a name?'

'The Whispering Men. Folk say you can't count them. The stones change their numbers to suit themselves.'

'You inhabit these parts?'

'I did at one time. But no longer.'

Now I could see him. And to me at seventeen, as then I was, he looked old. Though in truth he was but halfway to heaven. One score and fifteen. It was the silver of his hair aged him. That and his hunger. His eyes were sharp with want, his cheeks hollow. The man was plainly starved. And as if to confirm this perception I had of him his empty belly gurgled speakingly.

Said I, out of my soft heart, 'Would you eat?'

The fierceness in his eye increased. He nodded. 'I've had naught but a handful of unripe cherries since yesterday and even then the farmer chased me off.'

His speech was neither like a country man's nor that of a city man. So my third and last apprehension of him seemed the likeliest – here surely was a schoolman out of his academy? A gentle philosopher grey as an uncooked prawn.

I told him to follow me and jumped briskly over the stile. Oh, I was lissom in those days. I skipped across the circle to my favourite stone. Grandad the First. Here I sat myself down as heartily as any boy could have done and unbuckled my satchel. He came to stand before me.

'You step out like a girl,' he said.

I was vexed at this discovery he had made of me. 'What's that to you?' I said, making my voice yet lower and more masculine.

'An observation merely,' he replied.

'Here,' I said, and offered him the bread and goose-neck sausage I had thieved out of an open window that same morning.

He sprang to these stolen eatables like a wild beast, tearing at the sausage with eager teeth and gobbing huge mouthfuls of the bread. His appetite called to my mind certain Puritan clients I'd had when I was a Bishopsgate punk fresh to the game a year back. Dear God, they could not have enough soon enough. But as with them, this fellow's business was swiftly concluded. Both bread and sausage were gone with a sigh and a groan followed by a belch for which he apologised most fastidiously.

I said, 'Now, sir, why don't you sit and let your stomach settle?'

'Have you more?' was all his answer.

I took breath. 'Only a flapjack I bought yesterday with good money at Banbury market.'

Good money it assuredly was. As good as any I have ever hoisted out of a gentleman's coat in a back alley. And the half-cut young cully so urgent upon relieving his bladder, he never noticed the departing of it.

Once again I invited my new acquaintance to sit beside me and this time he obeyed. Whereat I broke the flapjack in two. His ration was gone in a minute and I was obliged, still so ravening was his eye, to bolt my share for fear he would snatch it out of my very mouth. After that I had nothing left in my satchel except a sponge, a bundle of toothpicks and a cake of soap. For though I am stained grievously with sin I am no slut. I have ever and always kept myself nice.

Satisfied I had no more food to give him he reached into his own pack and pulled out a silver flask. At the look of it I thought so handsome an object must contain aqua vitae or canary wine at least. But no, it held only water. None the less I was grateful for a sip before he thrust it at his mouth like a harvester drowning his thirst under a hedge. He gave another sigh and smiled for the first time. I cannot say this action transformed him in my eyes but he certainly looked rather more of a man.

He said, 'I thank you, sir, for my supper. May I know your name?'

Here was a fix for me. Should I reveal my true name, and so prove my sex beyond surmise? Or should I give him that other I had chosen for myself the day before? When I had got clear away from those students bathing in the river? Taking with me the best of their garments. To wit: one pair of close breeches, one holland shirt with ribbons at the cuff, one short vest of calf-skin (slightly worn), one cocked hat and a pair of understockings in need of darning. My shoes were still my own for the boots I had also made off with proved too large and would have rubbed my heels to blisters. I discarded them along with my skirts and petticoats being determined that in my new identity as Master Jack Jones I would have nothing of the woman about me except my hair (such is vanity) pinned up inside my newfound hat.

As I weighed my reply my new companion resolved my dilemma by pronouncing thus: 'I dare say you prefer not to tread the roads alone as the young woman I suspect you to be?' And his speculative eye fell from my beardless chin to my bosom which though covered by fine linen was too well shaped to rest entirely discreet. 'I suppose your present attire affords you some protection from carmen and drovers?'

'You're right, sir. It is for that alone, for my virtue, that I have risked offending the good Lord. For I was taught He abhors falseness of dress quite as much as that of word or deed.'

I confess I blushed a little to hear myself voice such hypocrisies. To listen to me you would have thought I was a virgin pure as snow and not the doxy London had lately made of me. Even so my lies had a grain of truth in them, in that, while I had been willing to sell my charms to please my protector there in Bishopsgate, once I had fled from him I had sworn to be no man's puppet ever again; I would rather be damned than pleasure any itinerant coxcomb. Besides in breeches I could escape the faster, I reckoned. And whereas formerly I had been content either to make love for love's sweet sake (as they say), or else for money, I was not now ready to be ravished for neither.

Said I, 'Since my sex is plain to you, sir, I need withhold my true name no longer. Nor shall I. I was baptised Sarah Susanna and I'm the youngest-surviving daughter of William and Judith Greensmith of Long Compton. But most folk call me Sally.'

'And I am known as Enoch Powys, sometime but no longer, of Trinity College, Cambridge.'

'There! Didn't I take you straight off for a scholar!'

'You did?'

'Aye. As you walked ahead of me I said to myself: There goes a poor twat of a schoolman down on his luck.'

'Poor is true enough, Mrs Sally. For I have been thrust out of my college.'

'For what?'

'Experimentation.'

I could not tell what he meant by this nor was I any the wiser when I heard his explanation. He told a tale of building furnaces, of buying coals and salts and sulphurs and causing noxious fumes by day and night. And all this in the service of another scholar – a man whom Enoch in his cloistered simplicity thought I must know of – a certain Mr Isaac Newton, the mathematical wizard and scrupulous alchemist, as he called him.

At this I got his meaning if not his man. 'You've been a-making gold?' I said. And my heart leapt at the thought.

For gold has the power to transform us all, has it not? It makes the old young, the ugly handsome, beggars kings, a whore a goddess.

'No,' he replied. And my heart returned to its place. 'We did not succeed. Alas, the great work is also a great perplexity. To practise it you must have a purse without bottom and the patience of a saint. But when a barrel of horses' urine I'd purchased on Mr Newton's behalf – for the preparation of phosphorus, you understand – when this same hogshead leaked its contents, all sixty-odd gallons of it, through the ceiling of the Master's chamber which lay below, I was disgraced and obliged to leave the college.'

'Didn't Mr Newton plead for you?'

'Oh, yes. Yes, he did. Most feelingly. But it was to no avail. For the horse piss was not my only crime. I fear I had also, in my position as secretary to the Bursar, well, I had *borrowed* somewhat on occasion, from the college exchequer. Fully intending, of course, to replenish the fund when I could. But that was yet to be. So this also told against me.'

'You're a thief?'

He hung his head. 'Harsh words, Mrs Sally.'

'But true ones even so?' I patted his knee to temper the stricture. 'Take heart,' I added. 'For at the least you've no cause to feel shame before me. I'm quite as much a malefactor as you.'

And I told him how I had, that same morning, cut my Banbury cully's pocket of fifteen shillings and sixpence, not to mention my robbing of those lads at swim the day before.

'But these thefts were of necessity,' he said.

'Well, surely, you had equal need of the money you stole?'

'Not entirely. For I got my board and lodging *gratis* as well as a modest *honorarium* for my labours as secretary.'

'For what then did you steal it?'

'For diverse studies of my own that I conducted in parallel with Mr Newton's.'

9

'You're an alchemist, too?'

He nodded and I perceived a mystical gleam in his eye like a Jack o' Lantern.

'You may call me a fellow huntsman of the Green Lion,' he said, staring up at the darkling sky.

I could make nothing of this answer and said so. Whereupon he informed me, a little to my surprise, that I must lack an instinct for the poetical. I agreed at once. It was true. I had little or no fancy in me of any sort. I had feet of clay. Nay, in those days I was *all* clay. But that said, I dare proclaim, when I looked in a mirror or listened to a hot gallant, that I found I had been shaped, in each and every part of me, by a master hand. Modelled thus I had no need of fancy. It was enough to inspire it in others. And I did. In men and women equally.

But you may rest assured I took no pride in my beauty. Well, only the little that was natural at seventeen. For in my heart I knew it was not of my creation. Nor of my parents neither who were and remain as homely as pigs in midden. No, my charms were heaven-sent.

My errant scholar's eye had turned again upon me and this time I could have sworn I saw a peeping admiration in it. Had he read my thoughts? Or was it because I had removed my hat to reveal my corn-gold hair? The next moment a breeze set with a knife's edge swept up the hill and round about us, rippling the grasses as the sun sank.

He shivered. I said, 'You feel the cold?'

'Most abominably. Even on a summer's night such as this.'

'Then we'd best seek out a warmer refuge, hadn't we?'

I rose up and we made our way to a haycock close by. It might have been put there for our convenience for it was built of last year's hay which had become soft as silk and dry as tinder. Moreover it had been eaten away, upon the leeward side, by winter cattle so that its cap of mouse-grey straw formed a ragged, jutting eave whereunder we could repose ourselves as snugly as we pleased.

As night engulfed us I wondered if my gentle acquaintance might soon turn less mannerly and offer me indecencies? Perhaps upon the rising of the moon? After all, he was a man. I had little doubt I could resist him if I chose. But would I? One half of me took him for a milksop while the other, that half that was so often in the ascendant, was hopeful of discovering the devil in him. Oh, I was a wicked child, full of the itch. But, in the event, my scholar offered me no worse than a series of inoffensive snores. In consequence I lay awake a good hour wondering whether I felt unduly respected or unjustly spurned.

Waking at dawn I found him gone. Quite gone. I rose up

indignant. What manner of gratitude was this? Had I not fed him to my own detriment the night before? Had I not been ready (here I stretched a point) to pleasure him in his beggary? Was this my recompense? To be forsaken without a word? How dared he insult me so?

As I turned angrily about me I saw his pack left as before beside mine where we had lain. And then the next moment there was the man himself stepping towards me across the dew-spangled grass. In his hands he held the oddest vessel I had ever seen.

'I thought you'd shogged off,' said I, 'without so much as a thank-you-kindly.'

He affected not to observe my displeasure. He bade me drink from his receptacle. I took the thing from his cupped hands. It was made of glass in the shape of an ovoid bubble with a lid on top from which a spout protruded. Within its glassy walls lay milk, at least a pint, freshly warm and frothed at the surface.

'What is it?' said I.

'Why, milk, of course. Straight from the cow.'

'No! That I see. No, I mean this vessel it's in. I never beheld its like before.'

'Oh that? Well, this is my pelican. Or if you prefer my alembic. In it all things may be distillate.'

But as you may imagine these words of his, like those earlier concerning a green lion, were Greek to me. For I was yet to be a familiar of his chemical cant.

Removing the lid he once again advised me to drink and at this second commandment I did. The milk heartened me, making good my sleep. As I wiped my mouth on my sleeve (for lack of a napkin) I said, my eyes into his, 'So you've been a-thieving again, Enoch?' And this was, I earnestly believe, the first time I used his name.

His answer was a sweet smile with much tattle after. 'No,' he said. 'I went upon an errand of rustic mercy. For the cowman had stayed slugabed, neglecting his charge. Therefore it was left to me to make good his error and relieve Mrs Buttercup, a long-horned matron of liquid eye but bristled muzzle, of a most grievous pressure in her teats.'

He spoke all this nonsense so pleasantly that I laughed and was tempted to embrace this new Enoch there and then and make of the morning what the night had lacked. But I did not. Some native caution stayed me. Have a care, thought I. Know this chance scholar better. Is he not perhaps subtler than you think? Surely he is like those lizards that live on air and suit their colour to their circumstance?

I restored his *pelican* to him with my thanks and watched him swallow what I had left of the milk. Our breakfast was done.

'What next?' I said.

'I'm bound for Oxford. I have a sometime friend there. I hope he may be of assistance to me. But what of you, Mrs Sally? Which way does your road lie?'

I did not know. I had no true destination. No mark to aim at. Nothing, except a half-hearted resolution to go back to London. A place I had vowed never to return to. But that had been when I had reckoned on a welcome home; only to receive insult and abuse. For in my absence my father had become the district's beadle. In consequence his newfound propriety could not tolerate beneath his roof a prodigal daughter who, he had it on report (this world is full of whispers), was become a whore at London. That the rumour was true did not lessen my pain at his repulsion of me. He and my brothers thrust me from the door despite my mother's pleadings and my sisters' tears. And all the while the true Christian folk of our village observed my eviction with eyes of stone.

Following this downturn of fortune's wheel I had wandered the country at a loss for what to do. I had travelled in something of a circle until I had come to the aforementioned conclusion that I must return willy-nilly to London and throw myself once more upon the mercy, such as it was, of my former sweetheart, protector and pimp: Mr 'Rusty' Ironside of Wrestler's Court, a rogue as hotly persuasive as he was quarrelsome. Of necessity I must make my peace with him, share his bed again and never mind his furious rages nor his other jades, trulls and minxes.

But then Enoch, recalling me to the present, proposed that I might accompany him to Oxford. 'Let us be comrades of the road,' he said. 'At least for today.'

I agreed heartily, thrusting out my hand to shake his. At his clasp I felt suddenly – it was like the sun rising – that we were indeed true comrades. Or rather that there existed somewhere between us, within us, affinities akin to those of blood. This revelation was as if (given my continued disguise) we were indeed veritable brothers. I seemed now to have known him all my life and even beyond. Before being born. We had existed like seeds of time elsewhere. In some other sphere. It was a most unexpected sensation. I ached to ask him if he too felt these things? But the time for that question was not then. As his comrade, as his brother on the road, I would have opportunity enough, soon enough, to get his answer.

We set south for Oxford and by nightfall we were there, having broken our march at Woodstock to furnish ourselves with provisions. We stole a banquet out of several windows. Enoch was quick to learn the art once I had shown him how to handle the rod I had cut from a hazel coppice. The practice of curbing (as it is vulgarly known) is indeed simple enough and has much in common with angling of the coarser sort. Firstly you should never take to the road without arming yourself with a pocket knife, a bent nail and a twist of twine. (These items I would advise you keep apart in different pockets lest the constables search you and put two and two together.) Then, secondly, when your belly reminds you of its requirements you cut yourself a hazel rod, bind your hook to the end of it and go fishing in and out of other people's windows. Some items such as sausages or bag puddings you may hook up as easily as tench or barbel while others you must play more cunningly, *viz.* a loaf of bread or joint of beef or pat of butter. Once, from a gentleman's parlour, I even took a silver jug full of French brandy. I hooked it by the handle and did not spill a drop.

At Woodstock we caught a cottage cheese a-drip in its muslin, a currant loaf, a bunch of spring onions and, as the crown of our endeavours, a roasted chicken hoicked by its truss string clean off a serving dish. We therefore dined like princes and would still have enough for our supper, should the need arise.

It did. For when we reached Oxford Enoch was suddenly reluctant to enter into the city. He would find out his friend in the morning, he said. We would do better to visit him by daylight, he thought. At this I was not only disappointed but puzzled; for I had understood that this old acquaintance of his kept a lodging house. So where better for us to present ourselves now the night drew on? But though I complained and, even though I offered to pay for our lodgings out of what remained of those fifteen shillings I had garnered in Banbury, Enoch would not hear me. My mild schoolman, my gentle comrade, had become adamant and I was obliged to relinquish my happy anticipation of sleeping in a bed.

We took ourselves off a short way and found shelter in a boatyard where we made ourselves easy in the open belly of a half-built barge: taking for our couch the great heap of wood shavings which lay at the bottom of the hold. Here we passed the night in mutual innocence since for the second time Enoch offered no rudeness to me and I no wickedness to him. We slept as honourably as babies.

But daylight brought stark mischief. Raucous. Savage. Double-shaped. Two crop-eared mastiffs stood above us barking furiously. Beside them appeared their master, the boatyard's owner. To my sleep-laden eyes he loomed hugely, broad and dark against the soft flush of dawn.

'Go get 'em!' he yelled out of a spittle-drenched mouth as ferocious as his dogs. His charges obeyed his command on the instant, launching themselves upon us, odiously a-squeal, legs out-splayed.

I swung my satchel vainly at the first of them as Enoch, finding his feet among the wood shavings, whistled with a shrillness that pierced the ear in that close space. The other mastiff that had already seized Enoch by the forearm fell back while mine froze as if struck. Enoch whistled again. Or rather I saw his mouth pulled taut across his teeth between finger and thumb and his lips vibrate though I heard nothing. But the dogs did. They whined, cringed, and hung their heads. Enoch whistled again and the one sank even lower while the other turned over on its back to show its belly. And all the while they keened like frightened puppies. We scrambled out of the hold to confront the boatyard man.

He was confounded. He stared at Enoch in fear and anger.

'What you done to my dogs?' he enquired.

'I schooled them. Would you have had them tear out our throats?'

'Aye. And why not? You was trespassing. You are still.'

'Not a crime worthy to be met with a fatal mauling.'

'You get out from here! The pair of you. I won't have no dirty beggars here! Maltreatin' my dogs. Get along with you!'

And he seized an adze that lay to hand, raising it to strike at Enoch. I confess I screamed, fearing murder. But to my further astonishment my comrade at once avoided the perilous swing of the instrument and took his attacker by the wrist. The man yelped just as his dogs had done. The adze fell from his grasp. In the same instant Enoch turned sinuously about and ducked so hard his opponent was somersaulted clean over Enoch's back to pitch headlong into the barge where a frenzy of barking greeted his arrival among his own kind.

We left the yard at a brisk pace with me in amazement at this latest transformation of my companion. And I began earnestly to ask myself who exactly this was that I had fallen in with? The man seemed protean. In the space of thirty-six hours I had discovered him to be not merely vagabond but scholar, alchemist, comrade and now, contrary to his seeming diffidence, dog-handler and warrior. And so, as we walked beside the river I asked him where he had learned that wrestler's trick which had overwhelmed the boatman. Enoch laughed and said he had enjoyed instruction from a sage of Japan now resident in Cambridge. Natives of that far-off country held such skills, he said, in a state of almost religious veneration. The art and practice of them were regarded as a ladder towards spiritual perfection.

'You reach perfection by hurling people over your shoulder?'

Again he laughed, saying he supposed so. Certainly knowing the trick of it afforded the practitioner an undoubted satisfaction when faced by a bully boy.

The sun was now up and gilding the water while in the meadows the dew was dispersing in a golden haze. The seclusion of the scene induced in me a desire to bathe and refresh myself after sleeping two nights in my clothes. Whereat, as if nature wished to afford me just that opportunity, the river path diverged to skirt a pretty backwater cradled among aspens and elder. Here was as serviceable a bathtub as any milkmaid or nymph or even Venus herself might desire and command.

I voiced my inclination to Enoch who at once agreed to afford me the privacy he presumed I craved. He would swim in the river while I bathed in the backwater. I almost said that we might, for all I minded, bathe together, that I was not the green innocent he supposed; that I both knew and liked, rather too well, all that men were. But again some premonition constrained me. What was this effect he had upon me? In his presence I seemed to find myself altered. Was Enoch, in some unspoken manner I could not encompass, seeking to reform me? Was he leading me by the nose back to the strait way I had deserted so cheerfully on first meeting Rusty? Going at this miraculous rate might I not soon, if this was Enoch's influence upon me, discover myself (whence came this thought?) once more a virgin? My virtue mysteriously, nay, impossibly restored?

However it was I bathed in solitary contentment with the riddle unresolved. Especially I enjoyed the water's cool embrace for I am naturally warm-blooded, being of the sanguine sort quite as much as the phlegmatic that is common to all women. But then, after some few minutes, an inner imp of my former wickedness urged me to swim out to the main channel. Why should I not? Were we not, Enoch and I, comrades? Must I constrain myself in a shallow backwater when what I wanted was a proper swim? No, I reasoned exactly as this imp of mischief intended, no. I would strike out!

Once launched upon the stream itself I could see Enoch nowhere. What was become of him? But before I could speculate further the current took hold of me and I was swept downstream. Had I had ten times my strength I could not have resisted this rush of water. I was borne inexorably towards a continuous roar of sound that grew louder by the second. The flood I was in was now smooth as glass and that noise ahead could only be a weir or sluice. The next moment I glimpsed a weed-shrouded post standing out of a sunbright bar of water. Clinging to it was Enoch. I doubt the man saw me. He looked half-drowned. The river's impetuosity was carrying me directly to him and I was powerless to change my course. I was projected at the very same spot he had been rushed to. In the instant I was at the post and as my hands grasped at it so was the rest of me swept against him. Never have I seen more surprise in a man's eyes than Enoch's. Here we were, brought into a violent proximity neither of us could have bargained for nor yet prevent. I cannot say I felt any pleasure at this sudden intimacy since our case was too desperate. For upon my body striking his all along its length Enoch released his hold on the post and cleaved to me. Over his shoulder I glimpsed a steep, silver bank of water that lay slantwise across the stream with an angry whirlpool below it. But already my arms were weakening. I could scarcely hold to the post. Nor was there time for words even if we could have opened our mouths without swallowing half the river. Nor in truth could we have heard each other such was the din. Here my grasp upon the post failed and, thus desperately embraced, we were flung down the weir into the cauldron beneath. At our headlong arrival there we were both sucked under and upon surfacing a yard or two further on I found I was alone and in reach of the bank. As I scrambled out I saw Enoch's head bob up out of the whirlpool's spume only to at once sink back. I leapt back in and on his second surfacing I managed to push, pummel and drag him with me to the bank. Somehow I got him up onto grass and there we lay, gasping and sobbing at God's good air.

We must have stayed there, naked as our first parents before they fell, for a quarter of an hour or so, before we were sufficiently recovered to sit up and look about us. At least I did. I looked at everything. Enoch. Our surroundings. While he for his part stared fixedly away from me.

My observation of Enoch gave me more pleasure than I had expected. He was of a firm, even physique. His flesh was remarkably hairless. A good point this. I dislike a wiry breast upon mine. As for those parts we look to first on a man, they appeared to be of a proper if not excessive proportion. I had no doubt I might receive a satisfactory service from them once they were heated for the fray. Our whereabouts also pleased me for not only were they happily secluded but I could see a short way off a cottage garden bordered by a lavender hedge whereon a full week's washing had been spread to dry. With these garments' help we might find our way back to our own effects without remark. But before availing us of this fortuitous bounty I determined to have some conversation with Enoch.

To achieve this I stretched out my hand and turning his face to mine I said, 'You may look at me if you wish.'

'Oh, I wish,' he answered. 'But good manners forbid it.'

'That they do *not*,' I said roundly. 'In fact, Enoch, you should know that it is bad manners for a man *not* to regard me. I was born to be admired.'

'How do you know that?'

'I can't say. But I do. I always have. Now look and you will agree.'

'You're quite sure?'

What could he mean? The question provoked a shiver like a tiny knife inside me. I said, 'Of course I'm sure. Why shouldn't I be?'

'Perhaps because I know more of what I am than you do?'

Here was more Greek. I said, 'Do as I say.'

At this his eyes obeyed my warm instruction and he proceeded to gaze upon me as Adam must have done upon Eve after he had eaten his share of her apple. Under his regard my first, familiar response was to bask as if warmed by love's fire. His look was a steady caress. I felt myself melting. But then, most strangely, most inopportunely, I found I was blushing. Next, in an absolute contradiction to what I had that moment requested, I began most earnestly to wish he would not eye me so. I raised one arm to my breast, placed my other hand at my lap.

I said, and my lips trembled, 'What's this? What have you done? What are you doing?'

'Nothing you have not commanded.'

'I felt something of this before we bathed. Now it's worse. Please, don't look at me.'

'Very well.' He turned his eyes to heaven. My blushes retreated. I said, 'In your company I've changed.'

'As I have in yours,' he answered. 'So it is that one works upon another. Are you changed for the better, do you think? Or for the worse?'

'I don't know.'

He fell silent. I got quickly up and ran to the hedge where I snatched a shift that I donned at once. I cannot express how glad I was to be dressed again. Then I took a towel for Enoch. Returning to where he sat I handed it to him. He covered himself, smiled and rose up. I felt easier.

'I believe I owe you my life, Mrs Sally? But for you I would most surely have drowned. What brought you to my aid?'

Even as in answer I uttered the word *providence* we heard a shout and together, turning, we saw an old woman, stout as a barrel, waving a stick and coming furiously at us. Plainly she was in pursuit of her washing. It was time to go. Enoch needed no urging. We both ran. But for him the towel was an impediment. He discarded it. The woman stooped to recover it and our race was won.

By good fortune Enoch's pack and clothes remained where he had left them but all my belongings were gone. I was indignant but Enoch urged me to reflect. Was it not justice of a kind for thieves to lose what they had stolen to others like them?

I said, echoing a sentiment of Rusty, 'Not in a decent robbing fraternity.'

But to say true I regretted the loss of my shoes, my sponge and my money more than my boy's habiliment.

And thus it was that I entered the renowned city of Oxford as a barefoot mawkin in her shift escorted by a down-at-heel schoolman of threadbare credentials. Oddly, so far as I could see, we excited no attention whatsoever. Oxford, it appeared, was a seat not only of learning but also of indifference. But while the beauty and substance of its buildings astonished me, the handsomeness of its students dashing everywhere about affected me even more. Seeing them Enoch's recent influence upon me was quite dissipated. I was my old unblushing self again. And I felt the better for it. Better to be a whole whore than a half-virgin. This reflection, however, I kept to myself.

When we got to the lodging house kept by Enoch's former friend his sour-faced widow informed us he had been dead a twelvemonth. But even so she kept the place in business and if we wished for a room – her eye was now directed to my ringless left hand – it could be ours for half a crown a night with not a question asked. On hearing this Enoch shook his head (for he had not a penny in the world and had I not just lost my Banbury money?) and declined. But I would have none of this, reasoning that widows are often open to an offer and that given the preponderance of young gentlemen in the town I could earn our keep for as long as we chose to lodge there.

I said, 'And for that half crown we may also expect our daily diet?'

The woman blinked and was about to shake her head before she thought better of it.

'You may sup here for that but find your own dinners abroad,' she said.

I agreed at once (knowing a gift horse when I see one) but with the proviso that we should inspect the room first.

As we went up the stairs Enoch whispered anxiously in my ear, saying he could not countenance our compounding to stay there without the means of paying but I told him to leave all with me; we would meet our expenses; I knew the world better than he did; and this town of Oxford, wicked though I had no doubt it was, could not, I was sure, match London. If I could live and thrive in London as I had this last year or so then I could ensure our comfort in this place. The folk here would be as university mice to city rats. Despite this reassurance he shook his head but whether in disapproval or incomprehension I could not tell.

The room proved handsome with good windows, fine cupboards and two beds both of ample size. There was even a closet adjoining wherein stood a basin and ewer with fresh towels hung ready. Upon seeing these conveniences I at once concluded the agreement with the widow, only requiring her to repeat her assurance concerning our security within the chamber. She did.

Next all I needed was to find my first gallant. Straightway I informed Enoch that I would go out to view the town while advising him to remain within doors and recover from his brush with fate that morning. He concurred without protest. Was this because since entering Oxford I had become all steel and fire? Perhaps. Certainly he had turned timorous schoolman again. Whatever the reason (which concerned me not) I departed, leaving this mutable creature as he fetched a book and spectacles from his pack and settled himself myopically, happily at the window to read.

To ply my trade or, if you like, to practise my art, I had need of certain accessories, *viz.* a new pair of shoes, fine stockings, something more of a dress, a hairbrush and a comb. To cull the means to get these I took myself first to the cattle market where in return for much rude pawing and cruel pinching from foul-mouthed drovers and ale-blown farmers I hoisted three pockets and lifted one purse. My haul was almost worth the ordeal being in total four guineas, two shillings and sixpence. Had I pleasured a dozen of them in a row I could not have earned more from this commonalty. But I, you may rest assured, aimed higher.

From the cattle market I directed myself to the most wholesome part of the town that is set beside the chief seats of learning. Here I soon purchased enough to emerge refashioned. With my hair newly brushed, my feet shod in calf and my person clad with lace, lawn and calico from France printed with cornflowers and moon daisies I was fit to *converse*, as the saying goes, with the first proper gentleman to afford me a second glance.

Several did and I chose to acknowledge one in particular who was transported in a chair. From the fullness of his wig, his rosy cheeks and easy smile, not to mention the livery of his chairmen I took him for the youthful heir to a fortune. And so he was. After a minute's speech with Lord Spark he invited me to take his place while he walked beside me. And thus was I borne in state to the street door of a substantial house that stood within a college wall. I took it for the Warden's lodge at least. But no, it was a mansion particular to my lord's family as founders of that institution.

Once admitted I was offered tea (no less!) and other civilities but it was evident to me that my noble patron had no real mind for expensive nicety. He might be veneered in silks but beneath he was all refulgent Adam. I, too, was impatient to have our business completed so I might return in triumph with my spoils to Enoch. And strangely, throughout the enacting of our wickedness, and despite the undeniable vigour of Lord Spark, I thought continuously of Enoch and of no other.

My new gallant imagined my transports were evidence of his prowess alone and therefore he was pleased to reward me with a purse of ten new-minted guineas. I pouted at the contents and immediately, for he was perhaps more callow than he pretended, he doubled the sum and begged me to return the next day at the same time. I assured him I would and fairly danced down the stairs and through the streets to Enoch, who was astonished. 'Did I not say,' I said, 'that you need have no disquiet about taking these lodgings? Why with this,' and here I poured out my gains upon the bed, 'we can find far better if we please.'

'No,' he replied. 'I'm content to stay here.'

And so we did for a fortnight. In which time I amassed a minor fortune by way of my daily visits to Lord Spark. Enoch, the while, made calls upon a variety of learned acquaintances he had among the scholars there, in the hope of securing a pension or even a fellowship. He assured me his capacities as mathematician, theologian and chemist were quite the equal of any of the most distinguished of them, but, alas, since he had no recommendations from that other place whence he was fled (could rumours of that unlucky tub of urine have preceded Enoch covertly?) he enquired in vain. With the passing days his hopes retreated, even as my confidence in my own professional powers advanced. Never have I felt so capable, nor so much the mistress of myself, as when I was a whore at Oxford.

At home with Enoch – for I had come to regard our lodgings as that – I lived in the most intimate chastity. We resided together as brother and sister. I found this way of life both comforting and irksome. On the one hand I relished his continued respect for me, since, despite my regular absences upon business, he nevertheless treated me as if I were the most virtuous creature in the world. On the other I yearned to lie with him as only I knew how.

Finally on a night when the moon was at her newest I could resist this heartfelt imperative no longer. I crossed the room to his bed. Once at length beside him I poured out my soul to him, declaring what you may well have concluded already, that I had discovered within me sensations of a kind I imagined I had felt before but in very truth had not.

What is love? Some say if you must ask this question you may never know. I cannot agree. The matter is of more complexity than that. My love for Enoch, for I now hereby acknowledge it, was greatly to do with that sense of affinity, like that of blood, I had felt earlier. In superficial character we were chalk and cheese but at depth, at heart, we were one. Was this why I had taken such pleasure in our original state, first as honest comrades of the road, then as chaste siblings of the hired bedchamber? But beside these two considerations there had lurked within me a third: my bodily desire of him. A desire which, having been awakened in the river, had now gone beyond my earlier passion for Rusty, although at the time I had thought this had betokened love without end. Not that I expected Enoch to show the same mettle in the breach as Rusty. My gentle schoolman was not of that mould. Rusty having been all martial bounce and war-like bang (not for nothing was he known to his Cockney cronies as Captain Steele) whereas Enoch was soft and sensible and as changeable as quicksilver.

My whispered protestations together with our continguity warmed us both and in short we soon passed from a state of sweet innocence to one of even sweeter iniquity.

Later I dreamed that we were re-enacting our crime, only on this occasion we lay not in our present chamber, but within the glassy walls of that vessel Enoch termed his *pelican*. A lively fire beneath it heated us in our carnal endeavours. But so absurd did this dream seem to me that I laughed myself awake before achieving that peak of rapture I had been labouring so eagerly towards. Thus was I denied by my own scepticism (that want of fancy discerned by Enoch) the very goal I aimed for. Fortunately the solution lay beside me. I therefore teased Enoch with a kiss and earnestly desired him to complete my broken fantasy. He willingly complied and this time I came to that summit even as Sol himself rose at our window. Whereupon, bathed in the dew of love's exertions, we lay in a sun-warmed silence more eloquent than any words I can here set down. We were now, I told him, truly wedded in a union blessed of heaven.

Two days later Enoch informed me he wished to leave Oxford and go to London where he had hope of pursuing his studies upon his own account and out of my earnings.

I was truly astonished. Quite robbed of words. Finally I said, 'You would have me continue as a harlot?'

'How else can my work be funded?'

'Why, you're no better than my former protector!'

'If I could win a stipend I would, Sally, but such doors are shut to me here.'

I was again at a loss for an answer since I had now begun to think of myself as something of a wife. I had even toyed with the thought of renouncing whoredom in favour of domestic seclusion and if God willed (though as yet, praise be, He had not) children.

Seeing me struck dumb Enoch said, 'Have you not told me you enjoy your compounding with others, especially with Lord Spark, for money?'

'I have done, yes. And sometimes I still do. Yet I know it is wicked and could wish not to be so. Besides being as we now are to each other, dear Enoch, I could begin to desire a different way of going on.'

He smiled and taking me in his arms assured me between kisses that his reliance upon me would only be for a little while. Once he had sufficient in the way of materials for his researches and a place in which to prosecute them he could subsist on very little and, who knew, his work could well attract the attention of a great patron?

'Never fear, my dear,' said he, kissing me again, 'but soon you will be the most respectable woman in London.'

'Why? Do you mean to marry me?'

'It is not impossible,' he answered. 'But first we must be established in that city, in the manner I have just given you notice of.'

And here he proceeded to certain other teasing arguments that were as persuasive as they were wordless and so it was I agreed to everything.

To conserve my Oxford money (I had earned in all 280 guineas) we resolved to travel on foot. London, when all was said, was but five days' easy walking away. For prudence sake, I put up my fine clothes and we quitted Oxford as we had approached it: as a poor schoolman and a country hoyden.

We journeyed peaceably without any incidents save those of our own making. Never have I known a sweeter time. The nights were warm, the days hot. So hot that we were obliged to rise early then find shade at noon under a hedge where the cuckoo called or in the woods where turtle doves cooed in one eternal murmur. Enoch told me (a thing I knew not) that the dove before it came to embody the Holy Spirit had been considered by the Greeks as the bird (along with the sparrow) peculiar to Aphrodite, that goddess of desire known to the Latin race as Venus. Whereupon I told him he was a tiresome pedagogue whose tongue might be used to better purposes. He sighed, but heeded my command, saying I was a perfect savage, a shameless pagan.

So was he for all his gentle protestations to the contrary. He might well, as I did, pretend to the usual manners of the world. He might equally, with me, yearn (from time to time) to live in a state of respectability and even godliness. But at heart, like me, he could countenance most sorts of wickedness without a blink. In a word the pair of us lacked what is called *conscience* and for the simplest of reasons: our appetites were so numerous that we could not for the life of us, let alone for the death of us, countenance anyone or anything that stood in the way of their satisfaction. This alliance of ours was therefore an ideal partnership, had we but known it, for crime.

But, as you may suppose, such moral considerations were no part of me just then. Or rather I should say I perceived them imperfectly as through a dark glass. No, for that time I was content, as Enoch was, to be nothing but a compendium of fleshly sensations whose satisfaction lay entirely at my command – or his. Thus on that journey to London we lived a midsummer dream tasting every pleasure love can afford.

But all too soon Tyburn's gibbet greeted us at the west end of the town. And, as if in reinforcement of this saturnine welcome, a storm blew up to drench us. Yet no sooner were we past the hanging posts (where the bodies of two men and a woman were dandled by the wind) than the sun shone out again and there was a sudden rainbow, as bright as any I had ever seen, set up against the dark-bellied clouds still piled upon heaps above the city.

On our arriving at Covent Garden I was anxious to lodge in that quarter, having no desire to go further eastward lest I might encounter my former protector again. When I spoke of this fear to Enoch he agreed at once for I had told him everything of my life with Rusty. Therefore he also had little or no relish of meeting my former admirer whose temper was as hot as the colour of his hair. In consequence we found lodgings in St Martin's Lane whence we proposed to look about us for such premises as might prove convenient to the practice of Enoch's art and, if need be, my profession.

I was now at liberty to translate myself again from country lass to town lady. I put on my Oxford clothes, purchased more at Westminster Hall, and taking Enoch by the hand led him, protesting, to a tailor so he might pretend to be more like a gallant than a vagrant. Attired thus we commenced our search for accommodation that would suit us. But it soon became plain that we would not find what we looked for in this western part of the town where the buildings were either too grand, too pretty or given over to government.

Like it or not we were obliged to look eastwards to the City at the risk of meeting Rusty. Should you continue to wonder at this concern of ours, I may perhaps convince you, when I say Rusty was a man who got himself everywhere within his own precinct. He was born in the street and he lived in the street. Or rather he had been found as the merest infant not a day old in Houndsditch whence he was rescued by a dung merchant who brought him up as his son, giving him his own name of Ironside. But Rusty had no gratitude and by the time he was of age he had broken with his foster family to become, I shall speak plain, a pimp. From that day on he enjoyed many shifting abodes from bawdy houses to gambling dens but his chief pleasure was to go about the streets day and night in surveillance of his dollies (as he called his whores) or in search of new ones. Certainly when I lived with him at Wrestler's Court he was scarcely ever at home except to swive me or rob me. But to everyone in the City from the highest to the lowest he was very well known and much liked, when not feared, in his character of Captain Steele – although I know it for a fact he had never yet served as a soldier for all his bully boy's huff and puff.

Enoch, the while, was astonished by the resurgence of the City. To me it was not so surprising for I had only fled from it a month before. All to me was familiar: the wide streets laid out, the buildings in progress of being new-made all of brick or stone, the continual pandemonium of the masons, the workers in lead high up on the roofs, the constant grinding of the carts bringing more stuff – scaffolds, cobbles, lime, sand. All this bustle was what I had ever known of London, for while news of the Great Fire had reached our village soon enough in '66, another two years passed before I ran away to seek my fortune in the capital. By which time it was in the way of comprehensive renovation. Enoch did, however, possess one advantage of me – he had witnessed the monstrous conflagration itself, travelling from Lincolnshire with Mr Newton expressly to observe it.

'The fire,' said he, as we passed the blackened carcass of St Paul's that was promised to be demolished to make way for a new church, 'the fire broke out upon the Lord's day of the 2nd September and not as is often supposed upon the 3rd. By that day, the Monday, news of the catastrophe had got to Grantham whence Mr Newton and I were gone on account of the plague being at Cambridge. At once my mentor was himself on fire to see the phenomenon. Therefore he begged me to accompany him at his expense, and nothing loath, I did. We came post-haste.

'When we got to Broxbourne we could already see the glow of the fire beneath a pall of darkness like the ending of the world. Coming closer by way of Enfield to Stoke Newington we encountered many citizens of every degree fleeing the fire with what goods they might carry in coaches, carts and wheelbarrows or else on their backs. And it was a marvel to note how many lugged with them diverse instruments of music such as lutes, virginals and even bagpipes. I had not thought us so musical a race, said Mr Newton. Nor I, said I. To avoid this ever increasing press of traffic we turned westward and so came by way of St Giles to Charing Cross. Here we were informed that troops under the command of the Duke of York had been called out to maintain order but the King was yet to view the destruction although he was promised every minute; meanwhile no one might pass Temple Bar though what man would? Also we learned that Westminster Hall was made a place of refuge for the dispossessed whom had otherwise sought respite in Moorfields or about Lincoln's Inn.

'Despite being weary from hard riding we determined to take a boat downriver at once but found all craft in such demand we were obliged to wait an hour and then pay an inordinate fare: the distress of many, as always, breeding money in the pockets of the few. And thus we came to inspect the fire at the closest possible quarter as night fell upon the second day of its raging.'

By this juncture Enoch and I were got to Cheapside. Which was now become a highway quite three times its former width yet still as multifarious a market as it ever was. Beyond the ancient booths and age-old barrows (since what is thought ephemeral oft endures) where you may buy anything you please, be they Kentish artichokes, Norfolk lampreys or French cundums – the purpose and utility of these last fish-like items I was obliged to explain to innocent Enoch, who, full of cheerfulness, at once bought three in a parcel as something for us to try at the week's end – beyond all this public commotion there stood a great row of tenements whose roofs and chimneys flouted heaven, built of rose-pink brick with tall *chassis* windows that could slide up and down to a height twice their width and therewithal glazed in broad panes of glass. These shining windows, set off by handsome copings of white stone, afforded these new edifices a dignity that was as orderly as it was modern. And quite at odds with the old-fashioned welter, noise and unruliness of the market set before them.

As we walked I cast my eyes every which way in fear of seeing Rusty while Enoch resumed his account of the catastrophe that had provoked this renewal of the town.

'Our avaricious waterman,' said he, 'got us smartly away and as soon as we rounded the great turn the river makes about Lambeth Marsh, we beheld, smelt, heard and indeed felt the fire – for its heat reached out at us across the water. There was a gale from the east tending south. Great plumes of firedrops spewed ever skywards leapfrogging one street only to descend upon the next, there to start new flames. Our waterman informed us (falsely as it proved) that the disaster had begun in a smithy at the corner of Botolph's Lane while another observer who sat with his family in a neighbouring boat swore truly that it was started in the King's baker's house in Pudding Lane. Thence it had first spread westward, he said, along Thames Street, consuming the houses that stood upon the north end of the bridge and thence all along to Blackfriars. Now it was going northwards as we could see for ourselves. This affable and informative gentleman also said that the Lord Mayor of London was run stark mad with the horror of it and that the rush of exodus had already claimed more victims than the fire itself. With that he wished us a courteous goodnight and moved on downriver saying he must see to his own house and goods in Seething Lane which were as yet unharmed although that might change if the wind did. We are become supplicants of nature, said he.

'The entire hill of the City with St Paul's at its crest was now most awfully ablaze. The rush and roar was incessant and as terrible to hear as were the myriad small explosions as flags and cobbles cracked in the heat. The sound was like muskets upon a field of battle. To them was joined at intervals the sudden thunderous roar (as of baleful cannons) when some close store of brimstone or oil in a cellar was ignited. The height of the flames was, I thought, impossible to compute, but Mr Newton assured me that those above and about St Paul's (whose roof was already fallen in) were in the region of three hundred feet. Surely here was no usual combustion? London was become a giant furnace stoked by Titans. The flames writhed in the wind with a violence that held one fixed between admiration and disgust while the smoke above obscured the stars and moon. Even as we watched we saw the steeples of first one then another church spurt like torches only to fall like Lucifer amid a torrent of sparks.

'This sight prompted Mr Newton to suggest that to contain the fire gunpowder might be employed to some purpose. The systematic razing of certain streets by prettily placed explosions would create a rampart or cordon of rubble less susceptible to ignition. When I objected that this destruction might be as bad in its effect as the fire itself he shrugged and said he spoke only out of necessity's hard pinch. One might after all destroy to preserve. And indeed the next day this same stratagem was attempted although too late.

'But if what we saw upon the north bank was hideous what lay all about us upon the water was pitiable. For here, in lighters and barges, were not only household goods flung in any-old-how, with their owners huddled among them, but also yet more stuff floating in the river itself upon a great ebb tide going towards the bridge where it piled up against the stanchions in heaps. Here was the piteous flotsam of a thousand ruined lives: chairs, benches, tables, baskets, more virginals, linen of all sorts and, to crown all, a birdcage with its occupant still in it – a grey parrot – shouting *God save us* in a litany of . . .'

But Enoch never finished his account of the Great Fire because as we passed out of Poultry (as busy selling fowls of all sorts as ever it was) into Threadneedle Street we walked bang into Rusty. Oh, dear. Words fail me.

♂

God's light, would ya believe it? There she was! The doll I thought I'd lost for ever.

My Sally. Sweet Sal. Sally the Alley. My Warwickshire punk. Could that one spin her flax? Could she turn yer spindle? Could she not! Answer yes and yes! And yes, yes, yes, again. What an earner!

But what was she come as? All done up in silk and ribbons? Who did she think she was? My Lady Cunny or the Duchess of Muff? And this cully wiv her? Who was this streak of goose piss?

I says to her, 'Well, well, what's all this I see before me? Is this who I think it is? Could it be *you*, sweetheart? *You*, Sal? Well, I never. You what shogged off last month wivout so much as a God be wiv ya? Well, what do you know? Wheel's come full circle. Here we go again, right?'

She says, all breathless wiv her pretty titties doing the double shimmy, 'Oh? Is that you, Rusty? Oh, you did give me a start.'

'And you me, Sal. You me.' And I kiss her on the kisser. Hot and strong. When I lets go, I says, 'Now you better introduce me, hadn't you, to your new friend?' And I give this bubber at the side of her a hard stare, the old basilisk eye, no blink.

'Oh,' she says, even more of a wobble and turning red, ooh, such a claret upflow from chest to cheek as gives me a stand like a frigging crowbar. 'Oh,' she goes on, 'oh, yes, well, yes, Rusty. Of course, dear. Yes, this is Mr Powys.'

'Oh, yeah?' I say, stern, still keeping his eye.

And what do you think he says for answer? He says, 'How do you do?' The cheeky bastard!

God's bollocks, I'll give him how d'you do. I say, 'Oh? You reckon you can address me direct, do ya? Straight off? Without so much as a by-your-leave?' And I was of a mind to give him the knee in the cods and the butt in the mug only Sally reaches forward, all honey, to touch my arm and like always I'm putty in her hands. Oh yeah. It's God's truth. Me, Rodney Ironside, also known as Captain Steele, the hardest man in town, I'm twist to her finger.

'Rusty,' Sal says, her voice throaty, her eyes wide, 'I'm sure we can be friends. In fact, I know we can. The three of us. Why not? Enoch's a schoolman. From Cambridge. And he's more than clever. Like really clever. So be civil, won't you? Enoch, this is Mr Ironside. But I've always called him Rusty.'

He offers me his hand. He says, 'I've heard much about you.'

What's he heard? What's Sal told him? God almighty, this could be trouble. So I say, big smile, some sweat, 'Oh yeah? What?' And I take his hand in my usual iron grip. Just so he knows who he's up against. But – would yer credit it? – his mitt's as slippery as a frigging fish and when I go to crush it, still all grin and seeming friendly, the slimy coxcomb withdraws it before I can get a proper grip.

'Mrs Sally tells me you're well known in the City?' he says, all grease. 'As a man of parts? With many interests? All lucrative? It is always a pleasure – indeed a privilege – to meet a man of substance beyond dispute, Mr Ironside.'

And he bows. And I think, well, mayhap this creeping sodomite's not so horrible as I first took him for? Leastways he's polite. Pays respect where respect is due. That's a start. So long as I get respect I stay easy. It's all I want really. Respect. Mixed wiv awe. Loadsa awe. Give me awe and I'll be as nice as pie.

Besides there'd been something in Sal's tone of voice when she'd said how clever he was. Like she was hinting he could be, you know, an asset or some such? Like in some new venture? For the three of us? As business partners? All matey-matey?

I say, 'I could sink a double ale. How about you, Mr Powys?'

So we took ourselves off to the Three Tuns and there I heard Sally's tale and then his. And they got mine. How I'd gone along much as normal after Sal had run from me, only (and here I laid it on thick) London hadn't seemed the same wivout her. And I give her the glad eye. She blushes. Nice. Also how I'd come by this new property down by the river at Pudding Wharf – I'd won half of it in a wager and paid for the rest out of my girls' earnings. Call it immoral if you like but then look at the King wiv his doxies, his gamblings. What I do is naught compared wiv him. And he's meant to be like an example to us all, in't he? Mind you, I once saw that latest whore of his, that Nell, on the stage. What a plum! Yum-yum. And a dead ringer for my Sal! They could've been twins. Only Sal's as fair as a fried egg on a gold plate while the King's new cunny is black as Newgate's knocker. But even so the likeness – uncanny.

But if my eyes lit up when I saw Nell Gwyn you should've seen Sal's when I mentioned these premises by the river. What was they like? Did I live there? They must be new built? How many rooms was there? All that. Quick as a flash.

So I say, like a stupid great natural, 'Why? You looking for lodgings?'

She says stoutly, 'Oh yes. We both are. Me and Enoch. Yes, Rusty. We need somewhere to live.'

'Oh, it's like that, is it?' And I can feel my temper rising as I think what I'm suddenly thinking which is of this slimy sod screwing my Sal. Not that I'm jealous, no. It's just that wiv seeing her again, and wiv feeling her knee under the table, I'm red hot, rigid and crazy for her, right? As I always was and ever shall be.

Sal notices (she was always quick to catch my mood) and she leans forward, all eyes, bubs and breath again, and says, 'You'll always have a special place in my heart, Rusty. Seeing how you was my first.' And then lower, so Enoch can't hear it, 'And you always will be when you want.'

So that's the quarter the wind's in? Well, this could make a material difference as the divine said to the duchess as she defrocked him. Well.

I say, 'You wanna see it?'

Did they want to see it? Can a shit-shoveller shovel shit? Away we went.

Viewing the aforesaid property through their eyes I came to recognise its advantages rather more than I had before. It'd been built for a ship's chandler's with living space above on two floors. On my acquiring of it I'd put in the odd lump of furniture and two of my girls. But a dead crafty pair they turned out to be. What we in the business call *flat-fucks* on account of them being more for each other than the game. After a week I gave 'em the push. You can't carry passengers, not in my line of country. Since when the place had stood vacant.

So now Sal says all twinkle and dimple, 'But it's handsome, Rusty. Just what Enoch and I need.'

'It couldn't be better,' says he, slimy as frog's spawn.

'For what?' I say, hard as rivets.

Well, now, this is where this Enoch takes a dirty great breath and I get the full schoolman's spiel. Jaw, jaw, jaw. And it's like my earholes can't take in what they're getting told. Except it seems he reckons he's one of your modern Enquirers or sincere searchers who get all stirred up about the Laws of This and That. Not *the* laws like you an' me understand 'em (the ones that'll get you dancin' on air as soon as look at you), no, Enoch means them other laws of nature. Those ones that govern the stars in their courses, the making of metals, the run of the blood in your body. All that mullarky. Science as it is now known. And he's looking for a place where he can set up his laboratory. In which he can build furnaces with flues so he can continue what he calls his sacred hunt for the Green Lion like he was at Cambridge, he says, before he dropped a hogshead of *urina equum* on some bastard's bonce.

I must've looked dumb as they come as I tried to discover the head and the tail of this history because Sal says to me, spelling it out as if I was some cheese-brained Froglander, 'Enoch means to make gold, Rusty. Gold. Right?'

Now here's a word I do understand. All four pretty letters of it. G.O.L.D. The bright stuff that never tarnishes. Warms your pocket. Heats your balls.

30

So I say, showing worldly caution outside but nursing hope inside, I say, 'Oh, yeah? Yer mate knows how to do that, does he? He can make gold, can he?'

'Of course. He's just said, hasn't he? That's what he was telling you. Oh, Rusty, you're thick as pig shit.'

I correct her. 'Pig iron,' I say. But what's become of her ladyship? All of a sudden? Here's my Sal slipping back into the old vernacular. I take this as a propitious sign. We could get back to where we was.

Enoch hems, haws. 'The gold I seek is as much spiritual as physical,' he says, looking like a Puritan consoling a widow.

To the which I answer, 'I bet. But you don't get the one without the other, do you? Or so I've heard.'

He nods. 'So it is said. But it's a long process. It demands of the adept not only perseverance but also humility and application.'

I think, 'Bugger them,' but I say, 'Just so long as you get there in the end, mate, that's all we can ask, innit?'

Sal says, full of faith in her man, 'Oh, he will, Rusty. I know he will.'

Now it's my turn to take a deep breath before saying, 'Well, maybe we better sit down and see if we can come to an agreement upon this matter?' So we sit. I continue, 'All three of us. All in it together like? All for one, one for all? Like I loan you the premises for free in return for a share of the proceeds? Like? Mm?'

Their eyes shine but, of course, I haven't told 'em what I've really got in mind, have I? No, tickle yer trout first then gaff it, that's my motto, always has been.

'Oh, Rusty,' says Sal and kisses me on the cheek.

'A most generous offer,' says Enoch.

Whereat we all shake hands upon the business and the next minute I've persuaded Enoch to return then and there to their present lodgings to fetch their gear over in a hackney as soon as he likes. And would you believe it? Yes, you would! The stupid cully agrees like a lamb. Leaving my old Sal all of a jelly, seeing how she's been getting my feel-up under the table all this while.

She says, 'I ought to go, too.' But her cunny-wise look belies her words.

I say, smooth as silk, 'Oh, by no means. I have need of you, madam, to advise me of what further appurtenances you may require to complete your comfort here.' What a frigging jawbreaker. Only sore need of you know what, makes me this mouth-musical.

Wherewith Sal blushes and off silly Enoch goes. And even as I bolt the door and turn about we're in each other's arms, slam-bang, locked tight. Next thing we know we're up the stairs at the high step and into bed. God's truth, I've never known a ladybird undress quicker than Sally. Or look more like herself once she had. I tell yer, that one wore nothing better than most do clothes.

If we'd never been loath before and we hadn't (save when she was vexed at me charvering me other pretties) then this time it's out of this world. We're right up there, right? Going up through all the seven heavens. And as we go we keep saying, wiv one voice, here we go again, God's light, it's been so long, oh Rusty, oh Sally, it's like we was made for each other, innit? Until as ever, words escape us. But after, when they return, I whisper in her ear, tell her she's my Venus and she says I'm her Mars. And then as we lie there I see – is it my fancy or what? – I see this baby-pink cupid, wiv rainbow wings and a grin all over his face. The cheeky little bastard's hovering above us saying, do it again, I want a brother. So we do. Laughing like fuck. And sure enough this next time when we break off there's two of 'em flitting about, giggling their heads off, and piddling pure gold all over.

Poetics to one side, our future was now settled. I let Sal and Enoch move in to Pudding Wharf and I advised Enoch I wouldn't require no rent, after all. This makes him reckon I'm the most generous landlord he's ever met while I inform Sal that she's the rent, understood? And Sal says that'll be a pleasure but we won't tell Enoch, will we, because he's so soft and sensible, not hard and thick like me? At which I go to thump her but she disarms me wiv a kiss.

So we don't say a word and Enoch gets busy about his laboratory. And by the time he's got it going, wiv three furnaces burning day and night – one for calcination, he says, another for distillation and the third for long digestions – then he's so occupied wiv his great work, as he calls it, that Sal and me can get on wiv ours. As and when. And that's how it goes for the first month. Lovely. But like I said just now, I'd got some other ideas, hadn't I? For the three of us?

To put it to you straight I wasn't going to wait for that Welsh cunny to make gold. Or find the philosopher's stone. Nor the elixir of life, God help us. I mean, I'm no scholard, as you will admit, but I'm not stupid neither. Nobody gulls me. No, my approach to our tripartite enterprise was simple: to make it show a profit as soon as maybe, if not sooner. Like I wasn't in the business of long-term investment and already Sal was coming to me asking for cash to buy Enoch yet more gear: coals, pipings, sand, horse dung, aqua fortis not to mention lumps of lead, iron, copper, tin – you name it he needed it for his science, oh Christ, yes. So I told her, look, goddess mine, Enoch can have whatever he wants just so long as he does what I say, right?

'What's that?' says she, taken aback. 'What's he got to do?'

So I let her have it. Bang. I say, 'Open his laboratory to the public.'

Sal's amazed. Eyes a-pop, jaw a-pop. She gasps. 'Oh, he'd never do that!'

I make wiv the quick menace. 'Oh, yes, he will, sweetheart. Once you persuade him.'

'Me? How?'

'I leave that to you, Sal. Far be it from me to teach you your trade.'

'But Enoch's work is secret, Rusty. *And* sacred.'

'So?'

'So he can't let every citizen Jack and Jill into his laboratory! Even you can see that? Surely?'

I'm getting heartburn, seeing red, but somehow I rein myself in. I say, 'I'm not talking about the common herd, am I? No, doll. No. you got me wrong. I mean the select few. The prime subscriptors. As chosen and invited by me.'

'For what?'

'I've just said! To see the work. And to get the spiel from Enoch. And then you and me invite 'em to subscribe in cash or goods. Right?'

'But what do they get in return?'

'A certificate giving 'em a share of Enoch's gold – when it's made. D'you see?' She nods, she does see. I continue, 'It goes like this – I pick the likely cullies, bring 'em to you as hostess. You charm them, wine them, maybe dine them, and then together we introduce 'em to the great work and Enoch who strikes them deaf, dumb and amazed wiv his experiments.'

'Whereupon they pay up?'

'That's it. You're there, doll.'

'What if they don't?'

'I'm tellin' you they will! Look.'

And here's where I produce my ace card. It's this certificate I've had drawn up in Lincoln's Inn by this lawyer's clerk who owes me. (Like he likes his rumpo but can't always pay on the nail for it and is too ill-featured to find it for free.) Does this certificate look impressive? It does. And real, too. What's more it reads like flaming Holy Writ. Like, for instance, it promises to pay the Bearer on Demand at a Date to be Determined that particular Share of the aforesaid Enterprise hereinafter referred to as the Powys Projection which shall or shall not in Due Course be Computed and or Deemed as such Equitable proportion division or percentage of that Initial Subscription as heretofore Subscribed but without Prejudice Let or Other Hindrance to those Absolute Rights inherent *ab origine* indivisible already held in absolute Trust by Powys Projection as Certified above throughout the cognate terrestrial Globe also known as the Earth together with the yet to be observed Universe. And so on. With more bollocks to much the same effect only this time there was these convenient spaces provided in which to insert any old numbers, signatures, seals and whathaveyou as required to hoodwink the subscriptor. Furthermore I tell Sal I've got a printer who's all ready to knock me out as many as we need in strict confidence. So how's that, I ask?

Sal says, 'Why aren't there any commas or full-stops in this certificate?'

I say, 'Because it's a legal frigging document, you stupid cow. You never have punctuation in this sort of thing. It could lead to clarity and understanding then where would all the lawyers be? We've all got to live, doll. Right?'

She agrees and I note how deeply impressed she is really, underneath. She says, all butter, 'Oh, Rusty, you are clever really, aren't you? You're more than just cods with feet on, after all.'

But me, I wonder, seeing where her hand's got to. Mine returns the compliment and in a flash we're off again, conjuring cupids.

Later the three of us sup together and I take my leave after extracting a final promise from Sal that she'll break my scheme to Enoch and what's more make sure the slippery so-and-so agrees. Because if not, not. Get me? She does.

☿

In the instant we encountered Sally's former protector I saw that she, whatever her recent heartfelt protestations, would once again embrace him whilst vowing to me that she did not.

However I was content to play the cuckold in the affair since there is ever for me a peculiar satisfaction in the knowledge that I am deceived. Does not the power of a secret work two ways? Upon those who think they keep it safe and upon them who know it but hold their peace? Besides, the bad faith of others excuses one's own. Nor was I discommoded in any respect, least of all in the field of love. For I soon discovered that my mistress's appetite for pleasure with me was not a whit diminished by her reunion with her *amator redivivus*. On the contrary, like Cleopatra, Sally's relish of the game was increased by what it fed on.

And so it came to pass that I was at liberty to prosecute my chemical enquiries while Sally divided her time and her charms between me and Rusty – as I soon learned to call him. Nor, I must admit, should I ever have enjoyed such commodious accommodation, let alone such an abundance of materials for the exercise of my art, had not Sally been as she was – an honest whore.

On top of this I was not unaware that the three of us, thrown thus together by chance, formed, in our newfound conjunction, a perfect triangle of an alchemical kind. For on the one side I observed in Rusty much – sometimes too much – martial spirit and on the other, in Sally, all that is venereal, whereas if you take me for the base line of this three-sided figure, then there is nothing in my nature that is not mercurial. Being as I am the eldest son of a Welsh gold miner and the third-wisest woman of Merionydd – the first two being wise enough to reject my father. Oh, and I was born under the sign of Gemini to boot.

I also took it for a pleasant augury that in this our triumvirate we mirrored not only the planets of Mars, Venus and Mercury but also those same mighty gods themselves. Were they not, in some measure, reincarnate in us? Looked at in this manner did we not become, at Pudding Wharf, a great force for something could we but discover what it was? Nor was this all neither, since here, signified in us, lay those metallic elements vital to the execution of the great work *videlicet:* iron, copper, mercury.

For let it be said here and now – before you hear otherwise from such as Rusty whose bias runs eternally contrary to mine (if only in that I have none while Rusty is nothing but) – let it be set up as if in stone, that I am true to naught save the sacred art of alchemy. Rusty may advise you, judging everything by his own gaudy light, that I was as much a mountebank as he, as much a bawd as Sally. But this was not so. At Pudding Wharf, as at Cambridge, I followed the path to chemical perfection not for gain but for its own sake and in the earnest hope of revelation. And I may say that in the end I got it but not there nor in the way I had looked for. But to say more at this moment would be to speak of a future already passed.

I will allow, however, that the very sincerity of my purpose enabled me to play the trickster with authority. Not that I was immediately compliant, quite the reverse, when, some weeks after our abiding there, Sally first imparted to me Rusty's stratagem. Indeed I protested hotly. I would not, should not, could not, I said, permit the public to view the work I had in progress. My laboratory was sacred, my holy of holies.

But Sally, between kisses, prevailed upon me. And in the process revealed herself to be quite as devious as my inmost self.

'Dear Enoch,' said she, her breath warm in my ear, 'do you not see how this may advantage us?'

'No, I do not,' I answered, eyeing my glasses – for I had three in the fire wherein I had fused the star of antimony (of a martial regulus) with silver prior to amalgamation with mercury – 'I see nothing of advantage to come of this. Rather we shall have nuisance, foolishness, tittle-tattle and all to satisfy Rusty's commonplace desire for gain. Does he not understand,' I said, waxing hotter, 'that what I seek here is beyond price? No, of course, he doesn't,' I added, answering myself before Sally could, 'he lacks entirely those mental powers necessary to such a comprehension being as he is both numbskull and rogue bound up together in one!'

'Hush, my dear,' said Sally not at all put out by my peevishness. 'Just sit you down and listen.'

But I would not sit down. I continued, 'And the vulgar sort he proposes to introduce here are as ignorant as he. They may well gawp and wonder but they won't understand.'

'Oh, I'm sure they would, Enoch. Once you explain the process. Your enormous mental powers will make up for the littleness of theirs. Besides, people love to hear what they cannot understand provided the explicator can make them feel they do comprehend it really. Why, there was a book appeared only last year that spoke of the stars and the heavens in double Dutch yet had such pretty pictures and nice diagrams that everyone thought they had got it whole. It sold like hot cakes, is even yet in print, and has made the author famous and the printer rich.'

'But I am no teacher,' I said. 'I am all research, a pure enquirer.'

'Nonsense, dear. You explain wonderfully. Have you not introduced me to the mysteries of your science?'

'Art,' I said correctively, just like the pedagogue I had sworn I wasn't.

'Further,' she continued without pause, 'have you not often expounded to me, whether I would hear it or no, that your sacred *art* as you term it, is as a rainbow arching the gulf which is set between earth and heaven?'

'A silly conceit to please a woman,' I snorted.

'And I made sure you did,' she replied with a giggle, nipping my ear between weasel teeth. 'And did you not also inform me but yesterday as I prepared your morning bath that alchemy progresses from the production of the philosopher's stone which is no stone at all but a mercury seven times sublimed that can turn any metal, howsoever base it be, into gold, which is not common gold at all, oh no, far from it, but is instead, the shadow of God Himself? By which time you had got me tumbled naked into the bath and followed suit yourself saying you must have your Venus as if at the sea's verge whereupon we made waves that quite soaked a good Turkey carpet and scared the cat?'

'True,' I said, quite mollified.

'Then, in that case, you cannot deny you are a good teacher,' she concluded. And put her mouth to mine.

In consequence I was in no position to reply even if I had wanted to. Sally's kisses have a combustious adhesiveness like unto brimstone and treacle.

When she released me from this embrace she said, 'So you see, my dear professor of everything that flies above and below, we may ourselves make money thanks to Rusty's itch for instant profit and then, at a time of our own choosing, leave him, taking our share of his knavery with us. For we shall have our share, Enoch, or I am not your future wife, after all.'

Had I heard aright? 'What new duplicity is this?' I exclaimed full of virtuous indignation on behalf of a man I half-loathed, half-liked and totally distrusted. 'Would you cheat Rusty?'

'Sooner than you,' she said.

I cannot say I took complete comfort from this answer since her words implied a relativity that was quite the opposite of love's supposed absolute. For Sally to prefer cheating Rusty to betraying me did not, to my mind, preclude her from doing the same to me in the future. Besides had she not continually deceived me with Rusty ever since we arrived at Pudding Wharf? Although, of course, I had known all along and had not minded it? Taking breath and calling inwardly upon Paracelsus to guide me, I put these doubts to one side and said, 'You wish me to agree to Rusty's plan so you and I may gain by it at his expense and then fly off with the proceeds without informing him?'

'How clever you are,' she said. 'And then we shall be free. Beholden to no one but ourselves. And we may live as we like, wherever we like. You can have another laboratory entirely your own and I shall settle down and have babies for I start to foresee a time when I shall grow weary of congress without issue.'

Would this woman never cease to astonish me? I had, of course, detected in her, at Oxford and upon our arriving at London, some unspoken smack of a would-be respectable matron. But not since. Yet here it was stated plain. And I must admit a part of me warmed to the thought of my Sally thus transmuted, with babies at her knee and another at her breast. And myself a sanguine *paterfamilias* content with his pipe before the glowing hearth. The vision had a certain charm even if at bottom I doubted my participation in it for I ever regret and yet exult in the knowledge that I shall never enjoy such a simple existence; that I must forever pursue my art abjuring worldly benefit until I hold the key to all knowledge in my head and heart.

I said, 'Very well. I agree to allow Rusty to introduce selected – I say it again – selected clients into the laboratory and I shall do what I can to illuminate them concerning the great work.'

'And you will let them subscribe to it?' And she showed me an imposing certificate Rusty had had prepared for those foolish enough to part with real gold in return for the philosophical variety.

I said, judiciously, 'I say neither yea nor nay. For I may not, given the sacred nature of the work, sully myself with any thought of gain. I must leave such inferior considerations to you, my dear, whilst I address myself to superior things.'

'So you may remain the humble adept, the virtuous philosopher, the modest schoolmaster I first took you for, and yet enjoy wealth beyond dreams?'

'You have said it,' I replied, not unmindful of Him who first pronounced this eel-like evasion of an ultimate truth.

Sally laughed, 'Oh, Enoch, you're a perfect hypocrite!'

'I hope so. How else shall I succeed in this world or the next?'

She laughed again and I with her and so our dealings were concluded. But upon the following conditions: *item*, I would only 'teach' or 'expound' twice a week. At all other times our clients must keep silent while within the laboratory and be assured that to speak directly to me would result in their instant expulsion from the place. *Item*, Rusty and she might promise them what wealth they pleased upon the accomplishment of the great work but I would not at any time be obliged to corroborate or confirm their speculations. *Item*, if Rusty should – as she intimated – encourage the public to bring forth gross articles of base metal for transmutation into gold these goods should be kept at his cost and sold off as and when and where they could, since such rubbish sorted ill with the intricate and precise quality of my researches. In other words my laboratory (whose state of artfulness was manifest) was not to become a mere shop for antique moveables, unwanted fire-irons or metal scraps. And *item* the last, I was to be addressed at all times only as Dr Quicksilver since I had no relish of Mr Newton or others of like distinction coming to hear of our proceedings.

With these provisos admitted by Sally and related by her to Rusty who at this moment appeared most opportunely from his usual alehouse, we proceeded to dinner in a most amicable tripartite complicity.

♂

Don't ask me how Sal worked it wiv Enoch the Adept but come the end of July we was in real business. All three of us, co-mates, perfect pals, in harmony. And what a circus it was! We couldn't keep the bastards away! The town fell over itself to visit the great work and view the great worker: who was now known as BA Cantabrigiensis Interruptus. Oh, yeah, it turned out he wasn't even a real scholard like he first told us he was. All that cods about him and Mr Newton. No, the varsity had got his measure as a student and given him the boot. Since when he'd done this 'n' that in and around the town of Cambridge but was never a real schoolman. Just a laboratory assistant. What a faker! I got all this from one of my girls' regulars – a peer of the realm no less, most respectable, age of eighty, what a goer! Not that I let on to Enoch, oh no! I saved that for another day, didn't I?

But that said you should've seen the lab. Enoch did it all up. Like it was on stage. Talk about Ye Olde Theatrum Chemicum – to coin a phrase as well as malooka and, boy, did we coin it – this one was like the King's Playhouse doing frigging *Macbeth*, Act One, Scene One.

Only instead of the witches' cauldron, bubble-bubble, Enoch sets up this dirty great load of glass pipes, tubes, carboys and bottles he's had specially blown for the purpose. Custom-built for conning. *And* – would yer believe it? – when all his gear's finally in place, rigged up proper, the whole mullarky looks like an enormous transparent bird! A kind of glass goose. Or is it? No, I tell a lie. No, it's more like it's a three-headed ostrich wiv a dragon's tail and legs with plates of meat on. Plus these big red ears on its chest – which is known as the great aludel apparently – wiv an old man's face done in blue glass between them. Very peculiar. But does it impress the public? It does! And how! They can't believe their organ-stop eyeballs.

I told Enoch straight – like I always give credit where credit's due – I told him his machine (as he called it) was worth its weight in bleeding gold. And I said that even before he'd got it working. When it was just standing there.

So what does our Welsh wizard do next? I'll tell ya. He pours into this monster various solutions of chloride this, sulphuretted that and decalcinated whathaveyou. Right? You're wiv me? Then he sets a nice little fire under the dragon bird's tail – just where its arsehole would be if it had one. Oh, don't get me wrong, when I say *fire* I mean nuffink much more than a medium-sized oil lamp sending up a gentle heat. Right up it, right? Well, after a while, wiv me an' Sal all agog, these different concoctions he's put in heat up and start bubbling nice 'n' easy. And then – and this is the cunning bit – these same liquids start to rise up through the pipes! And one lot is bright green like emeralds and the other is red as rubies but the two don't mix, oh no, they go on their separate, complicated courses through the tubes and you've got this incredible sight of these wonderful liquid colours sort of slowly coiling and dancing round each other but never mixing because if they did, Enoch said, they would muck each other up most horribly and reduce everyfink to a sort of cowshit soup. Which would be a calamity and brings me to Enoch's masterstroke.

Because we now realise, me and Sal, that our resident genius has so placed his apparatus that the sun can shine right through it. Of an afternoon when the lab's open to the public. And that in all those places where the tubes cross over each other the light of the sun shines through both the green and the red. Yeah. Do I hear some clever Tom, Dick or Harry say so frigging what? Well, you needn't 'cos here comes our crafty doctor's aforesaid stroke: the big plus, the extra extra, the Midas touch. Here's what hooks the clients, gets 'em falling over each other to subscribe in the venture, has us running out of share certificates in the first week – we had to shut the lab on the Monday while I got more run off at the printers. Yeah, here cometh Enoch's especial effect.

You see, and believe you me it's an eyeful when you do, where the slant of the sunbeams through the window hits these cross-overs you get these yellow reflections – they're like gold medals new minted – on the wall behind Enoch's creation. And there's so many of 'em – thanks to these little mirrors he's stuck up everywhere but out of sight so you can't see how it's done – they look like they're falling down from heaven in a golden shower. Incredible! And as you look the whole room seems to get bathed in this yellow shimmer, this shining glow, this magic effect his machine makes. Only it's all science really, right?

Enoch called it his *spiritus mercurialis*. Or to you and me and the average pisser the spirit of mercury. But the last laugh is yet to come. And this is when he lets on to me and Sal that, despite all these pretty opticals, and despite him informing the clients how this three-headed ostrich is the hub of his research, it isn't. Oh no. It ain't no such thing. No way. No. It's a nothing. It's quite immaterial to the great work. It's a flim-flam. A bauble. A toy.

So I say, 'Then what's it for then?'

And he says, 'To draw money out of stupidity, cash out of cupidity.'

'Here, I thought you said you was above money?'

'And always shall be,' he answers, smooth as silk about a great lady's bum. 'But the more this device makes for you and Sally the happier I shall be, Rusty. However, for me the machine's purpose is to distract the vulgar from my true enterprise, which is, of course, the great work itself.'

'Oh, I get!' I say, getting it. 'You're saying it's a blind?'

'Precisely. We blind them with science, my friend.'

Well, at this, I just fall about laughing, don't I? And so does he. And so does Sal. We're all so frigging merry it hurts.

'Fantastic!' I shout, doubled up, roaring all over. 'It's got to be the trick of tricks, the con of cons! Oh, Enoch old son, you're magic, mate, magic!'

And he pretends he ain't. All modest. And I'm so busy admiring his acumen I don't notice where his hand's got to, snaking up Sal's skirt, the sneaky, libidinous bastard. Like I said, was I a fool back then? Answer? Yeah. I was. Yer original cunning man's cully. Oh, yeah, I admit it. That was me. Back in '69. Yer cheater cheated.

♀

Through the hot weeks of August and September the town kept coming. And with them citizens from abroad: Hollanders, Polacks, Venetians, Muscovites, Turks. To entertain them Enoch was obliged to invent an alchemical discourse in Latin (this being the language of ultramarine scholarship) which made no more sense than his usual patter in English. But language proved no impediment to cheating and our foreign clients paid through their noses as cheerfully as any English idiot born and bred.

Our success was a wonder. And although it had already lasted more than six weeks it showed no sign of dissolution. Here was alchemy indeed, though more of Rusty's kind than Enoch's.

For Rusty was now proved a supreme man of business. And of enterprise, too. Here was his genius released. Thanks to him we harvested money like corn; not only from our admittance fees to the laboratory and from the continuing sale of our certificates but also from what he called, rather grandly I thought, his *satellite merchandise*. By which he meant the dinky little models he'd had manufactured in red and green glass of Enoch's magic ostrich together with scarves, gloves, kerchiefs, whatnots, napkins, dishcloths and even kidskin cundums all embroidered either with the sign of the pelican or those chemical symbols denoting the elements of iron, copper and mercury, *viz.* ♂ ♀ ☿. Or if you prefer, us. For Enoch had expounded the profound and peculiar nature of our threefold confederation to me and I cannot but confess it pleased me with an inward thrill to consider myself as Venus and to take bellicose Rusty for Mars and to have my mild, insidious Enoch as Mercury, the wing-heeled messenger of the gods, even though he was pronouncedly flat of foot.

Apart from the burgeoning sales of these souvenirs which soon showed us more profit than the admittance monies, Rusty made yet further gains from the variety of metal goods our customers brought, in their simplicity and greed, to have transmuted into gold by our renowned Dr Quicksilver. Many expected to see the miracle performed before their very eyes upon the very afternoon of their visit. And such was their vehement trust in chemical projection that Rusty and I were often hard pressed to explain to them that any mention of so commonplace a proceeding as the making of immediate gold would provoke Dr Quicksilver to a fury (the like of which was a hurricane) and they would be far better advised to entrust their fire-irons, brass buttons, coal scuttles, steel corsets, spare pruning hooks and any number of ancestral armours, not to mention an entire run of iron palings torn from the perimeter of an estate in Lancashire, to us. We would keep them safe until such time as the great work came to its finition whereupon we did not doubt that the formidable doctor would be of a more pleasant humour – having obtained his life's ambition – and might happily then turn such trifles into something of rather more value than they enjoyed at present which was, was it not, let us be frank, little or nothing?

Thus deceived they yielded up their treasures to us most obediently and Rusty had them at once conveyed downriver to the Isle of Dogs in a sail-barge rented expressly for the purpose. There, at his newfound depot, he sold off the stuff to the witless folk of Essex and beyond. So here again was what Rusty termed *another nice little diddly-do*.

Nor was that all. Have I not said Rusty had now shown himself more than a mere bully boy and – in his way – quite as much a genius as Enoch was in his? For next he leased the building adjacent to us and changed it almost overnight from a warehouse to a whorehouse. This he did by the simple expedient of hiring the cheapest carpenters he could find (all Irish to a man, poor souls) to construct three dozen wooden cubicles of a likeness to human hen houses. Once in place they filled the three upper floors of the building. Into these boxes he introduced beds, also made to measure (narrow – since it was deemed the occupants would be more upon than beside each other) and furnished with cheap mattresses stuffed with the wood-shavings left from the construction of the cubicles. And then, once he had purchased linen sold off for naught by the receivers of a bank-routed weaving house in Spitalfields, he brought in his pullets, assigning each a nesting box of her own and appointing me to be their mother hen, or, if we must speak openly, his brothel's madam.

Meanwhile every coxcomb who inspected the laboratory, whether Christian, Jew or Infidel, was discreetly advised of the pleasure house next door where, as a valued subscriptor, he might find himself entertained by a lady of his choosing (all being high-born, clean as whistles and virtual virgins) wellnigh *free of charge* upon the contribution of £3 to a most worthy charity but only now established for the succour – and care – of aged alchemists fallen into want on account of their selfless devotion to the great work. This sum to be entrusted to me, Mistress Copper (as I was now known), the adjacent young gentlewomen's cherished Mother Superior, as it were.

For here was a masterstroke to equal Enoch's: Rusty had dressed all our girls as nuns and novices save that their habits were split at one side as far as to the waist. This modestly immodest apparel proved more inflammatory than scarlet taffeta and again our clients paid up like lambs, often doubling or trebling their donations to charity, as they sought to make their choice from the devout but libidinous parade we had devised to greet them.

Our ground-floor reception *salon* (Enoch advised the use of the French term to add tone to our establishment) was handsomely appointed – unlike the flimsy boxes above – being furnished with pilfered rugs, stolen cushions, ill-gotten mirrors and chairs upholstered with horsehair. These last items had been grudgingly bought for real money since not even Rusty could promote the theft of so new-fangled a commodity which at that time was known only at Court or in the Lord Mayor's Parlour.

When on parade I would not allow my girls to sit but only to walk around in silence with heads bent low as if in deep devotion. Their eyes, however, they might shoot sideways as often and as eloquently as they pleased. Or they could, if so moved, sink graciously to their knees and with hands clasped in silent prayer allow their forearms to press up their breasts to a more fetching pronouncement; and, while their eyes sought heaven, survey any gentleman before them in all his parts – from top to toe. And in between.

But if our various enterprises showed no sign of faltering and seemed rather to expand like well-kneaded dough, they soon brought troubles of their own. Success can never be simple however much it may seem so to the observer shut outside it. Since, once I had filled every cupboard and coffer with golden guineas, silver crowns and copper pennies, I was obliged to have Rusty prize up the floorboards. Here we stowed our continuing flux of cash in stout linen bags until I noted the plaster of the ceiling below (of the laboratory itself) cracking so ominously with the weight of our success that it threatened to break open upon Enoch's head and dash him and his experimentations to pieces.

The safe-keeping of our wealth having brought me close to my wits' end, providence saw fit to send me a saviour. None other than Lord Spark. Yes! My young Oxford gentleman. Ushered in by Rusty at his most obsequious (all Cockneys love a lord) his eye fell not upon my girls but upon me. At once I was at pains to prevent his recognition of me in Rusty's presence. How my eyes spoke, how my fingers fluttered at my lips indicating the necessity of silence. All to no avail.

'Why, Mrs Sally,' says he, his face a-smirk with recollected satisfactions, 'what good fortune is this? To find you here?'

I pretended not to know him. 'Surely, sir, you are mistaken?'

'Never!' says he, taking my hand and bowing low over it. 'How could I forget my Sally?'

I heard Rusty's indrawn breath, saw his eyes spark flints, all Cockney deference gone.

'Know this gent, do yer, doll?'

'But of course, Captain, of course,' says his lordship out of purest innocence. 'This lady was my dear companion at Oxford not three months back.'

'Oh yeah?' says Rusty, jealous as an Egyptian.

Fearing cut and thrust any minute I say, 'Oh, but you've changed, sir. I scarce thought so short a while could ring such a change upon a man.' And turning to Rusty I add, 'Lord Spark was an invalid at

Oxford. So poorly. Quite incapable of – of anything. I was his day nurse.' And I keep my eye on Lord Spark hoping and praying he's taken my drift. For if not we're lost. Rusty'll beat us black and blue – never mind his rank or my sex.

'Oh, you was sick, was you?' says Rusty, not yet convinced. 'And what was your worship sick of, may a humble Captain ask? Was it the mulligrubs, the terms, the clap?'

'None of those, Rusty,' I say cutting short his insult. 'It was love – love, wasn't it, my lord? Pure but not requited love. You cannot but remember, can you? That beauteous maiden of the House of Campbell.' Surely he's heard me? Surely I've placed my words firmly enough in his sweet, guileless noddle? I cross my fingers, touch the wood of the chair behind my back.

He has heard me! He says, laughing, 'My dear Mrs Sally, you must mean the Clan of Campbell not the House. The Caledonians don't have houses. With them it is castles or nothing.' Then he turns, sweet as you please, to Rusty. 'Yes, Captain, I had conceived an *amour* for this Scotch heiress but she, *hélas*, was betrothed to another and would not break her vows to him despite my wealth outweighing his, hers and all of Scotland's put together.'

And he laughs again most richly while I thank my maker Lord Spark seems no longer to be so green as I had feared at first.

Rusty meanwhile has unknitted most of his eyebrows and when he speaks his tone is dulcet, soft as swan's down.

'Oh, is that so, sir? Your wealth's like that, is it? Sort of wide spread? Kind of substantial? Even massive maybe?'

'Oh, yes, Rusty,' say I, seeing our chance. 'Tell him, my lord, how – since you've come into your fortune – how the King himself comes to you, doesn't he, when he's skint?'

'The King – ?' says he before remembering himself. 'Oh, yes, the King, His Royal Highness, yes, dear Old Rowley himself, our majestical rakehell, yes, he often repairs to me when, yes, Louis of France or our own puny Parliament – what a house of whiners and cringers! – fails to oblige him.'

Rusty's jaw has fallen to his neckcloth. I say, all honey, 'Tell Captain Steele how much you lent His Majesty last July when we were at Oxford. Was it £10,000? Something of that order I'm sure it was? After all the King being so exalted could hardly borrow less, could he? It'd look, well, unroyal, right?'

'Quite so. Yes. No. Nor did he, Mrs Sally, no. Indeed it was – if my memory does not deceive me – it was, yes, it comes back to me now – it was in fact £20,000.'

I liked this latest touch of my lord's. His doubling of a figure I had plucked out of the air. It gave our game the smack of veracity. There's nothing like a detail corrected for conferring credence upon a lie, is there?

'Such a sum, of course, might beggar another man less smiled upon by fortune than myself,' he added.

'D'you hear that, Rusty?'

Had Rusty heard it! His ears were pricked like a mastiff's in a bear pit. Even so I thought I saw a green glint in him somewhere – at the back of his eyes. Rusty may be thick as the Tower of London but he isn't simple, oh no.

He says, quite subtly for him, 'And Mrs Sally, sir? How did she – as your day nurse – care for you? What services did she provide?'

I'm holding my breath. I want to speak. To make sure Lord Spark says nothing untoward but at the same time I know any interjection from me could make Rusty smell the rat that lies rotting behind the wainscot of our converse.

Lord Spark, God bless him, says with a very exact composure, 'Why, Captain Steele, sir, Mrs Sally cured me by her gentle counsel, womanly wisdom, her deep knowledge of the human heart and her chaste presence every afternoon for a fortnight. We took tea together. I import my own from China.'

Rusty goggled. He'd heard tell of this ruinously expensive new beverage but never drunk it. While to be fair to Lord Spark I had. That last part of his account was true enough. We most certainly had taken tea together – but on a sky-blue taffeta daybed, stark naked. Truly the truth may be selected like fine fruit.

'Oh, chaste, was she?'

'As the driven snow, Captain.'

'And so who did the chasing, my lord? You or her?'

At this threadbare banality I protested, 'Oh, Rusty! How can you be so coarse?'

'Comes natural wiv me, darlin,' said he. And still he'd got the ghost of a trouble-maker's grin all over the bottom half of his blunderbuss face.

I said, 'Can't you understand? His lordship and I enjoyed a harmless platonic acquaintance!'

'Oh? Like when poets put their dollies up on pedestals so as to peek up their skirts?'

I said to Lord Spark, fury my master now, I said, 'Take no heed, sir. Rusty won't never change. He's a foundling from a shit-heap in Houndsditch.'

46

But nothing could shake his lordship now. 'Assure yourself, Captain,' said he, 'Mrs Sally's spiritual ministrations enabled me to forget my Caledonian mistress and I recovered my usual appetites.'

'Right.' And I see that Rusty has at last renounced jealousy in favour of gain. 'And you've brought 'em wiv you today, have you? These appetites?'

'Most forcibly, yea, undeniably, sir.'

But his noble eye is still on me. If I knew how to blush I would, but I don't. So I say instead, 'We have much to nourish a man's appetites here, sir. Be they never so aristocratic.'

Whereat I indicate my circle of novices who as always are observing their daily offices before the appraising eyes of our afternoon faithful. And here may be the place to state without equivocation – for it is with me a matter of principle – that as my girls' Mother Superior I required them not only to appear enticingly demure but, once selected by a customer (be he practised liveryman, aged politician or raw apprentice), to give good value, be truly attentive to his animal requirements (and believe you me, your average Englishman can be in bed a most curious beast) and always without fail – this was the first rule of the establishment – always to offer the impression that he, that valued customer, during the space of time he'd purchased, was to them the most important person in the world. Our house must be a brothel with heart, I insisted. And no gentleman was to leave it knowingly under-satisfied.

This liberal policy I attributed to Enoch's emollient influence upon me. For he had so solicitously nurtured what was essential in me that I considered I had become the Goddess of Love herself and had gone quite beyond those common man-made restraints that weigh so heavily upon us women. Lasciviousness was now a crystal fountain of innocent joy to me. In consequence I felt obliged to reformulate each and every one of my girls in my own wicked yet innocent image. And I did. So that we were become a cornucopia of loose-limbed, honey-tongued Venuses and our nunnery was known throughout the City and beyond – even as far as Piccadilly – as the only knocking shop in London where a man of discretion might indulge the flesh without limit or disgust.

Rusty led Lord Spark withershins round the circle until he selected Sister Tabitha, a sweet mystery of fifteen just pulled in from Penge.

As they mounted the stairs to her closet Rusty said, 'Truly rich, is he? That one? Like stinking, up your fundament, rich?'

'Yes, Rusty. And do curb your language. It makes you sound worse than you are.'

'Codswallop! I am what I am, doll. So – anyway, you get his lordship to make a really malodorous contribution to our welfare fund for knackered alchemists, all right? Say twenty guineas minimum. See ya. Got to meet a man about a pullet. Be good.'

And he salutes me with a hearty smack on the backside before swaggering out, all brass neck and cods.

Some half an hour later, when Lord Spark had completed his devotions, he begged a *rendezvous* with me the following day. I assented on condition he pay twice the sum Rusty had stipulated. For I wished to remind Rusty that I could be quite as resourceful as he. Lord Spark disbursed the said forty guineas without demur and kissed my hand three times whilst assuring me Sister Tabitha was the neatest little strumpet but I was the love of his life, the chosen lady of his heart, his soul's necessity and I might be Lady Spark if I chose. I laughed and bade him farewell until the morrow but not, I confess, without a certain trembling of the knees at the thought of so much old money heaped upon one so young, so charming, so noble, and now, in his person, upon offer to me! I could be Lady Spark no less! Surely this was more than Enoch and Rusty put together would ever achieve? But even as I tasted this possibility, that most seemingly desirable of fortunes, I knew I could never accept it. Like it or not I was, in all but name, already wed. And not just to one man neither, but two, God bless me.

That night I lay with Enoch, but where at Oxford I had thought of him while embracing Lord Spark now at Pudding Wharf I envisaged Lord Spark while enjoying Enoch. What luxury! What transport! To have two lovers at once: the one in my head, the other in my cunny. Truly what flies above flies below, as Enoch's forever saying.

He, of course, had not recognised my Oxford gallant for the simple reason that I'd made sure he never met Lord Spark in that city. Therefore upon his lordship's viewing of the laboratory before entering our bawdy house so conveniently adjacent, Enoch had taken him for just another over-dressed young gent, complete with all the usual ignorances of the Sacerdotal Art of Alchemy. So he was – and yet his touch for coining gold, as well as inheriting it, was surer than any of us had at that time supposed.

I met him the next morning at the Exchange. But such was the clangour and dust of rebuilding we immediately took his coach (shining black with his crest upon the doors and blinds) to his mother's house at Westminster. Here I comported myself in a manner absolutely conformable with these matronly surroundings – indeed I informed him at once, on his proposing to show me the upper floors of the mansion, that I would not upon any account consent to a resumption of our former relations until I had had his sincere advice upon a subject of serious concern to me.

'And what's that, Mrs Sally?'

'Money,' I said, speaking out like a dowager.

'Money? Oh, have no fear. My boasts of yesterday were not idle. Though prompted by you to disarm Captain Steele.'

'I do not speak of your money, my lord. I speak of mine. My money.'

I would say his jaw dropped by at least an inch, perhaps more. Certainly I saw a pretty pink tongue and the whitest of teeth – two factors that for me do much to recommend a man. I do love a sweet mouth. But where am I? Oh, yes, he was speaking, was he not?

'Your money? You – you have money, madam?'

'God's life, I do, sir. Too much if the truth was known.'

'Impossible. No one may have too much money save saints and half-wits.'

'But I'm at a continual loss where to keep it safe, sir. And it weighs so heavy – especially the copper and silver. The gold, I agree, is less of a burden. But even so – we've got all these bags and boxes of it. Up in the attics, under the beds, and every cupboard, press and coffer's stuffed to bursting. So just lately I've had to hide it under the floorboards. The plasterwork upon the laboratory ceiling cracks horridly.'

'And all this from your convent?'

'Not all, sir, no. No. We have our subscriptors' money to hand too.'

'Not to mention, I suppose, the monies held in trust for the relievement of distress among aged alchemists?'

'Exactly, sir. And the income from admittance to the lab. Plus Rusty's flim-flams.'

'Flim-flams?'

'That's Enoch's name for them. Those mementoes and trinkets we sell to our female customers while their spouses and companions are contributing to charity next door.'

'Ah so, my dear. Now I comprehend. I had not thought your enterprise was quite such an El Dorado.'

'Oh, don't say that! Rusty's superstitious! He says you must never invoke that name. That's worse than having a black cat cross your path as you walk under a ladder on Friday the 13th.'

'But nevertheless your business, from what I hear you say, at Pudding Wharf, flourishes beyond your initial expectations?'

'That's right, my lord. Though if I'm fair I must admit Rusty always maintained we'd rouse the town. And we have. The thing's blown up like a sow in farrow.'

'But surely this delights you?'

'Well yes, as I say, but also no. On the one hand it would be against nature not to be pleased but on the other, well, it has brought with it a host of trepidations.'

'You fear you may be robbed?'

'Night and day. Yes. Well, I do. Rusty, of course, brags he's the match and master of every thief in London and no house-breaker would dare come near us. But that's just his piss-talk if you understand me. He may drink double ale by the quart but the fact is he's very small beer. Least he was before all this got started.'

'And Dr Quicksilver? What's his opinion upon the matter?'

'Enoch? Oh, he's not of this world, is he?'

'Is that so?'

'Well, you don't know him. But I do, and, well, what I mean is, he's too, you know, airy-fairy? Sort of elsewhere really. Nice but not always with us. Either he's got his eyes on the stars, or else there's his nose stuck in some old book, or then again, he'll be busy stirring sublime of this into root of that.'

'So everything rests upon you? Upon your incomparable shoulders?'

I nod and the next thing I know his limber fingers are dawdling about the nape of my neck and then spreading, firmly, nicely, to caress, gently to knead, the aforesaid incomparabilities: *viz.* my shoulders. For there is forever there a tendon or two grateful for considerate attention. Under this sweet influence I also let fall a tear, in part from my anxieties, in part for show, being still a whore at heart.

He says, all masterful man and from the look of him as anxious to have laid me as to aid me, 'My sweet Mrs Sally, do you not, have you not, thought to invest your money? Surely you must? This money that so irks you? Are you not aware that you may be rid of its base, material presence and yet by investment see your money increase?'

'Invest? Investment, sir?' I say, not knowing these words – at least in his way of using them. 'Do you suppose I should dress it up in some fashion?'

Lord Spark laughs. 'No, my sweet ignoramus, no. I intend the word in its modern meaning. It comes from the vulgar Italian not the noble Latin. From *investire*: to employ money in the purchase of a commodity from which profit may be got, or else to lend it to others against interest.'

'But that's wicked!' I exclaim. 'That's a sin. That's usury. You can be sent to hell for that.'

More laughter from him as at a child. And now that he speaks of money it is a wonder how mature he sounds. Clearly I have been mistaken in him – this is no longer a guileless student but the solemn owner of a mighty inheritance. His bashfulness of the day before I must now impugn to his astonishment, and pleasure, upon seeing me again.

He says, 'Usury is no longer a sin. To invest is today the honourable preoccupation of all gentlefolk. Besides, have I not said the word comes from Italy? And are not Italians all Papists to a man, woman and child? Who in the world knows more about sin than they? Yet they've forgiven usury among themselves, allow it and have renamed the practice "investment" and created, oh, since long since, unique houses known as *bancas* whence they lend out money upon interest to all the world.'

'And they do that safely, do they? How?'

'Upon paper, my dear. They give paper promises. No coin ever changes hands unless it is absolutely required.'

'Oh, like us? We give certificates to our subscriptors.'

'Not quite, no. These *bancas* or *banks*, do it both ways. Your way – that is to issue receipts against the money received together with a guarantee of its increase. And another way which is to lend out that same money again to others upon their promise to repay it to the bank at interest.'

'You may hire money?'

'Indeed you may.'

'Oh,' I say, at something of a stop now. Dare I tell him the truth? Or will he be so shocked he'll report me to the sheriffs? His hand has crept forward from my shoulders to my bosom. His fingers are soft and warm and clever. I sigh. And decide if I can trust his caresses I can surely trust the rest of him. I say, 'But Rusty reckons we won't ever pay our customers back. That isn't the way of it, he reckons. Not for us.'

Lord Spark's withdrawn his hand! Alarmed I turn to him. Have I offended his propriety? Does he see me as a common cheat? I'm going pink and white with fear. He kisses me sweetly on the mouth, I slip my tongue between his pretty teeth but he pulls back. My eyes quiz his. Is my secret safe with him? Is it?

He says with a grave smile, 'My dear Mrs Sally, your business is in its infancy, is it not? While I speak of full-grown enterprises in which there's no longer any necessity to play at fast and loose.'

'Why not?' And I take his hand to paddle in mine. I feel safer touching him.

'Because their profits have become so huge it is wiser, safer and indeed easier for them to abide within the law. You and your partners in your quest for breeching capital, as it is known – in that it takes your infant business out of petticoats and into adult attire – you have been obliged to operate outside the law. It is often so to start with. But no one in the City will think the worse of you for that. And now you have it you may become as plain-dealing as any alderman and as honest as the Lord Mayor. And I recommend you should.'

'We must send our money to Italy?'

'No. No need to go so far.'

'Is there not?'

'No. We have banks in England. Here in the City. As great as any in Siena, Milan or Amsterdam – for the Dutch also know a good thing when they see one. I can propose three to you at once.'

'What are they?' And I can't resist caressing his soft cheek where there's still no sign of a beard.

'Well,' he says, 'you have Sir William Rich upon Coin Street, the Brothers Gold at the sign of the Giant Locust beside Cripplegate, and possibly finest of all, Colonel Lucre's bank within Bleeding Heart Yard.'

It is my turn to smile. 'They sound worse than us.'

'Not at all, my dear. They are soundness itself. Beyond reproach. But you must have an introduction to them. They will not take just anybody's money, oh no. You must be known. Nor do they deal in petty sums.'

'Do you mean they'll ask where we've got our money?'

'Not if I vouchsafe you. And now is the time, my dear. Believe me, there has never been a better. For with the City rebuilding, more and yet more funds are required every day and therefore every day we may charge a little more for our money. And we do. The City is rising as a phoenix from the flames but the costs are prodigious. Yet so will be the rewards.'

'How is that?' say I, marvelling at his rising eloquence and guiding his hand into my bosom once more.

'It is so, my dear, because it is gold that buys bricks and mortar and pays the builders. Not to mention the architects whose fees are as ambitious as their designs.'

'But then your money comes back in sales and rents?'

'No. You gain new money. The interest upon the original sum which is your capital as we call it. And this interest comes to you so abundantly, so regularly, that you may turn much of it into capital and still live like King Croesus.'

It sounded better than Enoch's ostrich and I won't say I wasn't pretty much won over especially with my paps all a-tingle at his fingers' ends. I could feel myself melting but then I thought of Rusty. And I didn't see him liking it either way. I mean he'd been jealous enough of Lord Spark the preceding afternoon without my taking his lordship's advice and more today. Entrust our money to others? Rusty, I knew, would say 'Cods to that.'

I said with a shiver, 'Rusty would never agree, I'm sure.'

'Need he know?' said he, neatly unbuttoning my bodice. 'Could you not shift it out – ' Here my left breast fell plum into his grasp whereupon he kissed it most reverently. 'And carry the money out in parcels when Captain Steele is abroad?' Now my entire bosom was at his command and he spoke between such soft kisses, sweet suctions, gentle cuppings that I was shortly at a loss not only for speech but breath. 'And now I reflect upon it,' said he, 'you might be well advised to invest your money not in one but all three banks – Rich's, Gold's *and* Lucre's. Thus you would, as we say upon Cornhill, spread the risk.'

'Risk?' cried I, rising to my feet before he spread my legs. 'You never said there was a risk!' My tender emotions were gone. Fled in the instant. I buttoned my dress as swiftly as I could. Soon I was an honest City madam again. Modest from top to toe. At least in intent and provided I kept my distance from his lordship. What resistance I might offer should he mount another of his assaults upon me I could not tell. Very little, I guessed, for only the sudden fear of losing our money had diverted me from my true inclinations. Were he to reassure me handsomely I knew I would be lost again.

He did. He said, 'There is very little risk, my dear. For us of the City risk becomes entirely acceptable once the spread of the investment is wide enough. Your capital placed with all three banks would give you exactly the broad security you rightly crave.'

His voice was as soothing as any costly physician's, his smile sincere. But he made no move. I stepped forward, then remembered my necessary loyalty to both Enoch and Rusty, and stepped back again.

'Would you,' said he, ignoring my shilly-shally, 'have any notion, idea, estimate, of the gross sum so far achieved at Pudding Wharf?'

Here was another quandary. Should I tell him the extent of our gains? Lord Spark, noticing my hesitance, spoke softly as to a timid bride. 'Have no fear, dear Sally, your secret will be safe with me.'

'Oh, sir,' I said all a-rush. 'I fear to break a solemn covenant. For only last Wednesday Rusty made me swear never to speak of our success to anyone.'

'But, Sally sweet Sally, this covenant you have already broken. And most opportunely, too. For now you are on the road to a further fortune which Captain Steele will thank you for when you reveal our dealings to him.'

'*Our* dealings, sir?'

'Well, so I trust. For we have much to offer each other. In fact I shall now confide in you something of equal confidence.'

And he was rising up! 'What's that?' I hear myself say with my breathing all short again and my breasts and cunny doing what they forever do when temptation comes their way.

'I shall only say it if you first convey your secret to me.' And at this he takes both my hands in his and draws me to him so we are poised upon the cusp of an embrace. Was there ever so winsome a gallant? I am lost in admiration. And desire. 'In exchange,' he adds, 'you shall hear mine and I will hazard against all odds that when you do you will rejoice. Rejoice extremely.'

Well, by this he's close upon me and I am past all prudence. I say, 'Well, at our tally last night we stood at £198,913. 12s. 6¹/₄d.'

'Nearly £200,000?'

'Oh yes.'

I swear Lord Spark has grown pale at my words and I truly believe I can detect a measurable extension to his virile member pressed against me.

He says, quivering between love of money and love of cunny, 'But this is more than a fortune! This is a King's ransom! And I don't mean Old Rowley's. Who would pay out that for him? No, *Le Roi Soleil* at Versailles might command such a sum but not our waggish Charles. Two hundred thousand pounds! Oh, Mrs Sally, I had no idea of such a sum.'

I answer, much encouraged by what I'm sensible of laid next my belly – will it yet reach my navel, I wonder? – I say salt-sweet as an open oyster, 'Well, sir, now you have my secret, so what I beg is yours?'

He's as short of breath as me now. He says, 'Oh, Mrs Sally, you must know I am a partner in all of these three houses. So if you conjoin with me, I shall be your banker and invest your fortune to the utmost of my powers.'

His eyes penetrate mine and in the instant we are agreed, I'm upon my back upon the rug, my skirts are about my neck and our mutual contract is jointly signed, sealed, and delivered at all speed. There and then. Thrice over. Yes. We are conjunct once for each bank. What delight. Never, I swear, have business and pleasure been so combined. Hey ho!

Once I had got our money safely housed I felt much lighter. And mightily relieved that Enoch's laboratory ceiling no longer threatened to fall upon his head. Not that he would have noticed, so shut up was he in his alchemical world where symbols danced at his behest, metals walked and creation was new-made in bottle glass.

But while it is easy to set down here the deposition of our monies it was not so in practice. Indeed the transferment was a tiresome business fraught with several dangers. Danger of daylight robbery by the more ruffianly of the populace, danger of embezzlement by the less scrupulous of my girls, and danger from Rusty – for had he discovered my purposes I knew I would scarce survive his wrath. Therefore I devised a scheme to cloak the venture.

My device was this. I sent the most faithful of my girls each day upon an apparent alms-gathering mission. They would rattle their bowls for coppers up and down those streets and alleys which housed Messrs Rich, Gold and Lucre, crying, 'Alms for the Needy, alms for the Houseless, alms for the Crippled' – in fact they were under instruction to cry anything that sounded veracious enough to mask their true errand. Which was to meet Lord Spark. When he appeared the transaction would at once occur. In exchange for his ha'penny tossed in the bowl and the password 'God smile on your good works, sister' he would receive the bag of money fetched from beneath our nuns' capacious skirts. And straightway enter the bank with it. In this wise while September passed into October I got all our monies safely lodged upon most advantageous terms.

And each morning that I repaired to Lord Spark to assist at his levee he would present me with a statement of account of what was now gathered in. Each paper always showed precisely how much had been deposited each day (I would cross-check the totals and always they were correct to the last farthing) at which bank. Furthermore he itemised what instructions he had given for the deployment of these funds so that now our monies were invested in such commodities as tomorrow's cocoa beans, next month's potatoes, the coming year's corn, or such enterprises as the West India Company, the China Foundation Fund, the Speculative Development Society, Phoenix Bonds and *inter alia* as Enoch would say, the Established Church of

England for the rebuilding of St Paul's – though in this venture we had only a token investment, for Lord Spark was of the firm opinion, shared by the cathedral's illustrious architect, that the projected dome would fall down, its enormity being quite unsupported save by principles of force perfectly invisible to the eyes of ordinary men.

These statements I kept safe as necessary receipts for our depositions and also as guarantees of future increase. For only upon the presentation of these documents would the banks reimburse our capital and interest, should, as Lord Spark said several times, a rainy day arrive. But meanwhile these documents gave me a very keen pleasure, I gloated upon them like a self-satisfied miser, coin now seemed a vulgar medium prized only by hucksters and other such superfluities. I was above mere money. Like Lord Spark, and all other great persons whose greatness also guaranteed their goodness, I floated now upon pure paper.

He also taught me to refer – in a prettily assured tone – to this miscellany of certificates as my *portfolio* which by a curious transference of thought (for our minds have many a trick in them, have they not?), by an odd association of words and action, became my cunny.

He would say, teasing my thighs with prancing fingers, 'Oh, yes, Mrs Sally, your *portfolio* must come to a most prodigious fruition.'

'Pray God you don't get me with child,' said I, drowning in bliss for Lord Spark seemed every day to become a more accomplished lover. I do believe he performed better than that much-praised, over-puffed, self-advertised Lord Rochester who was (half a dozen of my girls having to my certain knowledge laboured in vain to make something of him) a gentleman more for heroic couplets than heroic couplings. It is often the case I find. The foul-mouthed rake cum self-styled poet strides into your *salon*, all hyperbole, paint and glitter, demands the best of your cellar, the rarest of your doxies and is at once a martyr to vintner's flop.

It was at one of these levees that Lord Spark again asked me for my hand in marriage. This repeated proposal threw me into confusion. For the truth was I had come during this interlude to care for the boy rather more than I had originally intended. And though he was older than me by some four years or so, I nevertheless looked upon him with an almost maternal solicitude, having seen, I believed, rather more of the world than he. And this was true up to a point. The point being, of course, that the world, as we call it, is in fact many worlds in one and it is easy to suppose that yours is the whole of it when it isn't.

But at that moment all I could think of was how to let Lord Spark down gently. For I was bound to refuse him however much his offer plucked at my heart strings, turned over my liver and churned up my bowels.

I said, 'Oh, my dear sir, you honour me beyond deserving. But what would your mother say?'

'My mother? To perdition with her!'

'No, you cannot, must not say that! No son may. She would know me at once for what I am – a country slut turned whorehouse madam.'

'No, Mrs Sally, no! I will not have you call yourself such names. You are a perfect nymph, an eternal goddess, Venus herself reborn. And as my wife you will be raised to my rank in society. I shall present you at Whitehall where you will put Old Rowley's floozies quite out of court. If Charles can have his Nell I can have my Sally.'

'But, sir, the King has not made a wife of his mistress, has he? And by such example nor need you. We are best as we are.'

'You prefer your present state to that of a wife?'

'My dear, I'm only me – naught else. Transmute me into a lady – create me Lady Spark – and I would be a false thing. Bawdy brass got up as gold. And you would be the first to suffer for it. The world would say: "There goes Lord Spark with his high-flown harlot" – and laugh at our backs.'

'I wouldn't care,' said he most fervently, kissing my belly button. 'Nor need you.'

'You may say that now, sir, but I think in time you would care. A gentleman's reputation is quite as irreparable as any woman's.'

'I warn you, Mrs Sally, sweet Mrs Sally, I shall not take no for an answer. Do you hear?'

And at this he pulled out from under a pillow a black silk pouch. Then he untied the purple drawstring and shook it over his open palm. Out fell a ring. And such a ring! It was of gold and carried a diamond as big as a hazel nut! Which burned fierce as a star outfacing the morning sun. Yet as I gawped upon it, it seemed to me to possess at its centre a core of iciest indigo. It was as if this diamond had a sapphire engendered in its crystal womb. People speak of living jewels but never had I beheld one as brilliantly alive as this.

Lord Spark took my left hand and slid the ring upon my wedding finger. 'There,' said he, soft and low. 'There. You may not refuse it. There, Mrs Sally. We are betrothed. And our marriage shall follow as night the day.'

I was left quite speechless and I would tell a lie if I did not say my heart leapt at the sight of it there upon my hand. Tears sprang in my eyes, my cheeks burned, my tongue yearned to say: 'Yes, yes, we shall be married,' but I knew I could not, must not mouth these words, so rather than speak them I bent my lips to his and then so worked upon him that he was obliged to riot with me again and so vigorously that after we were done he fell at once into the deepest sleep whereat I quickly dressed, drew off his precious ring, replaced it regretfully in its pouch and left it upon the rumpled sheets, close to his right hand. Then, upon tiptoe, I quit him.

As I walked back to Pudding Wharf I congratulated myself upon my handling of this business. Had I not renounced him as sweetly and yet as firmly, not to say honourably, as such a noble youth deserved? I told myself I had and I was sure that upon his waking he would understand entirely and entertain no resentment of me.

But then, the following Wednesday – a dark, pernicious day promising naught but premature winter – my faithful girls returned from their various expeditions with their swollen moneybags still banging their knees beneath their habits. Lord Spark, they said, had not appeared at his usual stations upon Coin Street, Cripplegate and Bleeding Heart Yard. He had been nowhere to be seen though they had rattled their begging bowls for hours. I redisposed these latest gains at Pudding Wharf and waited, thinking he was bound to send word, even if he did not himself appear.

I waited for a week, ten days, a fortnight. Then I sent him a loving message at Westminster by way of Sister Tabitha. I swore he meant almost too much to me, that I was his most compliant mistress, that I longed to have word of him, and he might send for me whenever he pleased upon the shortest notice. In other words I abased myself before him. Had I been a Cantonese concubine I could not have kow-towed more extremely. Sister Tabitha returned with my letter undelivered.

The house, she said, was quite shut up. Not even a servant there. I slipped my letter into the kitchen fire and told myself I must not be perturbed. Lord Spark, I told myself, had gone into the country for a while; his mother doubtless had need of him; he would return to me soon enough; I was his lodestar even if I could not be his wife; and, most pertinent of all, was he not my trusted banker? Had he not charge of all our funds save for our very latest gains? And being, as he undoubtedly was, a most noble gentleman he could not but bear such a burden honourably. My investments were safe. All that was required from me was the virtue of patience. He would return. And even if he did not I could always go to his bankers with my *portfolio* and reclaim everything. Thus reassured I addressed myself once more to my duties as the most successful brothel-keeper in London.

Thanks to Sister Tabitha I was fully cognisant of Sally's liaison with Lord Spark long before she saw fit to inform me of it herself. For Tabby would slip into my laboratory for a gossip whenever she had a spare moment which was not so often as I came to wish. The pretty creature was much in demand. She, I believe, regarded me somewhat in the way of being a father to her. Certainly she would sit most comfortably with me and ask a thousand silly questions and I, in return for learning what took place next door, would teach her the rudiments of the great work.

Surprisingly for one so young, and coming at that from Penge, she was quick to understand that the transmutation of metals was as much a spiritual quest as it was a physical practice. She could also comprehend that the stone of the philosophers was entirely different from the philosopher's stone – a subtle distinction usually apparent only to the seasoned adept. In fact so clever was she I soon came to tease her and say I would make her my apprentice. She would laugh and prattle, warming her hands at the Fires of Life as she called my furnaces, address me solemnly as professor, and see all manner of pretty fancies in my alembics: angels in castles, blue eagles, green dragons, self-consuming snakes and any number of crowned lovers, embracing each other most complacently. 'Heavens,' she would say, 'your laboratory is quite as naughty as our house next door.'

Tabby's visits pleased me extremely and I must confess I was often tempted to abuse her trust in me – for she appeared unheedful of her manifold charms, dressing and comporting herself with an innocent informality that would have aroused Old Adam in an eunuch. However, I controlled my baser inclinations, despite Satan whispering within me that I might justify surrender to them, given Sally's infidelity not only to me but to Rusty also. Further, as I reminded his infernal worship several times, whatever Tabby might say of the admixtures in my alembics, this laboratory was necessarily a sacred place that must remain undefiled. Here magical, mystical, chemical weddings were to be celebrated rather than mere fleshly ones. And so, in this manner, Sister Tabitha and I remained in a state of comparative innocence together; which, I believe, was a pleasant comfort to us both.

Meanwhile I kept Sally's secret to myself. Such caution is, of course, native to me and besides, one can never know when intelligence of this nature may be of use. Some have found this characteristic of mine dislikeable, too calculating, even reprehensible. But to such I can only say that I was not created merely to be approved of, nor to seem sweeter than I am, let alone liked. I was born to be me. For however human we may hope to be the truth is we are also elemental. Quite as much as metals are. And if we are to change then we must first be fired. What is more I have ever found as many who could love me as mislike me. Take Tabby. And Sally – in her fashion.

Therefore, knowing Sally as well as I did myself, I knew it was contrary to her powers to refuse any man of parts. Just as Rusty could not help being bellicose so she must be lascivious. Her renewed conjunction with Lord Spark was thus as inevitable as it was predictable. For, even without Tabby's apprising me of it, I had already recognised him. I had known him for Sally's Oxford lover the instant he walked into the laboratory, having glimpsed him twice in that city. Once as he bussed her most heartily in an apothecary's doorway as I returned from my bookseller in the Broad and second, waving to her from a window as she hurried from his door below.

But what I did not know initially (since Tabby, for all her pristine sweetness, had not been entirely candid with me) was anything whatsoever of Sally's fiscal dealing. This I was soon to discover for myself. Nor shall I pretend it was difficult to discern, since her stratagem was, if not quite transparent, then, at the least, hardly opaque. And somewhat of a puzzle – for why should whores go begging? As I observed her girls, so demure in their outdoor habits which, unlike their indoor garments, showed not a square inch of flesh save for their faces which had been scrubbed so raw as to appear as unknown to paint as any more honest brides of Christ, when I saw them pass along the Wharf, their progress struck me as oddly halting. These nimble creatures, who could lead you a dance as soon as look at you, waddled away up St Botolph's Lane like those flat-footed, long-bellied aquatic birds explorers write of that cannot fly, may scarcely walk, yet dive and swim like seals. But then, upon their return, their gait was lighter, their pace freer. *Ergo*, I reasoned that they must have gone upon an errand to rid themselves of a covert burden. Something had gone out beneath their skirts but not returned. What? After three days of this observance I asked Sister Tabitha, direct.

'What do you carry with you, child, when you and your sisters go a-begging?'

'Why, our bowls for alms, professor.'

'No, Tabby, beneath your habits?'

'Nothing, sir.'

And to demonstrate the truth of this she lifted her skirt to her waist affording me a glimpse of those secret charms the mature adept is expected to abjure.

I drew breath, averted my eyes. 'Dear Tabs,' I said. 'You must not be so frank with me, child.'

'Why not?'

'You know well enough. Or else your experiences next door have left you mysteriously untouched.'

'Oh, that's because Mrs Sally – Mistress Copper I should say – is always telling us we need have no shame. Our profession is as honourable as it's ancient. 'Tis only sad philosophers and sour Puritans who condemn it, she says. We may be as proud of our parts as the gentlemen are of theirs.'

I laughed and said that sounded very much like the Sally I knew and at once returned to my first question.

This time I put it thus: 'It appears to me, Tabby, that your regular alms-gathering is but a mask for another purpose. That when you go from Pudding Wharf you are obliged to take with you something awkward, of a certain weight that must be hid from view. What might this be, I wonder?'

To my astonishment the girl burst into tears. 'Oh, professor, please don't ask. I'm sworn to silence. Mistress Copper'll flay me alive if I speak.'

And she clung to me, though whether to distract me bodily from further questioning of her or to extract my sympathy for her predicament I could not tell. I did my best to be as stern as any father of good conscience and for the most part I succeeded.

'Would it by any chance be money, my dear?' said I.

'I mustn't answer,' cried Tabby, burying her face against my breast.

'You needn't,' said I, with an happy inspiration. 'All I ask is that you listen and only correct me if I'm wrong.'

She agreed tearfully and clung even closer to me.

I said, 'Would you and the other girls perchance be carrying the takings from our enterprises here to somewhere safer – to those houses known as banks where money breeds like rabbits in a warren?'

'Oh, professor, how did you guess?' said she, looking up into my face.

'Hush, Tabs, you've no need to speak, remember?'

'Oh, no, nor have I.'

'Perhaps you are instructed to meet an intermediary who relieves you of your burden? A gentleman, perhaps, whom you know and may trust to convey the money to its destined place? For I cannot imagine an innocent religious such as you entering a bank.'

'But I'm not, am I? I mean I'm no more a nun than Mistress Copper, sir. Am I? I'm a mystery. Least that's what she calls me.'

Now was my turn for puzzlement. 'A mystery? What's that?'

'An apprentice flower, sir. I've still got lots to learn, Mistress Copper says, before I can call myself a proper harlot. And I should be glad to learn from you, professor, if you should have the time. For all the girls say you must be a prodigious rake to pleasure Madam.'

I laughed. 'Oh, Tabby, Tab, Tabs,' said I. 'Is that what they say of me?'

'Yes, sir. They say you and Captain Steele and Mistress Copper form a – how does it go? – a manage ah twat, yes, that's it.'

'I believe you must mean a *ménage à trois*, Tabby. A French term.'

'I knew it was naughty. Do you?'

I ruffled her hair, quite forgetting myself and feeling distinctly unprofessorial – even mercurial.

'Perhaps,' said I. 'But you, dear Tabs, have avoided my chief question. Now, do you or don't you carry money to Mrs Sally's friend, Lord Spark?'

'But of course I do! We all do! How did you guess?'

'Oh, child, you have no guile at all. To that you had only to say nothing to confirm it!'

'Now you've got me all of a muddle, professor.'

And she looked up at me, wide-eyed. I held her gaze. Too long. Satan was gibbering lewdness at my inner ear, Tabby's lower belly was moving in a manner most irreligious and I was about to – I record here the words of the Lord of Hell himself – to go for it, when the door banged open to admit: Rusty.

'Doc,' says he. Then, 'Oh, busy, are we? Research, is it? Put one adept and one dolly in a stink shop, apply a generous heat when Luna's in Libra, and I'll give you odds on one of 'em will lay you a philosopher's egg.'

'Oh, Rusty,' exclaimed Tabby. But she was laughing.

I wasn't. I said severely, 'I was merely demonstrating in figurative terms the close interaction of certain vital elements in the alchemical process. Tabitha is a promising pupil, keen to learn as much as she may of the sacred art.'

'Looked more sort of profane to me.'

'That may be because your eye is untutored. What's your business?'

'Tabby. She's called for next door. One of yer regulars, doll. Some cully from Cambridge.'

'Oh, no! Not Eric the Cleric? Of Christ Almighty college?'

'Name of Knockitt, he says.'

'That's him! The pedant. He's awful. He'll as soon lecture you as lie with you. There he'll be poking away, all sweat and no substance, and meanwhile you've got to hear him carp on about poets. He hates 'em. Says they get everything wrong. 'Specially when it's history. Knows everything about history does Eric. Reckons it was all got up for him alone.'

'Come on, doll, he's waiting.'

'Can't Sister Clever Clogs do him? She's more his sort – all brains, no bubs.'

'He's asked for you.'

And with that Rusty hauled poor Tabby out and I reflected upon a woman's lot being a most unhappy one unless like Sally she can rise above it. And this thought led me to consider Rusty. Should I inform him of Sally's stratagem? I doubted he knew of it for he had been much abroad of late, either in quest of yet more harlots and clients or else at the Isle of Dogs where his trade in cast-off metals (iron, copper, brass and lead all bought for cash) had grown in equal measure with our businesses at Pudding Wharf. For while Rusty's clients still brought us their ridiculous household ironmongery in the vain hope of observing me transmute a pewter pisspot into a gold ingot and while I still refused to perform such trumpery tricks (though to conjure such a transformation would be child's play itself given the eternal gullibility of the eternally greedy) Rusty was enabled to ship the offending articles downriver to his depot. It was there that he not only sold them off but quite as often bought more from the voracious Essex folk who were, if anything, as urgent for cash as goods.

What had begun as a subsidiary commerce had grown to a major business. On the island Rusty now had great heaps of metal secured about with new-built walls and guarded day and night by wolfdogs from Alsatia. He was also busy building four mighty furnaces, to my design, in order to make cannon balls for the King's Navy – Rusty having met and supplied the Clerk to the Navy Board with a certain pretty molly who, by happy chance, was the spitting image of Lady Castlemaine. This affable gentleman, whom I later discovered was none other than the informative person Mr Newton and I had encountered upon the river in '66, was so besotted with the notion of Lady Castlemaine's incomparable beauty that for Rusty to send him her 'living double' (as he put it) was regarded by this Mr Pepys as a signal service worthy of recompense of a substantive kind. Hence the Navy's order for fifty thousand cannon balls.

But for all this I had become so intent upon my latest series of experiments in which I followed to the letter Mr Newton's notes (fair-copied by me against a rainy day some years since), that I kept myself apart, as far as I could, from the diurnal mundanities of Pudding Wharf. Though this is not to say my heart did not increase its rate of beat whenever Tabby chose to call.

The nub was I had found myself drawing truly close to the point of producing what we patient enquirers term a 'philosophic' mercury which is a goal every adept strives for but few attain.

My transcription of Mr Newton's proceedings, together with my own observations, have stayed ever fresh in my memory. Indeed I can even now turn these tablets over in my mystical brain and read them as if they still existed in the material world rather than having vaporised with me at that moment which for me is long past but for you, diligent reader, is yet to come. For you will recall that, within the human dimension, I remain mere ether, or, if you prefer, hot air.

My records of these experiments conducted in the fall of the leaf '69 read thus: *Imprimis scito minerale crudum et immaturum esse* ... oh, forgive me, I am forgetting. Future ages have abandoned Latin, have they not? The language of Cicero and Horace is no longer taught in schools save those of a rare but universally abhorred distinction. Very well then, from these my airy tablets I shall, I must, translate the manifold mysteries of the sacerdotal art into the vulgar tongue which now obtains in England and is, I hear, close to Rusty's manner of speech and yet is spoken by the highest in the land. For thus it goes, does it not? Time denies all things, but especially excellence.

My populist version proceeds thus, as though addressed to children: 'Well, for a start, take antimony. This is a crude, elementary, metallic body, sort of bluish-white but flaky. We oldsters call it *Leo Ruber*. Sorry – the Red Lion. But antimony can only be purified by the sulphur you get in iron, all right?

'So next you place two parts of antimony to one of iron in a furnace (and if alchemy sounds rather like cooking, well, it often is, with the adept as the temperamental chef!) and keep it there for six hours and forty-five minutes until the metallic part of the antimony is separated by the sulphur in the iron from all other constituents. You will see it shining at the bottom of your crucible. We call this residue the "star regulus". Now if you melt the star regulus with gold or silver the whole caboodle evaporates! Which, as Mr Newton has said, is something of a mystery. However we old-time chemists are never daunted, though sometimes down-hearted!

64

'Well, now we have got our regulus we put it in a pot with ordinary quicksilver on a low heat and then grind it in a mortar. You repeat this process eight times, flushing out the residues of the amalgam on each occasion with water.

'You are now close to making a very special mercury indeed. But first you must distil it seven times in a retort: a vessel made of heat-proof glass with one or two spouts. You may have seen one in an old picture or museum. They are sometimes called alembics or pelicans. The pelican being a bird much associated with alchemy on account of it supposedly feeding its young with its own blood. But back to the lab where something exciting is about to happen. Because now we are going to put our distilled mercury into a glass with gold! And what happens? Well, the gold and mercury combine and circulate in the bowl of the vessel making the shape of a beautiful living tree continuously dissolving then growing again. It is a multi-coloured mercury quite unlike the common kind. And the form it takes is nothing less, to my supposing, than the Tree of Knowledge; though others have called it the *Cauda Pavonis* – sorry, there I go again with my old Latin! – I mean the Peacock's Tail.'

And it was then, one late October afternoon, as I was contemplating this profound phenomenon and congratulating myself on having at last created my philosophic mercury or the universal agent, as it is also known, when through the enfolding silence of my innermost meditations I heard a noise. A peremptory rat-a-tap as of a walking stick banging ill-temperedly at my door. And in spite of the sign hanging without which plainly stated: Do not disturb.

How dared whoever it was? At once I was moved from the sublimest tranquillity to a tearing rage.

I was a sudden volcano, eruptive, incandescent.

With my heart pounding I strode to the door and pulled it apart, quite forgetting that I often work stark naked. Yes. Apart. For such was my indignation that I had a quite unlooked-for strength so that as I opened the door it fell to pieces at my feet. It was a stout, well-made, oaken door and yet there it was come entirely apart at its joints. If I was astonished (and I was) my unwelcome visitors were the more impressed. Four mouth-agape faces greeted me, pale as death and quite as soberly dressed.

'How now? What's to do? Can you not read the notice?' said I, still ablaze. 'Is it not plain? Do not disturb!'

'Our business with you, sir, does not admit of denial,' said the leading fellow, a bucket-faced grumpus of three score years at least. 'The name is Gibbet. Mr Justice Gibbet.' But although he seemed pleased enough to announce himself he did not afford me his hand. Rather he stepped across the flotsam at our feet and marched into my inner sanctum.

The next man followed him: a suet dumpling of a Puritan left over from the Interregnum, a sweated, greasy thing who had clearly risen high in his own estimation.

'And I am Brother Holier-than-Thou,' said he with a hard smirk and a Yorkshire accent. 'A Baptist but not a nude one. Cover yourself, sir, for shame.'

I said, 'Get out of here this instant.'

For answer the two others stepped in like obedient hounds, but obedient to Gibbet, not to me. The first was a knight of the Shires, Squire Manyacres, with red-veined cheeks and vinous nose. He looked friendly enough – if his friend you were. The second and last intruder was the tallest man I had ever seen, a concave-chested giant, six foot six at least, who spoke in a rattling whisper, as if the constant support of his extreme corporeal elevation left him no breath to speak with.

He exhaled most sepulchrally. 'How do you do, Dr Quicksilver? Lancelot Pinchbeck at your service. No need to dress for me.'

And he held out his hand most civilly.

This produced a bellow from Gibbet as of a bull in a ring. 'You're too damn'd polite, Pinchbeck!' And turning to me, '*Viscount* Pinchbeck to you, you mountebank!'

I said again, 'Vacate my laboratory at once.' And, to reinforce my demand, I seized a white-hot poker out of my wind furnace that was used only for the most ardent processes such as calcination or cementation.

'Peace, gentlemen,' cried Brother Holier-than-Thou, hands in air.

'Never! There'll be no peace here till you are gone, sir!' And I waved the poker under his baptistical nose. Then at Gibbet. But the Justice stood his ground.

'You would assault a Judge of the High Court, sir?'

'I admit of no rank here, Gibbet. Nor titles. Such worldly flummery has no place here. Here all men are equal in the eyes of God and Science. And those who step within these portals must become as innocent as naked children, abjuring all superfluous things. Leave at once!'

'Piffle!'

At this I could contain my wrath no longer. I fetched this presumptuous lawman a swipe across his umbilical parts with my poker, now reduced to red heat. He fell back in outrage crying he was

66

killed by a madman. But the hurt was to his pride not his belly; though the stench of his singed worsted and under-linen stank out the room.

His companions rallying to his support, begged me to forbear. But my blood was up, my stomach revulsed! Here was my laboratory defiled by worse than Gadarene swine! My best experiment disrupted! Why should I forbear? And who were these to command *me*? Me, Enoch Powys, the cunningest man of Wales since Owen Glendower, the spiritual heir of Ripley and Sendivogius, nay of Hermes Trismegistos himself, our Triple Master. No, I was not as they were!

And so I erupted at them, laying all about me with my poker which by this time was scarce warm enough to curl a lady's hair, yet in my delirium of rage as wicked a weapon as any bayonet flourished by a French musketoon.

'Was it for this,' I bellowed, 'that I have devoted myself for years on end to the royal and sacred art, renouncing all recreation in my quest for truth?'

But in pronouncing this expostulation, I had, I must confess, chosen to ignore rather conveniently the constant pleasures of my life at Pudding Wharf; in particular the manner in which Sally entertained me both in bed and at board. For she was almost as skilled a cook as she was a mistress. Truly Aretine would have been hard put to celebrate a more luxurious carrying-on. Who but the blessed enjoy scrupulous philosophical enquiry by day and fleshly indulgence by night? Surely it is a melancholy truth that honest rage can make hypocrites of us all?

However, as I hurled myself at my interrupters, I considered naught of this. I was become avenging fury, militant angel, pitiless scourge of God. Nor were Gibbet and his associates the only entities to suffer, although by this time I had lambasted Holier-than-Thou most vindictively; felled Pinchbeck with a well-placed stroke across his knees; propelled Manyacres into a tub of sal ammoniac in preparation out of ripe Egyptian camel dung; and smacked Gibbet twice upon the nose with my spare fist.

No! These deeds were not enough. Such was my anger I was also bound to strike out at everything I had held most dear. Yes! I was, as it may be said, moonstruck. Pots and pans, pestles and mortars, crocks and crucibles flew every which way, denying those attractive forces, those gravitical powers, that are coming ever more to be attributed to Mr Newton (whose expositions of the physical world may yet equal his alchemical achievements), while various pelicans which I had sent into horrid collision one with another exploded all together with such collective force that the Hall of Hell itself, great Pandemonium, seemed formed about us.

Nor did this combustion assuage my towering spirits. No! I had also to vent my indignation upon my *spiritus mercurialis*: at that meretricious effigy I had made to flatter and divert Rusty's clients (importunates such as this Gibbet and his cronies) from the true work in hand. That machine which Sally always called my glass ostrich. I hit out at it with that absolute venom reserved only to those who must destroy what they have made while despising themselves for making it in the first place. Hell is popularly supposed not to contain any fury like that of a woman spurned. I beg to argue otherwise. And will say there is simply no fury anywhere equal to that of an artist – for so we poor adepts term ourselves – against those things that paltry circumstance has obliged us to create in contravention of our true will and judgement. For in the face of what we call the *magnum opus* Man becomes at once both nothing and everything – mere putty in the Hand of God and yet as a god himself to lesser mortals. Hence my unlooked-for fury. First at Gibbet, then at his companions, next at myself and lastly, at my own works there at Pudding Wharf – the finest laboratory in London, nay, all England.

'May I speak?' said Square Manyacres, ashen-faced, from out of his tub of camel shit.

'So you keep it short, sir!' said I, appalled now by the efficacy of my own violence. Truly I had not known I had it in me.

'We are but a delegation, sir.'

'A what?'

'Or if you will a deputation. From others. We are not come here purely upon our own account. Do I make my meaning clear?'

'No. You do not.'

But now that I was cooled I felt constrained to extend a hand and help him from the tub. He emerged with a tremendous squelch that released an air so vile you might have thought hell itself had farted.

'Thank you, Manyacres, for restoring us to the purpose of our business here,' answered Gibbet oblivious to the stink. 'You, sir, you are under arrest. For assault and battery. Pinchbeck be so good as to fetch us a sheriff this instant.'

Pinchbeck hobbled from the room while Holier than Thou clapped a hand upon my shoulder.

'Any citizen may make an arrest. You, sir, you are apprehended!'

Suddenly my spirits were fled. I could not say a word, make any resistance. My passion, like that of Mr Milton's Israelites, was all spent, though I cannot agree with him that all is best though we oft doubt. In my experience all inclines to be worst without doubt being admitted to the equation. What we needs must do, is always to fix the result to our satisfaction before it arrives to our disadvantage. But I digress. For that moment, at that time, my fury was gone.

But Gibbet's wasn't. Oh, no. He was more than content to pronounce against me while awaiting the Law's material manifestation.

'Quicksilver!' he thundered, omitting my Doctorate of Philosophy, admittedly self-awarded but not the less appropriate for that. 'Quicksilver!' he reiterated, as if I were already convicted and about to hear his sentence upon me. 'I am here to expose a monstrous, fiscal malpractice. What we may term a financial fraudulence that could well de-stabilise the nation! Furthermore, I am not here merely upon my own behalf, or even that of my close companions, no sir! I am come upon the part of some sixty-seven – sixty-seven, sir! – disobliged, preyed-upon, impecuniated subscriptors to your enterprise! This mendacious enterprise, sir, this one, known as the Powys Projection! Registered here, sir. At this very address. Number 3, Pudding Wharf, in the Ward of St Mary Pudding, in the City of London, sir. A venture – you have assured us – it is upon written record – in which base matter will be transmuted by the latest scientifical principles as revealed by the Lucasian Professor at the University of Cambridge into 24-carat gold fine. But you, sir, we are now convinced, intend nothing to this end. All is a sham, a scheme, a fiction! Our monies have gone to line your pockets not your research. You and your accomplices have grown fat at our expense – for it is now discovered to us that your partner Rodney Ironside, also known as Captain Steele, is a notorious pimp and his companion Mrs Greensmith, otherwise called Mistress Copper or even Cyprus Sally, is nothing but a common brothel madam and a by-word for purest filth and prodigious fornication!'

At this slur upon my Sally all my newfound humility was gone again and my passion returned tenfold. But before I could translate my wrath into deeds worse than before – murder at least – Rusty appeared.

There he stood in the doorway, open-mouthed at the damage I had already created so feelingly. For once he had no immediate word to contribute, no ribald comment to offer. This Cockney soothsayer, this street philosopher, was struck dumb. I was glad of it but also wondrously relieved to see him. Indeed never more so.

At last he whistled eloquently and said, 'Good grief, mate. What gives?'

Fuck a duck, whatta shambles! Talk about blood on the walls, here was camel shit on the ceiling! And every frigging utensil turned over. All Enoch's chemical clobber broken and spilt and our famous glass ostrich – the spirit of mercury – just a crunchy carpet of glass splinters a-swim in its own ooze. And the man himself, our Welsh wizard, bollock naked, eyes rolling and steam coming out of his ears.

And wiv him he's got these three cullies – some preacher from the look of him wiv his nose all bloody, then this next one wiv the aforementioned extract of camel right up to his armpits and the last a sorta human gravestone wiv a gaping hole burnt in his breeches so you could see his belly button and worse. Nasty. Quite horrid. Very shamefully shameful. Like tact had gotta be required, right?

So I said, 'Gents all, I pray you, be my guests. Let us repair next door and sink a grateful pint.'

'No, sir,' yells Burnt Cods. 'We await the sheriff.'

I say, still the soul of frigging diplomacy, 'Oh, don't worry, mate. If the sheriff don't find us in here he'll come next door to the convent anyway. He loves the place. Devoted to it. A very devout fella the sheriff.' And turning to Enoch, I add, 'For Chrissake, professor, put some clothes on. You look a right twat in the altogether – I mean you ain't exactly hung like a horse, are you?'

This verbalisation got a grin out of Camel Dung and I reckoned I was on the road to winning the bastard round to my way of thinking but Burnt Cods wasn't having none of it, oh no, not him. He was all gravitas like he was some Judge of the Realm or similar sort of King's codswalloper. And, Mother of God, can our Charlie wallop his cods.

'No,' Gravitarse says. 'You must know, sir, I am Mr Justice Gibbet of the High Court.'

Oh Christ, I'm right. Jesus, I do hate it when that happens, don't you? Like you've got all the horrible facts of the matter together all in one blinding flash and every bleeding one of 'em's correct! This frigger's a frigging Judge! I'm dead, I reckon. Or at the very best, transported for the rest of me natural.

I say, as much a-quiver as Enoch was the moment before, only now he's got a shirt on and has at least one of his rolling eyes under control, I say, 'Well, your worship, your learnedship, your justiceship, I still think we'd be a sight more comfortable next door. It's like a convent *de luxe*, you know.'

Meaty pause for *cogito ergo* as Enoch would say. But fortunately

Dame Luck's in one of her better moods and Camel Dung's all agreement and then, of a sudden, so is Bloody Nose. Nice turnabout that. So next door we go.

But upon entry we very nearly have another nasty moment when the divine Bloody Nose, now known to me as Brother Holier-than-Thou, reckons he's about to penetrate the portals of a genuine *Papist* convent. I assure him the place is full of straight-up English pussy not your purple Roman variety and he's all smiles again, saying it is now incumbent upon him to lead these ladies back to the ways of righteousness and along the paths of virtue. Phew! So far so good. On we proceed.

And then, thank Christ, there's Sally in the *salon*, all genteel, and so respectable you'd think she was Someone's Lady not Mrs Anybody's. And the first thing she does is command her three craftiest cunnies to dispense sisterly tenderness, innocent kindliness and homely cleanliness towards our three cullies. Bloody Nose gets his conk washed down and dried off, Camel Dung gets scrubbed in a bathtub and given a big silk nightgown to wear while new clothes are found. And even the Justice submits to his belly being wound about with a mighty silk cummerbund (leftover from a passing Maharajah) which more or less covers the nasty rent in his breeches. And all the while our best canary wine gets poured from bottle to glass to throat. Very solicitous, mellow and, for the moment, wholesome.

All this hospitality gives me the chance to advise Sally of what's occurred in Enoch's lab, God help us! The which is further illuminated when Enoch himself slides in, cool as a cucumber once more, and all dolled-up in his best silver velvet – what a quick-change bastard that artist is! And with him is this Viscount Pinchbeck – the nearest thing to a talking giraffe I've ever seen and with him, thank Christ, who but the Sheriff of Pudding Ward in person, otherwise my best mate and oldest drinking muckraker, Mr Montague Cruikshank, the finest urinator this side of Temple Bar. For Sheriff Monty – and I tell you no lie – given six pints of double well sunk, can piss you higher than your head. The wagers I've lost to that man. Betting he couldn't water the flower baskets hanging above the front door of the Crooked Billet. He could, I couldn't. Or else in Pissing Alley itself behind Smithfield where you can see the meat-porters' wall marked up wiv all the levels attained and the date, and your name. Since way back. Monty tops the lot at six feet three and five-eighths of an inch. What a performer. My best yet is only five feet eleven and three-sixteenths. So you can see my old mucker is in a class of his own.

So we do the usual 'Look who's here' and 'What's wiv you, me old cock' palaver, shouting, laughing, back-slapping. And I'm real loud on purpose so I can slip him the hard news underneath our Cockney carry-on, sorta in between, aside, *sotto voce* as the Ities say. I tell him I'm in dead schtuck re. Gibbet and company and so is my mate Enoch the Adept not to mench my one and only Sally the Alley. Monty gets my meaning – like all we've worked for is under threat – tips me the wink, and I can breathe easy again and start matching him pint for pint and get ready to lose another pair of sovereigns to the bastard when it's time to take a leak outside.

Also by now Sally's girls are coming the old allure, their habits are slipping – off here, up there – and already Holier-than-Thou is leading two of 'em, giggling their tits off, up the stairs for what he calls further religious instruction but they tell him, slap, tickle and laugh, the rule here is very, very strict, especially for sins of the flesh discovered in gentlemen of the cloth. Meantime the Squire's got Sister Tabby on his knee if that's the name for it, while Viscount Pinchbeck is hanging on Enoch's every word about the sacred art of us three getting rich at the expense of gullibles like him. And the Judge – well, give praise where it's frigging due – our Sally's giving him the full Cleopatra, charming him, plying him with more canary, and he's addressing her as his gracious lady. I tell you I can't hardly bear to watch or listen but I know that between her and Monty our bacon's saved for another dinner.

And all this intercourse gives me room for manoeuvre, as the general said to the colonel's widow, and I'm able to convince the Judge – with Monty offering weighty grunts of support – just how close we've got to success with the Powys Projection. Like it's cast-iron, copper-bottomed, guaranteed. And the subscriptors' money is safe as houses – the Great Fire excepted – and they'll get it all back wiv buckets of interest very shortly. Like when Enoch makes gold. The process is extremely delicate, of course, very, very advanced, way ahead of its time – and here Enoch chips in, thank Christ, wiv a spiel so frigging scientifical it's gotta be true, and at last I reckon we've got the big fish hooked! We've got Gibbet nodding agreement! Wiv Pinchbeck and the Squire following their leader. Nod, smile, grease, nod, charm, nod. Lovely. Only then Gibbet asks – like a shade too nicely? – if we can give him a date for the successful completion of Dr Quicksilver's research? A date? I ask you! Some people! Some hope! But that said – ouch. Kinda awkward.

I look sharp at Enoch, who smiles sorta boyishly, and is about to unload another heap of natural philosophy when I can sense (like in my water) that this ain't gonna wash, not this time round, no, sir. If

I'm to keep the evening as nice 'n' tidy as I've at last coaxed it into being then the Judge has gotta have a date. Like it or not the old dog needs a bone. So frigging toss him one else he'll be barking again, won't he? Stands to reason.

So I come on stern and firm. I say, 'Next month. Four weeks to the day, your honour. The 23rd. No sweat. We'll have gold. Of course, we've gotta get the laboratory put to rights but Dr Quicksilver will be on target, hitting gold four weeks from today or my name ain't Captain Steele. Right?'

But in spite of this very necessary show of strength Enoch coughs. A nasty, sceptical, doubtful kinda cough. So, natch, they turn to him, don't they? And there's our schoolman all academic demur! He can't concur! The cunny's shaking his stupid head. But I'm not having none of it, God's cods, no! Like we must have confidence or we ain't shit. First rule of business, confidence. How else do you pull the cullies? Doesn't Enoch know nothing?

I say again, sterner still and louder, 'The professor can do it, I know he can!' And I make sure I've got my hand on the bastard's knee, all matey looking but gripping it like in a vice, so he gets my gist. And I add, big sick smile at Gibbet and Co., 'You know these scholards, gentlemen. Too modest by half. In fact the more modest they come the more like geniuses they perform, don't they? Least that's my experience wiv the Doctor here. One minute he says it can't be done, the next he's showing you the peacock's tail and under it the philosopher's egg. As for his elixir of life, we're giving it to the girls here right now, did you know? Like testing it before it goes on sale to the public, right? Mistress Copper swears it's working wonders wiv them. Makes every single one of 'em into a right little goer. All that youth they've got already plus this new mixture. Jesus! Jig-a-jig ain't in it!'

Yeah, I must admit I larded it thick but what else could I do wiv Enoch sounding the alarm when least needed? Sally, God bless her, backed me right up. Like real loyal she was. Whatta woman.

She says, 'Oh, Dr Quicksilver's everything Captain Steele says he is. He was taught at Cambridge by Mr Newton, you know?'

Viscount Pinchbeck's heard a lot about Mr Newton, reckons he's the cat's whiskers, and immediately asks Enoch to tell him more. This stroke of Sally's works the business. Enoch is now well and truly deflected (he likes nothing better than to jaw on about his past mentor and patron) and Sally, Monty and me – we can complete our reassuring of Judge Gibbet and Squire Manyacres. Like tucking babies down for the night like. I reckon if we've convinced them two we've convinced 'em all. What with Holier-than-Thou getting his upstairs and the Viscount deep in Newton's laws of celestial bodies in motion.

The Squire is only too ready to agree especially as now he's got Sister Tabby purring pussy noises into the crook of his neck and Gibbet, with Sally's hand patting his, finally pronounces that he will suspend further action until November 23rd but should the projected result be unachieved by this aforesaid date it will be his duty to prosecute us without further ado – and with the utmost rigour, ahem.

We all agree upon this and with a nudge to me Sally beckons Sister Lettice across (she being a high-born harlot and just the job for his justiceship). Lettice slides in like a boa constrictor upon Gibbet and suddenly he's found that despite his being a learnèd lawman, he doesn't know his arse from his elbow after all, though both appurtenances are feeling nicer than they ever have before, and somehow he's sorta floating up to heaven with clever Lettice. Papists talk about the assumption of the Virgin – but that was as nothing compared wiv the sight of Gibbet ascending to the Honourable Lettice's nesting box.

This main matter concluded it's now time for me and Monty to repair outside and I lose as per usual while Monty assures me he'll keep an eye on Gibbet and advise me straight off if he gets restive again though we both reckon the danger's past and agree Sally handled the whole thing like the duchess she ought to be. And in we go again for our next session.

But what's happened? Something has. While we took our leak. Well, for a start the saloon's gone dead quiet. Sorry, *salon* I should say. Which at this hour of an evening ain't that unusual, it being the first shift (as our girls call it). Most of 'em are upstairs hard at work and Sally's gone into the office to balance the books, someone's playing 'Nymphs and Shepherds' on the portative organ, and here's Enoch all alone, sorta waiting for me, in the middle, like he's a menacing silver ghost.

I say, 'All right, mate?'

He says, 'No.'

I say, 'What's the trouble?'

He says, 'You.'

'ME!'

'Yes, you, Rusty.'

'Why, what've I done, for Chrissake? Nothing. Except repair the bleeding damage you've done!'

'I'm not talking about that.'

'Then what?'

'I'm talking about you making a promise to a third party on my behalf without consultation with me. *Viz.* to Justice Gibbet that we shall achieve projection by the 23rd of next month.'

'Well, we had to say something! Thanks to you going pot-herb loony in the lab! What was the big idea? Apart from being like frigging stupid. You put us all up the conduit!'

'They interrupted me.'

'So what?'

'I was about to achieve it.'

'Achieve frigging what?'

'The universal agent that digests gold – the philosophic mercury – '

'*Digests* gold? We don't want to digest gold do we? We wanna frigging make it!'

'It's part of the process. According to Mr Newton – '

But I've now had enough of bleeding Newton! And I shout, hot 'n' strong, as the Jewboys say, 'Do me, professor! Yer lab's all cods, innit? The times I've told you!'

'Yes! And the times you haven't listened, Rusty!'

And now – would you credit it? – Enoch's gone wobbly again. Like he's trembling all over. He's a-quiver. And his eyes – words can't do justice – it's like they burn! And he's at me! This long streak of pedant's urine is trying to stick one on me. A fist in the gob! A knuckle toothful upon Rodney Ironside, me, yours truly, Captain Steele! And though I may have been baptised a simple Rodney I ain't one, that's for sure. Oh, no. If you should ever bump into me I'd advise you to call me 'Sir' first, then 'Rusty', and if you're a chick 'Rod' later. Next – if you wanna get real familiar 'Rod Ironside, sir' said wiv the correct degree of cringing respect could well answer. But remember, never 'Rodney' on its own. Like I said, I expect awe, right?

Only I ain't getting none from Enoch. Oh, no. This one's got instant murder on his mind. Though I don't see what I've done. If you ask me I'm the injured party. I may be thick as pig shit – and how often does Sally tell me that? – but as I see it, at this particular moment of Anno Domini '69 I've saved the fucking day at the eleventh hour. Saved it from Enoch's stupid stupidity. Jesus Christ – the Welsh! They gotta be the trickiest scumbums on earth!

Well, by this time, he's either beating a tattoo on my chest with his puny fists or else swiping me round me iron jaw with the back of 'em. And calling out like a girl, 'Take that, Rodney!'

This, of course, is it! Enough is enough. So I shove him back wiv my left arm – all sheer, unhurried authority 'cos might is right, right?

– and ball up me other fist to fetch him a classic right-hand cracker to the jaw. So he'll be out like a light. And when he wakes up he'll have learnt his lesson: never punch outside yer weight.

But will you believe it? The bastard grabs my fist wiv both hands, turns his back on me, cracks my arm over his shoulder and the next thing I know I'm flying! I'm a body in motion! I'm describing an arc! I'm in orbit in Sally's saloon! Only now I'm not, am I? No, the warrior has landed. Kerump! I'm all of a heap on the floor!

Needless to say I'm back on my feet in a flash and coming for Enoch. And like now I mean trouble, real meaty trouble, know what I mean? Enoch's gonna wonder what's hit him. This is to be ugly. Nay, brutal.

But every time I go for him he ain't there. The slimy sodomite's dodging and weaving like an eel in a barrel. And he's taunting me. Shouting rude things like I'm all balls and no brains and I realise he's kicking up such a racket that all my girls and their customers are popping their heads out of their closets and peeping over the stairs and through the banisters to see what's to do down here.

And they can see I'm getting the worst of it! Like the mad professor's making a monkey out of their protector! And now here's Sally come out of the office! Oh, no, this is too much, this must not be, this is worse'n the pillory. He'll be clipping me ears next! Enoch make mock of me? Never!

I lower me head and go for him, catch him at last in the chest, knock the breath clean out of him. He's down, I'm on top. He's out from under. I'm up again. Only not so mobile. Great. I wind up me killer blow, throw it, straight at his gob – I'm gonna smash his pearly teeth in – and wiv me other fist, here's where the brutality comes in, I go for his kidney – a low-down, alley-rat stroke, I know, but I gotta win. No question this time. If I don't win I'm a laughing stock. Just listen to them religiouses – shrieking like bats!

But what now? Oh, no – can it be? – me ankles are knocking together, Enoch's tapped 'em wiv his foot! And I'm falling forward, no, I'm not. I'm going over his shoulder again. Oh Jesus. Only this time it's different 'cos he's spinning on his heels and suddenly – I swear I tell you no lie – I'm being swung round and round him by me arm. He's got this sudden strength. Where from? I'm off the ground – all twelve and a half stone of me and every ounce of it sheer muscle and bone is gyrating in orbit round this pathetic little smartarse. And as I fly I feel myself growing redder and redder with the anger, and the shame of it. God in heaven, I'm like a red-hot ball on the end of a lumpa string – Enoch's string. And my head's full of stars, shooting this way, that way and there's others too going round in velvet darkness, all blue and green or silver and gold, going wiv much the same motion as me, in the same direction, and all the while I can hear and see these airy spirits – like are they nice as pie angels or dirty demons? – pissing themselves wiv mirth to see me so humiliated. Me. Sally's God of War.

Then he lets go and I'm hurtling to my doom hitting my head on this big oak newel post we got at the bottom of the stairs.

I hear Enoch say, 'You may speak for yourself, Rodney, but never for me. Never again.' And he stalks out, head in air. How's that for gratitude when it's at home? And all of this in front of Monty, too. Kinda shaming. Shee-aye-it.

♀

Men! Enoch and Rusty fighting like tom-cats! And if Sheriff Cruikshank had not been with us we should have all been carted off to Newgate by the neighbourhood's watch. Me, for keeping a disorderly house, and them for making a civil disturbance. Not that there was much that was civil about it, with all my ladies laughing their heads off, their gentlemen likewise, and my two common law turkey cocks gobbling at each other. Not at all what we expect from a respectable house of pleasure in the City of London where a man of business may restore his spirits after a day with Mammon.

However, Monty and I – between us – soon had Rusty restored to sense of a sort and our girls back where they belonged. Though I confess I could not but sympathise with their intense satisfaction at seeing Rusty put down. After all, had he not, in the first instance, put each of *them* down, and then most inexorably deflowered them? Whores ever love a pimp's comeuppance. And I shall ever be the last to blame them.

Also I must set it upon record here that I owe a lot to Monty Cruikshank. Apart from anything else he was my very first paying gentleman and stayed a regular pal after. And it was Monty who now, straightway, got Rusty drowning his shame in more strong ale – or was it barley wine? No matter. The result was the same: peace on earth, goodwill to all men – which allowed me to seek out Enoch next door and make certain he retired to bed with a good book and stayed there. He said he had only stood up for his principles. I told him we had had quite enough of *those* for one night, thank you.

An hour after with Rusty himself again and determined to prove it with Sisters Chittyface, Rumper and Bunnybum – I can say one thing for Rusty quarrelling and drink never depleted his ardour nor his performance of it – I was able to retire myself and, discreetly, reward Monty, on the house as we say, for his protection of us. And so honour was at last satisfied on every side and Pudding Wharf could echo the watchman's cry: 'twelve o'clock and all's well.'

Even so it took me three entire days, and nights, to effect a reconciliation between Enoch and Rusty. First the one said he would but the other would not, then the first changed his opinion while the second thought he might have been too easily won round. And when, at last, I had inveigled the silly pair of them to shake hands and drink a pint of sack together – 'dago's widdle' Rusty called it – even then I was in no wise secure in my mind that they were become once again the comrades they had been. Although they swore they were. Most assiduously. For where formerly a sincere warmth had grown up between them (the attraction of opposites, perhaps?) now there seemed to be little but the calculated affectation of amity for mutual advantage. It was always painful for me to see Enoch try to be too vulgar; just as it was never right when Rusty tried to be polite. In other words they were oil and vinegar which will amalgamate most effectually if whisked hard enough but left to themselves will very soon separate. When I was there to stir them together I felt at ease, but when I was not, I knew they grew apart.

However, despite these provisoes, our life at Pudding Wharf returned to its former pattern. The laboratory was put to rights, although neither Rusty nor I could persuade Enoch to build another spirit of mercury. Strangely, some of the materials which had been spilled and spattered during Enoch's fit of fury, were, he said, improved by the excitation. Especially the sal ammoniac that Squire Manyacres had sat in. According to Enoch the indignant warmth of his posteriors had acted upon the camel dung to effect a residue (or lees) at the bottom of the tub quite remarkable for its concentration and its purity.

Much of this time Rusty busied himself abroad. Such had always been his habit, of course, but now he was more than ever out of doors. His enterprise upon the Isle of Dogs commanded great attention, he said. He even took Enoch with him one afternoon for further advice upon the four furnaces he was building and they returned in apparent good humour together. But the next morning Rusty was sour as a crab apple, saying all Enoch the Adept was good for was the spending of money, not the making of it. Enoch, I soon discovered, had advised the lining of the furnaces with a brick of a particular density that was ruinously expensive.

So our days passed with the convent doing as well as ever while the laboratory drew fewer and fewer visitors. I put this down to the absence of the glass ostrich. And also to Enoch's flat refusal to discourse upon the sacred art. A customer would now pay good money to enter our Holy of Holies only to discover a dull, workaday place, not unlike a smithy, inhabited by an irritable adept who said little and explained nothing. Such visitors, not surprisingly, came away much disappointed, and did not recommend Pudding Wharf to their friends nor their acquaintances. Nor did they buy our latest certificates which Rusty had got newly imprinted to accommodate our latest date of projection which grew nearer by the day.

One way and another I felt the spirit of our joint enterprise had departed with the destruction of Enoch's miraculous machine. I said as much one dinnertime but he pooh-poohed me saying the glass effigy of Hermes the Mystagogue had been the toy he had always said it was. A pretty emblem and a charm for the ignorant, but in no wise to the purpose or the true end of the vital process. His bleak denial (though scientifical I had no doubt) gave me no comfort. Was not the soul of the place quite gone? I retreated next door and devoted myself demurely to the management of my house of pleasure. For after all, when all's done, we may say of a well-appointed brothel that it does, at the least, enjoin us to the exercise of love and so, in the practice of it, who knows, some of us may achieve a true contentment?

Yet happiness was still far from me. I dwelt in a continual unease. Unsure of my co-mates, of our money and my future.

One night, after I had lain in bed alone for several hours, always expecting Enoch to appear, I rose up. The moon was full. My unwelcome thoughts in need of dissolution. To speak sincerely I needed comfort. For while I was assumed by all and sundry, but especially by Enoch and Rusty, to be a supreme and accomplished comforter of men, the truth was, is, and shall be, that I too have need of consolation upon occasion. Who does not? So wrapping a tawny silk gown about me I went downstairs to hunt out Enoch.

He was, of course, at work, silvered by moonlight, in his shirt. He was intent upon watching one of his pelicans bubbling on top of one of his furnaces. He looked like an anxious cook worried that the sauce might curdle. I smiled, then giggled. He looked up so harassed, so intense of eye, that my heart melted.

I said, 'Come to bed, my sweet.'

He shook his head, sighed, said, 'I can't leave this. If I can achieve this interfusion, this matrimony, this imbibation, then – ah!' And he interrupted his speech, lifting the pelican from the fire. 'There,' he said in a softer tone and with a less agitated air. 'There. It is done. Now we must add this to the cross-let – ' Again he broke off as he tipped the emerald-green liquid from his pelican into a crucible in which dwelt crystals sharp as diamonds.

This operation concluded he then took a ball of pastry he had by him (purchased from the now resurgent royal bakery up above Thames Street) and rolled out a strip as deftly as any royal baker. After pressing this around the rim of the crucible he placed the lid firmly upon it so it was extruded all about. This, he now informed me, like any housewife, was to seal the casserole. No air, save that already present, must penetrate the vessel during the next stage of the experiment: *viz.* incubation.

He then placed his precious stewpot in his sand furnace where it was to bake amid a constant but dulcet heat for five hours and as many minutes.

'Are the last five minutes for luck?' said I.

He smiled indulgently and his smile said that I was no adept. Nor am I. At least not with base metals.

'Now,' he said, 'I must refresh my memory of what it was Bernardus Trevisanus observed – '

But here I put down my foot – hard upon his. 'No,' I cried. 'Bernardus Whomsoever can wait. We must talk, Enoch. Talk!'

'Of what, Mrs Sally?'

'Many things, sir.'

And to my surprise he set aside his worm-eaten book and said most candidly, 'Very well, my dear, for you the great work can wait.'

I said, 'Will you swear to keep what I say secret?'

'Even from Rusty?'

'Especially from Rusty.'

'Very well. I swear it.'

I took breath. 'We must be gone, my dear,' I said. 'Before it is discovered there is no gold.'

'But mayhap I can make it?'

'You can't believe that, Enoch!'

He sighed. 'Sometimes I do, at others I don't. Yet Mr Newton was convinced it could be done. In the material sense as well as the spiritual. And surely we have no need for flight – have we not Rusty's friend the sheriff to protect us?'

'Yes, but if there is no gold by the 23rd then I doubt even Monty can save us from the gallows.'

'The gallows?'

'Most surely! Justice Gibbet is no idle name, my dear. And there's another thing – quite as secret, swear again.' He sighed at my earnestness but gave me his word anew. I said, 'All the money – well, the most part of it, is not here.'

And I told him of Lord Spark and his *bancas*.

'Yes, I guessed as much,' he said.

I was flabbergasted for I thought I had done so well. And so secretly.

'You did? How?'

'Now it's your turn to swear, Sally. You will not punish my sweet informant, will you?'

'One of my girls?' I was indignant, nay, beside myself. I had thought my novices were all mine.

'Swear,' said Enoch, implacable as old Saturn.

'Which one – ?'

'Hush. Give me your word. For it was I wormed the truth out of the simple creature. You may blame me not her.'

'Tabby? Of course! Sister Tabby!' exclaimed I.

'I say neither yea nor nay.'

'I'll roast her alive!'

'No, you shall not, my dear. Promise.'

And he gripped me by the arms. Being me I had to battle not to embrace him, to remind myself I had other business quite as urgent. I nodded and he released me.

I said, 'I propose to go tomorrow and withdraw sufficient funds for our departure. The pair of us. You and me. Together.'

'But I cannot depart. I have no purpose save this.' And he patted a chamberpot in which dwelt two toads.

'But with our money you can start again somewhere else.'

'Travel again?'

'Or hang, Enoch. We may go back to Oxford. Or Bristol, perhaps. Or even north to Edinburgh. Somewhere we are not known and yet may live decently. Or abroad. At Paris! I could run a lovely nunnery at Paris.'

'And in this we shall deceive Rusty?'

'We have no choice, my dear. Not if I'm to be Mrs Powys one day. Nor is it only Rusty. Oh, Enoch, the offers – the more than handsome offers – I've refused on your behalf. Out of love for you. Lord Spark, Sheriff Cruikshank – '

He was pale now, shaken I think. He said, 'Is this true?'

'Would I lie to you? To all the world if I must. But never to you, Enoch. Will you come with me? Will you?'

He gazed upon me a full minute by the clock before he said, 'To the world's end, Mrs Sally.'

And then he reaches out to stroke my cheek. And, of course, the next instant we're embraced, my tawny gown is off, his shirt torn from his back and we're *in puris naturalibus* in a pool of moonlight on the lab floor. And for some reason quite hidden, quite beyond me, this is quite the most exquisite congress I have ever enjoyed. And I have, of course, enjoyed more than most. Nevertheless, that said, I cannot easily relate what heights of sensibility I attained there upon the floor of Pudding Wharf. And as at Oxford, when I first lay with Enoch, I was granted visions. This time we embraced in an emerald garden upon a perfect lawn in summer sunlight. And as we strove to tie love's knot there strolled three times about us Enoch's translucent ostrich. His *spiritus mercurialis* running with gold within, sparkling with gold and fire without, flapping its gaudy peacock wings and with its serpent's tail entwined about its three necks while its three heads chanted one after the other: 'The seed is sown, the womb shall conceive, great Sol is generated.'

Back on earth as we lay, breathless on the laboratory floor, bathed in silver dew, I whispered, 'Did you see it?'

Enoch had not. 'See what, my dear?'

'Your glass bird. We were conjoined in a garden and he was stalking all about us and calling out things: things like, the seed is sown. At least one of his heads did. The one with the hooked beak. "Squawk," it squawked: "The seed is sown."'

'Well, so it is. The first head would have been Luna, of course, the second Sol. What did he say?'

'"The womb shall conceive."'

'And the third head would be the Conjunction of Sol and Luna in Taurus, the House of Venus. Did you hear him speak?'

'The one with the long beak like a stork's? Yes. He said, "Great Sol is generated." Oh, Enoch! What if it's true? Me with child. Oh, no. Me. I know it sounds unnatural but it doesn't seem natural, not for me. Let alone me carry Great Sol. What does that mean?' And I clung to him like a green girl, I mean fire in your belly is one thing (especially for fellows like Rusty) but not the sun. What woman wants to nurture the sun inside her let alone give it birth? I trembled in Enoch's arms. 'It's just fancy, isn't it? Another flim-flam? Only in the mind this time?'

'Certainly,' he said in just the voice I needed, slow, sure. 'It is not the destiny nor the quality of Venus – and you are my Venus, Sally – to be with child. What you felt was not conception in the carnal sense but the spiritual creation of Mercurius. Your vision sprang from remembrance of my effigy of him. No, my lady, you were made to be born anew each morning at the sea's edge and to possess an absolute purity of lasciviousness. Your fate is to be eternally beautiful beyond all human expectation, to be the perfect object of your sex – ' And here he was kissing my neck and left ear so intriguingly, with such flittermouse delicacy, that I felt myself altered beyond resistance all over again '– but not to bring forth flesh and blood.'

'Yes,' I sighed, 'yes. You have such a gift of tongue, Enoch. You have words at your fingertips while your lips – oh, my dear.' And I, for one, could speak no more.

The next morning when I woke I was in my own bed with a dim recollection of Enoch carrying me to it like a bride. But now he was gone again and though this time I did not stir myself (being too imbued with languor) to go down in search of him I nevertheless found myself recalling his words concerning me. They made me both sad and glad even as I felt them to be true yet false. Perhaps I should accept them simply as the effusion of love? Nor was I convinced I was not with child. We would see, I murmured to the pillow.

I must have slept again for the next thing I knew Enoch, stark naked yet clothed in sunlight from the unshuttered window, was dancing and shouting in front of me, looking twenty years younger, he could have been a boy of fifteen not a scholar of thirty-five.

'We've done it, Mrs Sally! We've made gold! True gold!'

And in his hand was cupped a tiny nugget of yellow metal no bigger than a peppercorn. It certainly looked like gold. It rolled prettily in his palm. He explained how it had come from the crucible he had placed in the sand furnace; how he had made every essay of it he knew and it was proved. He, Enoch Powys, had achieved Mr Newton's dream. And he was sure our making of love beside the furnace whilst it cooked had been intrinsic to the process, since it had been as chaste as it was lascivious.

But now my difficulties were begun anew. No, made worse. My persuasions of the night before were quite forgotten. For having achieved this scientific miracle – although the market value of so small a particle was negligible – Enoch insisted he must continue night and day, for as long as it might take, until he had found a method to produce a greater quantity. My task was to show this sample to Rusty who, in turn, must show it to the sheriff. Our subscriptors, informed of this spectacular success, were to be powerfully enjoined to further patience and all would be well. More than well. The age of gold was truly about to return. The date Rusty had imposed too precipitately upon the project must be revised to conform with science rather than Mammon, and we would not be taking our leave just yet. Oh, no, never fear, all would be well!

And with that he descended to the laboratory again, leaving me with a sinking heart. And even more doubtful of our future than I had been the night before.

In the late afternoon of that same day I found a moment to notify Rusty of Enoch's success. He declared the nugget a fake. Dismissed Enoch's claim to have justified his researches as yet another fairy story. 'The bastard's a faker, doll,' he said three times over. 'You know it. I know it.'

Did I? I said, 'He doesn't.'

'Maybe. But that's his choice. Like he's welcome to fool himself but not me. Besides this little knob won't satisfy nobody. Not Monty, not Gibbet.'

I was bound to agree. Rusty was voicing my own reservations. I said, 'You must tell him, Rusty. Tell him to his face. Tell him we've got to go. He'll never make it in time.'

'We both will, Sal,' he said, with that highway grin of his – all teeth, eyes of ice. 'Like now.' So we went in to him.

But would Enoch budge? No. Rusty and I argued this way, that way. And all honour to Rusty, he kept his temper. Despite everything. Even when Enoch told him to have faith, that what was false could be true, base metal could be gold. Finally we both of us told him he must mind the consequences since we would not. I had had a secret hope this last throw would make Enoch reconsider. To my dismay it did not. My sweet wizard was become as deaf as the toads in his chamberpot. I ran from the laboratory in tears.

Rusty came to me and I cleaved to him. I was glad of his common touch, his common sense. I told myself to put Enoch's ambiguities behind me – they were of the devil. I wanted life not philosophy. Whereat Rusty astonished me.

He said, 'Maybe you and me – we oughta do a moonlight, Sally? Just you and me? Cut our losses?'

Had he read my mind? For I confess I had asked myself if Enoch would not flee with me then perhaps I might do worse than persuade Rusty we should depart together? If one wouldn't the other might? However, I answered that I must think upon it; that such a course might do, but I hated to desert Enoch. Rusty said he understood and I believe that for this once he did. He really did. He said he would await my answer.

Thus was I truly torn; my loyalties more divided than ever. Before, I had extolled Enoch to Rusty's detriment but now I found more to admire in Rusty – his resolve, his practicality. Whereas Enoch had proved himself more wedded to dreams than to me. This disquiet was further stirred by Sheriff Cruikshank coming to the salon one quiet supper hour, when all our usual young whoresmen were gone to some gaudy night at Whitehall, to confide, in strictest confidence, that he was now under what he called 'the iron fist' of Mr Justice Gibbet. He had been sent for to the Judge in his chambers that very morning and been advised that if the matter at Pudding Wharf was proved, by the first hour of the date agreed upon, to be moonshine in a mustard pot (*viz.* a trick by three bags of scum: that was – Rusty, me and Enoch) then he, Gibbet, would require him, Monty, as Sheriff of St Mary Pudding Ward, to an absolute and rigorous performance of his duty. In plain words, arrest us. And while Monty regretted it had come to this, he was bound to recognise his duty when it was pointed out to him by such as Gibbet. If not then he, too, might come, like flies on a bull's pizzle, unstuck at the crux. Meantime the least he could do was to give us fair and friendly warning. Right?

I said, 'But why are you telling this to me rather than to Rusty? I thought you two were the oldest pals in Christendom?'

'Because, my dear old Sally, such a tricky business is better handled by a clever lady like yourself.'

Well, Monty might try to butter me up but I'm no parsnip. I said, 'You'd have me do your dirty work for you? No, thank you. With such a message I'll get a black eye at best from Rusty – if not a good kicking.'

'No, no, Mrs Sally,' he protested. 'Rusty will appreciate that I can't be seen with him no more.'

'But you may be seen with me?'

'Of course. For to be seen with you, my dear, may always be put down to Cupid's dart, right?'

And he smiled lasciviously while his right hand was already straying upon a feeling errand. I set it aside.

I said firmly, 'This is no way to make love to me, Monty.'

He said, 'But surely I deserve reward? Haven't I offered you what we call "red-hot, indoor information"?'

Well, I've lived long enough in this vale of tears to comprehend that some insinuations must be attended to. And as you will have noted I had no insurmountable aversion to our double-dealing sheriff. Therefore I gave Monty what he craved, though I cannot say my heart was in the performance, yet at our conclusion he appeared gratified enough. As we dressed I said to him, a little ruefully, 'Well, that proves Rusty's old proverb, doesn't it?'

'Which one is that, my dear?'

'His favourite. He's always saying it: There's no such thing as a free fumble.'

He laughed, kissed me cheerfully and was gone down the stairs, whistling like a blackbird. I wish I'd kicked him.

So, being now in possession of all the facts and having enough common or garden sense to realise I could not afford any further indecision, I decided to confront Enoch at a final interview. Once and for all.

The next morning in the laboratory I told him that Monty had confirmed my worst fears. He nodded but did not break off from pounding eggshells in a mortar. I said we must therefore, without further ado, depart that very night, taking what ready money we still had stored at Pudding Wharf – this being the Lord's day and therefore not a time to take my receipts to Lord Spark's money houses. He nodded again, shaking calcified mouse-droppings out of a curcubite and coughing at the pother he had made. I said our case was urgent. He nodded as if in agreement with himself. I asked him if he had heard me? No reply – he was raking ashes out of Athanor, his sixth furnace. I stamped my foot, and told him if he would not answer then I should, for my own safety, leave him to face Gibbet alone and flee the city with Rusty who in this matter had more sense than him!

I thought this last admonition might bring him up short as a colt on a leading rein but no. He nodded again. At this I lost all my customary forbearance. For though I am a country girl traduced by the town I have always tried to keep my mouth as clean as my person; a coarse-tongued harlot is invariably a cheap one, I believe. Rude language sits better on a pimp like Rusty.

But now I forgot my usual manners and cursed Enoch furiously, stamping not one but both my feet and weeping buckets. Hearing me he grew as sullen as Saturn. Next I cajoled, I wheedled, and eventually I even – oh the shame of it – sought to seduce him once more among his furnaces! In the full light of day and upon the Sabbath at that! May the Lord pardon me. But despite all this Enoch was unmoved. He remained as heavy as lead and duller than ditchwater.

When at last he spoke, he said, as if I were a convocation of the Royal Society rather than his mistress, 'You should understand, madam, that I am bound by my art to pursue my quest until fulfilment. Your claims, or Rusty's, or the subscriptors, can have no weight at all with me, nor with the *magnum opus*. The great work is sacred. If you must go then go you must, but I must stay.'

Beyond myself upon the receipt of so many *musts*, I screamed like any fish-wife, 'Then you stay, you fork-tongued, lying, creeping bastard! And may you dance on air!'

And upon this unseemly yet satisfactory blast of abuse I left Enoch to his doom, taking a boat downriver to the Isle of Dogs. There to tell Rusty all.

I had not visited his depot before and so was quite unprepared for what I saw both of it and in it. I had heard him brag of its size and contents, but had considered this Rusty's usual hyperbole and quite discounted half of what he said, assuming it a dump. How wrong I had been. Here were stout brick walls topped with iron spikes, tall gates of studded wood, ten vicious wolfdogs, the great furnaces Enoch had designed, and such towering heaps of discarded metals as quite beggar my powers of description. Suffice it to say that one pile stood higher than Queen Eleanor's Cross at Charing and consisted of nothing but antique andirons left over from the kitchens of King Henry the Whoremonger and his daughter Good Queen Bess.

But if I was astonished by the place, the sudden, unlooked-for sight of Monty Cruikshank in earnest converse with Rusty surprised me even further. What was this? Had not Monty sworn blind to me the day before that he must not be seen with Rusty? Had his oath been nothing but a falsehood to get me on my back? To say that I boiled over with indignation would be to understate; I was ready to expostulate even more vehemently than I had already that morning at Enoch. But before I could approach them Monty slipped away through a side gate and I was left to face Rusty alone.

'Why, Rusty,' I said, 'was that not Monty I saw with you?'

'Did ya?' he said, full of no expression at all.

'I'm sure it was.'

'What's wiv you, Sally? Why've you come down here?'

I decided for the moment to allow Rusty to evade my question concerning Monty. I would return to it later. Nor would I answer his just then. Rusty was as prickly as a hedgehog. Something was astir.

I said, 'I had no idea you had such a venture down here. How clever you are, Rusty. How resourceful.'

'But I told you, doll,' said he, saluting me upon the lips.

'It must be worth a fortune.'

'It is, doll. Come and look.'

And he takes me by the hand and leads me past the furnaces to a wide space beyond as square as a parade ground at a barracks. And as trim – the gravel finely raked. And upon it there stood pyramids of cannon balls, all polished and oiled. Some were as big as bowls, others the size of billiard ivories. I counted twenty of these pyramids. They were ranged in rigid ranks with an area left vacant for one further rank.

Lost in admiration I said, 'Why, it's a work of art, Rusty.'

'Well,' said he, flushed with pride, 'the Navy likes things neat. You've gotta be shipshape for the Admiralty or they'll flog the skin off yer back for breakfast.'

'There's hundreds of them!'

'We can make fifty a day.'

'And all so shiny.'

'We buff 'em, then grease 'em. So they don't rust. Yer rusty ball in the breach is a slow ball, the sailor boys tell me.'

'I wouldn't say so, Rusty, not with you, not in my experience.' And I tickled his manhood for an instant just so he understood my pleasantry. He did. We embraced like old spouses happy in the feel of each other. At this rate I felt sure we might soon speak of what truly concerned us.

Rusty said, 'We've delivered two thousand so far.'

'Has the Navy Board paid you?'

'Well, no, not yet. But my mate, their Clerk of the Acts, says there won't be no difficulty. And if there should be, which there won't be, he can always have a word with the Duke of York about it. So I'm not to worry, he says. And he should know. Affable fellow. Full of chat. And a real ladies' man. But short of sight.'

I was astonished to find Rusty so trusting of the Navy. For after all, it is the King's Navy, isn't it? And they say King Charles's word isn't worth the breath it's spoken with. Charm, all the royal charm in the world, they say he's got. But rely on his promise? Never.

Rusty, suddenly come round to the purpose just as I knew he would, said, 'You was right, Sally. That *was* Monty just now.'

I said, biding my time, 'I thought as much. What did he want?'

Rusty snorted. 'A slice of this.'

'Of your business here?'

'Yeah, the sly sod. Like he's heard it's a gold mine, he says. And he wants me to cut him in as an old mate. On a significant scale, as he put it. Oh, and I wasn't on no account to tell you, doll. He was dead bothered when he caught sight of you coming. Couldn't wait to shog off. But he did say we'd gotta have another chat later. I didn't like it. I still don't. Not with him hinting he knew something I didn't and I better go along with him or else. I told him he was talking like some Scotch border bandit.'

'Blackmail?'

'That's the word, Sally. There ain't no other fits the case. Imagine! Monty, my old muck-mate Monty, putting the screws on me! I still can't credit it.'

He sighed, kicked a cannon ball, cracking his toe upon it, swore, then fell silent.

I said, 'Monty came to see me, too.'

'He did? When?'

'Yesterday.'

'Why?'

I told Rusty why. Told him how Monty had warned me, in all apparent solicitude, about Justice Gibbet's desire to string up the three of us if Enoch failed in his projection of gold. How he had pressed me into promising to break this news to Rusty, which even then I had – and how, in return, in recompense, for Monty's calculated confidences, I had been obliged to grant him a free slice of me.

Rusty balled his fists. 'The bastard! That's cake and eat it, innit? The both of us taken for a ride. Right! That's it! I'll kill him!' And he started off towards the gate. But I pulled him back, I said, 'There's more to tell, Rusty. Listen, I beg you. And after, you may do what you please.'

He simmered down to bubble heat and I continued my tale. I confessed that I had tried to persuade Enoch one last time to come away from Pudding Wharf. But out of regard for Rusty I omitted to mention that I had intended to go only with Enoch and not with him. Without actually saying so I contrived to imply that I had proposed our departure as a tripartite evasion of the law. I concluded by saying that I was now of Rusty's previous opinion and that he and I should depart together as soon as maybe, indeed that very night, and rebuild our lives elsewhere. Leaving Enoch, Monty, Gibbet and all our subscriptors to stew each and everyone of them in his own juice.

To my surprise Rusty did not answer at once. He appeared constrained by thought. And in this most unusual hiatus I realised, only too suddenly, and clearly, that by telling Rusty of Monty's interview with me I had stoked the furnace in him to my own disadvantage.

At last, having turned brick-red and spark-eyed he said, 'You and me, doll, make a run for it?'

'Yes,' said I fervently. 'Like you said yesterday. It's that or the gallows, Rusty. Say yes, please!'

'No.'

I swear I have never heard his voice sound more measured. Nor seen him look so commanding. It was as if he had added a cubit to his stature which is, as the Good Book tells us, quite impossible. Except now Rusty was suddenly become the complete warman he had always said he was. It seemed he had tempered his whole ardent, braggart disposition in iced water and come out pure steel. To tell true, at that instant, I was frightened to look at him.

'No?' I said, shocked into trembling query.

'Never, Sally. Me leave our winnings so Monty Cruikshank can collect them? Enoch's lab, your dolls' house, this depot? My contract with the Navy? All for Monty? Oh, no, Jesus, no. I'll kill him first and swing after if need be! But never that! No! The two-faced son of a bitch! Waits for years, making out he's my best mate. Holds on until I'm really on the up, really rolling in it and then, bingo, the squeeze! And who do I blame as well? Enoch. Oh, yeah. Like he humiliated me in front of Monty, didn't he? With them low-down, dirty, Nipponese wrestling tricks of his? Yeah. Gave Monty the idea he could put one over on me, too. And on you. Oh, I see it all. But if Enoch's horrible, Monty's worse. Christ Almighty, verbalosity fails me, doll. Like Monty's evil. He's gotta go. Oh, yeah. Nobody does this to Rusty Ironside and lives. Like the contract's out for him already, right?'

I begged him to reconsider although I knew my words were quite in vain. Rusty was now bound by himself and custom to conclude his grudge against his erstwhile comrade. For within their fraternity such treasons have always called for death. Rusty's reputation was put at hazard; soon, if not already, the word would be out that Cruikshank had challenged Ironside for the mastery of every profitable mischief in London. War was declared for the controlment of all high road bamboozles, back alley cheatings, city lane cogs, front door swindles, and park walk chicanes. In consequence Monty would have by now recruited yet more bodyguards and put a pair of eyes at every street corner. In other words, the battle lines were already drawn up between them and I was left in the middle and in danger from both sides.

This being the case and since neither Enoch nor Rusty would come away with me, then I must, I now realised, act urgently upon my own account while there was still time. I might, I supposed, go to Monty for protection. But even as I thought it, any comfort in this reflection vanished. For, if Rusty overcame Monty, then Rusty would surely kill me for such a betrayal: and if Monty beat Rusty then I knew I could never live with myself after – I could never be the mistress of Rusty's murderer. Therefore, willy-nilly, I was obliged by necessity to safeguard myself.

Rusty said, 'You'd best let me alone to think, doll.'

Here was the last confounding of all my hopes. So I said I would do the same; that I, too, must take thought for the future. Whereat, after offering him a kiss so disconsolate it barely brushed his cheek, I took my leave of Rusty and the Isle of Dogs. Indeed of everything I had so far known.

♂

It's still the talk of the town. Oh, yeah. Even now. It's become the stuff of legend. It was in six broadsheets – wiv woodcuts, two in colour! They even made a ballad of it. 'The Battle of Pudding Wharf', it's known as. I sing it to myself sometimes. Like it cheers me up.

Not that I'm down-hearted. Oh, no. Newgate's sorta comfortable. Always has been to those who know how. I mean I've still got plenty of mates both on the in, and on the out, as we say. And like cash is never a problem, not wiv me pullets still putting out like it was Easter time – which now I think of it, it nearly is. After all, today is All Fool's Day, so chocolate fish, marzipan bunnies and painted eggs can't be far behind, can they? Yum-yum. I've always had a sweet tooth.

So one way and the other I still enjoy my creature comforts. The girls are forever calling by wiv hot dinners, warm cunny, fresh linen. Like I tell you, they really provide a service. No, all I lack is liberty. 'Cos the fact is stone walls *do* a prison make, and iron bars a cage. Oh, yeah, believe you me. Trust a frigging poet to get it arse about face. Anyrate, rest assured, I'm working on the liberty angle. Like I gotta be out of here before I'm called to trial, right? That's imperative. Get me? Point taken? Good. But that's still between you, me and the chamberpot, all right?

However, before I get started, honoured squire, gorgeous squiress (book-lovers both), you really need to know the back end of the story, don't you? Like how exactly did this famous battle, dust-up, riotous assembly, barney and/or public affray (take yer pick) come to be what it was?

Right, yeah, well, here we go: when Sally left me, back in November last year, all on me ownio on the Isle of Dogs, I was in mid-ponder, wasn't I? There was me thinking, right? Remember? Reckoning how I could get even wiv my erstwhile mate and fellow pisser, Monty Cruikshank, who wasn't just asking for a slice of my metal business but had also intimated he would shop me to Judge Gibbet if our Welsh wizard, Enoch the Erudite, didn't come up with the goods by the 23rd of the month. G day as I called it. G standing for gold, of course. And Gibbet. And Gawd help us.

Nor was that all. Oh, no. Because there was my Sally telling me she'd had to put out for Monty. Oh, yeah. That conniving bastard had presented his blackmail of me to her as if it was really a friendly tip-off to us both. And therefore worthy of reward. Like one good turn deserves another, so on your back, duckie.

Call it peculiar but Sally's the only one of my girls I can ever get jealous of. Where are you, doll? A letter wouldn't come amiss. Just address it here to Captain Steele, the Portcullis Room, Newgate Prison. That'll find me. And while we're on the subject – where's Enoch? Because he shogged off, too, didn't he? Come the 23rd? Only question being who wiv? Was it wiv you, Sal? I didn't see you. Was you in league wiv him again? I wouldn't put it past you. But one thing's certain, doll, once I'm out of here I'm coming after you. And him too. Oh, yeah. That's a promise.

But back to yours truly, all a-thinks on the Isle of Dogs after you'd gone. Not that I stood there long. No. Because all of a sudden I had this flash of inspiration. I was like illuminated. I knew what to do. And that was take a pair of oars up to Lambeth and look in at the Old Green Dragon – as fraternal a boozer as you'll find anywhere – if you're one of the fraternity, that is. Nice 'n' quiet. Cool. No singing allowed. No frigging lutes neither. Just quiet chats wiv old china plates and useful new ones. And every bastard vouched for, right?

And the landlord's a pearl among men. Don Rocco he's known as and the *Don* isn't short for Donald, oh no. It's for respect. Like it means 'sir', right? Even to me. The word is he's the bastard son of a Sicilian slave-trader and a Neapolitan contessa. Could well be. He's all charm. And muscle. One thing's for sure – he keeps an orderly house. Nobody pisses in Don Rocco's fireplace wivout permission granted, if you understand me. And if you need to know who's where at any given moment, friend or foe, in or out, or who's ripe for employment upon any venture you care to name then Don Rocco can always supply you with the right fella at the right price. You could call the Green Dragon a job exchange, really. With Don Rocco taking ten per cent of whatever the job's worth. He also runs a tidy little protection service for everyone doing business at Foxhall Pleasure Gardens just along the road from him. But that's another story and need not detain us now.

So upriver I went and even though the tide was on the ebb and the river jammed solid with traffic at the bridge my oars got me to Lambeth in under the hour. The lads was all of a willing sweat so I gave 'em tuppence over the odds (they was my sort, really) and they was so pleased they swore to drink my health that night – the lying sodomiticals.

Don Rocco was his usual suave self. Whatta magnifico. And, yeah, he had just the jokers for me. A coupla Poles lately out of Danzig. The Krosno twins. Not possessing too much English but with loadsa *lingua franca* and urgent to get some gelt – *viz.* cash. They'd do anything for ready money and never fail. Slit a throat, that'll be a groat, right?

So I say to Don Rocco, 'Where do I find these sons of bitches?'

'Right here,' says he.

'When?'

'Give me an hour,' is his answer. So I do. I settle myself down in a corner wiv a jar of his best double ale (magic) and absorb it gently while trying to decide if I want these Krosno twins to bring me back just one of Monty's testicles or both? *We'll see* is my mood. Sorta meditational.

Three jars later in they come, this Polack pair. Don Rocco's been as good as his word. And what've we got? What do I see before me? Well, for a start, a double chunk of corporeality, really. Not too tall but broad in the shoulder. Could be they was built for real in-fighting. Two flat-iron faces plus four pig eyes sharp as needles. Greasy hair chopped short. And dead identical. Ditto their clothes. I doubt even their old mum coulda told 'em apart. So – so far so good.

Except their breath! God in heaven, it blew me away! 'Struth, burnt cabbage kept on a warm stove for a week wasn't in it. It was like they'd put their rectums where their mouths was. Jesus puked! Me, too. But, but, but, let me be humanistic, this eager duo was far from home, down on their luck, and only wanted to earn a dishonest penny, right? And like their brows was bedewed with eager compliance. They couldn't do nuffink too soon for yer. No matter what.

So I apprise these Krosno comedians of my requirements. I paint 'em this portrait of their quarry, warts 'n' all. And, boy, has Monty got warts. Two on his conk and three on his chin. Like he makes the Old Protector seem he was really Adonis De Luxe. I also tell 'em where Monty resides when he's at home (Number 12, Bun Hill), point out what boozers he prefers – wiv special reference to his favourite, the Crooked Billet by the Artillery Ground, saying how if they see, by the light of the moon, this big bastard watering the flower baskets above the door, from below, like he's a fountain wiv feet on, then that's their man. That's our sheriff.

But, I say, kinda serious now, but, I shall require material proof of them duffing Monty up. Oh, yeah. Like I shall need a token of their success before I part wiv the moolah. Understood? It's to be cash on the nail – or rather on receipt of Monty's signet ring wiv his little finger still in it, 'cos, upon reflection, I've decided to be merciful, after all. Like since we was once old muckers, fellow urinators from Temple Bar to Tower Hill, I'm prepared to leave Monty's unique standpipe wiv its highly regarded dependencies in place. At least for the moment. Is that clear? Have they got their horrible Polack heads round that?

They nod. I give 'em half-a-crown in advance wiv double to come on delivery of the aforesaid digit. We make wiv the shakes. Their palms are hot 'n' dry – a point in their favour – I like a choleric humour in a hitman. And off they shog, all need, greed and evil. Nicely. I relax. Sink another quart and take my leave of Don Rocco's meritorious establishment wiv expressions of mutual esteem on both sides.

But, oh dear, where am I when they come back to me three nights later? At one o'clock in the morning? I'll tell yer – back at my old pad in Wrestler's Court where I'd installed my latest pudendum. A Liverpool lass. Eager to learn but already a natural-born harlot. Lascivious as a civet. So when these little pebbles rattle the leaded lights I'm not best pleased, am I? However, patience being a virtue I ever aspire to, I contain my ardour, ease myself out of my Scousie's embrace and take a look-see out of the window.

And there's these Krosno comics wiv their heads bandaged up so they look like a pair of Turks on a pub sign. What's more, one of 'em's got a crutch up his left armpit while the other has both of his arms in a sorta double sling, for Christ's sake. Nor do they appear overwhelmed wiv joyfulness neither.

So I take a deep breath, shovel myself into a pair of breeches and I'm down the stairs, five at a time, to let 'em in before I'm a laughing stock all over town if I'm not already.

'What's bleeding happened?' says I.

'Boo hoo,' says they, all down in the mouth, bruised 'n' beaten.

'Did you find Monty?'

'Ya, ya, mister.'

'And? You did him over? Roughed him up? Sorted him? Where's his ring? Where's his finger?'

'Nah, nah,' is all they could say, shaking their horrible headpieces and moaning like distant foghorns up an Essex estuary. And now I'd got a coupla candles lit I can see their bandaged brainboxes are all bloody at the sides. Oh, dear, again.

94

'Plis, mister, plis, we go to man,' says Numero Uno – or is he Numero Duo and does it matter? No, it does not. 'We find heem like you tell. We hit heem. We knock heem on floor, ya? He go quiet like leetle mouse. I go to take ring – '

'And?' says me, waiting for the catch in the fabric of their yarn. Like here comes the dirty great hole in it.

'Plis,' says the other one. 'Plis. This man. This sheriff, he having friends he was, ya? Out come they of the beerhouse, ya? All one, two, three, four big beef buggers, ya? You know them, mister?'

'Yeah, like I can imagine, yeah. And? What then ensued?'

'It bad.'

'You don't say? But how? Just how bad was it? You don't mean to tell me they did you up 'stead of t'other way about like you was hired to do? Like?' I can be real mean when I want. You know, ironical.

'Ya, mister.'

'Not only,' says the next one. Seeing how there's only the two of 'em they come on plentiful. Must be on account of it being the middle of the night and me being pulled off of the nest to get a load of the unwelcome. Like their news is so bad it's worse'n the Dutch blockade. 'Not only,' adds this one for emphasis, 'but also as well, please, ya, mister, they do cut away the ears, ya?'

'*Your* ears?' I query, meaner than ever. 'Yours?'

Whereat they both nod, would ya believe it? 'Course you would, like you're the smartarse reader, and me, I'm only the stupid narrator, right? So on we go, you've got it now and me, too.

And this is it. This one wiv the crutch takes the best part of a Krosno earhole out of his pocket! Then another! Then two more! Four curly bits of gristle he's got in his hands. They lie there in his palms like something the cat's brought in. Ug. Nay, ugly.

'We shamed,' they shout – the pair of 'em in unison. All indignant, even bellicose.

Well, I can concur. Me too. I'm also furioso. I mean this reflects on me as well, dunnit? And Don Rocco. That's four of us that Monty Cruikshank's heavies have made a monkey of. Like it's embarrassing. Like we've been humbled. Like we don't like it, do we?

'Don't worry, lads,' says I. 'You'll get satisfaction or my name ain't Rusty Ironside, the Cockney captain you can't afford not to trust.'

And I give 'em their money even though I can't pretend they've earned it. But my reckoning is they did try and they was outnumbered. Besides, if ever a pair of desperadoes needed cheering up it was them unlucky Polacks that night. Also I advise 'em to get a periwig each – the sort that hangs right down, like what the King wears. That kinda headgear can cover a multitude of absentee auricles. And, come to think of it, now ear-clipping's all the rage (both lawfully and unlawfully) you'd think your full-bottomed wig had been invented specially on purpose to save unfortunate lughole losers further humiliation. All right, I know the fashion's come from France really. And over there, at the court of King Louis, they wear 'em well below the knees, and in bed, too. But that's the dirty Frogs for you.

Anyrate exit the Krosno twins and I retire upstairs where I find my latest fancy asleep and dreaming. But I leave her be 'cos I've gone kinda critical. Sorta cosmic. Inside. Like where before my quarrel wiv Monty was local, territorial – just a grudge fight, a falling-out between old city mates – now it's on another plane. Like it's like war in heaven. Up among the spheres.

I mean I can't, I won't, have Monty exulting all over town over me. Oh no. Not again. That is not admissible. No. Insult has now been added to injury, right? And while the Lord may well say vengeance is His I'm not leaving it to Him neither. Suppose his Son was to say: 'Leave off, Dad'? Rusty has seen the light and it is red. I'm gonna have a slice of my very own revenge. A big, fat, juicy, personal slice. And this time you can forget little fingers, ears and even cods. This is to be entire dismemberment.

So I cogitate. And make a list of those villains what owe me a favour. It's surprising how many do. I discover I've seen to a lot of people's welfare since whenever. Lent a crown here, succoured somebody's mum you know where, greased a magistrate's palm there – all that. So pretty soon I've got twenty merry bastards I can call on. At least on paper. For a start there's Abe Shemozzle and Randy Randolph, not to mench Kipper Manly, Slim Arnold, Will Toplady, Brendan O'Bryne, Edge Venables – you name 'em I've got 'em pricked down for action. What a troop.

And that's just from my side of the town – the east end. I'm not even counting Don Rocco's fellas south of the river. But I reckon he'll come across wiv as many again. After all, he not only runs Foxhall, Lambeth and Bankside, he also masterminds the watermen, fisher-men and lightermen. And nobody comes meaner than them, do they? But like they reckon the Don's a force to be saluted, old Father Thames himself. It's oh, yes, Don Rocco, you're quite right, Mr Don Rocco, would you like a barrel of salt-cod, Sir Don Rocco, can I ferry you up west, Lord Don Rocco, there's these firkins of brandywine fell off of the stern of the Lord Mayor's barge only last night, King Don Rocco etcetera. Need I say more? No, you get the sampler, don't yer?

By sparrow-fart I'd got my strategy drawn up. And like all great battleplans it was a masterpiece of deceptive simplicity. But getting there took quite a bit of thought. Oh, yeah, the old noddle took a hammering. What I had to do first, you see, was to work out not just what day it was but what hour of what day. And like when I got there St Ethelreda's opposite was banging off six o'clock in the morning of the 21st day of frigging November, right? Which meant I'd got exactly forty-eight hours before the dawn of G day, the 23rd, when Sheriff Monty would come wiv the full majesty of the Law to Pudding Wharf to collect what wasn't there and never would be, on behalf of Judge Gibbet and our other gullibles.

Now the big question was: Would Monty expect me to be there? I thought no. No, no, no. My reckon was he'd be counting on arresting Enoch, maybe Sally and her girls (but only so they could work their way out of trouble wiv him and his cronies), and impounding all remaining goods and chattels before sticking up wanted notices for me all over both premises.

But suppose I *was* to be there, wiv my mates, lying in wait? Like in ambush? What then? Yeah. What indeed. I can tell you: big surprise. The first principle for military success. We could all be there, quiet as death, waiting for him, lurking, hunkered down in the pussy palace. And not a pullet in sight for Monty and Co. because I'd have told 'em all to vamoose well before dawn. Like they could doss down for the moment at Wrestler's Court. It would be a squeeze but a nice one. A real giggle. Once we was victorious.

Right, so there we'd be, like them Greeks in that horse while, in the meantime, and, boy, do I intend this time to be mean, Don Rocco's forces glide in under cover of the morning mist in a magnificent flotilla from the South Bank and we'll have Monty like in the steel jaws of a dirty great mantrap. Ker-runch. Because, as we burst forth out of the hen house, each and everyone of us fell as death as they say, Monty'll be so astonished he'll retreat into Don Rocco's fellas as they leap ashore.

And for weapons we'll have knives, crowbars, catapults, and the odd pistol just in case. Not that I'm planning on a shooting war as such, more a bruiseful, unhumane, bloody ruck as in football. Lotsa crippling but no sudden deaths as such unless by accident on purpose, right? And in this mêlée I shall aim only for Monty – Monty here I come.

Right, that was my strategy worked out. Now all that remained to do was to salute my neat little marmoset from Liverpool (or if you prefer my squirrel from the Wirral, since that's where she hailed from), who, in the soft dawnlight, was looking most amiable, amenable, malleable, not to say amable, what with the sheets pushed back all a-rumple, and her charms akimbo to the view. Phew!

Love's call to arms fulfilled, I'm away down the stairs again and abroad. Back where I feel even more at home. Out on the street. Recruiting. Only this time it's warriors I'm after, innit?

First call Abe Shemozzle. He's got this co-operative society of unpaid lacemakers in Petticoat Lane. Like these old dames don't get cash for their labour, oh no. They get kind words and promises instead – dead charitable it is. But this respectable enterprise is just a cloak for Abe's real business – supplying cadavers to doctors of anatomy. Like your ambitious medical man or Royal Society philosopher will pay solid money for soft flesh (male or female, young or old) provided – and this is some proviso – it's still fresh. The more it smells the worse it sells – right? Which is where the hard graft comes in. For Abe. Like it stands to reason any sharp-witted sodomite can rob a grave. I mean they're always at it, aren't they? Where else do antique rings and cameos come from? But the corpse itself is another matter. Like invariably too far gone. So for Abe, graveyards are not applicable. No, his dealing is otherwise. Wiv them as arrange interments for the bereaved. Abe has befriended every frigging undertaker in Britain. And coffinmaker. In other words Abe robs coffins, not graves. Like he's in there, post haste, *before* the parson's even said, 'We brought nothing into this world and it is certain we can carry nothing out but meanwhile I've got these three very handsome benefices, thank you very much.' Yeah, Abe anticipates the funeral, supplying wax effigies (often of a speaking likeness) to replace everybody's nearest and dearest, who then get carted, packed in ice, up or down, depending whence the cadaver's coming from, to London. Well, to the Mile End Road in point of fact, because that's where Abe has his deep-dug ice house for the reception of this oh so perishable merchandise. In this way your Yorkshire auntie, who only asked to be laid beside your Yorkshire uncle, comes south to further science. As did her spouse before her, had she but known it, only she never did, did she? 'Course not, your uncle being long since anatomised, right? Jesus Christ, how them professors and their students fell about when they saw his vitals laid open – they reckoned his heart a hoot, his liver a laugh, his spleen a splutter, and as for his gut, well, that was not so much an educated giggle, more a learned grin. Great jokers your medicals even when not on the beer.

At Abe's substantial residence I get the full Yiddisher welcome plus breakfast. But after it has subsided and I'm up to the gullet in variously preserved relatives, pickles, bagels, fish 'n' beef – so salty –

no wonder the world's circumcised love nothing more than several gallons of their own kosher *vino* to wash down their nosh, like they cut the throat of every single grape – did you know – and let it bleed to death? Oh, yeah. I tell you no falsehood. That is it, straight up from the Promised Land. From which we Gentiles may gather that when Jesus changed the water into wine at the wedding feast it was a bit more of a miracle than at first appears.

But the reverse of Abe, the patriarch, is Abe the corner boy. Though wealthy and well settled (two kids and another on the way), Abe still likes a decent rumpus; he's of the view that a proper dust-up once a month keeps his hand in and his pecker up.

So family respects duly observed we toddle out for a morning draught and I tell Abe the tale of Monty's perfidy. Well, given my eloquence, he can't wait. Like he volunteers for action before the words are half out of me gob, and what is also germane to the matter, he reckons he knows of three other stalwarts of the Chosen people who'll come in wiv us, no questions asked, and just for the exercise. How about that? So don't you never tell me your Yiddisher can't be a gent. And a fire-eater, too. Nicely. After the which, we gargle the state o' the nation for a bit. Like, as ever, it's going downhill in a handbasket, and have I heard the latest? This present Parliament (for want of a politer word – like they say it's in the pay of Louis of France) this load of landed freebooters is reckoning on raising a new tax. A tax not on goods but upon services, can you imagine? It's a continental idea, of course. Rumour has it some bastards in the Low Countries thought it up. Like the moment somebody does anything for you, they tax the effort involved. So if one of my doxies pleasures you for half-a-crown, say, you've gotta pay another twenty per cent on top (another sixpence!) which goes to Parliament so our lords and masters can fuck for free. And people call me a villain! All very politic, equitable. Just the thing to keep the nation stable.

Yeah, well, the fat chewed, the lantern swung, I'm off again. I'll see Abe and his mates the following night in full battle gear – leather jerkins, leather breeches, boots, gauntlet gloves wiv built-in knuckle dusters, crowbars, chivs and, last but not least, masks. Like we don't aim to get recognised, do we? Oh, no, anon is the name of our game or we swing else, don't we? Where was I?

On my way to Billingsgate, that's where. Aiming to meet my next recruit. I ought to find Kipper Manly swilling down the slabs – for as of now the market will have been and gone (it being well into the fore noon) and Kip's job, when he ain't stuffing fishguts into barrels for manure, is washing down. Oh, it's hard graft down the market, I can tell yer. Wet fish is a mean labour. It's ever a wonder to me how fishmongers stay so waggish. Me, I'd rather work in an abattoir. At least there the blood's warm.

But Kip's gone. And I don't mean home. No, he's in frigging hospital. St Thomas's. Cross the bridge, turn left, you're there. So I do and find Kip looking horrible (like ghostly white) and talking in this high-pitched whisper. It seems he got on the wrong side of some fish-factor's galloway nag who smartly gave him the kickback you know where – twice – the equine equivalent of the old one two. Whereat all of Billingsgate enjoyed a mighty merriment (even the fresh boiled lobsters creased themselves) except, of course, poor old Kip who was not feeling quite so manly all of a sudden. Like he's had to postpone his marriage to pretty little Primrose (an ex of mine, natch) while the doctors try to re-jig his wedding tackle. Like it's touch and go whether it'll ever be good for anything bar pissing. Sic transit gloria Manly, as your scholard might say.

So Kip is *hors de combat* and I go on to rout out Brendan O'Bryne. Now here's a lad after me own heart. A truly hard nut through and through. Your veritable Celtic warrior wiv the fair skin, the shiny dark hair, and the pitiless blue eyes. Just to see him is to sense trouble on its way, coming up, like thunder.

Brendan's a scaffolder and roofer when he ain't rollicking, drinking, versifying, and fighting. I found him on top of the Royal Exchange flashing out the leads. There he was beating hell out of these lumps of docile metal (lead always reminds me of Enoch on a bad day, don't ask me why) so they would lie snug all round the joints of these magnificent new chimneys, this rebuilt temple of Mammon's put in place to keep its right worshipful jobbers and brokers warm.

Brendan and me, we top o' the morning each other, horse around a bit, make wiv the anecdotes, like 'Have you heard the one about the deaf Presbyter and the Dutch widow?' until I get to the purpose: like is Brendan O'Bryne, illustrious nay royal descendant of Brian Boru (and on the right side of the blanket at that!) ready for war? What we might call a major confrontation wiv the powers that be, in which me and him, plus an elite corps of proven hardmen, duff up not only the local law in the person of Sheriff Cruikshank but also that of the realm, in the horrible shape of Judge Gibbet, not to mention those stupid subscriptors of mine who've now had the impertinence to try 'n' call me, *me*, Rusty Ironside, to account for cheating 'em rigid? Oh, and I expect there'll be quite a few constables, watchmen and other ambulant garbage to abuse as well. How about it, Bren?

Well, what can I say he said? In all honesty I don't think I can surprise you and report that Brendan O'Bryne said 'no', can I? No, I can't. The welcome news is his eyes flashed wiv an icy-blue light. The perpetual frost in them glinting wiv the sorta inner fire you associate wiv ill-got diamonds. And I tell you, to see such sparkling evil light up a fella's countenance, on a grey November morning, on top of a building site, is to experience what makes villainy truly worthwhile.

Right. Now. To cut this history down to size I can relate that by the late post noon I'd laid on more'n a score of loyal lads for the following night. We was all to foregather at Pudding Wharf as the clocks struck midnight (St Mary Pudding's always two minutes ahead of St Mary Overie across the river but no matter) when the 22nd instant turned into G day, the 23rd. G now short not for Gold but for Guts for Garters.

That much achieved at my end of the town I tooled across to Don Rocco's parish again. Where he readily agreed he, too, had been insulted by the drubbing handed out to the Krosno twins and that prompt retribution was essential if law and order (our style) was to be maintained. Like crooked sheriffs and fornicating justices needed a short, sharp shock, so they know who's truly in charge, right? Don Rocco opined he could provide a flotilla of a dozen boats wiv six brutal watermen to each. That should answer prettily enough. And he would command in person. Whereat we supped in great content and I lay that night at Lambeth dreaming dreams as hot, dry and barbaric as I ever have dreamt but when I turned over in the morning who should I find beside me but this clever little punk from Southwark, thoughtfully procured by the ever-resourceful Don. And so charmful was she I got up to face the day almost too full of the milk of human kindness. However, by the evening, I'm glad to say I was my usual combative self again.

I got to Pudding Wharf well ahead of the lads. My intent being to make sure my pullets was well clear of the premises before battle commenced. Nor, come to that, did I want them distracting any of my desperadoes from the real business in hand. But what do I find? No one. There's not a single nun or novitiate to be found anywhere in the Convent of the Sacred Pussy. What haps?

But then I clock a letter, stuck with a hairpin onto a cushion in the saloon. And it's addressed to me and Sally. And that tells me Sally hasn't been here since – since when? Dunno. Anybody's guess. Like when she left me on the Isle of Dogs maybe?

So I read this aforesaid missive in the hope it will furnish me with some cognisance of what the fuck's going on. I reckon it's in Sister Lettice's hand – she having the learning for it. I read, don't laugh, I can. It says: 'Sir, madam, we the Undersigned hereby declare that having been left to Fend for Ourselves these last Four days and nights – '. That proves it, Sal hasn't been back '– with never a Glimpse of our Master or Mistress, and, having continued in the Exercise of our Profession here at Pudding Wharf, with as much Application and Diligence as we should have employed had you been here to Supervise and Succour us, we now Consider that it is Time for us to Discharge ourselves from your Service, not only for Reason of your Neglect but because it has come to our Notice that the Sheriff of this Ward in the City of London is due to call tomorrow at Dr Quicksilver's Elaboratory – ' *Elaboratory*! how high-faluting can Lettice get? '– which Lieth next door to Us and we do not wish to be exposed to the Rudeness which He and his Officers will surely use against us, since it is Well Known that honest Whores are considered Fair Game for crooked Lawmen. In plain words, if the Sheriff fails to receive satisfaction at the Elaboratory, he will seek Another Kind with us. This being a Most Likely Outcome (for we doubt Gold can ever be made next door, even by the Ingenious Doctor whom we all Love dearly) – ' I don't believe it! My pullets partial to Enoch? All of 'em? What's he been at? I tell you that fly bastard could get adepts a bad name! '– We have Resolved together to Divide all our Earnings between Ourselves equally and then Depart – some of us Severally, others Together in a Company. We have Resolved this in a Spirit of Sisterly Communion and we Trust that you, Mr Rusty, and you, Mrs Copper, may approve our Proceeding since, willy-nilly, we have been Obliged to Act upon our own Behalf without Benefit of your Firm Protection or loving Counsel.'

There you have it. That's what I read. My first thought was, how dare they? But then reason prevailed and I reckoned what they'd done was unusual but logical. But even so I blamed Sally. She shouldn't have deserted 'em; they'd looked up to her and she'd let 'em down, the poor little cunnies. And I shared their view that Monty and Co. could well take dirty advantage. After all, they wasn't to have known what I'd got in mind, was they? I mean they wasn't party to my battle plan? So, given the likelihood of such unwelcome attentions (for I never knew a constable yet who expected to pay for his nookie) I concluded they'd done right. After all, as you know, I'm all for a degree of mayhem between fellas but I draw the line at multiple raping of the ladies, right? Like my doxies ain't yer Sabine women; they deserve better than forcible fumbling. Like me, they require a proper regard for their accomplishments and cash in advance. Whereupon my thoughts turned again to Sally and if she'd been there

I reckon I'd have smacked her right across the room but as she wasn't I was forced to contain my ire for later. 'Rusty,' I said to myself, 'bottle up yer bottle, mate. Save it for Monty.'

And I did 'cos here was Brendan O'Bryne along wiv Abe Shemozzle and his cronies. Christ, do they look war-like. In all their leather. Plus studs. Big boots. And carrying these dirty great axes like you fell trees wiv.

I says, 'Lads, lads – you better take the heads off of those and just use the handles. Like we're aiming for incapacitation not decapitation, right? I mean we don't want none of us to swing after, do we? That'd be a sad end to a merry ding-dong.'

Says Brendan, 'But I'm looking for bloody revolution and death to the Prods.'

I answer, 'Me too, mate, but Cromwell's dead now and we've got our King back, right?'

'That makes no difference to me, boy. I still need blood. Blood for Drogheda, blood for Wexford. Blood for blood till the end of time, begorrah.'

Yeah, Brendan did say it. No kidding. He said *begorrah*. Dead consistent the Irish whatever you may hear to the contrary. If you need a standard expletive apply to your nearest Paddy.

I say, 'Sounds like you've been talking to Abe here. His lot's even worse'n your lot. They want everybody's blood, everybody's money *and* the promised land.'

I'm right, Bren and Abe have been stoking each other up in the righteous-cause arena. Like they'll be musket-running to each other next. From Holy Mother Ireland to Holy Moses. And back.

But in the end they do like I say and ease off the axe-heads and assure me there's enough weight and whip in the ashwood hefts to open a skull or two anyway. So honour is satisfied on their side and mine.

Come four o'clock in the a.m. we're all present and correct. Every single volunteer of us is on parade. Hooded, masked, primed. So I call 'em together and give 'em my battle plan. And do they enjoy the beauty of it! They really go for my nutcracker strategy wiv Monty's mob caught between the devil (us) and the deep blue sea (Don Rocco). Though the colour of the Thames just here is more your goose-turd green, of course.

Orders given and received we settle down to wait, passing the rum toddy round to warm our animal spirits. Not that I want us intoxicated, just nice 'n' toxic.

As quarter to five strikes my lookouts glued to the peepholes in the shutters report the enemy's on his way. In fact we can all hear 'em – their boots on the cobbles ain't what you'd call dainty. And what do I see next? Six sheriff's officers and Monty on a white horse, the poncy git. But I must say I expected more opposition than this. If this is all we're gonna have, my fellas won't scarcely get their danders up.

But then we hear the really heavy tramp of boots en masse and the trot and jingle of a troop of horse. Music to our ears. Whatta turn-up. Whatta privilege. Cruikshank and Gibbet have called out the militia! Here comes a squadron of mounted pikemen reinforced wiv a platoon of musketeers led by a young captain. So it's like they've got the firepower while we've got the willpower. And the surprise. Suits me.

But what, I ask myself, was they expecting Enoch to do? Our tame adept? Then even as I wonder I realise. They've brought the militia along to safeguard the gold they reckon he's made for them. It being, as agreed, the 23rd. G day. They ain't expecting resistance or trouble as such – oh no. Rather they anticipate a happy how-do-you-do; a sweet but business-like encounter: Congratulations, Dr Quicksilver. How many hundredweights of 24-carat gold fine did you say you've got for us? Twenty? But that makes the ton! Most exceptional, nay, miraculous. When the King hears of this he'll be onto you in a flash. You'll get ennobled, for sure. And elected President of the Royal Society *nem. con.* And, by Special Appointment, you'll be Chief Adept in the Sacred Art to the Court of St James. Imagine that! Did you know, His Majesty has just commanded a special laboratory to be built for you right underneath his privy closet, so he can shag his lovelies above while you sweat your guts out below? How about that? Don't you feel proud to be British? There you'll be creating wealth untold for old Rowley (after all, he only gets £1,200,000 per annum, you know) while he rolls all over Nell Gwyn?

Thus did my fancy roam but even as it dallied wiv this conceit, the other half of my brain, the martial side, was weighing the odds. Surprise, it told me, was a fine weapon but a volley from them musketeers could mow my lads down like standing corn. Got it? Well, I can't have that, can I? Oh, no. After all, we're cunning villains, not stupid soldiery. So what to do, Captain Steele? Think fast. Think logistically. Think ordnance. I've gotta have extra thump. Where do I get thump?

Which was how I came to remember them grenadoes or hand-bombs some of our soldier-clients had left wiv Sally in lieu of payment. The poor bastards had been granted furlough but no pay. And Sal always loved a soldier. And these grenadoes was like iron pineapples on wooden sticks. For safety I'd dumped 'em in the cellar meaning to take 'em downriver to the depot one day. Only I'd never got round to it, thank Christ.

So down I go to find 'em – swiftly, wiv dispatch. And there they are – the pretty little runticles. A baker's dozen of 'em stacked in the wine racks. Like I get 'em upstairs and ask Brendan and Abe how they work. Is there a tit you hit or what and how much time have you got before they blow your head off instead of your enemy's?

Well, Brendan knows all about grenadoes. He would, wouldn't he? And he points out a little ring on a string which when pulled snaps the flint that ignites the gunpowder inside the pineapple. As for time, you've got none at all – it's pull, throw, duck, hope, bang. Bren reckons they are possibly the most dangerous weapons around – for the grenadiers, he means. Your foe mostly laughs and shouts: Pull the other one!

However these are what we've got. Beggars can't be choosers (though that hasn't always been my experience – I've known some of that craft as hard to please as Lord and Lady Muck once it comes to spending their day's pickings) so I decide these hand-bombs are worth a go; do or die.

Bren, Abe and Will Toplady agree to share the risk of 'em wiv me and we deal 'em out between us, three each to them, and four to me, and we settle down to wait – masked and wound up – for Don Rocco's signal that he's got his waterboys nosed in snug at the wharf on the rising tide. And like us, ready for action.

Nor are we the only ones waiting. Monty's mob, and the militia captain wiv his men, they're all on the *qui vive*, too. But waiting for what, who? Five minutes go by, then ten, then another twenty. And still no signal from Don Rocco. This is sticky. I'm getting, you know, sorta prickly. The enemy's tightening up, too. You can tell it from the increasing stamp of boots and hooves on the cobbles. Plus horse snorts. And all the while the dawn mist's rising on the river, acrid, evil and as grey-pink as pigs' swill.

Next thing we know Judge Gibbet arrives in a sedan. So that's who Monty was waiting for. Of course. It would be. And out the bastard steps from the chair looking as gruesomely judicial as ever. Nay, I tell a lie, more so, 'cos he's got these three lumps of paper in his forepaw wiv wax seals and red ribbons on 'em. Well, you can guess what they was. (Yeah, you're dead right, readeress – didn't I say you was as brainy as you was beauteous? All them charms and intelligence on top. Challenging!) Yeah, three fucking warrants for our arrest – us, the magic threesome – me, Sal, Enocchio.

But where's the Don's flotilla? Where's his signal? Like how much longer must I wait for his pyrotechnicals? Didn't we agree he'd let off these dirty great rockets (or *flares* to give 'em their military style) – red, green then yellow – as an unmistakable signal that he was in position? So where the fuck are they? This is not like Don Rocco. This delay is starting to give me, even me, your Iron Rodney, a squirt of the squitters. Like I need the Lord of Lambeth's support or my strategic masterstroke's up the proverbial. Like I've got half of King Charlie's standing army up against me. So where are these frigging oars wiv their fireworks? 'Cos, like, if Rocco's let me down – only he never has before, has he? Has he? Think, matey, think. Have a hard me-think. This is worrisome. God's bollocks, he has! Oh, shit. It just shows, doesn't it? The allowances you make for your mates? Jesus! Here am I forgetting the Krosno twins. Didn't Don Rocco assure me they was just the lads for the job? Sharp, clever, deadly? And didn't they come back wiv their stupid aliens' ears cut off? So maybe – oh, dear, oh dear, I've got all these niggly little doubts running round my head like cockroaches in a slut's pantry –

Whoosh! There the rockets go. Praise the Lord and pass the pineapples. Red, yeah, green, yeah, and the third is like a little shower of gold sparks. Pretty. Oh, am I glad? Am I relieved? I thank the King of Lambeth Marshes, after all. I do. Because now, now it all happens at once, dunnit? 'Course it does, for this is war, right? And if one thing's certain in war, it is concerted, simultaneous, bloody confusion. And he who blasts straight through it, wins. And this time you better believe me. For I speak from experience and wiv authority, as General Mars, no less – a title I adopted later. But that's a future kettle of cat's piss and need not distract us now. Not at this point in time, no.

I'll say it better hadn't! Fuck me, this here present is quite enough to be going on wiv, I can tell you. Why? Because Don Rocco's rockets mean it's my turn, it's down to me, to make wiv the frigging leadership.

I shout 'Now!' And at this the lads at every window of the pussy palace shove the shutters wide open even as Sheriff Monty, Judge Gibbet and the militia captain, flanked by six musketeers, advance on the door to Enoch's laboratory.

Out goes our first volley – sticks, stones, them axe-heads of Bren 'n' Abe's, bottles and any other throwable clobber. And just as I'd calculated we do have the advantage for the moment. Like Monty and Co. are caught hopping. They duck, weave, swear and shout. But the pikemen and the rest of the militia are out of our range, and at once I hear their sergeant shout: 'Load!' Ominous.

So now is no time to frig. Not wiv all of that, plus Monty banging on Enoch's door and shouting, 'Open in the name of the Law!' While me, I'm bawling like a lunatic, 'Right, Bren, Abe! Let's go!'

And leaning out of the window I address Monty direct. I shout, 'Morning, Monty. Get a load of this!' And, wiv an inward prayer, I pull me pineapple's string and hurl the bomb straight at the two-timing, double-crossing, hypocritical Sheriff of Pudding Ward.

Alongside me Bren and Abe have done the same. So we've got three of our grenadoes in the air, on the go. But do the little bastards bang? Bang they do not. Oh, no. They've gotta be frigging duds. Mine's already hit Monty in the chest as he's turned to look up at me. Now it's at his feet. While Bren 'n' Abe's bounce off of the lab wall and roll towards Judge Gibbet. Useless. Just like the Krosno couple. Seems like some sodomite's giving me the evil eye. Am I jinxed or what? And Monty – this tops it all – Monty laughs. At me! Your friend and my friend, me!

'Well, Rodney, it's gotta be you behind that stupid mask – who else would bother? So what's wiv you this time, matey? More mouth, as ever?' How's that for barbative? Like there's no enemy like an ex-mate, is there?

As reply I grab me next hand-bomb. But before I can pull the string, my first one blows! Then the other two! And, boy, how they do blow! You ever seen a second split in half? Or an instant smashed to smithereens? Well, I did, in that triple explosion! And was it joy? Like it was undiluted. Like it was the perfect murder you dream of. All them pretty pictures, all at once, dancing before your astonished gaze: there's Monty blasted wholesale through the main window of the lab wiv its fifteen panes of glass breaking all round him in a myriad splinters while Judge Gibbet's just fallen to bits. The Law's in pieces. His head's going one way, his torso another and that's his legs still standing – just for the minute – wivout the rest of him. Whoops. Over they go. As for the warrants he's got out for us, why, they burst into flame and fly away like they was them birds that hatch out of disaster. You'll know their name but I've got no time to remember it because now I hear the militia captain shouting orders and his musketeers are ramming their balls down their muzzles and I reckon me and the lads better issue forth or else. Like it's now or never.

'Charge!' I yell.

And out we go – the whole mob of us, our blood up, crowbars at the high port, axe-handles swinging, grenadoes ready, and all of us shouting our agreed warcry: here we go! here we go! Simple, dead obvious, much used, but you don't need nothing original for a field of battle, do yer? It's always either 'here we go' or 'kill the bastards', innit? Least, in my experience it is.

And that's what we hear! Coming from the wharf! 'Kill the bastards!' Don Rocco's mob's ashore! And yelling just that! There they was looming out of the mist. What a cohort. All these dark shapes. Menacing wasn't in it. And what was they whirling round their heads? Lumps of chain. Ship's chain. Medium gauge – not too light, not too heavy, just deadly. Like steel flails to wipe your face off, never mind the smile on it. Jesus, did I feel admiration. I was really proud of Don Rocco's party. What an ally even if the bastard had had me on tenterhooks.

But all that's behind us. Our pincer movement, my nutcracker battleplan, works like a well-oiled miracle. Do we have our enemies in a squeeze? It's more a mangle. This is merciless. The poor sodding musketeers can't get their load off even though they kneel, raise their guns and the sergeant shouts: Fire! And why? Because if I reckoned our grenadoes quite a stroke, Don Rocco's got another – for the pikemen's horses. Like as the musketeers go to volley us to kingdom come so the pikemen charge Don Rocco. Whereat he reaches into this satchel he's got and throws out loadsa marbles. Kids' marbles! And these little glass balls go skipping and rolling over the cobbles and under the horses' hooves. You ever seen twenty horses fall over all together and roll on top of fourteen musketeers as they shoot off? Magic. Pure chaos. Unalloyed mayhem. Our enemy is his own enemy. We don't hardly have to do nothing except stroll about knocking this one over the head, or whip that one round the chops wiv a chain. Like the mobs rule, right? Mine, Don Rocco's. If this was up Westminster this would be a mighty revolution. Plebs versus Nobs. And I must say I can see Brendan's enjoying himself, using one of his grenadoes as a cudgel. Can he lay about him? Can a dog fart? And there's the Krosno twins handing out their revenge, too. Like they've got knives and seem to be going for the sergeant's ears. Kinda biblical of them – only in the good book it's eyes you go for, innit?

Some of the other lads have got the pikemen's horses under control while me and Don Rocco meet in the middle of the carnage – bodies everywhere either inert or begging for mercy. There we are shaking hands. We've done it. We are the victors of Pudding Wharf.

All that remains is to take a quick look at Enoch's lab. We go together. No need to use the door, we walk in through the window. Well, I've seen it worse. As when Enoch himself went off the handle and smashed it up. But even so Monty and the grenado's blast have done a fair bit of damage. It looks like Monty became a sorta projectile in himself. There he lies beside all Enoch's glass retorts, all smashed, loads of 'em, and their contents spewed all over the floor. And would ya believe it, it's a great big glistening puddle of a sort of mercury, only bright yellow, instead of silver?

'Is that liquid gold?' says Don Rocco, a greedy glint in his eye.

'No,' says me, knowing better. 'That's your philosopher's mercury.'

'What's that?'

'The key to the next stage of the process. You see wiv the *magnum opus* as it's called by the adepts there's always another stage. The process never ends.'

But now Monty moves. His eyes open. His lips vibrate. He's trying to say something. Only he can't. I step in close.

I say, 'We won, Monty. Mind how you go.' And wiv that I turn on my heel and me and Don Rocco leave the sheriff to his fate among the ruins of Enoch's dream and my moneyspinner.

And it's just as well we did leave then because here's Abe Shemozzle looking kinda urgent and telling us it's time to vamoose before the Lord Mayor's trained band arrives. They'll be coming down Fish Street any minute and though I'd said I didn't want fatalities the fact is he and Bren have counted eight dead and fourteen badly wounded among the enemy (them Polacks have had a real party) while on our side we've got one sprained wrist (I don't ask what from) and a shoulder in need of a bone-setter. So now our valour's proved maybe we better use some discretion?

I agree. So does the Don. And seeing the mist still clings to the river like a punk to her gallant we reckon it's best to depart by water. That way we can all disappear if not into thin air then thick air. Nicely. We embark.

And I find I'm in a boat wiv the Krosno duo and they're all smiles wiv this kerchief full of soldiers' and watchmen's ears. Which they count between gulps of aqua vitae and offering it to me. I'm nothing loath and it goes down like water only then you get this wonderful warm belly effect and start wanting to sing.

But as for that we've got the Irish to do it for us. For suddenly somewhere behind me in the fog I hear Brendan O'Bryne's voice lifted in song. Like that Paddy patriot's already putting our exploit into verse. And now as the Thames and Don Rocco's watermen run us softly up to Lambeth I hear 'The Ballad of Pudding Wharf' for the first time. It goes like this:

> 'Twas of a morning early,
> On the quay at Pudding Wharf,

That Rusty's mates and Rocco's mob
Gave battle in their wrath.

Our blood was up, our pride at stake,
The militia out in force,
With Justice This and Sheriff That,
Each one upon his horse.

We caught 'em in a trap of steel,
They scarce could fire a shot,
Our hand-bombs took 'em all apart,
Made bloody mincemeat of the lot.

For if you want a handsome riot,
'Tis ourselves you're looking for,
The corner boys, the water boys,
Who hate the frigging law!

And here Brendan shouted, 'All together now!' Whereat we all of us joined in. Whatta chorus!

The corner boys, the water boys,
Who hate the frigging law!

And I may say that was just the start of that ballad. The polite start of it.

We celebrate all that day, that night and the next morning. But when eventually I get back to Wrestler's Court to see how my Liverpool doxy is doing I find these six bulky City Officers wiv a warrant for my arrest. And I'm cornered. Six to one, I ask you. Even I have to respect adverse odds like that. And, of course, I reckon at once this is all on account of my revenge on Monty and like I've been a fool to come back here, which I have been, but on the other hand home is where your latest cunny is, right? If I've a weakness (and I have, I admit it) it's flesh, female flesh.

So there I was under arrest, after all. Me that was so proud, so witty and so wise, as the poet puts it. But not for murder, oh no. Nor for mayhem. No. Oh, no. I'm committed to custody for what we might call a technical or administrative offence: for failing to pay my annual licence to the City Fathers (them fat cats at the Guildhall wiv their fur tippets and gold chains) in order to keep a bawdy house for them to cavort in. The services me and Sal have laid on for that lot! Why, on one occasion, we had to provide two dozen nymphs to dance in their birthday suits all over the Lord Mayor's banquet table.

And entertain his gentle guests after. And what do I get? This aggravation. Oh, it's a naughty world we live in, right?

Well, natch, I offer these characters the money on the spot. Then offer to double it and suggest we sink a pint together, why not? But no, oh no. They refuse. They may not accept gratuities. The Law of the City of London in its self-governing wisdom, has deemed it convenient (for them) to put me up for trial at the Guildhall sometime next year. Mayhap by Easter if I'm lucky. And the penalty if I'm found guilty? Transportation to Virginia.

Meanwhile I gotta rot in Newgate. Though as I admit that's putting it a trifle strong. Except, like I've said, I gotta be out before the trial. I mean we can't have Rusty Ironside go down for a mere fribble, can we? For not paying twenty titsy-bitsy oncers to twenty itsy-bitsy aldermen with a Lord Mayor on top. I mean, I know life can never be said to be fair, but that'd be frigging diabolical.

But who's this tapping on the door? Not another doxy? I'm shagged out. Least for the moment. Like there's no peace for the wicked, is there? Not even in jail. 'Come in,' I sigh.

And, courtesy of my favourite warder who – for the right price – can turn you a blind eye as quick as any key, who do I get but Abe Shemozzle? Enter Abe wiv a load of life's little restoratives for Gentiles: jellied eels, oysters, whelks, lobsters, winkles and a firkin of double ale. Also fresh bread, butter and watercress. But that's not all by no means, no. Abe has got an idea as well. A merry device. And like it could be the answer to this prisoner's prayers, like. See ya on the out!

♀

The day after I left Rusty, Enoch, and Pudding Wharf for ever I proceeded to those banks proposed to me by Lord Spark. For in them was all our money. Well, mine, now.

From these establishments I expected to withdraw something so that I might live for a while without whoring. But all three of them declared my certificates of deposit unknown, if not fraudulent. Indeed I was obliged to leave the last, Captain Lucre's bank in Bleeding Heart Yard, in haste, since the Clerk there threatened to call the constables. At all three I was doubted as an impostor, my precious certificates were decried as forgeries so inept as to be laughable, and as for Lord Spark, well, they had never heard of him and he was certainly no partner of theirs, good day, madam. And so it came about that I discovered I had lost all that we had amassed at Pudding Wharf. A good £200,000 carried patiently by my girls to a pretty young gentleman I had rather cared for and imagined I could trust was all gone. Had he not asked me to be his wife? And had I not declined his offer as gently and lovingly as I knew how? I do not think I have known a blacker day than that grey November Wednesday.

As I walked back to Westminster, where I had lodged overnight, I was ogled several times by various hot gallants but I was too distressed to profit from their licentiousness. My usual appetite for the game seemed quite departed – at least for that moment. My head was full of Lord Spark. Was his proposal of marriage part of his plot against me? Had he, from the beginning, intended to deprive me not merely of my money but also of my honour? Here I stretched the truth of the matter like a doeskin glove – but only out of need for a modicum of solace; for a certain reparation of my wounded pride. For there lay the seat of my distress. My pride lay in pieces. Had I not always counted myself as the victor, never as the victim? Just as Rusty always did? And Enoch, too, once you dug deeply enough? Hence our essential harmony. But now all this, all my former life, was in ruins. Lord Spark had cheated me; Monty was even now determined to cheat Rusty; and Enoch, oblivious of everything save his sacred art, was about to be cheated, perhaps of his life, by our subscriptors and the vengeful Judge Gibbet.

At this I stopped short and asked myself most earnestly if I should return yet once more to Pudding Wharf to plead with Enoch for the very, very last time? But, having thought upon it, I decided it would be of no avail and so I continued on my way.

But before I came to my lodgings I passed by that house belonging to Lord Spark where, in my comparative innocence, I had sported so liberally with him. Now I wondered if that house was indeed his mother's. Or was it but a part of what Rusty would have called his lordship's 'frontage'? For just as a greedy pawnbroker will present a handsome window to the public so a needy gentleman will endeavour to convince you of his property and worth the better to fleece you of yours. All the worst of Rusty's confederates were ever at pains to appear solid, sober citizens. And did not Rusty himself dress most fastidiously? So that he might live up to his self-appointed rank of Captain? And had not I – a mere bawd and brothel madam – gone in silks as grand as any Court lady's? Although many of those are no better than they ought to be. And was I not even now, sailing, as we say, under false colours?

These thoughts had caused me to halt again – this time to observe the house that had prompted them with rather more care than I ever had before. Certainly it was a mighty mansion and given its situation here in the heart of the City of Westminster, close to Whitehall, it betokened wealth of precisely the kind Lord Spark had sworn was his. Which if it were so, why had he cheated me of mine?

The place looked shut up – just as Sister Tabitha had said it was on her calling there on my behalf the month before. Yet even so I felt an urge to knock once again at that handsome door. So I did. And pulled the bell pull. No one came. My half-hope that a caretaker or maidservant might still be housed within was disappointed. I stepped back into the street to be greeted by a greasy fat man in a greasier waistcoat bearing a bunch of keys.

'May I assist you, madam?'

'I'm looking for Lord Spark.'

'Who isn't?'

'What do you mean?'

'I'm his caretaker. Every day I get somebody banging at the door. Gents he owes, lasses with bellies out here – ' He patted his own in a pertinent illustration of their condition. 'Oh, I tell you, madam, his lordship's a terror.' The surface of his speech was gentle but under it lay common Cockney.

By this time he had gone past me and unlocked the door. Now he held it wide. And smiled obsequiously. Would it please madam to enter, he enquired.

I answered that it wouldn't, since Lord Spark was not at home, was he? He agreed, still smiling. But if I entered he might be able to divulge his whereabouts. We might share a glass of his lordship's best *clairette* together? And by now his true intent was become manifest. His eyes gleamed lasciviously, his brow, his baby-fat cheeks, his upper lip, all were broken out into a pearly dew of sheer lust as he gazed upon me.

I considered. I had had no inclination for any of those pretty rakehells who, upon my way there, had made a leg at me or twirled their handkerchiefs to catch my eye. If they could not affect me, what hope had this lump of perspirant lard? But then a truly wicked fancy entered my head. Might I not venture in, learn what I could of Lord Spark, and still cheat this creature of his satisfaction? To achieve that would provide me with a degree of pleasure, albeit of the meaner sort. For, as you may recall, I had, until that fateful morning, always held it as a point of honour to offer honest harlotry. To give fleshly value for money. And so I had taught my girls. What a sentimental madam I had been.

But now, now that I had been so cruelly cheated of all I had (I quite discounted Rusty and Enoch's share of that £200,000) why should I not take what revenges I could upon the world?

With this unworthy thought safely lodged in my brain I smiled as falsely as a fish-wife, and agreed that I might, after all, enter the house. Whereat he bowed me in.

The place was empty. Devoid of all furnishings upon the ground floor, upon the first, and upon the second. Only upon the third was there anything approaching domestic comfort.

As we climbed the stair I asked my panting, grunting, sweating companion (did the shortness of breath he exuded come from his corpulence or his venereal expectation?) if Lord Spark had had the house's moveables removed?

'No, that was me,' he answered. 'By which I mean I've sold 'em off.'

'But you say you are the caretaker here?'

'So I am. And the name's Ralph. Ralph Butts.'

I ignored this information; I had no need to know him. I said, 'But you've taken no care of these furbishments?'

Here, as we passed it, I indicated that chamber where Lord Spark had offered me a diamond worth half the Indies – now it was become a box of echoes.

'Oh, no. I've taken great care.'

'How?'

'To get the best price I could. They was lovely chattels, you know? Walnut, rosewood, ebony. Not to mention the Turkey carpets, bibelots, damasks, all of that.'

His gentility was dissolving even as we ascended. Soon he would be his lower self in all its beastly entirety. At the second landing he paused, but not, I thought, for breath, despite his huff and puff.

'Go on, my dear,' he said. 'After you.'

But I would not have that. I had no relish for such a proceeding. Had I not already observed, with disgust, how his hands trembled and twitched to paddle at me? If I were to mount ahead of him they would surely be scooping up my skirts?

So I smiled, but with *hauteur*, like a duchess at a grocer. I said, 'By no means, sir. You must lead the way. That is the prerogative of a caretaker.' And I held his eye, obliging him to obey me.

He complied and I reached his quarters without molestation. Here some furnishings remained; notably a bed (unmade), a chair or two, and some twenty boxes of good French wines. The floor was carpeted with empty bottles, broken tobacco pipes and the crumbs of at least a dozen meat pasties mixed with mouse droppings. The place stank.

At the sight and smell of this accommodation I had some difficulty in keeping to my purpose. Every instinct in me told me to depart at once. But then next to the chamberpot I saw a small, brass-bound money chest half-hidden beneath the bed. At this my smile, and my resolve, returned.

I said, 'The abode of a bachelor, clearly?'

He said, mopping his brow with his sleeve, 'I don't stand on ceremony. Not when I'm alone. What will you take? A pretty claret grown by the Ho Bryan family close by Bordeaux? Or would you, as one of the fairer sex, prefer a sweeter draught? I have a Sauternes here goes down like nectar.'

'You sound like a wine waiter, sir.'

'Ralph, please. Let's have no formality here – not between you and me, my dear. But, to tell true, I was apprenticed to a wine-shipper – as a lad, you understand?' And he smiled boyishly in my direction. A sight truly horrid. Given his horse teeth.

'I'll take a glass of claret,' I said, calculating that I might persuade him to drink rather more of that than the sweeter wine. He might well regard it as a man's drink, God help him.

Eagerly he complied. Never have I seen a bottle uncorked more quickly by the simple device of pushing the cork into the bottle with the handle of a candle-snuffer. Some of the wine spattered his chest and belly but of this he took no heed, merely upending the bottle at his mouth and shaking it so that the cork bobbed upwards to release the wine.

Having gulped several gulps he offered me the bottle and said, 'There, it'll drink easier now.'

'Is there no glass?'

'Glass?' He sounded astonished.

'To drink it from.'

'Oh, no. Sold all the crystal.'

'I can't drink from that.'

'Suit yourself.'

And he sucked again on the bottle, grinning most libidinously the while. I took heart at the sight. For at this rate he would soon be incapable of offering me harm. A dozen slurpings later the bottle was empty and he opened another in the same manner; but not before inviting me to sit at ease upon the bed.

To gain time I said, 'But you promised to give me news of Lord Spark.'

'Tunbridge Wells.'

'Is that where he's gone?'

'With his mother. She's as bad as him. A real vixen. The word is – ' and here his voice sank to a vinous whisper ' – the word is they poisoned the old earl so Spark could inherit. Could be. His dad was a tight-fisted, opinionated, tyrannical old sot. What simple folk call a real aristocrat.'

'They murdered him?'

'That's the rumour. I don't say it's correct but I do say it's not impossible.'

With this he advanced towards me, leering venereally. I stepped back to avoid him. Fortunately he stumbled upon one of the empty bottles strewn across the floor and fell forwards onto his hands and knees. Suddenly he looked like that King Nebuchadnezzar who thought he was a beast of the field.

I said, with more hope for myself then concern for him, 'Are you hurt?'

'No,' he said, wobbling to his feet. 'Must sit down.' And he waddled, panting and blowing, to the bed. 'Come on, missus, I've told you what I know, now it's your turn to do me a favour.' And he patted the place beside him.

I said, still determined to evade him, 'Have you no fear that Lord Spark will return and discover you have sold his goods?'

He grinned. 'No. I'm off tomorrow. You could come with me if you like. I can treat you nice. I'm not short of the ready. Not no more. Oh, no. Take a look.' And with his foot he pushed the money chest towards me. 'Open it. I don't lock it. See for yourself.'

I said, my mind working furiously, 'But I believe you, sir.'

'Well then, come on, girl. You know what I want and I reckon you know how to bestow it. Right? The minute I laid eyes on you I said to myself: I bet that one could turn you a trick or two, Ralph old son. What your name, darlin'?'

By now he was entirely Cockney and had begun to unbutton his breeches. And it was then – I thank providence – that I observed two tasselled cords that lay beside the pillow. All was suddenly clear. His eye followed mine. He giggled.

I said, 'Are they your chiefest pleasure?' And I fear I could not keep the contempt from my voice. He nodded.

To recount what followed with any decency is scarcely possible. However I shall attempt it. Any omissions I make are therefore deliberate but can, of course, be made good by the fancy of the reader. All I shall say is that I allowed that tub of fat to strip himself stark naked and that I then tied his hands and feet together with the two cords. If the sight thus afforded reminded me of anything it was of a pig trussed up for market. Certainly he squealed with delight to find himself thus restrained. But then I took my kerchief and tied it about his mouth so tightly that he could not speak. At this he shook his head in vehement remonstrance but I was stone. Next I opened his money chest and before his popping eyes I took from it, with more pleasure than I can say, a purse into which I counted no less than a thousand pounds in gold. It took me half an hour.

My delight in this was threefold. Firstly that I obliged my trussed-up drunkard to watch me steal his money; secondly that this small fortune belonged to Lord Spark; and thirdly, that if anyone had a right to it I did.

My immediate prospects now repaired there remained yet one thing more to do if my revenge was to be complete. I took that caretaker's bunch of keys and used them, teasingly, to excite his manhood (such as it was) into a state of tumid expectation – but no more.

This achieved I blew him a kiss and departed, leaving Ralph Butts bereft of speech, liberty and carnal satisfaction. And that, I believe, is the only time in my life when I have been truly wicked. Never have I done a worse thing. But I doubt I shall ever repent of it. For it seemed to me then, and it does still, to have been an act of absolute necessity for my soul's sake; part of a process set in train by forces outside myself. Can evil bring forth good? I know it isn't meant to (how the parsons preach!) but all I can answer is that at that minute it seemed it had. I felt I was set anew upon the high road to that citadel called Self-Esteem.

There is, despite its name, but one well at Tunbridge Wells and that a mere pissing conduit of muddy water impregnate with iron. However I soon discovered it was entirely within the character of this upstart village to pretend to more conveniences than in actuality it possessed. Nor is November the time to visit it. For then the *beau monde* is hardly to be seen. The reason is evident. At this wintry season those favoured by birth and wealth are busy abusing their stomachs elsewhere so they may come here in midsummer to repair them. Also their depleted fortunes. Either at the gaming tables or by marriage to some spinster of the Shires made desirable (no matter how uncomely) by her pedigree, *viz.* 10,000 acres.

The lot of these country virgins is quite the reverse of your town harlot's. For here the fair sex pays the unfair, with a prodigious dowry, to be fumbled most religiously as a bride only to suffer neglect as a wife whose means have now become her spouse's. At least a whore may keep something of her body's earnings. I surely did. Even with Rusty for my protector. And so did my girls.

My first purpose at Tunbridge was to find out Lord Spark. So, having taken lodgings, I went at once to the source house, since I presumed that even if he were not there then those who were might know where he was resident. And I was almost right. Yet what a mighty little word is *almost*.

For whom should I find in this watery tap room but his mother? A lady not yet of truly advanced years but nevertheless feeling the pinch of age and visibly grown anxious of it. She was seated at a table sipping the waters with an air of solemn obligation. I cannot say the general mode of dress was flamboyant. I saw at once that I was the best-dressed woman present. Also the most handsome. Since the majority were twice or thrice my age, and those few whose years matched mine looked – how can I express it with discretion? – they looked pinched and unfulfilled, as if those tender parts of their persons they sat upon were rather a misery to them than a joy.

But it was not they who took my true attention. No, my eye was drawn at once to the man seated with Lord Spark's mother. For beside the water was a jug of coffee and a glass of brandy. Clearly here was someone of a more sanguine temperament than those about him. He was of a most upright bearing, too. In spite of his age, which was, I thought, at least three score and five. Later I learned that he was over eighty – being born in the year of the Armada. When I asked him in all innocence what was that, he looked at me in amaze and said, 'Child, have you no knowledge of your nation's history?' At which I answered cheerfully, 'None, sir, I'm too young yet for old times.' Whereat he explained the Armada to me and I fell straight asleep. And thus I remain, even now, none the wiser upon that score.

At this initial view I took him for a retired Royalist and I was not mistaken. He spoke ever respectfully of our first Charles (he who lost his head) calling him King Charles the Martyr, and reverencing him far above our second one, our present King Charles the Satyr, as he termed him. His substance was in Somerset and it was obvious that Lord Spark's mother, the Countess of Wavenhoe, for so she announced herself, was intent upon enjoying it, if not its owner. Having disposed of one husband (presuming the forked tongue of rumour is to be believed) she was now in full cry after another: this upright gentleman. Who was presented to me as Colonel Bancroft.

After effecting these introductions – and enquiring discreetly who was who of the majordomo as he dispensed the water which, at sixpence a glass, amounted, I thought, to a practice close to aqueous alchemy – I learned that my quarry, Lord Spark, was gone abroad. And not just to the Upper or Lower Walk or the Common thereabout but far abroad. Upon inheriting his fortune, his mother said, he had proceeded immediately to sea, determined to circumnavigate the globe, heartlessly leaving her, a grieving widow, with all the cares of the estate at Wavenhoe. In consequence her health was broke and she was come there to restore it. How could a mere woman, bereaved of a husband and bereft of a son – here her liquid eyes fawned upon Colonel Bancroft like a royal spaniel's – how could such a frail creature be expected to bear so onerous a responsibility?

Bancroft heard her out with any number of solicitous grunts and nods but it was already plain to me that it was I who commanded his attention. And as soon as he decently could – that is when the Countess's complainings, hintings and eyelid battings had run their course – he made enquiry of me. What brought me to Tunbridge Wells so out of season? Surely it could not be for my health? For never had he beheld such a picture of female well-being as I displayed. I could not be in search of a husband, surely? Since I must have suitors galore? If I was not married already? And at this his sharp eye quizzed mine in a manner I could not mistake.

Seizing the occasion I responded that I was a poor gentlewoman from Warwickshire who had come to London as a companion to a rich haberdasher's widow. But she had now remarried and cast me off, for fear I might take her new husband's fancy. Again our eyes caught. And, yes, indeed, I was come to Tunbridge in the hope of finding some new society, since I had none in London now. I had staked all my small savings upon this removal and I would be deceiving him were I to say otherwise.

And as this last pretty falsehood escaped my lips I allowed my eyes to dwell in his in such a way as has never failed me yet with any man worth his sauciness.

But what, demanded the Countess, had I to do with her son that I should come there to enquire of him? And her jealous eye stole to my belly as if to impute I might be with child by him. As well I could have been, if not by Enoch or Rusty or even Sheriff Cruikshank, but the ordinary truth was I was not. Even that pregnant vision I had been in receipt of with Enoch at Pudding Wharf had proved false.

I smiled and lied, 'Madam, fear not. I met your gallant son but once. At the theatre with my former benefactress. It was then that he informed me that he would be staying here with you and, if it were convenient for me to pass some days here also, we might come to know each other better.'

'Oh? You're a fortune hunter?' said she.

At this insult I was tempted to dispense with any further falsehood and inform this sneering matron of the truth! That in this instance, her two-faced son was the fortune hunter, not I! And had stolen £200,000 of me!

But providentially, Colonel Bancroft forestalled my remonstrance (or else this Countess and I should have had a public skirmish) by asking me my name. And equally opportunely, by placing his hand upon my knee – below the table and out of sight of Lord Spark's mother. His question and this action both gave me pause. For several reasons, as I shall explain.

During my journey there from London – which is a mere two stages in the coach upon an excellent new road – I had had time to consider my motives in searching out Lord Spark. And concluded they were mixed; or if you will, a muddle.

On the one hand, having got myself by foul means enough money to travel and accommodate myself in wholesome comfort for many months, I was impatient to confront him and demand restitution. On the other, my black mood that had led me so to abuse that foolish caretaker, was now diminishing and, as we trotted through Chislehurst, I was prepared to own that, despite the wrong he had done me, his lordship was, in his person and parts, a pretty fellow, and I had had an undeniable affection for him. In truth, had I not been sorely tempted to accept his marriage proposal? Why, it was even possible my refusal – although I had thought it delicately and feelingly done – lay at the root of his betrayal. His theft a lover's pique. Thus, by the time we changed horses at Sevenoaks, I was ready to forgive him pretty well everything – provided I too, having made peace with him and become his wife, might share in the fortune he had seized on.

But these silly fancies were soon vanquished by a sterner thought. Which was now proved prescient. Suppose, after all, I did not find Lord Spark at Tunbridge Wells? Suppose my information was false? His caretaker could not necessarily be relied on as a fount of truth, could he? What then would I do? This reflection curbed my enthusiasms even as we galloped pell-mell through Hildenborough. But then, after another mile or so, when our pace had eased again to a trot, I decided that if this fear were realised, I must seek a substitute for Lord Spark. That I had a true need of a man of means – and of mode – to support me in a new life as a lady, but in the comfort and style to which I had become accustomed as a brothel madam. I would, I swore, get me a husband to outdo any – even Rusty or Enoch!

With this resolve my spirits rose and the last vestiges of that blackness which had seemed to imbue me, and consume me, in London were departed. Quite vanished. And then it was that I remembered a thing Enoch had told me, which is that in the great work of alchemy, there comes a moment, called Nigredo, when the whole process seems at an end before its time. But as with the proverbial darkness before dawn, this terrible negation of everything is in fact the precursor of inevitable success. Whereat, in my mind, I smiled upon Enoch and kissed him, bidding him farewell. Henceforth I too would be made new.

To achieve this, and also for prudence's sake, I required, as once before, another name. But something in me could not quite dispense with all of my former self and in the end I chose a partial alias: a *nom de guerre* of demi-veracity for what I now foresaw as a likely war of the sexes. At Tunbridge Wells I would be known as Susan Smith rather than by my full name of Sarah Susanna Greensmith. Whereupon we reached our destination and I stepped down from the coach as this new person and took rooms under that name in Frog Lane. Which brings me back to Colonel Bancroft whose hand has advanced a little higher.

I say, 'My name is Susan. Susan Smith.' And I dimple at him while gently restraining his hand. Since in my new character I am determined to be something more of a gentlewoman – if not by birth then by the control of my animal inclinations. At least until marriage is upon offer. He beams delightedly despite my denial of his adventuring but I cannot pretend that the Countess is equally enamoured of me. In fact so dagger-like are her glancings that I rise from the table, thanking them both for their courteous reception of me before adding that I shall not inconvenience them further.

My calculation is that my absence may inflame Colonel Bancroft the more whereas my presence can only gratify Lord Spark's mother the less.

I say, 'I trust we shall meet again during my stay here. But for the moment I am fatigued from my journey and must rest at my lodgings in Frog Lane.' This ragbag of truth (my whereabouts there) and untruth – I am not in the least fatigued – I direct at Colonel Bancroft alone.

He rises to kiss my hand, well, the air just above it, in the cavalier manner, and I go, inwardly advising myself not to swing my hips in saucy triumph. For I now know I have made an absolute conquest.

Nor was I deceived. That night at supper I heard my landlady speak with someone below that made enquiry of me: Was a Miss

Smith within? Two minutes later the woman appeared with a letter which was most precisely addressed and sealed with a crest of a winged lion – something to give confidence to any maiden on the make.

I opened it and discovered my aged admirer was a poet as well as a soldier. But then what else should we expect of a cavalier?

> Dear Nymph e'en now arrivèd at my View,
> How may I not your Virtue celebrate?
> While these your charms swarm all about you
> Can I, your Swain, stay celibate?

To which was appended a brisk *post scriptum*: 'Liaison. Tomorrow. 29th inst. Noon. Upper Walk. Third elm tree sou-west Mother Macey's coffee stall. Do not fail. J.B. (Col.)'

Next day, as you will imagine, I was at the spot upon the very first stroke of twelve. But to my surprise my rhyming colonel was not to be seen. Five minutes later my indignation had begun to mount in earnest. Was I, after all, disdained? As a nymph I have ever demanded punctuality from my swains, whether in a public place or a private one. Two more turns around the elm tree and I was about to depart in rage when I saw him hurry out from behind Mother Macey's stall in a most peremptory manner.

Without a word he seized me by the elbow and hurried me down to the Lower Walk, paying no heed to any of my questions. Thence he drew me by green alleys and wicket-fenced byways to the Common. And, given his age (as I then supposed it), I was astonished how little this violent excursion affected him. Never once did he huff or puff. Of course, had I then known his true age I should have been even more impressed.

We came at last to a quaint heap of yellow rocks greened by moss, rusted by lichen and fringed about with ferns. There we paused and I drew breath while he did not. Instead he apologised both fervently and elegantly, explaining how the Countess had harried him all morning; how for a week now she had presumed herself as good as betrothed to him, the which she most decidedly was not, and never would be; and how, such had been her tenacity – she had clung to him like that famous creeper from Virginia now become common here – he had been obliged to declare his bowels in danger of imminent dissolution in order to get free of her. And he thanked me for staying so faithfully for him. Other ladies of less worth would not have waited, of that he was certain. And again he begged my pardon.

I laughed and assured him I had been at the point of a most indignant departure but now that I knew the facts of the matter I was ready to forgive him because I was sure that as a soldier he valued punctuality quite as much as princes are popularly supposed to do?

He agreed he did but added that he had heard our present prince was the exception which proved that rule, save when it came to horse-racing and whoring. I, in my new character of Miss Smith, blushed hypocritically saying I knew nothing of such things, whereupon he pronounced himself ashamed of speaking so loosely. And fell silent.

This hiatus allowed me to ask, with a further increase of feigned innocence, what next he intended towards me? And had he answered that he wished to embrace me there and then among those pretty ferns I swear I should have cheerfully complied so fetchable was he. Fortunately he did not (being an old-fashioned gallant) and I was able to keep up my impersonation of a virtuous spinster out of her parish.

In answer to my question he took my hand and sighed. So this time, to encourage him, I said I had thought at first he had intended to abduct me and had wondered where it was he might be taking me? And again all was said with a breathy innocence which allowed my bosom to palpate demurely yet promisingly. For old Eve will out if she can. Especially if old Adam is in view.

He replied that his dearest wish would be to take me home to Somerset. For never in his life had he beheld a more beauteous creature and that if external attributes were indicative of the soul within then I was a perfect goddess. And although he knew there was no fool like an old fool he had nevertheless spent the previous night composing verses in praise of me and perhaps I would have the kindness to cast an eye over them?

'Here? Now?'

'Would you?'

I nodded. At once he produced from his pocket a much folded leaf of paper and handed it to me. I sat myself down upon a convenient boulder to study his profusions while he stood before me – his eye bright with animated expectation.

There were five poems in all, but two stanzas will suffice to show their mettle, which was as heartfelt as it was constrained.

Upon Phyllis (viz. Susan)

Could I but bind thee to me, cruel Phyllis,
Love's sickness would be fled;
For thy removal all my ill is,

Such absence leaves me almost dead.

I said, 'But I'm not cruel, sir. And I haven't removed.'

He said, 'Figures of speech, Miss Smith.' And shifted his footing like a boy at his lesson. I read again. This second was warmer.

Again upon Phyllis (viz. Susan) after Petronius

I love a miss will make me bold
Her charms within my arms to fold.
To press her close and also kiss,
To sigh, and burn with eyes that wish
For that which could I once achieve it
I'm d——d if I would ever leave it.

I said, knowing wickedly too well, 'What does *d-dash-d* stand for?'

He blushed most delicately. 'An old soldier's oath, madam. I was feeling strongly at the time. But say. Do. What do you think of my efforts? No need to spare me.'

In response I rose, quite forgetting my spinsterly imposture, and was upon the brink of embracing all him, all at once. For the truth was, that having received these verses as a lady, my instinct was to reward them as a whore.

For never in my life had I had a poem written to me. I was overcome with pleasure. Flattered beyond words. But luckily the gods (especially Hymen) remembered my maidenly pretensions for me, thus securing my future.

Their succour came in the shape of three barking balls of canine fluff – one black, one white, one grey. They came yapping out of nowhere, halted within a yard of us, and from this prudent distance gave vent to an animosity as violent as it was petty.

I began to laugh but my gallant Colonel did not. He grabbed my elbow again and cursing these miniature furies (I was glad to hear him lose something of his ancient decorum) he bustled me deeper among the rocks into a sort of grotto.

Yet I was astonished. This was surely unlike my brave cavalier – to retreat from danger? Especially a danger so impotent?

'Why, sir?' said I. 'I cannot believe three such creatures can harm us?'

'Not in themselves, of course not, my dear – I mean Miss Smith – no. No, no, no. But they are the Countess's lap-dogs. Her damned lap-dogs!'

'Oh, that's what *d-dash-d* stands for?' I answered, laughing.

This time he laughed too, but added it was not a word he should have wished to utter before a person as innocent as myself. Inwardly I sighed and yearned to tell him I had heard far, far worse; that the language of Pudding Wharf was so vicious as to be a match for the Court itself.

'Hark,' he commanded.

I obeyed and as we listened I felt the Colonel's grip upon my elbow relax. For the yapping was drawing further off.

He said again, bitterly, 'Her dogs. Diana Wavenhoe's dogs. But they are gone. And she with them, I thank God.'

Now I was at a complete loss since the impulse fate had so providently checked two moments before was now returned more forcefully than ever and, what was worse, in a place entirely suited to the purpose. Once more my cavalier seemed eminently worthy of embrace.

But this time Colonel Bancroft, rather than gods or dogs, came to rescue me from my fleshly self by asking again for an opinion of his verses. And thus were the urgencies of blood distracted by the tranquillities of ink. Such poetical considerations afforded time for me to draw breath, draw back, and even draw a veil over my ever-refulgent feelings. I said, in all sincerity, I was honoured, and would henceforward treasure his paper, keeping it either in my bosom or under my pillow. Receiving my praises he beamed and assured me he had many more within him to write upon me but now he thought we should leave that spot since he was reasonably sure that the Countess would, by this time, have gone for her dinner. Which she never missed.

Hearing this I took thought. Was not this grotto too convenient to vacate so suddenly? And, now, now I was once more in command of my inclinations, might I not employ it to press my suitor, not to a bodily demonstration of his passion, but to an even more vital one, to wit a declaration of his devotion? Possibly even a proposal? For that, after all, was my object with him, was it not? And I had the impression it would not require much ingenuity on my part to have him fall upon his knee.

Therefore I said, 'But, sir, we have so much to speak of. And this spot affords us a most pleasant seclusion.'

'You don't wish to leave, madam?'

'No, I do not. And please call me Susan.'

'Then you must call me Jeremy.'

'With all my heart.'

'In that case let us sit for a moment.'

And this time we both sat, but I ahead of him (there never was such a gentleman as Jeremy Bancroft) upon yet another convenient boulder.

I said, 'Am I to conclude that you do not care for the Countess of Wavenhoe?'

He exploded most satisfactorily. 'Wouldn't give tuppence for her. She's an adventuress, you know? A widow on the rampage. Pretending to more than she's got which is nothing at all. I've made enquiry of her. The Earl's estate was entailed to the last blade of grass. There's even a whisper she poisoned him. But I must not speak of such things to such as you, my dear, dear Susan.'

And he ventured to take my hand. Whereupon I decided to seize if not him, then fate by the forelock.

I said, 'May I speak of her son to you? Of Lord Spark?'

He blenched. 'I pray you're not enamoured of him?'

I smiled. 'Oh, no, Jeremy. You may rest easy on that score. I detest him.' He exhaled relief. 'I hate him as a thief,' I said.

Anxiety returned so quickly to him it was comical. 'A thief? Of what? Not of your honour, God forbid!'

If that thought was unwelcome to him it was even more so to me. For how upon marriage to him could I dissemble the loss of my so-called virtue? So longtime lost (way before Rusty) under a hawthorn tree in full blossom with a drover's lad whose name was quite forgot. But then I took heart and decided to face out that small localised difficulty if and when it was arrived at. Doubtless the arts of love would come to my aid.

So I pretended to a blush and murmured most virginally that that was not the case. But made sure to add quickly (so we should not dwell upon the subject) that Lord Spark had tricked me out of my fortune. As you might expect I did not explain either how it was got, or its extent. Instead I embroidered upon the plain fabric of truth: saying I had gone to him for advice as to where to place, in safety, my money but he had advised me so badly that I had lost it all save for a little I had kept by me. And indeed, given the circumstances, I could only conclude that he had stolen it for his own use, taking it abroad with him. And it was for that reason that I had chiefly come to Tunbridge Wells.

Jeremy called me a brave girl for attempting to seek out my deceiver while I felt a twinge of guilt at my continuing deception of him but the next moment these considerations were set aside as he asked me if I could contemplate removing from there to Somerset.

'Go alone with you, sir?' said I as silly Susan. 'But that would ruin my character.'

126

'No, child, it would not. For I would have you marry me.'

I doubt I have ever kept a more decorous silence. I held my peace for almost a minute while my admirer dared not speak another word. Finally I averred that before I could answer so momentous a question it behoved me, as a poor defenceless woman alone in the world, to know rather more of him. I knew he was a soldier and for that I honoured him. I knew he was a poet and for that I admired him. And I knew his estate was in the West Country but I had no notion of what it consisted and lastly, what was his heart's history? For such a man of parts must have loved and been loved many times?

At this he smiled and nodded, saying he had been married twice but had no surviving issue, nor indeed living wives. For both his dear spouses were deceased, one in childbirth and one of the smallpox. The income from his estate in Somerset, and in the New World at Virginia, where he had a thousand acres under tobacco, amounted to some £7,000 per annum, and if I were to marry him he would at once charge his attorney to redraft his will entirely and comprehensively in my favour, for though he was in excellent health and had all his faculties and parts in what might be termed full battle order, nevertheless he must admit he was no longer as young as he had been when he first took up arms for King Charles the Martyr.

That said he drew breath, sighed deeply and still clasping my hand, sank to his knee, and, with his eyes upon mine, asked me yet again if I would marry him – for he loved me with all his heart?

Reader, I said yes.

I dwelt five years in Somerset as an honourable wife before my dear Jeremy died in my arms. For despite his age (and I have told before how he was born in the age of Elizabeth) he was a most consistent and considerate lover. My dilemma concerning my non-existent virginity dissolved upon our wedding night in mutual pleasure, and after, little by little, I came to tell Jeremy everything of my history and although he was at times astonished (especially concerning Pudding Wharf), never once did he upbraid me. My husband was indeed a perfect cavalier and so noble was his nature he should have been a knight. Even now I dream of him.

Born a country girl I had at first expected to detest Somerset and yearn for London. But this was not the case. For I discovered there is a world of difference between life in the country with wealth and the same without it. I was a rich landowner's wife and could do as I pleased. I even learnt to refine my cooking at the instruction of a sulky young Frenchman whom Jeremy had hired from La Rochelle to supervise his kitchen. The boy was a bully, but he knew his business, and though I was his mistress (in the mastering sense) he forced me into culinary correctness *viz*. the French way. And to tell truth he was right. His methods were the best and very soon, I am pleased to say, I had learnt all he had to teach me, and begun to experiment with further receipts of my own. And soon became as proprietorial of my kitchen as Enoch had been of his laboratory.

From time to time, between country diversions (I drew the line at riding to hounds for I pitied the poor stags and foxes), memories of Rusty and Enoch would float into my head but then they would float out again. I did wonder, in a sort of bucolic matron's dream, what might have become of them, but nothing from that time past seemed as pertinent to me as the next harvest supper, or the Twelfth Night ball at Yeovil, or dressing the church for Ascension. Or, most engrossingly of all, upon the two occasions when I thought I was with child (wishful pregnancies, I fear they were) and the one occasion when I actually was, but only to miscarry. Alas, whatever venereal talents I possess they do not include conception, which formerly I had counted a blessing, but not then – for Jeremy longed for an heir. He would blame himself declaring his spermatic juices were less plentiful than they had been while I assured him he had enough left for the purpose, which was true. And so we would try again – enjoying what may be called the consolations of infecundity.

And thus it was that my idyll was brought to an end. By our very endeavours upon this score. For in '74 while in congress Jeremy expired. Even as he cried out 'I die!' he did. And while I shall not pretend it was a decorous end I can say it must surely be the best that any man may hope for? Certainly I was glad for him.

After I buried him and heard his will which he had had remade in my entire favour just as he had promised at Tunbridge Wells and, after making sure his estate in Somerset (which was modest) might be left safely with an agent, I determined to travel to Virginia to view his tobacco plantation whence the bulk of his income, now mine, derived. Therefore I took a maidservant with me, for company, propriety and service, to Bristol. And took ship for the New World.

We were not three days out at sea when I saw Rusty. But I scarcely recognised him. And if he knew me he gave no sign.

To say my heart missed a beat is to understate. It missed three. In horror. For how he was changed! He had been brought up from below with others to take the air. He was heavily shackled and his clothes, such as they were, hung in tatters. His head was shaved, his eyes red-rimmed yet dulled by privation, his beard grizzled prematurely, and most of his right ear had been either cut or burned away. And he was thin as a rake.

Upon enquiry I discovered Rusty was one of a gang of prisoners condemned for their crimes to transportation to America. And their destination was Virginia. At once on impulse I took up pen and paper and wrote thus: 'Take heart. All is not lost. Be of good cheer. The new world will bring us both a new life.' And I signed it by an old endearment of his for me: *Cyprus Sal.* And I swear to you that even as I signed it thus all my six years of gentility slipped away and I felt myself transmogrified back to my younger self when I was a happy, spirited, adventurous whore; a female pirate upon the high seas of male cupidity. And I laughed for the sheer unexpected resurgent joy of it.

A young midshipman was soon inveigled into conveying my message to Rusty and two days later when he and his miserable fellows were brought up again I contrived to be present, albeit high above him on another deck, and he looked up and this time his face broke into that grin of his that could undo a bishop's daughter at twenty paces and I winked down at him and felt my bowels melt as they had ever done at his proximity.

Furthermore that night I dreamed of Enoch! And though I am not overly superstitious, save for such things as crossed knives, spilt salt, new shoes on tables, walking under ladders, hawthorn in the house, gloves on a bed and the new moon spied through glass, I nevertheless took my dream for a sign that, just as I had encountered Rusty once again, so I might discover Enoch anew. Though where or when this dream did not reveal. We were lying in a wood under a midsummer moon in a sweet languor and dishevelment after love. And he was whispering curious words to me that seemed to caress me with a power superior to that of any lover's lips, or fingers or tongue. And in the morning, to my astonishment, I found I must have risen in my sleep and noted down his words, which in the light of day remained pretty yet had lost their power and made no proper sense: 'In this Wood are found two Doves for then the Soul of Mercury ascends with the Soul of the Dissolved Gold and these are enfolded in the everlasting Arms of Venus.'

This paper I kept by me in the hope that upon a day he might explain it to me. I had no doubt it was poetical (though I much preferred my dear dead Jeremy's verses which were plain as a pikestaff), that it referred to his sacred art which had put us to so much trouble and that whether Rusty and I liked it or not we, too, were as necessary as Enoch to its completion, though what that might be I had no means of knowing. For if I have learnt anything at all about alchemy it is this: alchemists never talk straight. Compared with them your ordinary crooked bully or bent doxy is a paragon of God's truth.

Eight weeks later we made landfall at Virginia after a voyage so uneventful as to be generally esteemed miraculous and I bought Rusty for £50. No, he was not a slave, that was the indemnity I was obliged to place upon deposit at the governor's house so Rusty might work out his term (fourteen years) on my upcountry tobacco estates which proved well ordered, comfortable and boring.

Needless to say, once we were removed there, and I was installed as mistress of my inheritance, Rusty graduated from convict to common law husband. But not before a decent interval had elapsed and we could act with discretion. For as a colonial widow of substance I soon became aware that I had inevitably a certain status within that New World community – a community that was far less liberal than any in Somerset.

This enforced respectability, however, had one advantage. It provided time for Rusty's health to mend, his hair to grow and his vigour to be restored. After a month or so he was as robust and as cheerful as he had ever been, although with an added weight or bottom, as we say, within him. He was no longer quite the cocky captain he had been; more a New World general. I took to calling him General Mars while he in his turn named me Madam Venus. But only in private. To the outside world beyond the plantation I remained Mrs Bancroft, widow, and he, Mr Ironside, confidential secretary to the estate – to wit, me.

Naturally we rehearsed many times each other's histories from Pudding Wharf to the New World but of Enoch neither of us had any intelligence at all. He seemed dissolved without trace. Lost somewhere in that gap of time which lay between our tripartite life at London and this twofold going-on in Virginia.

☿

Sailing in upon New York, with my Nubian Ganymede at my side, I was in receipt of a vision. A phenomenon as unwelcome as it was potent. And all the more provocative because by that time I had renounced, most irrevocably, anything we choose to term spiritual, in favour of everything we know to be material.

Let me not mince my words: I, Enoch Powys, had consigned the royal and sacred art of alchemy to the scrap heap.

It was a dirty March evening in '75 and at this first sighting New York appeared much as I had feared it would: mean, huddled, paltry. One minute veiled, the next revealed by the intermittent blasts of sleet and snow. Manna Hatta was nothing if not itself: an earnest, servile, dull-spirited trading post presided over by a makeshift fortress built of wood (in this age of steel cannons, I ask you!) from which flew the cross of St George; an absurd emblem already torn to shreds by the climactical fury of the New World.

Below this sodden edifice there stood a row of tumbledown shacks more fit for beasts than persons while beyond it a tawdry windmill was churned by the gale beside a church, clenched as a pugilist's fist, out of which the thumb-like spire seemed rather to give a fig to heaven than signify God's benison poured down from above. In the East Road weatherworn ships and workaday barges lay close-hauled at anchor in a stewpot sea of boiling lead. I doubt I have ever contemplated a more disgusting prospect. And I cursed myself again at accepting this errand for Mr Newton.

Abednego, as I named my catamite, whom I had had as a gift from the chief librarian at Cairo, said, 'How bad it look, effendi.'

I was bound to agree, but even as I concurred, the wind of a sudden abated, and the sun – that formerly I might well have described as Great Sol himself clothed in western glory – shone out for the first time upon that fateful day. The star's beams shone through the icy squalls that still spewed from the bellied clouds above. Yet such was the refraction of this emergent light that it seemed these precipitate down-pourings, which before had been either forcibly slanted or irregularly tossed that way or this by the wind, were now translated into standing columns or vertical pillars, which were quite unshaken by the storm's force, and full of shining eyes.

To my sceptical gaze this puny settlement which had previously abased itself before the elements was grown in a blink into a celestial city, a mighty New Jerusalem of impossible proportion and ungovernable power. I scarcely knew how to perceive it. All my latest reasonings were, at a stroke, at a stop.

For now these transcendent columns showed themselves not as shafts of rain but as great bastiments which, in spite of gravitical force, thrust themselves skywards with a gigantical turgidity not seen upon the earth since the raising of the Tower of Babel. But here was not one tower but an hundred! And these impossible edifices reared their heads like rockets and within them I thought I did perceive many persons at work and play and worse – all revealed through rising ranks of great glass windows. What was more, these fenestrations were of an immense dimension. They were big as matrimonial bedsheets which was a self-evident enormity since I have never yet discovered a glassmaker that could fashion a pane of glass any larger than a neckerchief. And these same transparent implausibilities were set at levels one upon another that rose as many as twenty, nay, forty, why, even sixty storeys into the sky! These proud towers were, I thought, beyond the vaunting dreams of any architect. I doubted even Dr Wren, intrepid calculator of all physical forces though he be, could have envisaged them. And emblazoned thus by the shooting beams of the declining sun these rain-dashed columns (that were but the rain itself) were become incandescent. They burned like almighty red-hot pokers a-gleam with liquid coatings of mercury and copper. Here, I swear, was an alchemical city such as even Mr Newton could never have imagined, and which seemed to mock my latest pretensions to practicality. Unless – and here a notion struck me with the force of a thunderbolt – unless this vision had been granted me as a demonstration by the organical of what the mechanical might achieve? But then, in a final flash, the sun was gone, the wind restored, darkness returned, and that impossible city nowhere to be seen.

I said to Abednego, striving to sound as drily sceptical as I might, 'Did you see any of that?'

'See what, effendi?' murmured he, snuggling closer with a soft rustle of his quilted petticoats. For little Abednego in his silks and velvets (not to mention his wig with the curls wired) answered most prettily and exactly to his description on the ship's list as Mrs Enoch Powys. And many an envious glance had I received of the sailors and my fellow travellers who to a man imagined I enjoyed a black Venus as my bedfellow. That I did not was no inconvenience to me, of course, because the charms my sweet boy slave afforded were quite a match for any woman's. And I do not discount Mrs Sally's nor Sister Tabitha's.

But the fact that he had witnessed nothing of what I had seen disturbed me. Was I to apprehend from it that this illumination (if that was what it was) had been shown to me alone by providence? And if so for what purpose? Perhaps to dissuade me from my newfound scepticism? If so I resented and repudiated it.

And in this mixed mood I set foot upon America for the first time.

We made our way to a woebegone inn called the Wooden Horse. Not a name, I thought, to carry great conviction with those of a Trojan temperament (as I had previously counted myself) but acceptable enough now I was become as it were a bustling, thrusting Greek. But these reflections were at once proved superfluous since the place was already full of a party of Sephardic Jews that moment arrived from Brazil and there was not a room to be had. We were directed to another even less commodious establishment upon Pearl Street where a gross wooden duck dangled on a rusted chain above the door. This object was painted blue and once we were within doors we were informed it was a dove, a blue dove, not a duck (many visitors had thought this but they were wrong), since this hostelry bore that name: the Blue Dove. Our apprehensions thus set to rights we were offered the last and worst room available – for cash in advance despite the evidence of our baggage.

The room was well enough if you considered yourself a bat or a barn-owl and were prepared to roost amid rafters. The bed was concealed in a cupboard with pierced panels as if for the preservation of cheese. It was scarcely wide enough for the two of us but when another was revealed stowed away beneath it I decided I might enjoy Abednego in the first and consign him to the second once I was satisfied. The which I did with some force thanks to the consumption of a seafood stew so full of clams and potatoes it would have occasioned lust in a lollipop.

The following morning we went out in our best (Abednego resplendent in silver brocade) to view the town more closely. And stepped straight into the mildest spring imaginable. The sweet season was come with a sudden clarity of light and a gaiety of blossom that quite astonished me. Yesterday's black tempest might never have been, the vicious edge to the wind seemed an ungrateful memory and the heaving sea that had tossed our insides out from Plymouth to Manna Hatta had transmuted itself into sparkling wavelets under clouds as guileless as newborn lambs.

As we strolled beside the East River the place appeared to be rather more, indeed much more, considerable than I had first supposed. For now I discerned well-set pebbled streets (pebbles from the foreshore being used for want of granite cobbles) and the numerous shacks that had first disgusted me were here replaced by good houses of brick built in the Dutch manner with stepped gables and staircases to the front doors. Clearly bricks and tiles might be manufactured in these parts as abundantly as in Bedfordshire. Nor had the original settlers' art of husbandry forsaken them since everywhere we looked we glimpsed, behind walls and wattle fences, most orderly gardens and vegetable plots meticulously tilled and mathematically trenched.

Having viewed something of the strand we turned about to go down towards the fort and shortly were come to what, upon first viewing, delighted us most: a canal that passed from the East Side to the West behind the fort and its adjacent windmill. It was at this time high tide and the waters within it reflected the houses that stood upon each bank. It was traversed by four bridges, two of stone and two of wood. This was indeed a true and most respectable imitation of Amsterdam – until the tide went out. For then, we were later informed, it became only too apparent both to nose and eye that here lay New York's chiefest sewer and one ebb tide was not enough to cleanse this open conduit of its quotidian filth.

After observing the fort (that was an even punier construction than I had previously suspected) we viewed the church of St Nicholas which, though curiously slope-shouldered, proved upon closer inspection, like a Dutch matron, handsome enough when surveyed all about. It was an edifice that was entirely roof – very like an inverted W. The oak shingles that covered it were weathered to a grey soft as the breast of any turtle dove.

Again we turned and again we found ourselves upon Pearl Street which led us back to where our tour of the town had commenced. Only this time we looked, rather than glanced, across the East River to the opposing shore. There, beyond all manner of high- and low-stomached shipping (the tonnage at anchor was more impressive than I had initially conceived) we saw another settlement which stood against wooded heights. We soon learned it had been dubbed Breukelen by the Dutch, which since it lay uneasily upon the English tongue, was now pronounced Brooklyn. A ferry crossed the sound eight times a day yet the settlers over there already despised their opposites upon Manna Hatta. What is it in us that makes us ever desirous to be better than our neighbours? Especially as we know, if we take a moment's thought, that true superiority lies in a precisely calculated modesty? These sophisticated notions, however, were and are quite unknown to the New World, and I dare say always will be.

Pearl Street brought us to the market which was still at business despite it being already ten o'clock by the bell above the court house. Below it, as a sharp reminder of justice ever ready to be applied to those who cannot pay to avoid it, stood the gallows. They were set upon the foreshore so that if you were not fully hanged at ebb tide you might be inexorably drowned at full.

But such sombre reflections were swept aside by the view we now had of the citizens of New York. What a consort, or, if you will, concert of sounds and sights! I swear I heard a dozen languages spoken in as many minutes. And the dress, both of male and female, might have come from the wardrobe at the King's Playhouse. Some talked and looked like the strait-laced, baggy-bottomed Hollanders they were (true Butterboxes) whilst others were a crazy burlesque of London's fashions at the Exchange or Westminster Hall or in the Park. These persons sported every kind of waistcoat, cloak, periwig and hat and to me it seemed that they had been preserved in amber since '69 when I had left Pudding Wharf for what Mr Milton has called 'fresh woods and pastures new'.

Such a crowd puts description to the test especially for a man such as myself not overly concerned with fashion. Everywhere I beheld velvet and lace, steeple hats and embroidered caps, not to mention French *sacs* of silk for the finer women and petticoat breeches for their strutting consorts. Ringlets flounced before full-bottomed wigs while be-ribboned walking sticks struck out at stray dogs, street urchins and other superfluities. Here also were Jews severe as crows, negroes black as Jews (compared with them my Nubian blackamoor was purest gold), pale-pink French, yellow Spaniards – and even a Turkish vizier, green as an emerald, borne in a litter for whom all the world made way. Which was hardly surprising given that he was escorted by twelve enormous bodyguards seemingly built of bronze bearing naked swords. Indeed it may be faithfully recorded that the only persons in New York who could be truly described as white were I and such others as sailors, tosspots, soldiers, dairymaids, costermongers, fish-wives, preachers, pick-pockets, fur-trappers, pimps and whores.

These last were everywhere. Between one market stall and the next you could purchase cunny as conveniently as haddock. The very air of the place breathed concupiscence. And the reason was at once clear for now I saw a party of straw-hatted tarpaulins come that instant off an English man of war. And it was plain to see that once upon the town these sailor boys wanted naught but women and booze. Why not half an hour later when Abednego had already been goosed three times (and me gandered twice) we found one of this nautical fraternity with his doxy *in flagrante delicto* hard up against the wall that had been built to keep the native Americans out. And I state only a natural philosophical truth when I say that the entire structure shuddered – along its length – at the vigour of their exertions.

By this time I bethought I had taken some measure of the town upon which I had adventured. And while this second impression was better than my first (setting aside that trick of the light that had transmuted it into a celestial city) I was of no mind to rest there long. *Ergo* I at once made enquiry at the waterfront for a boat to transport me to my errand's ultimate destination – a place but recently founded by a former acquaintance of Mr Newton. A gentleman of the name of John Winthrop the Younger who by then was become an American big-wig, *viz.* governor of the neighbouring state of Connecticut. For it was to him that I was bound to direct myself upon my old mentor's behalf.

My goal was a sea-port called New London. An ambitious name which led me to suppose that Mr Winthrop might well have established it to rival New York, since it stood little more than an hundred miles up-shore from Manna Hatta.

I soon found a sea-going wherry that would put in at New London on its passage to Boston. Its master, a cheerful Swedisher, informed me he would sail the next day at four in the morning so we were best to come aboard that evening. We did, and after an agreeable supper of lobsters and aquavit, passed the night in a tiny cabin as snug as buggers in a lugger.

We made a pretty little voyage of it by way of Long Island Sound and were never once beyond sight of land whether to port or starboard (though which is upon the right hand and which upon the left I shall never know, having no aptitude for nautical knowledge). The coasts we passed reminded me of England and I soon advised Abednego, who in yellow and scarlet was looking as juicy as a ripe nectarine in a forcing house, that when I had accomplished my present business with Mr Winthrop we would return as soon as we could to the Old World. For I had no inclination to become a colonial.

In addition (though this I did not admit to him) I now dared consider that sufficient time had elapsed since the events of '69 for me to reside once again in England without fear of being called to account for that irregular enterprise (and its violent dissolution) at Pudding Wharf where, it seemed to me, I had been inveigled into what I might term 'a false position' by the connivances of Mr Rodney Ironside and Mrs Sally Greensmith, both of whom, it was now apparent, had cruelly betrayed me by going clean away together, leaving me to my fate, which would not have been less than a good hanging at Tyburn, had not Sister Tabitha come to my rescue.

I cannot pretend, however, that I was at that time grateful to her. Life, after all, is ever something less than purely simple, though Tabby was. The sweetest little whore you could hope to slip a crown to and, despite her trade, as innocent as a sea anenome. No, upon that fateful morning of the 23rd November '69 I was truly put about by her intrusion.

I was, you may recall, still engrossed and entranced by the *magnum opus*. I had not yet come to the dark process of disillusion, followed by despair, in whose footsteps comes distrust, upon whose heel treads doubt, which can lead even the most dedicated adept towards disgust with the whole damned thing. And in my case to a fierce disputation with Mr Newton who resolutely rejected my newfound scepticism.

But that was later. When Tabby arrived I was still the credulous adept who had achieved not just one manifestation of the universal agent (which is said to be the necessary intermediary element by which art and science beget riches and therefore eternal youth) but thirteen. Yes, I had *thirteen* retorts all proclaiming the mystery. All showing within their glassy walls that sublimed mercury which is said to be nothing less than that beauteous, golden, apparently self-generating tree of knowledge (here fancy and hope become one) which I had previously observed in a single vessel one lunar month before when Rusty's impatient subscriptors burst into the laboratory and I expressed my indignation in a manner as abruptly astonishing to me as it was to them.

In that November dawn of '69 it seemed to me I had succeeded upon a scale unprecedented since the days of the Canon of Bridlington (thirteen mercurial miracles all in a row upon as many sand furnaces) and my mind was quick with any number of analogies from the past that appeared to illuminate the present with a light as bright and white as magnesium, and I felt myself to be a true alchemist at last, and upon the brink of an inner comprehension concerning the entire nature of the universe, its very construction and purpose – a revelation that has been termed 'philosophical gold' – when Tabby stood before me.

At first I did not recognise her for she was no longer in her usual naughty nun's habiliment but dressed as a lady, becloaked, and carrying a portmantle.

'Why, Sister Tabitha,' said I. 'Are you dressed for a journey?'

'Enoch,' she said, her voice a-tremble. 'We've already gone. All of us.'

'Gone?'

'We left last night. After we'd met together. All the girls. On account of us not seeing Mrs Sally or Mr Rusty for days on end. It's likely they've deserted us. So we decided, well, if they can shog off so can we. Like it's every cunny for herself now. We divided up the takings between us, fair shares all round – '

'A whore's republic? Very proper.'

'And left. Yesterday. Only I've come back.'

'Why?'

'For you.'

'Me?'

'You've got to come away, Enoch. There's a lot of men out the front. All over the wharf. And I reckon there's others inside the whorehouse, too. It must mean trouble.'

I said, 'What day is it?' For truly until that instant, I had not had any thought for time in its diurnal dimension.

'Don't you know? It's the 23rd!'

'Ah, well, that explains all. Rusty's subscriptors are come for their gold.'

'Have you got it?'

'Not yet. But I have made the universal agent, the sublimed mercury that can generate gold. It only remains to – '

'It doesn't!' she interrupted, grasping my hands. 'It's now or never! That horrible Judge is out there! And the sheriff! And soldiers, Enoch! Soldiers with guns! And horses! And pikes! And Sally and Rusty have deserted you, too. Don't you see? They've left you to carry the slop bucket. But we can still get out at the back. It's come with me or get strung up, Enoch. It's me or the rope! Come on!'

And if Sister Tabby's urgencies had not been enough to move me (they had) then the measured tramp of steel-studded boots approaching the laboratory door was. Three heavy-handed bangs upon it followed and these peremptory thumps prologued a voice that could have challenged hell's town crier for the job. It demanded openness in the name of the law.

Whereat, as if these very words were inflammatory, all *horrida bella* broke loose. We fled and even as we vacated the premises I heard a great banging back of shutters next door, then shoutings and a mighty clatter as of hostile objects hurled from windows together with soldierly voices organising war. Next came proof of it because as we scuttled up Fish Street Hill we heard three huge explosions and glancing back saw in the sky a burst of coloured fire of a pyrotechnical nature cascading down upon Pudding Wharf.

'By God, it's Armageddon,' I said in admiration.

'Come *on*,' said Tabby, tugging me away.

Tabitha and I lodged briefly together at Epping, proclaiming ourselves to the villagers as brother and sister. But that was not how we comported ourselves once we were alone together. It should have been a sweet time (and in that way it was) but in truth I was too perturbed by what had occurred at Pudding Wharf and fearful of retribution to rest easy, and Tabby, while fond of me and as corporeally ardent as any man could wish, was anxious to put her past behind her. She had conceived a desire to return home to her evangelical parents at Penge, there to confess her harlotry – she declared our temporary union to be based upon affection, not money – and to beg their forgiveness, and God's. She would plead, like Winifred in the old play, that she had been 'but a young thing drawn arsy-varsy into the business'. I advised her against this course, urging her to remain my loving companion in obscurity, but she would not listen, thus demonstrating that blood is not only stronger than water but also of more consequence than quicksilver.

And so we parted with many kisses, sighs and regrets on both sides – Tabby to the sober hillocks of Surrey; I to the severe flatlands of Cambridge. For I had determined to travel there discreetly so I might privately inform Mr Newton of my recent manufacture, in unusual quantity (thirteen alembics!) of the philosophical mercury, thanks to the use I had made of his receipt or *clavis*.

But being in no particular hurry and not having a superfluity of money – Tabby and I had maintained ourselves frugally upon her share of her earnings and, at the last, divided what remained between us: £4. 12s. 6d. each – I took a carrier's cart full of uncured cow-hides as far as Puckeridge. Mercifully the season was frosty otherwise the stink would have been unsupportable. From there I was of a mind to walk but the weather turned against me and I was obliged to lie up in a place called Barkway until it abated. I should not have thought of this malodorous hamlet as a nexus for news (no coach stopped there) but alongside the fleas and the bedbugs I found a broadsheet left behind by some other benighted traveller.

And in it was delineated in a block of nine woodcuts what was called 'The Notorious Battle of Pudding Wharf at London in which a Parcel of Rogues put paid to the Forces of Law and Order'. And in these pictures I saw the unmistakable likeness of Judge Gibbet albeit all in pieces at the explosion of a fire-bomb; my glorious alembics smashed and broken; the mighty figure of a masked participant labelled a Rascal said to be a certain Captain Steele, together with horses in heaps, militia men firing into the air and yet more men jumping out of boats. Beneath these representations of the scene was printed a coarse ballad of which, I regret to say, I can still recall the last stanza:

And when we'd slaughtered one 'n' all,
We vanished in the fog,
To sink a quart at Rocco's house,
Close by old Lambeth bog.

And below that there was an account in prose which succeeded in combining an absolute disapproval of the occasion with a total relish for the violence of it. It was to be understood, I learned, that three constables and twelve militia men had been wounded, six pikemen rolled upon or kicked by their own horses, a Judge of the Realm exploded and a sheriff was even then lying in hospital but unlikely to live. While the Perpetrators of this Enormity had got clean away in the Morning Fog. And the whole report was attributed to an author who signified himself as Janus. Thus, in this manner, my apprehension of an explosive confrontation between Rusty, Monty Cruikshank and Judge Gibbet was confirmed. Which led me to wonder if Rusty yet remained at liberty and what might have chanced to Sally? But as the broadsheet had no answers to these questions I could only put them from my mind and continue to hope that my part in the affair had not been adverted. And I thanked providence that I had chosen to be known at Pudding Wharf as Dr Quicksilver rather than by my true name.

Next day the sky cleared and I continued my journey. On arrival at Cambridge I made enquiry of Mr Newton, suddenly fearing what I had quite forgot, that now Christmas approached he might have departed for his house at Grantham. But no, I was assured that the great philosopher was not gone from his college and upon proceeding to Trinity that evening I discerned lights in his rooms beside the chief gate and in his laboratory below. I cannot express what satisfaction I drew from this. Simply to stand without and know my master dwelt within! Now all I had to do was to enter the college unobserved by the porters at the gate for I had no doubt that that servile breed would delight in betraying me at once to the Master and Fellows for my part in the great equine-urine mishap of the previous spring.

Between Trinity Street and Mr Newton's chambers lay a little garden which stood beyond the light of the lanterns at the gate. Into this shadowed space I stepped and once safely there I tossed a handful of gravel at his window whereat he opened it with an asperity I had expected but which I hoped I could ameliorate by the announcement of my identity.

And I was right. Upon hearing my name his aspect softened and in less than a minute I found myself admitted by a side door and heartily embraced by my dear mentor.

He hurried me upstairs to his main room and having installed me before the fire and regaled me with sherris sack (it is said the entire university floats in this unctuous liquor like an unborn babe in the amniotic fluid) he demanded to know everything of my life since I had left, while simultaneously reprimanding me for not having written a single word to him.

I gave him an account of my experiments which suppressed all details of a doubtful nature. To hear me you would have thought I had passed my time in pure research while earning an honest crust as a respectable clerk at Whitehall. But now, I said, compounding falsehood, that job was lost to me by way of a sudden reformation of the civil service – it was said the new order was going to be more economical of human resourcefulness and therefore of benefit to the nation. But meanwhile I had come close to starvation and been forced to abandon my laboratory and I was come to Cambridge to ask him if he could procure me employment of any kind, however humble, so it were of a chemical sort?

By way of answer he complimented me upon my success at achieving the philosophical mercury and brought out his own notes upon the process, questioning me closely, even urgently, concerning the precise amounts, both by weight and volume, of the ingredients I had employed, their proportions one to another, and the timings I had adhered to in their manifold distillations and purifications, together with the temperatures to which they had been subjected. That I had created the universal agent out of the star regulus amalgamated with common mercury was entirely in keeping with his own experiments in which he had followed the method of Thomas of Bologna but he was amazed to hear that I had achieved it thirteen times over and surely there must be significance in this number? However it was a great pity and a loss to the world of science that I had been prevented from continuing by poverty inducted by mere political policy. I had come, he said, as far as any adept of the sacerdotal art and I was to be most warmly congratulated, since he knew what a never-ending labour it was.

But, alas, he could not employ me there or allow me the use of his laboratory. He needed it for his own enquiries and, besides, if I were discovered his position might also be endangered, for not only did opprobrium still cling to the name of Enoch Powys, but also the rumour had got about that he, Isaac Newton, fellow of Trinity College and Lucasian Professor to boot, had certain heretical doubts concerning the tripartite nature of God – the which he would neither confirm nor deny, not even to me in the privacy of these rooms late at night with the oak sported, since there were those who might well exploit this gossip for their own ends. The college was full of placemen, fools and dullards, whose vicious envy and petty despite of exceptional men knew no bounds. The place was a nest of academical vipers – its denizens never at rest until they had succeeded in quelling or dismaying excellence. So he must perforce be ever upon his guard.

I might, however, lie there that night in his bed while he worked at a paper he was preparing against Descartes (whom he had begun by admiring but was now come to abhor as overly mechanistical) and he bethought what else I might do in order to lead a life worthy of my proven chemical talents. Meanwhile had I supped? No. Very well, he would send down to the buttery for me while I remained concealed in his laboratory. No one, not even the Master, dared enter *there* without permission.

I swear I could not have enjoyed a more sincere reception. I slept that night away like a baby and in the morning, after we had breakfasted upon hot chocolate and doughnuts, Mr Isaac asked me if I had an inclination to travel? If I had, he said, then there were several errands I might accomplish for him. Imagining by this mild enquiry that he meant merely a return to London, or possibly a visit to Oxford, upon some scholarly mission, I was, to say the least, surprised when he announced that he wished I would journey on his behalf to Paris, Frankfurt, Venice, Alexandria and Cairo. He could fund me, he averred, not luxuriously but decently, providing me with letters of credit and introduction, while in return I would conduct research of an alchemical sort at the major libraries of those cities.

For example, and here he presented me with a list as long as his arm – or yours for that matter, human arms being much of a length. There were five particular texts at Paris he required copies of; three at Frankfurt, several more at Venice although they might well be corrupt, while these eight in Egypt were likely to be the nicest of all – since when it came to the crisis he trusted the Greeks and Arabs above all others. For alchemy to them was as water to ducks. Was not the very name derived from *al khem* meaning mud of the Nile? Liquid life-giving gold – at least when the sun was setting? Or so, he believed, it appeared.

Would I accept the commission? How, given such eloquent persuasion, could I refuse? Oh, Mr Isaac had a tongue on him that Satan himself would have envied, with a mind to match. And I dare say the lord of hell admired both. For my master's intelligence seemed not of this world.

He imagined my travellings might take four, if not five years (but time, in this instance, was not of primary account, and could well be said to be relative, especially when measured against the resolution of the riddle of the universe), so what did I say? He could think of no one, not a soul, more suited to this task. And in conclusion he considered it a sign that I had presented myself, out of the blackest night, at his door. It was as if circumstance had conspired to aid him. For the texts he required transcripted must needs be done by an initiate – for one unfamiliar with the sacred art would merely confound what he copied with ignorance. And here he smiled so sweetly that I was become yet again his disciple and I agreed.

And so in the spring of that new year I crossed the Strait of Dover to carry out his commission. And was away as he had predicted for five years. I read every text (ancient and modern) upon his list, made transcripts, concordances, notes and commentaries, sending what I could back to him by way of anyone I encountered who was travelling to England and might be trusted with the manuscripts. Finally at Cairo I found a letter from him awaiting my arrival in which he expressed his gratitude for what I had achieved thus far and assuring me that my researches had strengthened his belief in the *prisca sapientia*, which is that knowledge enjoyed by the Babylonians that had now been for the most part lost but yet might be pieced together by a rational examination of such ancient texts as I had already sent him. Such studies, allied to scrupulous experimentation in the laboratory, would, he was confident, enable him to decipher the significance God had imprinted so cryptically upon His creation.

I confess his enthusiasm nettled me. I should have been gratified by his praise, but I was not, because by that time, after three years of ruining my eyes and applying to these texts the very kind of rationality Mr Newton recommended, a mood of disillusion, even of black doubt, had come upon me. It was very like a melancholia or accidie and had been occasioned, I decided, by my researches. By too much poring over old books which were written with such deliberate obscurity in so many languages not native to me that they promised the student of them lunacy rather than illumination.

I asked myself what was it they purported to convey? Was their subject science or poetry, chemistry or religion? And did these things mix? Great alchemists like Mr Newton believed they could; lesser ones, such as I, had begun to doubt. Perhaps two incompatibles were here confused to the detriment of both, and the sooner matter was separated from spirit the better?

Whereat I said, 'Physician, cure thyself.' And at once prescribed for myself a regime of unalloyed pleasure and self-indulgence which was not difficult to initiate or sustain in a city as seductive as Cairo. I was done with dusty books, creaking parchment, crumbling papyrus, pen and ink. And I swore I would never read another word of Cornelius Agrippa, Theophrastus Bombastus Paracelsus, Johann Andreae, or Basilius Valentinus, let alone Bonus of Ferrara, Flamel of Paris, Raymund Lull of Majorca and least of all would I ever again consult Plotinus, Jâbir Ibn Hayyân, Senior Zadith or St Albert the Great. I wanted life, not the Turba Philosophorum nor the Emerald Tablet. Which was how I came upon Abednego who served as third kitchen slaveboy to Cairo's chief librarian. When I expressed admiration for the lad (at fourteen he was Adonis incarnate) he was at once presented to me as a gift I could not refuse and we proceeded upon an extended holiday of delight, save for a wasp sting on my nose at Giza, surveying the antiquities of Egypt hand in hand. For in that country the love of men for boys (and vice versa) is deemed as natural as breathing while in Abednego's homeland of Nubia women are kept for the procreation of warriors and to work the house and fields. Which does not mean they are not beautiful – they are prized by the slave-traders and fetch high prices at auction. Often they are sold with their children which was how Abednego grew up in the household of my Cairo host.

On returning to that tumultuous city I decided I must proceed to England. I might have exchanged the great work for a small boy but I still considered myself Mr Newton's emissary and whatever my newfound distaste for the sacred art I was obliged to report to him. Besides I had amassed three coffers full of transcripts it would be dishonourable not to deliver.

Abednego and I sailed first to Sicily but there, at Messina, our close affection for each other soon earned the oddest looks. Surely the Sicilians must be the most bullish mothers' sons on earth? For them honour, family and babies are everything. Impugn any of these attributes or even suggest another manner of living and you will find yourself nothing but a pool of blood on a dusty road. So I bought Abednego a dress.

For safety's sake, you understand? To say Abednego was delighted would be but half a truth. He revelled in that garment, begged me for more like it. I indulged him and he soon became the prettiest travesty you could wish to behold. Especially when I got him a boned bodice fashioned out of silk and rounded out with two deep sea sponges, not to mention three wigs, a muff, a feather fan and high-heeled shoes. Why, at Barcelona, the jade persuaded me to part with the bulk of what money I had left so I might supply him with yet more female gee-gaws and girlish fripperies. And had I not had the foresight, earlier in my travels, to borrow for future research against a rainy day – as we travelling scholars put it – certain invaluable texts from every library I visited, things might have gone hard with us. For I confess I was besotted with the boy and indulged him shamelessly. In particular because I had discovered it caused certain *frissons* within me to see a perfect woman on the outside while knowing that underneath stirred a tireless boy. Furthermore, I realise now that we were lucky to have put in at Barcelona rather than elsewhere since I was able to sell those precious texts in that breezy Catalonian city without a single question asked. It seemed the place had been founded by the Great Anarch himself in favour of free trade. And so we were enabled to continue our voyage homeward in some style. As Mr and Mrs Powys.

At Cambridge we stayed at the Eagle and Child in Silver Street. That name refers, of course, to the great god Zeus, who in this ornithological form, carried off the child Ganymede from earth to Olympus to be his male concubine and cup-bearer of his favourite nectar – much to his wife's annoy.

Once settled in our room I gave Abednego strict instructions to behave as a most proper matron and at no time to flounce his parts as he was sometimes wont to do. I warned him that the students at Cambridge were like the Egyptians in their amatory predilections. In other words they would not give a fig if they discovered that under his skirts he was as they were. Indeed they would at once strive to debauch him while considering his womanly disguise a merry jape in keeping with their own puppy notions of wit – for they were all without exception indefatigable coxcombs and mummers. How did I know? Because I had been one until I failed to matriculate – what time I had been forced of necessity to pretend to certain academic qualifications I had not got. But, interestingly enough, by way of this life-long pretence to learning I had acquired more true knowledge of science than many who might claim, upon university record, to be Bachelors, nay Masters of Arts or even Doctors of Philosophy. Thus it is wise, I advised him, ever to keep faith with fakes.

That evening I went, under cover of dusk, to Mr Newton. But he was not there. He had gone to London to address the Royal Society upon his Hypothesis of Light. Therefore I was obliged to wait in the dark, since I preferred to remain, as it were, *subfuscus*, until he returned.

Three days later he was back and received me at once. He professed himself eternally in my debt for supplying him with virtually all those transcripts he had asked of me. Although it was a pity I had not had opportunity to copy the B text of the 3rd Testament of Synesius held at Cairo.

So grateful was he and such was his continued enthusiasm for the sacred art that I was at pains to conceal those doubts which had overwhelmed me in Egypt, leading me to renounce all my former convictions concerning it. But from my mentor nothing can stay hidden long, and he soon laid bare my scepticism. At which we had a fierce, even painful dispute. For surely there is no rage like an intellectual rage – especially when it blazes forth from a mind such as Mr Newton's? I admit it – I was scorched by something close to Heraclitean fire. How could I, he demanded, his gifted apprentice, deny his most profound belief that the secret of the universe, nay the very substance of it (and the two might prove to be the same thing), could only be laid bare to the mind of man by research of a poise so exact between profound knowledge, scrupulous experimentation and divine inspiration as to defy any fool who placed a limit upon what might be comprehended? Therefore it behoved us as scientists *and* adepts to keep our minds open and our apprehensions pure. Why else had he devoted so much time to the sacred art while at work upon his mathematical principles? And further (and here I was incinerated as in a wind furnace such as I had myself once built for him) was it not conceivable that my loss of faith in the alchemical art denoted not so much an unusual enlightenment as a commonplace diminution of my intellect? A condition suffered by many natural philosophers upon the advance of age?

Pounded thus I departed in great dejection to find no consolation in food, wine or bed. Abednego caught my mood yet none of his pretty ways could alleviate it. But in the morning came a note from Trinity in which Mr Newton apologised for the savagery of his attack upon me, though not its substance, while requesting me, if I could find time, to sup with him that night in his rooms.

In a mix of love and hate I sent back that I would wait upon him, and at six o'clock I went, albeit warily.

Would I, he enquired, over our boiled mutton and buttered carrots, undertake a final mission for him at his expense? To cross over to America (he spoke as if the ocean were not there – and to such a vaunting mind I dare say it is not) to call upon a friend of his? The man concerned (for now we are almost come full circle) was a colonial by the name of John Winthrop the Younger. He had met him at the Royal Society upon several past occasions but not this latest time, for Mr Winthrop was presently much occupied in the New World where he was the governor of Connecticut. The man had an informed layman's knowledge of the sacred art and a magnificent library which held within it three important texts he still lacked. If I would go there and transcribe them he would be once more in debt to me and who knew, perhaps these further studies might rekindle my faith in the quest for the Green Lion who, in the words of the Vicar of Malden, can wed the Sun to the Moon?

I knew not what to say. In part I wanted to agree at once, but pride and a certain dismay at the thought of another journeying held me back – especially of a further two months at sea. I said I would sleep upon his proposal at which he nodded and told me he would respect my decision whether it was yea or nay. Whereat we parted in a spirit of cordiality revived, if not entirely restored.

But when I consulted Abednego he was eager for the adventure, as he had heard that in the New World bread grew upon trees, the natives were coloured red and the race of life was to the swift. Such was his youthful enthusiasm I was persuaded and the next day I informed Mr Newton accordingly. He in his turn was delighted and furnished me handsomely for the voyage and for my sojourn there.

Thus, on the 15th of January '75 we embarked at Plymouth and got tossed by the elements as far as the Bermoothes where we lay up for a week thereafter to fly before half a dozen storms born one from another to Manna Hatta and that vision of a celestial city which I was now, upon reflection, come to believe to have been instigated as an antidote to my disbelief by my mentor, Mr Newton, in league with his mentor, God.

New London was set within a pleasant inlet and could already boast two jetties, a church, some clapboard cottages and a general store, together with a house of grander proportions set somewhat apart from this new settlement – undoubtedly the residence of John Winthrop the Younger.

My letter of introduction secured us a courteous welcome. Mr Winthrop expressed himself a venerator of Mr Newton and his fellow alchemical adventurers as he termed them at Old London. Especially Mr Boyle, Mr Locke and Mr Hartlib, now unhappily deceased. And he understood that even our King Charles, that prodigy of energy, was of a like mind and had commanded a laboratory to be built expressly for the purpose of experimentation.

I forbore from suggesting to my kindly host (who clearly thought evil of no one) that this particular royal enterprise was probably, if not certainly, prompted by material greed rather than any desire for philosophical understanding. For our sovereign is a great believer in getting rich quick where and when he can. Why, if gold were to be detected beneath Windsor Park, he would turn the place to a desert so he might mine for it.

Abednego and I stayed at New London for ten weeks in considerable comfort while I made the transcripts Mr Newton had commanded. And as I worked upon the latest edition of Albineus's Bibliotheca Chemica Contracta I am bound to admit I experienced certain stirrings of renewed interest in the sacred art. I shall not call it a revival of faith but rather a modification of that materialist position I had adopted, along with Abednego, at Cairo.

When we took our leave the governor showered us with gifts for ourselves and Mr Newton – favouring Abednego with a beaver-lined cloak. For somehow the old boy had never once discerned his true nature, addressing him throughout our stay either as 'my dear lady' or 'ma'am'. And when he spoke of him to me, Abednego would become, upon his lips, my bride. 'Your sweet bride,' he would say with a smile as if he were the pastor who had just married us. Meanwhile Mr Winthrop's wife had, I thought, had her suspicions but held her peace. Though whether from social propriety or secret outrage or both I cannot say.

And so we returned to New York there to run slap bang into Rusty and Sally, thus disproving the old historian's adage that history never repeats itself. It does – quite as frequently and pungently as pickled onions, cucumber or smoked mackerel.

Sally was still Beauty's self but she looked older and had put on weight. She was clearly in the best of health, however, and well if rather soberly dressed. Beside her Abednego seemed a butterfly. Rusty looked almost distinguished in a cassock coat of military cut and a full-bottomed wig that was quite majestical.

They were as startled as we were. And I have no doubt that three out of the four hearts there present leapt in a mutual mêlée of delight and distrust at this unexpected reunion. Certainly Sally's eyes upon Abednego were as sharp as hatpins.

'Well,' we three said in unison while Abednego gawped. 'Well, well, well. Well. Oh, really! Well.'

♂

Talk about fate delivering the old one two or, as we say on this side of the pond, the double whamoozle! Wow! Here was Enoch the Adept wiv this sodomite in a dress. Wiv a cod female, I ask you!

Straight off I say to myself them tits ain't real. Next, if that's a mount of Venus at the lower front of this slice of bummy side up it's coming on a bit strong. Like it'll wave to me in a minute.

And during all of this we're doing the fancy-meeting-you-in-the-New-World routine and it's clear to me our erstwhile Welsh wizard is in no mood to hang about. He's dead shifty, not making wiv the eye contact, the feet are going one way, his hands the other, wanting off.

So I say, 'Why so shy, Enoch?'

'Not at all,' answers he. But that don't seem to follow somehow. Could it be the poor old professor can't manage the here and now? If so, odd. He used to be fly as they come.

Then I get it. Of course! That's it. Yeah! He's ashamed to be seen by Sally wiv this boy on his arm. 'Cos she's twigged too. After all, if I reckon I'm an expert in the hold-door trade, then what's she? I mean, given her experience running Pudding Wharf if she can't tell beef from cheese at a hundred yards in fading light, who can?

Sally says, all grace and favour, 'Enoch, do introduce us to your friend.' Ooh, and the tone she put on *friend*. Like it could freeze your balls off.

'I'm Mrs Powys,' says the lad.

Whereat we all laugh. Least I do. But loudly so it does for all 'cos Enoch is not moved to share my merriment.

He says, po-faced as a po, 'My friend is called Abednego. He comes from Nubia in Africa. And I dress him like this and have named him Mrs Powys for security reasons.'

Again I laugh. I shouldn't, I know, but I can't help it.

'Christ,' I say, 'you'll be telling us next you gather intelligence for the Crown.'

'Not quite,' says he severely. 'The security I refer to is of a social nature. Society here and in England is not yet ready for an association such as ours. In Egypt it is different of course. Civilisation is older there. As for intelligence I gather what I can, albeit of a purely scientifical nature, for Mr Isaac Newton. We embark for England tomorrow.'

'It's lovely to see you, Enoch,' says Sally. And this time she smiles at him that smile I've never been able to resist nor no fella else neither. When Sal turns that on, I tell yer, you're gone. That is it. You are as good as in the lap of the goddess. Christ Almighty the power of that woman.

Enoch's no exception to this rule. I see him go weak at the knees. Like he's a-wobble and I almost put out a hand to steady him but in the instant he's recovered himself and is saying in a different voice, his old and easy one, that we might all toddle over to the Wooden Horse for a jar. The which is apt and nicely since that's where Sal and me are staying. Off we shog.

♀

The wheel had come full circle. Here were the three of us reunited in New York with only the presence of Enoch's negro boy to spoil the symmetry of the occasion. I shall not pretend I took any pleasure in the sight of this creature, although I can say with my hand on my heart (how it skipped at the sight of Enoch) that I had not any disapproval of the liaison in itself. If two persons of any sex can enjoy each other, good luck to them, the world is full enough of sorrows without worrying if one generative organ should be preferred to another.

No, the fact of the matter was worse. I was jealous, furiously, madly and immediately jealous. This emotion was as violent as it was unexpected. To see Enoch with another – never mind who. Another! Someone else! A person not me! Oh, it was horrible. And Rusty, I could tell, felt the same. Here was something sprung again between us close to that sensation of consanguinity I had felt on first meeting Enoch all that time ago. Only now it was shared between all three of us. At one level, blood level, Enoch, Rusty and I were one.

Abednego's presence at this reunion was a defiance of natural law. How dare Enoch bring to it a male concubine when he had me? Or could have. For I wanted, with every fibre of my being, to lie with Enoch there and then. I could not endure sitting there, sipping small beer and making small talk!

'Really? And how was Paris? Venice is a handsome city, I believe? But somewhat wet. Oh, me? Well, I lived in Somerset for a while.' No, I wanted none of that piffle. I wanted to be upstairs a-bed with Enoch, stark naked.

Rusty sensed my need (and to be fair he understood it, too) so I was not as astonished as I pretended to be when he suddenly rose up, very masterfully, pulling Abednego to his feet with him.

Said Rusty, 'Me and this one, we're going for a little walk, right?'
'Are we?' said the boy.

'Yes, mate. We frigging are. Like we've got a few things to chew over.' And turning to me, he added, 'Reckon it could take most of an hour. Maybe more. See you later, doll. Be good. Ta-ta. Rub-a-dub-dub.'

And with a wink that was better than a nod he hauled little Abednego out.

All this while Enoch had not said a word. There had been not a peep of protest from him at Rusty's high-handedness. Nothing. He'd sat as still as the corpse at a wake but his eyes on me had spoken volumes, nay, were even then speaking whole libraries.

I took his hand. His eyes pierced mine. Could I speak? My breath seemed gone. Yes, I could.

I said, 'Shall we?'

☿

Five years and more confounded in an instant. Simply no longer there. Gone as if they had never been. And I in Sally's arms again.

As we embraced amid a rumple of sheets and the deep swell of pillows I adduced that destiny had brought us thus urgently together for a purpose. And that purpose was to do with the royal and sacerdotal art. Why else were these pretty visions of lovers conjoined (who were none other than ourselves) crowding into my head as into a pelican while we conversed so corporeally together? Could Mrs Sally's charms, which now seemed quite as rare as ever they were, could they be bent upon transmuting me into my former self? All my doubts dissolving? Was I become a god again? Mercury revived in Venus? It seemed so. Once more I was a star, an element, deceiver, adept, fool! And this consummation, that was become as mystic as it was plastic, had been brought about by Mars himself. Mars, otherwise known as Rusty Ironside, earthly pimp and elemental bully boy. While Sally was no longer brothel madam turned colonial widow but once more the brightest and best of heavenly bodies, Venus, sweet, ductile, ingenious Venus.

At last as I lay upon Sally's incomparable breast, quite spent, I felt myself infused with a devotion so powerful I could only murmur as lovers ever do, 'I was not born till now.'

Sally said, cool and crisp as newly starched cotton, 'Oh, yes, you were, Enoch, you can't fool me.'

151

At this we fell to laughing immoderately and so began our coil again, with an increased compassionate heat, generated out of remembered times together which we had both thought lost to us, but now were here regained.

♂

Right, you horrible, idle, book-loving reader, you! Yes, you, wiv yer bum in a chair! I want it clear. Frigging crystalline. As of now! Are you receiving me? You better be 'cos this is your General Rodney Mars speaking. Like I'm in charge, right? In overall command, got it?

You have? Good. Keep it that way. From here on in, we are not, repeat not, playing peace-lovers. No, sir! As of this point in time I wanna see loadsa loyalty and blood on the bayonet, understood?

Excellent. Yeah, well, first off, we make an appreciation of our own forces, don't we? Like that's the procedure. And that's us, innit? Me, Sal, Enoch. Together again. In harmony. United. As one. The old triangle. Jingle-jangle. And if we act concerted we're unstoppable, invincible, sorta magic. And we shall. We do. Hup, hup, hup!

Which was why I didn't pause for thought when I saw that young saucebox wiv Enoch. Oh, no, it was action that instant. I mean you could see that boy was trouble just looking at him. So I said to myself, Rusty, this little homoerotical's gotta go. We don't need no spare pricks at this heaven-sent reunion.

But no, I didn't tie him up in a sack and sling him in the river – standard practice round here, they drown 'em like kittens. No, I was quite merciful really. Like I may act decisive but I ain't vindictive. It wasn't never personal, not wiv Abednego. Just inevitable. Sorta written in the stars as we say.

So, well, only the day previous, I'd clocked this youth – no, not Abednego, pay attention, book-lover, this other fella – holding up a doorpost down by the riverside wiv his snakeskin belt kinda loose, his leather breeches skewif and his hand in his cods. Well, natch, me being Mr Streetly Wiseman, I put this 'n' that together and reckon he's gotta be offering custom in kind, know what I mean? Like to a fellow-feeling sailor passing by or else to some mustachioed racoon-hunter on the trail? Which, I swiftly reasoned, meant, as wiv the females of the trade, this young cockalorum had to have a protector. Like that's the way the world wags, dunnit? There's always a Mr Big somewhere ready to mulct Mr or Mrs Small of their winnings, right? And doubtless this protector could use another male pullet, get me?

Like the more cherry-pies he has on the job the more rewards he gets? Least that's how I've always figured it wiv my cunnies.

I'm right. When I lug Abednego down there I'm directed to this saloon where there's these characters playing cards and letting this large one win. And when I say large I mean large. Like he's got a gut on him the size of a bread oven, four chins instead of a neck and the daintiest hands you ever saw covered wiv enormous rings. Not to mention ferret eyes, melon cheeks and rosebud lips. And yet hard. A man of mighty contrasts, clearly. Name of Arnold Jay Stone. Remember it. Like Arnold Jay personifies quite a lot of the New World.

We size each other up, kinda cool. There's a load of 'Hi, stranger,' and dead eyes all round, but in the end, once they've had the dress off Abednego and looked him over like he was a bull calf at market, we agree on twenty silver dollars. And I've done my first New World deal. We sink some raw spirit purporting to be whiskey and I'm away, leaving Abednego to his fate. Which could be a hard one, I agree. But that's the way it waggles. Life is tough. And there's only one enemy, right? Yeah, you've got it, poverty. Like wiv cash in hand you're on top, wivout yer just something unwelcome someone else has stepped in, correct?

So that's our own forces appreciated – us three plus twenty dollars, and whatever Enoch's got about him. Enemy forces? None really, except the above-mentioned, ever-present threat of penury.

But do I hear you say: Hullo, I thought Mrs Sally, lately wife to well-heeled Colonel Jeremy Bancroft, deceased, was a rich widow, with tobacco estates in Virginia? And didn't she rescue her old lover, that ever-resourceful, charming, happy-go-lucky Cockney rascal, Mr Rusty Ironside, from fourteen years' hard labour? And now are they not come to New York, so surely they must have a modicum of where-withal about them? Answer me that, squire.

Yeah, well, good point, attentive reader. You know, there really ought to be a regular prize awarded to an ardent booker like you – I mean, just for staying wiv a story like this. Though I will say one thing for it, at least it ain't frigging literature. But you're spot on, you've hit the gold, as the butt said to the arrow.

Sal did rescue me. Only life in Virginia did not turn out to be a goose-feather mattress, let alone a bed of roses, no. First there was the locals, then there was the natives, and which was worse I know not, but both were frigging horrible. Your Puritan farmer – forget him. All crop yields, potato blight and bless this house. And as for his spouse wiv her mouth shut tight and her chest fallen flat – I tell you a washboard's like sinful compared wiv one of them. And their kids! Don't tempt me, just bring back boiling oil is all I say. And, as you can imagine, these plain folk were soon giving me and Sal plain looks whenever we rode down to the plain store or the plain church or plain whathaveyou. Oh, yeah, we tried to fit in, but no, oh no, we was interlopers, and kinda fetching, so sod off, newcomer. Like America gets quite old-fashioned up the back-end of Virginia.

As for the Indybums! Oh, Christ, didn't they look painful. Feather hats, feather skirts (his 'n' hers), feather leggings, feather armlets, feather necklaces, and any flesh left over painted wiv funny eyes and dead peculiar zig-zags. And they'd scalp you soon as look at you. Mind you, a wig can fool 'em, which is why I'm here to tell the tale.

Oh, yeah, they attacked. Like they was always attacking. Every full frigging moon. We was on their warpath, right? The poor sods – these our feathered friends – wanted their land back. Jesus! How naive can you get? I mean I know I'm thick – I've lost count how many times Sal's told me that – but these lads was so natural it hurt. Didn't they know they was up against our neighbours? The aforesaid plain folk, who'd shoot the pecker off any Indian warrior impertinent enough to ride over the land they'd just fenced him off of? And which he still reckoned was his?

Not that any of this sympathy helped Sal and me. Your average New World native don't bother to distinguish between colonialists. To his mind we was all white and all for the chop. So after they'd attacked the farm twice, me stout in defence, and burned the crops thrice, me with an arrow through me shoulder and minus periwig, I said to Sal, enough is enough, like I want out, how about you, darlin'?

Sal shed a tear or two (like she'd been devoting herself to the dump out of respect for her old Somerset cavalier's memory) and put it up for sale. And didn't the locals laugh. But we didn't care. We left, wiv it still unsold, sod it, telling ourselves we'd make a new fortune in New York which we'd just heard had become Crown property once more. Like Britannia ruled again. And the frigging Dutch was nowhere, glory be.

What I had in mind for New York was a nice little cat-house, sorta club-like, wiv cards and dice attached. Get the idea? A wholesome place where a gent could have a flutter after his fumble wivout his old lady being wise of it. Discreet. Respectable. Not gaudy. Oh, no. Them days was past, I reckoned.

After all, Sal and me had come up in the world, even if it had let us down again just lately. But I reasoned, wiv the little we had left, we could set up like modest, and then start coining it like immodest. On top of which I can't say I was exactly averse to pulling the odd town pullet again. I mean I'd been used to my creature comforts in Newgate, lost the lot, then got 'em again wiv Sal in Virginia, but there's nothing like a bit of variety, is there?

And talking of Newgate – just for the record and so there's no loose end left lying about, as Lady Golightly said to her husband's tailor as she tucked him into her placket – yeah, I had intended to escape out of Newgate, hadn't I? Remember? Courtesy of Abe Shemozzle, right? That's where I left it wiv you, didn't I? Way back? In '69? Wiv me all agog and full of hope?

Hope! That's something to make the cat laugh. I mean, life just loves her little ironicals, don't she? 'Cos Abe's idea was really good. Ace. Like of a very considerable beauty.

It went like this: I was gonna get mortally ill of an unknown malady, Abe would send in his tame doctor, together wiv an undertaker to measure me up for the you know what. The doc would declare me dead but highly noxious to the health of every bugger else inside, and out we'd go in the made-to-measure coffin wiv me lying in it while the governor and his screws held their hats over their noses and prayed they hadn't caught the deadly contagion what had supposedly done for me.

And this we did. And it was a cinch. We got all the way to the main gate and was processing out through it when suddenly, just like that, I get this fit of the sneezes. The most explosive series of the bastards I've ever had. And it's all Abe's lousy, cut-price coffin-maker's fault for leaving a load of sawdust inside the bleeding box, I ask you!

So there was me, the corpse, erupting wiv these cataclysmic snorts, like a volcano wiv the lid on, just as we're doing our funeral march past the aforementioned authorities. Well, natch, those carrying me (Abe, Brendan O'Bryne and a coupla hired hands) start looking about them, don't they? Like they lose their solemnity. Can't believe what they're hearing? Wonder what gives? Ask themselves what the fuck, why's this coffin jerking every which way, etcetera?

Well, I could've told 'em, only I'm too busy pretending to be dead yet subject to these funny turns. A-tishoo! Next thing I know the bastards have dropped me on the cobbles, the lid flies off on impact, and I'm sitting up, racked wiv these spasms (like I'm seeing stars as well) and gazing up into the unforgiving regard of Governor Padlock. No, that ain't his real name, but he was a good bribable bloke, is still there, and you never know. However in this instance I'd kinda gone beyond any further help from him. I knew it, he knew it. Like a prison governor must sometimes do what he's paid to, right?

Meantime Abe, Brendan and the others are long gone down the street. They're far away and I'm left to tell Padlock it's like a miracle, innit? Me? Alive? Fancy that! But, take care, I'm still infectious – these sneezes prove it's the plague I've got, so don't come too close, I'd hate you to get it, etcetera.

But it don't wash. This time round I'm not credible, am I? I've lost out and this is it. The heavy hand of the Law (well, ten hefty warders' mitts as a matter of fact) is upon Rusty's shoulder again. And they're bringing all these chains, as well. Looks like they could mean it.

They did. From then on I wasn't just guilty of not paying the licence on Pudding Wharf to be a place of recreation for rampant liverymen within the bounds of the City of London, but I'm also up for attempted escape from Newgate as a living corpse. Jesus Christ, did I feel undead. Well, He should know. Sorry, I digress.

Either offence can, of course, get you transported to America. But the first carries only seven years. Only! While the second means fourteen. So what do I get? After five years waiting for trial? Fourteen. Still, let's be grateful where we can, I escape the noose 'cos nobody's got hard proof it was me at Pudding Wharf. Monty lived despite all, but never pressed charges. Don't ask me why. Maybe he reckoned enough was enough and anyway he'd made sure he got my business down on the Isle of Dogs (all right for some).

So that's it. No, it's not. My left ear. Bet you'd forgotten that. I hadn't. Never will. I miss it. I lost the poor old lobe onboard ship. Just before Sally saw me. In a dust-up below deck wiv another prisoner over a remainder biscuit. Me, I was fighting fair, head-butt, knee in the cods, when this fella makes wiv the teeth. Most uncalled for. But then what can you expect from a common criminal?

The rest you know. You've got it all now. That's the situation as it was before our new campaign got going in New York. And what an operation it turned out to be! Forget Pudding Wharf – that was chicken feed. This was the big one! At our house of pleasure upon Pearl Street. Yes, sir!

♀

By mid-June we were established in a business – Rusty, Enoch, me. And how complete I felt, having the two of them about me again. I counted myself the luckiest girl on earth. Oh, yes, girl. For it seemed to me I was back as I was when I first set eyes on Enoch. And so seemed he. And Rusty, too. We were all three become our former selves. Was this, I wondered, the effect of the New World? In which all things seem possible? I couldn't tell, and yet each day, and night, proved better than the last.

The house we rented on Pearl Street was a solid Dutch residence that had been built by a fur-trader lately removed upriver to Fort Orange. It had sixteen rooms upon four floors, not counting the storehouse and stabling at street level. It possessed an imposing stoop of fourteen stone steps outside, and a fine oak staircase inside. When Rusty first saw it, he whistled, and was of the opinion it was perfect for our purposes. It's like it's quality, he said.

In order to establish ourselves at such a place we had pooled our monies. Enoch was possessed of nearly a hundred guineas, I had still some thirty pounds and Rusty a dozen silver dollars left from his sale of Abednego. The other eight he had spent on wining and dining Enoch and me at the Wooden Horse. Lord, what a night that was, and how surprised, yet gratified, I felt, to find myself a-bed between the two of them, when I awoke the next morning. But of that I shall speak no further, lest I offend the apprehensions of the modern reader – for I have heard that he, or she, has grown not only politic but correct beyond the reforming zeal of any Praise God Bare-Bones or Zeal of the Land Busy. And thus are age-old pleasures renounced in favour of the satisfactions of new-made righteousness.

Our intent was formed by Rusty. Upon Pearl Street we would establish that which, he assured us, New York sorely needed: a house of refined recreation for the better class of bloke. He was right. His eye for a new niche in the market had not failed him. For while the town was full of sailors' molls and common harlots – the waterfronts swarmed with them – it lacked, what I might term, horizontal ladies of a certain cachet.

But where to find such? Rusty said, never fear, he'd go out that instant and fetch 'em in. Enoch and I agreed. For you should understand that at this initial stage of the business Enoch was as eager a participator in the adventure as Rusty and I. For the moment the other-worldly adept was, like a dormouse, sleeping deep within him. Off Rusty went.

Back Rusty came. With five of the profession. He tried to crack them up to us – expounding upon their merits as if we couldn't see them for ourselves. Their dyed hair, painted cheeks, bravely boned-up bosoms, and dirty fingernails were each in turn fulsomely advertised to us. They were, he assured us, natural blondes, pure peaches and double cream, new-plucked apples, and clever hands, clean as whistles.

I was obliged to reject them all. But, to be fair to Rusty, he made no fuss about it, since he knew as well as we did, that these poor drabs could never answer our new purpose. He promised to look again, and a few days later he returned to inform us that he had fallen in with a school mistress. A nice lady of much learning, quite a number of years (maybe even thirty) and a look in her eye that was what he called promising. She was French and said to be a baroness. Sort of up our street, he reckoned. Like class, was how he put it, and no, he had not made love to her in the how's-your-father sense, no, not so far, no, just the verbal, all right? But she'd lapped it up like fuck, right?

Out of discretion I shall call this lady (lady?) Madame Souligny, for I would not have any of Rusty's descendants distressed by what follows. Oh, yes, Rusty soon had his way with that one (he would, wouldn't he?). She got pregnant (she would, wouldn't she?). And the last thing I heard on this earth was that she was delivered of a lusty boy as bone-headed and as short-tempered as his father.

Madame Souligny's school was for young ladies. That is for the daughters of those New Yorkers who already considered themselves better than most by virtue either of wealth or birth or race – or all three put together. For some were rich from their own hard work, others simply by being born or by marrying money, while all considered their country of origin provided them with an inborn grace, superior to that of any save those of their own kind. In other words they were clannish. The cream of New York society.

Their daughters required what their parents called a proper polish, so they might be ready for a lucrative marriage either in the New World or back home in the Old. For there was much trafficking to and fro, especially in early summer, when the trade winds were favourable. To this end these young and tender flowers, as Madame Souligny called them, were drilled in all the usual gentlewomanly accomplishments – except the one that really matters.

In other words, as Rusty was at pains to emphasise, they were that highly marketable commodity – nicely bred, delicately reared, virgins. We might ask much, he said, for their services, if we could but think of how to fetch them to the house.

To which I answered, 'But that's impossible, Rusty.'

'Nothing's impossible, doll. Is it, Enoch?'

'No,' answered he with a weasel's smile.

Rusty grinned and winked at me, reckoning he had just acquired a potent ally. And it was at once clear he had, because Enoch promptly appended a proposition to this assurance.

He said, 'All that's required to entice these delectable young creatures here is a lure, or a device.'

I expostulated, 'Like what? What sort of trap, or bait, have you in mind?' For of a sudden I had no taste at all for their cocksureness. I even felt a twinge of conscience. Were we really obliged to plot against such maidenly simplicity? Must these frail lilies be smutched? But this, I fear, only went to show that I knew less of New York than I thought I did. Those young and tender flowers proved me quite wrong. But not knowing this then, I continued, 'I cannot see any way of bringing these girls here to Pearl Street. And even if you were to succeed in such a debauched enterprise how on earth could we hope to use them as whores when they're expected to be at school? And I, for one, would refuse to supervise them. Being Mother Superior to a heap of common nuns on Pudding Wharf was one thing, but this, a calculated seduction of pure-blooded young gentlewomen, is quite another!'

I admit I exaggerated and I admit I had become rather more of the outraged cavalier's widow than I had meant to be, and had either Rusty or Enoch said, 'Oh, come off it, Mrs Sally!' I should have deserved the reproof.

But neither did. Rather I was greeted with a silence that was eventually broken by Enoch who spoke as though I had not.

He said to the ceiling – as if the rather fine plasterwork might answer him – 'They might, of course, be, erm, what shall I say? erm, yes, mm, afternoon ladies.'

'And what,' I demanded, all Somerset gentility gone, 'are *they* supposed to be? Afternoon ladies?'

'Only a notion, my dear. A toy in the brain. A fancy.'

'Garbage!' said I. 'You always know what you mean *and* say it!'

'Not so, Sally, not quite so. While I agree I do at times say what I mean, at others I incline to mean what I say.'

'Can we just get to the point, professor?' said Rusty, whose brain wasn't built for philosophy.

'Oh? Yes, very well. Yes. *Ephemerae*, we might propose them to be. To our more discerning clients, especially those of a certain age and wealth.'

'Dirty ole men? You're reckoning on catering for them?'

'As I say, it's a thought, Rusty.'

'A knocking shop for the older gent! Yeah! I like it!'

'I don't,' said I, but yet again to deaf ears.

'I see these creatures of a postmeridian hour prettily masked – to conceal their identity – but diaphanously dressed – to reveal their youthful graces. They might well perform dances of an innocent yet pagan character arranged to appeal to such clients. Who knows we might entertain the odd sugar daddy come up from Jamaica?'

'Fuck it, I love it!' roared Rusty, punching the air. 'You've got it, Enoch mate! Yer a genius! And when they've done their titsy minuet in butter muslin, they could – oh, Jesus, I'm the frigging genius now – they could slip out of them gauze-like gowns, nicely, cleverly, sorta now you see it, now you don't, and dance wiv fans. Yeah! Big feather fans! So yer eye don't know where to look next, right? Holy Smoke, as the Algonk said to the roasted missionary, the old boys'll have to keep their hats on their laps – like we could make it a rule of the house, whaddya reckon, Sal?'

I said, 'What will their mothers say?'

Rusty laughed. 'Leave them to me. And their school marm. Now, Enoch lad, how yer gonna make this dream reality?'

'Me?'

'Yeah, you. Like it's your idea so you're the one to make it happen, correct?'

At this Enoch proposed as a preliminary measure that we should offer dancing lessons. Rusty would introduce the idea to Madame Souligny and the young ladies could be brought here for instruction. Again I objected, asking who would teach them? Enoch confounded me (and Rusty, who gawped) by saying he would. He had seen a book on a market stall only the other day which purported to give all the correct steps for all dances in vogue at the Courts of England, France and Spain. He would learn them; I might, too. And there we were: we should also need to hire a pair of virginals – here Rusty guffawed predictably and ever after the girls were known to him as Enoch's virginals – together with someone, preferably blind, to play them.

And so it came about. Even the blind musician, who first played for Enoch and me as we learned the steps we were to teach. To our delight we found we liked these exercises. Soon we were become devoted to them, even quite accomplished, and Enoch ventured to invent some measures and variations of his own. He made me laugh as he demonstrated them to me but then, when I performed them under his now professional eye, I am bound to confess I found they awoke various warmer appetites within me. Furthermore they excited him too, and upon several occasions we were obliged to cut the rehearsal short so we might retire upstairs for an animated performance of what Enoch's choreographic art (as he grandly called it) had so insidiously implied.

During this while Rusty succeeded in wooing his noble French school marm. His Cockney coarseness, that would have offended any English gentlewoman, was to her a source of amusement, bemusement and outright laughter. Inevitably these pleasant verbal encounters, in which she was said to have half-heartedly attempted to refine

Rusty, soon escalated to what you already know. I could have told her, of course, knowing Rusty. Once you start laughing with him you're lost. Not that Lucille, as she now was known, minded. Quite the reverse. She became so enamoured of 'my Engleesh rascal' that I grew almost jealous but fortunately I had Enoch, now translated dancing master, to fall back on. In time of need.

Our plot was complete. It had succeeded precisely as Enoch had predicted it would. Soon we received our first class of girls from Souligny's Academy – twelve in all, and all as demure as guinea pigs. And as lumpish. My heart sank. I had expected gazelles.

But Enoch got them moving and soon the music, the steps (at which they proved apt) and his gentle but firm instruction, pointing a hand there, a foot here, straightening backs everywhere, had them transformed from animal lumps into something very like butterflies, and it seemed to me, in my role as fellow instructor and chaperone (for so I had declared myself), that thanks to Enoch's unlooked-for genius as a dancing master and the girls' eagerness to learn, we might after all be able quite soon to invite our first clients to observe them. A prospect I no longer viewed with my initial distaste having become as devoted to the dance as any of these girls; and had I been their age rather than getting on for five and twenty (the Lord preserve my charms from time's decay) I swear I should have wanted to perform with them.

They were measured for their costumes; we found a milliner who was as happy to make masks as hats; and Rusty discovered a source of magnificent feathers for their fans – he said they were of a rare bird with only three toes. But Enoch was of the opinion that Rusty had misheard and that these plumes belonged to the rhea bird or Patagonian ostrich. But however it was, they were huge fluffy things that were a pleasure to stroke and if they brushed your arm or leg you might almost swoon with the soft touch of it. The girls adored them.

But when they saw their flimsy gowns they were abashed. And one, the most assertive, who was, as we may say, the head girl among them, announced she would not upon any account wear hers, for with no bodice let alone petticoat beneath, it would be indecent. Whereupon all her fellows were at once of the same mind.

I was bound to agree and knew not what to say. But Enoch did. Or rather he knew what to do which was even more efficacious. And here I am bound to tell you that had Enoch not chosen to follow the path he did, he might well have had a future in the creation of musical and theatrical performances in New York. But, as it happened, his chief destiny lay elsewhere, along with ours, and this present enterprise was, as Lucille might have said, a mere *bagatelle*, a *divertissement*, a *jeu d'esprit* from a master spirit.

What Enoch did was so simple it was astonishing. I was a-gape with admiration. He assured the girls they need have no shame in wearing these delectable dresses for they were, when they danced his dances, not themselves, but a bevy of beautiful, classical ladies renowned for their perfect poise and social grace. What was more, during their performance, and this would make all the difference in the world, they would wear masks.

And now for this rehearsal, he announced, they would wear these very visors. But given their understandable shyness, remain dressed as they were. And view themselves in mirrors so they might see for themselves how they appeared. Whereupon we gave them their pretty masks. How entranced they were. How they gazed in wonder upon themselves and each other. And as I watched it seemed they grew into these new, strange, reflected faces made of satin, brocade or cloth of gold. For each mask had a different character and into that character each girl entered. They began to move differently, their laughter changed, their voices, too. They were no longer who they had been. In a way it was as if they now considered their usual selves quite gone, rather as children will cover their eyes and then maintain they have disappeared. Or at least become invisible.

Enoch, behind their backs, prompted our blind musician to play a lively dance. And very soon our masked vestals were, with one accord, treading a measure of their own impromptu invention. How freely they performed! Their limbs seemed loosened beyond all former constraint. Next, as the music's tempo quickened (again at Enoch's supervisory instruction) they were flouncing their skirts, loosening their chemises to an artful negligence, and kicking up their heels like Maenads, until their sweet perspirations were running everywhere. For it was a boiling hot day and yet, despite this, Enoch had insisted we keep the windows shut.

As this extempore rout rose to yet another height of abandon Enoch clapped his hands like pistol shots. A rat-a-tat so startling it commanded instant attention, silence, obedience, stillness. Never had I seen Enoch so imperious. He was become a perfect tyrant. All eyes, behind those masks, were upon him.

But then, with the girls' absolute allegiance achieved, he began to speak in that insidious murmur that had wrought so many wonders with me. It seemed to caress your very soul. And he was advising them (oh, that cunning man) to suppose, to fancy they were now nymphs beside a shaded pool in Arcady. That the day was hot. The banks soft with fragrant moss and scented thyme. The waters sweet. And there was not a satyr to be seen, let alone a peeping shepherd or unreliable demi-god. Why might they not – oh, the kiss of these cool waters to their toes – surely they could, they should refresh themselves among these glassy, cool, translucent waves? I learned later that he had cadged that last bit from Mr Milton – a poet even I had heard of. But now, and here his voice grew yet softer, now might they not, in this perfect privacy, divest themselves of these stifling, ordinary, mundane garments that so little expressed their true selves, their true desires? Might they not divert themselves, among themselves, in a dance reflecting this Arcadian reverie – this pretty game, this gentle dream of an antique perfection long since departed from the earth? After all there was no one here they could not trust and besides this exercise in the extempore had but one rule: that while they might dance naked in this *balette* for bathing beauties, they must – must – must keep their masks.

His speech soon had these impressionable young creatures in that stifling room crooning and sighing like turtle doves and even as these sighings and murmurations escaped their lips in time with the rhythm of his words – or incantation as I must call it – so their limbs escaped their clothes.

I was almost as spellbound as they. The air seemed a-shimmer with sensations: Enoch's subtle insinuations (so persuasive), the slide of silk, the rustle of linen, the fall of calico, and most spine-sharpening of all, the twangle of the virginals, which now, upon Enoch's further whispered advice, was providing a disjunct accompaniment of individuated notes of such skin-prickling intensity, at intervals so unpredictable to the simple ear, yet so strictly correct to the musical, that one's very bowels were altered. So it was no wonder at all to me that our twelve virgins (were they wise or foolish?) were soon quite as much in their birthday suits as any practised doxy at a broker's banquet with Mr Dryden as the guest of honour. Another poet familiar to me. A hearty man, a regular at Pudding Wharf, who always asked for Sister Cecilia, but lived in fear of his crazy wife *and* his regular mistress, poor soul.

Now they were dancing, with Enoch moving like a Will o' the Wisp among them, exhorting them to become as water ripples or dappled sunlight; as dragon flies or darting minnows; as willow leaves fallen upon the stream or the flowing weed beneath. And again his beguilements had their effect. And Enoch, I thought, was himself changed. The spirit of mercury had returned to him but in a different guise. Now he appeared pure dancing master.

Next he gave our pupils the fans and informed them they were become doves about a dovecote – perfect emblems of Peace and Love. Again, at these reassuring words they were transformed. The air was full of waving, fluttering plumes. First they fanned themselves, then each other, and, having discovered the teasing delight of these feathered caresses, they cooed and bobbed and strutted accordingly. And laughed and sighed. The very room was made into a parcel of air. It seemed both an ethereal element and a vibrant azure cage in which there tumbled these sportive yet innocent birds. Surely here was any man's secret fancy? Why, it even touched inward parts of me, prompting certain tinglings that ever herald desire.

But Enoch's next device topped all. He clapped his hands once more, the music stopped, a breathing silence fell.

He said, 'Girls, you have been water sprites, you have been turtle doves and fantail pigeons, but now you are to be priestesses of Eleusius celebrating Demeter, great goddess of plenty and fecundity. And for that you must be clothed in flowered gauze.'

Whereat we brought forth those pretty but transparent gowns which before they had refused to wear. But now, thanks to the masks and Enoch's tutelage, they donned them eagerly and found no shame in them at all. I offered to sew more flowers upon them in those places that hitherto had seemed too unconcealed but now they would have none of that. The gowns, they said, were perfect. All they needed now was to know the dance. So again the virginals throbbed and twangled, again Enoch led them into the measure, and soon they were become a flight of butterflies above soft, seeded grasses trembling in a summer's breeze.

In this manner we were able to devise our first performance. To be viewed by Rusty before presentation to our clients. The dances, or *balettes*, as Enoch called them, were performed in reverse order, thus providing an escalation of gentle yet provoking libidinosity for the perceptive spectator. The girls (who now referred to the whole business as a 'show') appeared first as the floral priestesses; then as the fan dancers; and last as the river nymphs in the babbling Arcadian brook. This presentation lasted twenty minutes and when Rusty had witnessed it he pronounced the thing a triumph – like it was, he said, the nicest, politest, naughtiest prick-pleaser he had ever seen. Especially the last bit. Them mermaids! Wow!

Yeah, Sal and Enoch worked it a treat wiv them girls. Like before they hadn't known their wotsits from their you-knows. But after – well, like they did, didn't they?

And me? Where was I while they was teaching 'em the way of it, the knack of it? Good question, squire. Answer? I was deep in service to the girls' head mistress. And that, I may tell you, was no joke, no, sir. Lucille, for all her starched looks, boned stays, couldn't get enough of yours ever. But then as we all know the Frogs are notorious for it, right? Least so Brendan – gimme liberty – O'Bryne always said. And he was right. Like Bren had once travelled as far as Paris in search of – don't laugh – honest employ, not to mention self-respect and food. He got the lot. Plus merriness. By day he worked for good money on the roof of a church called Nôtre Dame and by night on a dame called Our Pauline La Poule because like I say the French demand their rumpo like we do our beer.

But to our muttons as the sheep-shagger said to the shorn lamb. The girls' mothers. Yeah, you heard me, squiress. Their mothers. Christ! Like some girls do have 'em. And how!

It went like this. Once they started doing their dances regular – afternoons only, three times a week on account of them supposedly being at their dancing classes not showing off their arses – Sal allowed them, just for half an hour after the performance, to mingle wiv the clients. Like sit on their laps, toy wiv this or that, maybe allow a wrinkled hand a little liberty – but no more. Oh, no. Because Sal was determined to keep her delicate charges delicate. There was no question of any of 'em going what Enoch called the extra mile though our gents were going down on their bendeds for it and we had the accommodation upstairs: six nice boudoirs.

But no, Sally said I'd gotta find other occupants for them; that her girls' maidenheads were not for sale even if the rest of them was. She even had a name for what they were – nice little *demi-vierges*. French again, it would be, wouldn't it? They, of course, loved the whole business. The attention, the tickles, the sheer naughty of it. And I reckon over half of 'em would have been easy game but I behaved myself and gave hard thought to Sally's demand for another sorta cunny for our enterprise.

But where to find it? Given that New York was either dead low or dead grand. No in between at all. Then the masks Enoch had got our virginals to wear gave me an idea – a blinding notion. Like if wearing one of them could ease up them tight little lovebuds, what would they do to their mothers? Jeez, just the thought of it made me boggle. What a challenge! Even for General Mars himself. Me, pull their mothers. Think of it. Them at it above, their own daughters prancing below! And none of 'em any the wiser! Nor their gentlemen neither, who could well be paying them, and us, good solid money for half an hour's fumble wiv their own wives? God Almighty, what a stroke! Like it would be another legend to my name.

For them I'd get these moggie masks, right? In grey fur, correct. 'Cos all cats in the dark are grey, agreed? Then subtly suggest, me at your most persuasive, that maybe they'd like a little amusement of an afternoon that would augment their purses? It would be a pretty pastime. And naturally very exclusive. Indeed so discreet was the house on Pearl Street that no decent woman might enter it unless she wore a mask.

Well, nothing venture nothing win and if you don't try you don't happen, do you? I got a coupla masks made up as samples and picked on two of the mothers who were great mates wiv Lucille. Like they was always clucking together over their dear little daughters' progress. Some progress! That pair was red-hot wiv the fans. Like they almost gave one of the gents a seizure, after which Sal had to tell 'em to cool it. Anyway their mothers wasn't bad neither, once you got past the hoity-toity. And, since Lucille had time for me they did, too. Like I reckoned they'd guessed what went on between us. And this had got their juices going, right? I do that to the fair sex and I swear I ain't braggarting about; it's the honest truth – like some have said I'm just a force of nature really.

I'll go wiv that, and I did one day, when them and me was in Lucille's apartment. I mentioned this new association of gentlemen meeting under certain regulations (like keeping their hats wiv them at all times) at a house of entertainment upon Pearl Street for social intercourse, know what I mean? This mouthful said with the odd sparkling eye and the occasional mobile eyebrow for heightening of effect. And as it so happened – Dame Fortune was at her best that day – Lucille was happily obliged to take delivery of some etchings she'd ordered a good year before, what had just arrived from France. Like to add lustre to her salon. And these, as I helped unpack 'em, turned out to be of a thoroughly French nature. Dead classical, of course, but dirty wiv it. Small. You had to peer real close to spot the jolly bits. And all of 'em depicted bare-chested fellas wiv pointed ears and shaggy legs making antique hay wiv lissom dollies of your usual ideal variety. Human nature never changes, does it? For which I thanked Christ since if it did I'd have been out of a job, right?

Well, these prick 'n' bum pictures got us going wiv talk about art.

And then of artists. How naughty they was but who could blame 'em? And I said if I was a painter wiv a model like that one – and at this I indicated a whoopsadaisy nymph laid out across a log – well, I said, I reckoned I would ... Only here I broke off, making a moment of some moment, right? And then added, I was sure they, being two ladies of beauty, experience and discretion, would know what I meant? And while it wasn't for me to say, me not being an artist, even so I'd chance my arm, here I flexed my not unimpressive biceps, and swear that they themselves was so lovely they was fit to pose as nature had made them in front of any artist in the world.

To which they said, eyes bright, faintly flushed, well, yes, perhaps, maybe, who knew? But such an occurrence was rather unlikely in New York, the town being hardly yet a Rome or Florence. Tinkle laughter, brush down of skirt, twiddle of pendant, tip of tongue through teeth.

This gave me the opening I was after. And coming on the suave, cosmopolitan rakehell – wine in one hand, nibbles in the other – I informed them that the private house of entertainment I had earlier spoke of was perhaps a place they should take a look at? That it aimed to provide a civilised venue for both sexes so long as they was of an artistic inclination. And this time I looked 'em both up and down and round about, before turning once more to admire Lucille's etchings. And adding, like an afterthought (though it wasn't, it was vital to the deal) that while, as I'd said, it was a rule of the house that the gents had to hold on to their hats, so there was one for the ladies, too. Pause for them to ask, oh, yes, what? Another pause. Always increase dominance where you can, and then I say that the rule for the fair sex in that house was to wear a mask at all times, whatsoever.

'Why?' they said in unison.

'So,' I replied wiv me very best leer, 'so you can feel free to have a ball. A masked ball. Like.'

That got 'em. They peeled wiv laughter, saying I was the wickedest coxcomb they had ever met and Lucille must lend me to them the very next afternoon, could she spare me?

Tricky instant. But Lucille graciously agreed provided I joined her for luncheon first. And I'll leave you to guess how Lucille's lunches went. Yeah, you're there! Wine and oysters in bed. Phew. One tough, demanding dame that one.

However come two o'clock on the morrow them two was there at Pearl Street wearing the moggy masks I'd given 'em. They looked great and you could tell they fancied themselves, too.

First I let 'em take a peek at the dances, thinking, Jeeze, if they only knew they was watching their own daughters! But as it was they nodded and giggled, said it really was most artistic, and declared the girls quite shamelessly pretty and their dancing so graceful it seemed entirely natural, spontaneous and somehow propriety was no longer quite the question, was it? Oh, those fans. Doing that. What would they think of next?

As we mounted the stairs one of 'em declared that the one thing New York had wanted until now was debauchery with style. But this house clearly intended to make good this lack. Why the place was acceptable to all persons of breeding and discretion, wasn't it? And I felt her hand creep into mine and her fingernail tease the palm.

As arranged Sally greeted us upon the first floor and together we showed them (wink, wink) the salons and boudoirs we'd done up. They did look nice. Freshly painted, clean, very high class. Fine linen on the generous beds (not like my cut-price jobs at Pudding Wharf), loadsa mirrors, rugs, you name it, we'd got it. 'Cos we'd really invested in this venture, like every dollar we took we ploughed back into the business, I'd made sure of that. And here was the first pay-off. These ladies was impressed, intrigued and reassured. And if that ain't a recipe for success I don't know what is.

When we got to the pink boudoir (they was all done in different colours) the one wiv her hand still in mine sighed as if in an ecstasy of admiration.

She said, 'Why, I declare, it is exactly like my own bedroom. Oh, my goodness, I do feel so at home.'

Well, Sally got her meaning quick as me and wiv a complicit smile (what a hostess!) told the other one there was a distinguished gentleman who would dearly like to meet her upon the floor above in the blue salon. He had admired her below and had requested this introduction with a most charming impetuosity. He was of a certain age to be sure but wore his years well. A fish factor now retired who had made his fortune in cod.

So while I toyed wiv the first he sported wiv the second and after showered her wiv compliments and cash. Mine did it for free, of course. And I will say she was a fine body of a mother and keeping that mask on all the while really made it different. As I told Sally that night, we'd have to get the bedsteads strengthened. Yer older cunny in a mask was quite a tornado.

Business blossomed, burgeoned and bore very fruity fruit. All the mothers, enjoined by the first two, was soon coming oftener than their dancing daughters. And you could say, that wivout knowing it, they was in the business of preserving the girls' virtue by selling their own. For what my one called pin-money 'cos it pricks, ha, ha, ha. Like she had a really crude sense of humour once out of her habiliments. And so in this wise everybody got satisfaction thanks to the mask bamboozle and our business became the best open secret in town. To keep it select we made it very pricey, required the correctest of attire upon entering and in all public rooms whether in the *salon de danse* or the *salon des jeux* and hired six bouncers to man the doors front and back. 'Cos some of our better-known whoremongers (old patroons, councillors, merchant adventurers, lawyers, brokers, etcetera) preferred to slip in by the backstairs. However once inside they was assured of confidentiality. Another rule of the house. And like Enoch said one evening over a cosy three-way supper it was something of a paradox that a house of such liberality and licence should require so many rules.

Sal said, 'I blame Rusty.'

'Why?'

'It was your bright idea. Bringing in my girls' mothers.'

'Well, you said we'd gotta have cunny wiv tone. And there wasn't none else. Besides it's worked a treat.'

'So far. But it's high risk, Rusty.'

'Never. Not wiv Enoch's masks.'

'One day one of them's going to slip.'

'No, they love 'em too much. It's the masks that give 'em the real thrill. Like they enhance the sensation, right? I know, you can wear one tonight, doll. You'll see.'

Our Welshman said, 'I think you're both wide of the mark. Since I am certain human limbs and private parts are quite as readily recognisable as faces. But that, of course, is the point of all intercourse conducted here upon Pearl Street.'

'Like they all know it really but nobody says?'

'Precisely. The mothers who entertain their spouses, or their spouses' cronies, or their fathers-in-law, know it absolutely and derive the more pleasure from it since on these illicit occasions they're earning handsome money, while for the gentlemen the pleasure resides in suspecting, for a virtual certainty, that this professional lady in the mask is really his wife or relation or better still, a fellow client's spouse or relation, from whom he's just taken thirty dollars at the gaming table. The fact is it suits both sides of this equation to preserve a most fastidious ignorance. Here masquerade is carried to its logical conclusion and no one within the know will, I believe, wish to destroy such a satisfactory hypocrisy.'

'There!' said I, thumping the table. 'D'you hear that, doll? The professor has spoke. There's no frigging risk at all.'

'Well, I only hope you're right. Both of you. But speaking for myself I do wish we could've found some other sort of whore.'

I said, 'But we can't, doll. This new land ain't like London wiv the country doxies coming in on every carrier's wagon hoping to be Nell Gwyn. I mean the most we'd get here would be Algonk squaws but they're forbidden the town and beside our gents wouldn't touch 'em any more than you did them waterfront brasses I first pulled in.'

Here I rose and said I had to go and see a man about a pig. True. That's straight up. 'Cos this pig was a fast runner – went like the wind, he'd said – and I had this hunch there could be malooka in racing pigs. Watch this lumpa space.

☿

From the moment of my reunion with Sally and Rusty rarely a day, let alone a night, went by without something pertaining to the sacred art arriving unbidden in my head. I was both plagued and entranced by insights, visions, dreams.

Once when supervising our girls in their fan dance I was suddenly confounded by the inner sight of the Sun and the Moon in combat. The Sun was mounted on a lion while the Moon rode a gryphon. They were jousting with lances and shields and in their clashes created a thousand stars. I cannot tell you how inconvenient this insight was. The rehearsal was brought to a stop and the girls wanted to know if *Sir* was all right. I recovered, of course, and the dance continued. But later I was obliged to reflect that such mental visitations were not without significance. After all, this conflict betwixt that which was firm and that volatile, *viz.* the Sun versus the Moon, was naught but my fancy's depiction of the chemical collision of sulphur and mercury. And was not the gryphon the Moon rode upon that fabled beast believed by the ancients to be the guardian of all Scythia's gold?

By July I could gainsay these portents no longer. Clearly they were sent to lead me back to the practice of alchemy. To advise me by revelation that I had deluded myself when I had repudiated the sacred art and that I could never be an entirely mechanistical being. But whence came this sorcery? From God, the devil or Mr Newton?

One night I conveyed this intelligence to Sally as a pillow secret. I whispered that I would have need of my share of the profits at Pearl Street to establish a new laboratory and that I had already surveyed the storerooms below the house which could be, with some adjustments made, suited to the purpose. On hearing this Sally sighed and kissed me as if I were a child.

She said, 'Must you? I like you as a dancing master. Much nicer than a dusty old adept.'

I told her smartly it was all her fault, since when I lay with her my visions multiplied inordinately – why, it was as though our very sport was the *magnum opus*. She said it was and it had better continue that way. And laid her thigh across mine. Whereupon, as she knew it would, speech flew from me.

Later I resumed my confidence in her by relating how, during waking hours, there appeared in my head a pelican that was not a retort or aludel but the bird itself which was sacred to Hermes Trismegistos. And this creature presented a most pitiful sight in that she continually pierced her breast to feed her chicks with her own blood. From my own former readings, and my recent further research for Mr Newton, I knew that this particular sign only appeared to adepts who had faltered in their necessary allegiance. It came from Hermes who was, after all, myself in an earlier guise. In plainer words, I was urged by my own inward essence to return to the practice of the art.

Sally, washed silver by starlight and the newly risen moon – for the night was warm and we had left the window up and the shutters wide – gazed long and calmly upon me as if she were become Lady Luna herself.

Finally she said, 'You must be Dr Quicksilver again?'

'No. This time I shall be known, if known at all, as Professor Mercurius.'

'And I, what shall I be known as? For surely I too am part of this practice?'

'Essential to it. You will be Madam Venus, of course.'

'And Rusty?'

'What he already styles himself – General Rodney Mars.'

'How grand we sound.'

'How grand we are.'

'And our demis? Will you neglect them? For who will supervise their dances?'

'You must, Sally.'

'Me? But you're so much better at it than me. You're always inventing new steps, new positions. And besides the girls adore you. They can't wait to have you turn an ankle or tuck in their bottoms.'

'Well, I'll come up to attend them when I can for I confess I'm fond of the choreographic art. It has proved a most happy diversion. But Sally, my dear, this that I've told you must be an absolute secret between you and me. Rusty must not know of it.'

'But isn't he, like me, part of it?'

'Of course. But his part may be played unknowingly.'

Sally sat up, full of doubt, hugging her peerless knees.

'You can't mean it,' she said, her voice quite changed. 'Even you couldn't keep a whole blessed laboratory belching fumes a secret.'

'I intend to follow a rather more sophisticated method this time,' I rejoindered, miffed.

'Even so. Rusty may be thick in some respects but he's sharp in others. He'll smoke it out straight off. No, we must tell him, Enoch.'

'But he'll demand I open it to the public view and then, well, we could end up as we did at Pudding Wharf.'

'What about all your stuffs coming in? The sulphurs, the salts, the sands, the horse-dung, the sea-coal, the toads, the rotten eggs? Not to mention all those other things whose names I can never remember. And you'll have to have a chimney and air vents else we'll be stunk out! How can you keep that hidden?'

I sighed. Sally was right. In my new-fired enthusiasm I had chosen not to think of practicalities.

I said, 'Very well, Rusty must know of it, but I shall inform him that this time there will be no visitors and no subscriptors. I cannot have the great work turned into a vulgar amusement nor a fraudulent bubble.'

'Will it be expensive?'

'Not once gold is made – although for me that is not and has never been the primary object of the enterprise.'

Sally laughed, tossed her head so her hair brushed my cheek.

'Go on, pull the other one.'

So I did. But by this I do not mean her leg for all this while I had been crooked upon an elbow idly teasing her right nipple in an elegiac, post-coital manner.

I said, 'Yes, it will cost us dearly and rather more than in London but such is our success here in New York that I'm sure we may do it. And at least our money will be safer invested in the *magnum opus* than in Lord Spark's *bancas*.' For by this time I had heard the entire truth of that sorry business.

'Well,' said Sally with a pretty ventilation fetched from the lungs that lay behind that teat I tweaked. 'Yes, but *that* we need not tell Rusty.'

'Not if you think not, my dear.'

'I do. We'll let him understand it will cost much the same as at Pudding Wharf.'

'Good. We are concluded.'

'No, we are not,' said she, turning to me, her sweet breath mingling with mine, and the moon in her eyes. 'To ensure you will not neglect me for your sacred art I must have your word I may come down and demand satisfaction of my dear adept whenever I choose.'

'You have it and shall have it, Madam Venus.'

'And whenever is also *now*.'

Whereat we laughed and laughing put ourselves yet again at each other's convenient pleasure.

Rusty raised no objections at all. I was surprised, even a little suspicious. But no, he said he was all for my resuming what he called heavy metallic research, and he quite understood that this time round it should not be made public, and there would be no need of subscriptors since we were coining it more than handsomely and besides he had got several other schemes either in operation or lively preparation. Sally and I might calculate the sums involved between us. All he required was to be kept informed.

In other words he told me to carry on and I felt like some newly commissioned ensign who had just been addressed and dismissed by a very superior officer indeed. None other than General Rodney Mars, of course.

When I told Sally of this, her first response, like mine, was one of doubt. What had Rusty really got in mind, she wondered? But later, once she had found opportunity to speak with him (for as ever Rusty was always out and about), she confirmed to me that he had certainly meant what he had said. The reason, she exclaimed, was that Rusty not only had his own affairs on hand but also that this time he believed I really would succeed in making gold. He had said he could feel it in his bones.

This I took as an excellent augury. It was a confirmation of our tripartite pertinence to the process I was about to put in train. Once more it was made plain we had been brought to the New World for this.

I wrote to Mr Newton informing him of my revived appetite for the work, and sent him copies of the plans I had made for the laboratory. Of course I would have to wait many months for his reply but I felt I could not begin before I had at least sent him this intelligence. It eased my soul and from it I concluded that while I had ever considered myself a singular spirit or free agent I – or at least some part of me – was also an eternal apprentice. But then what natural scientist is not, as it were, apprenticed to Mr Newton?

That done I made enquiries where I might purchase materials in New York and was directed to a builders' store upon the waterfront (or rather a large clapboard shack) where I found bricks, timber, sand, lime, salt and aqua fortis (but only single not double) together with lead, copper and iron.

Next I made my way to a glass foundry where I discovered I might command superb retorts, alembics and other important utensils to be blown into any shape I pleased, for the master glassblower there was a Venetian by birth and had learnt his craft upon the island of Murano. His name was Antonio Stella. Hearing this I at once commanded three score vessels of various specifications to be delivered the following month with more to come.

My third enquiry was at an apothecary's upon the Gentlemen's Canal where I found I might purchase antimony, sulphur and sal ammoniac as and when I pleased but they were clean out of common quicksilver (it was much used to cure the pox) and they knew not when the next shipment would arrive. I called upon three other druggists but their answer was the same although at one I did find double aqua fortis for which I was thankful.

That evening I told Sally of my lack to which she said had I not thought to enquire at the glassmaker's? For surely he made mirrors and was not quicksilver used with tin to make them? How right she was! How myopic I had been. Truly the mind is the oddest organism. For mine had been so fixed upon the idea that only an apothecary could supply me with mercury that I had not thought to ask the glassmaker. It was as if I had been earnestly looking for a pot of honey in a cupboard and not seen it because it was right in front of my nose. And who knew, I reflected, but in this there might be a moral for a resumptive adept?

I repaired to Master Stella the next morning and, at a price, he was prepared to part with some of his store. We haggled but even then I was obliged to pay twice as much as my old friend Mr Stonestreet by Bow Bells on Cheapside would have charged. I also purchased tin which, oddly, was somewhat cheaper in the New World and this, in part, made good the excessive cost of the quicksilver.

Now that I was in possession of, or knew for a certainty where I might get the raw materials and necessities of my art, I set about the furnishing of my laboratory. And by August it was replete with furnaces (eight in all from the fiercest blown by bellows to the mildest heated by hay), a *Balneum Mariae* where the glass sits in boiling water and a *Balneum Vaporosum* where the glass hangs in steam, together with tubs, receivers, mortars, and crucibles.

For I was determined to proceed with my researches into the true whereabouts of the Green Lion with a diligence that would surpass all my previous endeavours. Besides, to further me in this resolution, I now had a copy of a regime or method that Mr Newton had but recently prepared from his own universal studies, fortified by the readings and transcriptions I had made for him during my travels in Europe and Egypt. He had pressed it upon me before I set sail for America begging me to wear it against my heart for he was of the view that one day I might wish to act upon it, despite my recent repulsion of the art. At the time I had not taken him seriously but it had lain ever in my trunk and now, upon my reconversion, I had read it many times. It went far beyond his earlier *clavis*.

In this manuscript he had, like a true philosopher, distilled into essence the live-long thoughts of Hermes himself, Morien, Artephius, Flammel, Ripley and many more equally worthy of respect, if not complete veneration, such as Abraham the Jew, Scala and Maier. I might cite many more but if you know of them you have no need of such a recitation; and if you do not more names would be tedious. Suffice it to say that we may trust Mr Newton to have drawn only upon the most reliable authorities, ancient and modern.

Since Mr Newton's method will only be comprehensible to initiates I am safe to offer a digest here. Yet even I feel obliged to cloak certain aspects of the regime in secrecy since the sacred art is not for the vulgar, and the future world has already become, I am informed, entirely at the disposal of the common people who openly enjoy scientific miracles allied to a base and turbid polity. But I have expressed something of this before, and must contain such old-fangled doubts. But not my pity. For this future age I speak of may contain some curious eye which is even at this moment conveying these words to the inner ear of a perfect stranger who hopes for illumination.

But enough of speculation – though it is the nature of mercury to slip towards anywhere – here is Mr Newton's alchemical method expressed in seven precepts. Let he who runs read.

One: the Work is of two parts; the first being called the First or Gross Work which by Imbibation and Putrefaction purges the Matter from its Faeces and exalts it highly in Virtue and then Whitens it.

Two: the Second Work resembles the First – purging that which is already purged. Both Works have the same linear process.

Three: the putrefaction or disintegration of the Second Work

175

lasts about 5 months and is done by 7 imbibations or at most by 9 or 10. To promote this process the Spirit is drawn off at the end of each imbibation.

These three precepts seem to me of a crystalline self-evidence but now Mr Newton, with some help from me, expresses the remaining four principles mostly in the Hermetic Style. For both he and I were of the opinion that this precise knowledge could prove dangerous to the stability of the nation's economy if known too widely.

Four: in both Works the Sun and Moon are joined, bathed and putrefied in their own menstruum, and in the Second Work by this conjunction they beget the Young King whose birth is in a white colour and ends the Second Work unless you shall think fit to decoct one half of it to the red.

Nota bene: the *Magnum Opus* proceeds *inter alia* by way of blackness, whiteness, redness: the three colours held by the Ancients to be sacred.

Five: the Faeces, which in the Second Work are separated by the putrefaction, fall to the bottom of a white water and must be separated.

Observation: there is less residue in the Second Work and the Adept must therefore be yet more meticulous in his procedures. Much may be done by the use of the tubular glasses and pipettes.

Six: the new-born King is nourished in a bigger heat with Milk or White Water drawn by distillation from the putrefied matter of the Second Work. With this Milk he must be imbibed 7 times and then decocted to the White and Red. And in passing to the Red he must be imbibed once or twice with a little red oil to fortify his solary or sunny nature and make the red stone more fluxible (*viz.* apt to flow). And this may be called the Third Work – the First going no further than putrefaction or the black, the Second as far as white, while the Third proceeds to red.

Comment: it is typical of the *Magnum Opus* that beginning in two parts it suddenly becomes three. Truly the great work is never ending.

Seven: the white and red sulphurs are multiplied by their own mercuries wherein a pinch of salt is dissolved.

And there you have it. Given this recipe I say you also may, with application, humility and prayer, make gold. Good fortune guide you.

Sally was of the view that I would have need, in due course, of some veritable silver and gold in order to essay my white and red philosophical mercuries. Since it was, was it not, only by the deliberate, calculated, and precisely monitored dissolution of these precious metals that my experiments could be proved? And the inmost parts of these unique elements discovered, counted and apprehended in their most fundamental natures? For only by achieving that knowledge would it be possible for me to reconstitute these metals – or rather, as the complete adept, make them falsely yet truly in the laboratory, so that they would be indistinguishable from those found so perfectly made by God in the bowels of the earth?

Hearing this I stood thunderstruck.

I said, 'Where got you such wisdom, Sally?'

'Why, from you,' said she. 'You're forever talking in your sleep. The times I've lain awake and heard you say what I've just said.'

'Mayhap. But still I stand amazed. For this was no parroting of what I may have spoken inadvertently but understanding of it, too. And that, in a woman, comes as a lightning bolt.'

♀

Great God in heaven! Men think we have no brains! They suppose we're entirely melting parts. Which I admit I often am. But that does not mean I cannot think! My head is quite as active as my heart, my mind just as receptive as my cunny, and my comprehension as quick as any prick, no, quicker!

I said, 'How dare you suppose that because I am of a rare blonde beauty I am also dumb? How dare you?'

'I was so astonished,' said he.

'Well, just you be advised, Enoch Powys, that my knowledge does not come alone from you, a-babbling in my bed. But also from within me. I start to know quite as much as you. I am no longer the young punk you met at that circle of old stones – '

'The Whispering Men? Above Oxford? How long ago that seems.'

'It *is* long ago. Now you listen and do not seek to divert me. I am quite as aware as you that we are set here upon this New World for a purpose and that just as you are bound to me, so am I to Rusty as he is to you and me and so on and on! We are as a triangle set within a sphere. And that being so no single one of us – no, not even you, schoolman though you are – may lord it over the other. We are equal in the business. So let me hear no more from you of how clever I am for a woman, since if I am indeed Madam Venus, as you so frequently say I am, then it is not necessarily to be supposed that that deity had no brains!'

'Antique statues of her often lack a head,' he answered.

'I am not joking, Enoch. And do not say I am twice as beautiful when I'm angry.'

'You aren't.'

'Good.'

'Are we concluded, madam?'

'No!'

And here I drew from my finger the wedding band I'd had of my dearest Jeremy. I held it out to Enoch.

I said, 'Keep this safe till the time comes for you to essay your philosophic mercury. Use it then. And after, if you can, return it to me not as it is – 24-carat fine from Wales – but as I now wish it to be, made new, by you, of laboratory gold.'

I swear he blenched at my words but he took the ring, holding it in his palm and gazing upon it intently.

He said, 'Perhaps my father dug out the gold that made it?'

'If so it will have a value for you almost equal to that it holds for me. For I had it of my dear deceased Somerset husband.'

He smiled and kissed it, then put it in his pocket.

I said, 'When will you start the work?'

'Tomorrow at the rising of the new moon.'

'Then you have time now to supervise the girls. I already see them arriving eager for the dance.'

And I could, through a low window Enoch had caused to be constructed to afford light to his work at the front end of the laboratory. Beside it were the steps up to the main door and up them several pretty feet set upon neat ankles were stepping in a froth of lace petticoats and silks.

'Why, Enoch,' said I. 'Now I see why you set this window here.'

He laughed and announced that even the most devoted adept required an occasional diversion. And with this quip he tried to embrace me. But I was in no mood for it, and besides there was no time.

I said, 'No, look, the girls are here. You must get whatever fleshly consolation you need today from putting them through their paces. They need it. Come along!'

Briskly I took him by the hand and marched him up above. But what we had both failed to notice, as the girls tripped so lightly up the stoop, was the man who stood beyond on the other side of Pearl Street. It was only later that day the girls told me of him. He made them uneasy, they said. He was of a grotesque appearance, huge belly, small hands with many flashing rings and his hat worn low over the brow. He was often there. And twice had been spotted outside the school. Indeed Madame Souligny had once gone out to him and told him to take himself off. Whereat he had departed but only to reappear on Pearl Street a week later. Some of them feared he might be a trader in female flesh since it was rumoured that many settlers up in the sticks (as the more desolate parts of New England are known) will pay good money for white virgins to be their wives. I advised them always to walk abroad in groups together, and promised I would speak of their uneasiness to Rusty. For we could not have our house's main attractions abducted to the wilderness. That would be a crying shame for them and a mighty monetary loss to us.

When I told Rusty he said, 'Yeah. Sounds like that was Arnold Jay Stone, yeah.'

'Who's he?'

'A ripe son of a bitch, Sal. I sold him Abednego. Right. Leave it wiv me, darlin.'

♂

I'd been smelling trouble ever since my ace racing pig – It's an Ill Wind – fell over and died after leading the field for the best of four furlongs. And what pig went through to win? You got it – Delaware Demon. Owner? Arnold Jay Stone. Result? I not only lose the hundred dollars I'd got riding on Windy but I'm obliged to hand the prize money – a cool five hundred dollars – to Arnold Jay. *Ergo*, as the prof would say, a less than sanguineous Rusty.

I got the horse-doc, 'cos I hadn't got a pig one, to look the corpse over. Like me he was full of dubiety. After all, Windy was a healthy three-year-old wiv a scrotum packed full of balls, deep in the chest and strong of haunch. Like also he had a battling humour plus a really good turn of trotter. And whatismore, squire, he was by Tomahawk Fort Orange out of Big Bella of Boston. You don't come bigger 'n' bolder than that. Not in this sport I'd just got started in

New York. You know on a proper footing, wiv me in charge. Aye, aye, nod, wink.

The doc reckoned he'd best do an autopsy. I concurred, natch. But strong man though I am, I confess I wept to see my Windy opened up from arsehole to breakfast time. And what did Doc Sweetman find? Yeah. Untowardness. A foreign substance in the gut. Mind you, not many substances are foreign to a pig. I've got one owner swears by an exclusive diet of seacoal and whale blubber two days before a race. His pig's been known to win, too. But all of Windy's upper, middle and lower enterons was bung full of a massive dose of oatmeal laced solid wiv digitalic essence – foxglove to you. And very naughty. *That*, opined the doc, was what stopped Windy's great heart just as he gave it the gun on entering the final furlong. He had, as we say, been got at. But whodunnit? That was the question. Well, I can give you an informed guess. It had to be Arnold Jay.

'But where's our proof?' said Doc Sweetman as he washed up.

'I don't need proof!' I roared in my grief.

But that said, and me calmed down in front of a quart of double Pegleg, what was best to do? Well, to answer that I haven't got no choice but to explain, have I? And that's the real bluebottle in the unguent, innit? I mean – to really and truly get a hold of what's bugging you in life you gotta keep going back as well as forward, like you're still in the same place but rotting yourself wiv motion, right?

Well, Arnold Jay Stone was the fly in my ointment, no question. Though I dare say he reckoned it was t'other way round. After all, till I got there, he'd ruled the town. East Side, West Side. Like he ran the market on Whitehall Street protecting the stallholders from his own bully boys, kept his male henhouse going at a tidy profit, and was lord and master and chief bookmaker of every race, game of billiards, and cockfight in town. Consequently he was rolling in the malooka. But he hadn't thought of pigs.

So, anyway, once we'd got Pearl Street on the go and all the fashion, I started to look about me for other openings, right? And me being me, well, I reverted to type, didn't I? I admit a high-class cathouse cum gaming saloon had been my first idea, and very successful it was, too. But it soon dawned on me I was missing a proper rollicking, down-town whorehouse. I needed a home from home. Like I was born in shit, right? So, feeling the lack, I set up one by the barracks, employing them very pullets Sal had rejected as too downmarket. And straight off felt much more myself. Mind you, I still had to service Lucille, else knowing her there coulda been trouble, but she could see from my clothes and the odd jewel that I was on the up and that gratified her, too. Like I might be her bit of rough but I was successful rough. The other mothers didn't bother me no more because they was getting theirs wiv their own or his brother on Pearl Street. I do sometimes think that really was my best stroke ever, my finest finesse, to take a dirty great percentage out of what's normally done for free in the privacy of the conjugal bedchamber.

But back to the bordello by the barracks. Or rather to next door but one. To my new betting saloon. Here I offered odds just a shade more attractive then Arnold Jay did. On *his* races. Got it? Nicely. Soon I was taking a lot of his business – my margin of profit was narrower than his, of course, but the volume of bets placed soon made up the difference. I also hired a coupla personal bodyguards – ex-pressed men who'd jumped ship. Mean as they come. Known as Mick the Mick and Aguma M'Kubwa. Not that I was scared of Arnold Jay but I reckoned it politic to play safe. After all, he wasn't used to competition and I figured that if I was him I'd be inclined to eliminate it before it grew any bigger.

The which it did once I got into pig-racing. And as I say my rival hadn't thought of that. But the fella I'd gone to meet the month before had turned out to be a good 'un. And modest wiv it. When he'd said he got a running pig to show me, what he meant was he'd brought along one of his best out of twenty – twenty bollocking boars! They was originally Spanish hogs from Extramadura brought over by the conquistadors but he'd crossed 'em wiv yer good ole Wessex Belters. And the result was a racing stable of rampant porkers wiv stamina. He kept 'em up at Spring Valley. Also he knew another farmer at Kingston who bred racers out of other breeds – Virginian Shortbacks and Danish Dashers wiv a touch of Creole Hog for extra piquancy. The pair of 'em raced their pigs against each other for small sums but the sport was catching on locally and he reckoned it could be something for New York. Was I interested?

You bet! But I didn't let on. Oh, no. I hummed and ha-ed over a coupla jars and then allowed myself to be persuaded to travel up to Spring Valley the following week to see his porkers run. Certainly the one he'd brought down to show me was a beauty. Not pretty, you understand. But lean and mean wiv this dead cunning look in his eye.

I say, 'What makes 'em run?'

He says, 'A sow in season at the other end.'

I nod. 'Like you've thought it all out?'

'Yes, sir.'

So upriver I go. The farm is a picture. Whatta spread. And everything's painted white – the house, the railings, the piggeries. Wiv lovely green grass all over and mature arboreals.

And the track. A gorgioso. Like it's five furlongs set across a flank of ascendant ground so the course rises for half its length but declines gently over the other half down to the finishing post. This way my new friend explains the course itself provides for fast finishings. Adds to the sport. And the whole length of it is closely fenced wiv white palings so the pigs can't shog off. Not that they'd want to given what's on the breeze.

Well, after a good dinner wiv Farmer Broadbent and his neighbour from Kingston (for in the New World you count anyone a neighbour if he resides within a day's ride from you) out we go to the track.

And whatta sight. While we've been regaling ourselves on pork wiv crackling followed by apple pie and cream the farmhands have got four boars lined up, the sow all set at the other end and it only remains for us to place our bets. I get a bit of advice from all and sundry and finally settle on the pig Farmer Broadbent first showed me. I put ten dollars on him at five to one and they're off! Can those hogs move! Like it's astounding. Their snouts snorting, their dirty great ears flapping, their trotters pounding at the ground – these bastards weight in at a good eight score (that's 160 lbs to you) – and they're gone. We charge across to the finish and in less than a minute here they come over the crest, my pig's lying a handy third on the inside rail wiv Broadbent's two fancies giving him a length or so and his neighbour's bet is trailing. So now it's up to mine. I'm yelling, come on, sweetheart! Give it yer best, you bastard. Let's have you, etcetera. And, do you know what, that pig's heard me? He's coming down the hill like shit off a shovel, he's past the one lying second and he's putting in the late challenge to the leader. Will he make it? Come on, cochon! I yell 'cos that's what Lucille often shouts out when we get close to the finish. And he understands French, too! He's there, it's neck to haunch, neck to collar, neck to neck, is his snout in front, is it? Yeah! He's through! He's won by a bristle. My beauty! And I'm fifty dollars to the good. And drained. Truly emotively drained.

I say, 'Farmer Broadbent, you're a frigging genius. If this sport don't take in Manna Hatta I'm a Dutchman wiv brewster's droop.'

So he supplied the know-how and the initial livestock and I put up the finance. I also found a stretch of ground to rent just outside the wall close to the old Dutch Governor's farm in the Boweries. Here we set up the course. And not just for pigs neither, though they was the first attraction. No, we raced horses there, too. And dogs. And I wanted to try Algonk racing, too, you know, brave versus brave, but Sally put her foot down, saying they was humans like us not brute animals. We had quite a barney about it, but then Farmer Broadbent came in on Sal's side and went on about some ole treaty wiv the Gonks (as the older colonials termed 'em) that had held good for quite a while now and it was best to let things lie. So I bowed to superior wisdom. Like I'm not always obdurate, right? And set up a cockpit instead, which soon provided even more profit than the pig-races.

Next thing I know, given that the entire town is now either coming to Pearl Street for the high-class ogle, the superior other or both, plus high-stake cards 'n' dice; or else putting in downtown for a rough old roger and a poor man's flutter; or otherwise coming out all together, high *and* low, for a day at the races; given all this I'm making a mint, aren't I? You bet. I'm at the receiving end of admiring glances tinged wiv envy. And now's the time I get the serious look-over from Arnold Jay Stone.

Does he come on grand? No. He comes on spectacular. In this dirty great open coach, all spit and polish, drawn by four high-stepping gee-gees exuding breeding, unlike their owner. Whatta ponce. And sitting wiv him is this prauncy little shortarse known as Councillor Ambrose, who's gonna be the next mayor of New York, he reckons. Jeeze, whatta loudmouth. All glad-hand, fizz, and 'Hi, how y'are doin', fella?' But diminutive firecracker though he is, the bastard's big in furs, tobacco, and ox-hides. And he dresses to prove it. While chewing his own tobacco. Non-stop. Wads of it. And spits high, wide and ugly. And who's this he's got sitting beside him, who's introduced to me as Mrs Ambrose? Yeah, you're right. Abednego, looking like the cat that swallowed the cream. All in pink wiv pearls and this dirty flash diamond on his wedding band finger. Seeing me, Christ, does his fan flutter. And parasol tremble. But he doesn't acknowledge me, oh no, just stares right through me as we say how do you do. I can't say I blame him. I was sorta brusque that time we first met, but on the other hand, from the look of all this it's turned out quite nicely, I'd say. Here he is allied to two of the town's big wigs and looking worth at least a thousand dollars, which I dare say he is. And if you didn't know what we know, you'd take him for the genuine feminine article, you really would.

But I've got no more time to spend on Mrs Ambrose because here's this other coach drawing to a halt behind Arnold Jay's. And out of it step six dead-eyed dicks. Your unmistakable, undeniable heavy men. Dark-suited and every single one of 'em wiv a pistol stuck in his boot.

Well, me, I'm profoundly wishing I hadn't given Mick the Mick and Aguma M'Kubwa the day off, but I tell myself, look, Rodney, it's just a show of strength, this bastard's not gonna try anything on here in public, is he? Not wiv everybody passing by, smiling, bowing, and curtseying, and saying, 'Good day, General Mars,' or 'How do, Mr Stone?' or 'Hi there, Councillor Ambrose.' Like yer New Yorker, male or female, can't wait to grease up to power and success when they sniff it. And therein lies the rub, dunnit? Between me and Arnold Jay. Like we're both in the business of power and I'm the new boy. And it could be he don't reckon the town's big enough for the two of us? Whereas I do, once I've cut him down to size. Like diminutive. Nay, minuscule.

Hence this visit. Backed by his hired bully boys and a tame town councillor. It's to show me, on my own turf, that *item*, he commands private muscle, and *item*, public influence. At the sight of which I'm meant to quiver and feel all sewn up already. Only instead here's me burning up but telling myself don't go inflammatory, mate, stick wiv it, play it long – at least for now.

He says, 'Why don't we have a quiet word together, son?'

Son? I'll give him 'son'. He's not much older than me once you get beyond the basket of gut and the ferret eyes.

Says I, sorta deadly, 'If it's just the two of us, why not?' And I let him follow my eyes across to his six bastards.

Given which, he grins and tells his boys to go get themselves some sport. And doles out a load of silver dollars to 'em for the flash of it. Like to impress me with the dash of it, the sheer ready cash of it. I tell you, this fella's a showman. Worse'n me. Anyrate, his musclemen slope off and I wish I was at liberty to go fix the next three races and the four o'clock cock fight so they lose the frigging lot. But maybe they will anyway? At the least, whichever way it plays, I get my cut so I'm not entirely unhappy. Once again my sanguinity's shining through.

This established, me and Arnold Jay take our leave of the Ambroses and step over to a seat beneath a spreading walnut tree and I invite him to put himself at his ease. He does. But I stay on me feet. Like poised. So he's gotta look up at me with the light of the declining sun behind. This position gives me the mystery and the menace, right? Also like this I can act that much quicker if he's got some other stroke up his lace cuff.

I say, 'Right. What's on yer mind, mate?' 'Cos I'm not giving this one the compliment of a name, for Chrissake.

'Call me A.J., son,' says he. 'All my guys do.' Big-mister smile.

Well, there's a reply to that but I eschew it. Like this is not a conversation where the ball gets returned too pat, right?

Says I, 'Like shit in the pot or else get off but don't expect me to wipe your bum.'

Crude, I agree. But effective. He gawps. He ain't used to being spoke to like this. Better still I can now see he's got a problem containing his ire. Neat one. On I go.

To insult I add grievous verbal harm, I say, 'You got two minutes, fat boy, to make yer pitch. You're keeping me from my legitimate business.'

Like now he is seriously wondering where his breath is coming from. He rises, puce as a stewed plum.

He gasps, 'Look, sir, I came here to offer you the hand of friendship. Maybe a deal. I had supposed we might work together. I know this town . . .'

Do I bust in! I laugh in the frigger's face.

'You know this town! Do me, mate! Maybe you better know where I'm coming from? Like I'm from London. Real-old-rough-old-London! In real-old-rough-old-England! So don't you tell me this lump of minor America compares wiv *that*? This pisshole's in serious need of organisation, mate, plus improvement and expansion! And it's getting held back by pricks like you!'

Trust me to blow it! Just when I'd sworn to myself I wouldn't. What got into me? Mayhap it was seeing him wiv that would-be mayor and Abednego? Like it was too like parish pump corruption, know what I mean? When what I'd got in view was big-city vice and undreamt-of urban naughtiness.

He pulls himself to his feet. There's sweat on his brow, his button nose looks pinched, his eyes gleam wiv despite.

He says, 'Sir, you've made your position plain. Allow me to state mine. From here on you're in big trouble. Have a good day.'

And off he wobbles. And I'm left cursing myself for not following my first inclination to play it long, cool 'n' deadly. Like outwit him not lecture him. Let alone make an enemy of him straight off. Now I reckon I'll have to give real thought to raising my own mob of irregulars. And suddenly I'm missing Bren and Abe let alone Don Rocco.

However nothing else of note occurs that day, nor the next, nor the next. In fact the only difference I can see is that Arnold Jay becomes quite a race-goer. He's always there, cutting me dead on my turf, but entering good horses, dogs and finally pigs. He's found a source of runners down on Delaware Bay. I wonder whether to tell him he's *persona non grata* on the course but decide not. After all, he pays his dues, and the sport's gotta be seen as open to all or how else do I make it pay? And so it continues – like it's neither war nor peace between us – just an evil, brooding, armed truce. Wiv me meant to feel more and more unnerved by his waiting game. Well, I don't. Only Sal sometimes asks if everything's all right and I ask why? And she says I seem sorta on edge. Whereupon I go and have a drink wiv Mick and Aguma and they promise me they're still on the lookout for some more bodyguards for me but they ain't come across none just yet. Which they've said before. More unease. Are they telling me sooth?

Then Windy drops dead. And that means the truce, if truce it was, is now at an end. The day after I hand Arnold Jay his ill-gotten winnings (that five hundred bucks still hurts) I send word to him down on the waterfront that he's no longer welcome out at the course, after all.

No reply. When I ask Mick the Mick what did he say? Mick says he didn't say nothing. Just read my missive and then crumpled it up in his ring-encrusted digits and dropped it sorta carelessly over his left shoulder. Like I say, he's a real show-off.

Next, to add to my concerns, I hear from Sally that some fella sounding very like Arnold Jay himself has been eyeing up our virginals. And they reckon he's aiming to abduct 'em. All too likely. It'd be a shrewd stroke. From his point of view, that is. Do us real damage. Upset the mums, the dads, Lucille, the lot. Could cause closure on Pearl Street. And while I've told Sal not to worry, leave it wiv me, the fact is I'm uncertain what to do, which in war is fatal, innit? Like could I be losing my bottle? No. Unheard of. Quite impossible. I'm me. Rusty. Ironside. Steele. Mars. Anything else would be a contradiction in terms. Why, even as a transported felon done up in shackles and kept close below deck I was still choleric.

Eventuaneously – I can hardly bear to tell it – I break down, like Samson did when that Delilah cut off his hair, and I confess my fears to Sal. I boo-hoo in her embrace. And she cuddles me like I'm a child again. Oh, dear. Who'd have thought it? What's got into me? Most untoward. Where's my morale gone, mother? Blub, blub. Who'd have thought the New World would do this to me? Of all people?

♀

I tried mollycoddling Rusty; I tried scolding him; I tried making him truly nourishing dinners; I told him to lay off the beer and take more exercise; all to no avail. Like him, I couldn't believe it, my Rusty a prey to the dumps?

Which reminds me, I even had to take over the running of his latest adventure, so listless had he become. Fortunately it was a legitimate, if dirty, business: town garbage disposal. Rusty had invested in a whole caravan of huge, six-wheeled dirt carts (he'd got twenty in all) and also built these wooden cribs to take their contents down along the West Side shore where he reckoned the next increase in the town's expansion would occur. Like the shit's gotta go some place, doll, he'd say. And he who makes the place, makes the action, huh? And that was another thing – his way of talking was changing. He was using all sorts of colonial expressions mixed in with his native Cockney, and I must honestly say it grated on my ear. And I told him so. I said he wasn't being his true self using all these American words, which sounded much more manful than they really were, and perhaps that, too, was part of his malaise? All he answered was: Get lost, babe.

So there was I, trying to rebuild my man and run his new garbage and shoreline extension business while supervising Pearl Street. In other words I was run off my feet from dawn till dusk and then at night, when at last truly and properly off them, I had to busy myself reassuring Rusty he was still the man he was, in the usual time-honoured way, on my back. And I'll say this in favour of that position – it really does mean a girl can unplait her toes. But to tell true, he wasn't what he was. No, even in bed, Rusty was losing his thrust.

In the end I confided in Enoch, who by now was more and more engrossed in his laboratory. He had got his furnaces going night and day; but he worked mainly nights – don't ask me why. Something to do with stellar rays being more powerful during the hours of darkness, he said. Once Great Sol's gone down there's less competition for lesser stars. I didn't argue. Rather I told him how concerned I was for Rusty. That something was seriously wrong. He had lost, was still losing, all his proper bravado, and only because he had run up against the local opposition. And at this rate, everything we'd achieved there in New York would soon belong to Arnold Jay Stone – and that included our dancing girls and his lab. These last considerations pierced his preoccupied, alchemical armour. Suddenly he was looking me in the eye, instead of gazing upon one of his toads. I tell you I've never known an adept with more faith in toads than Enoch. He had to have them with him in the lab. Mind you, I've never known another adept, for which I thank my Maker.

But now I had his attention and once I'd described everything about Rusty from the colour of his eyeballs to the condition of his fingernails; to whether he suffered from nightsweats; and were there signs of flatulence? There were. My God, Rusty had started farting furiously. So much so I had told him he ought to apply for a job with the rattle watch – for it was the custom of that town to have the watchmen twirl clattering rattles instead of handbells to tell you what small hour of the night it was just when you'd have much preferred not to know.

Enoch handed me a phial full of a colourless liquid which was thicker than water.

He said, 'It sounds to me as if Rusty is a heaven-sent recipient of this.'

I said, 'What is it?'

'I should prefer to answer that, dear Sally, once we have observed its effect upon Rusty. Two drops in his breakfast small beer and evening wine for a week should suffice.'

'I wish I knew what it was,' said I, doubtfully.

'Me, too,' was his reply. 'But Rusty's response to it will tell us everything I need to know.'

'It won't hurt him?'

'Oh, no. At the worst it will have no effect at all.'

'I wish I could trust you, Enoch.'

'In this you may.'

'Cross your heart and hope to die?'

'Cross both our hearts and hope to die.'

And here he made the sign of the cross so tenderly across my bodice that I was fain to rip it off there and then. But my concern for Rusty was such it overcame this fleeting moment of desire and I returned upstairs wondering whether to taste Enoch's medicine myself before administering it to Rusty, but decided not, since surely it was prescribed for him alone? Thus plain cowardice vanquished moral scruple and I put two drops as prescribed in his small beer the next morning. And in his wine that night whereupon he slept like a mighty Yule log for twelve hours at a stretch.

Three mornings later I woke up to discover him stark naked, touching his toes, running on the spot and then lying on his back clasping his knees. A most indecorous vision that made me laugh immoderately.

'What are you doing, Rusty?'

'Me exercises, doll. The professor gave me this list of what to do. Last night at supper.'

And he handed me a paper covered in drawings of a small stick man making the movements Rusty was performing so strenuously.

'It's a regimen for restoring musculature, he says. Phew! This one wiv the knees up's a killer. But you gotta sweat at it.'

When he had finished he poured a jug of water over his head, letting the water run all down him while he towelled himself briskly, grinning at me the while. And I was thinking, could this elixir of Enoch's have done all this? So soon?

Whereupon I had immediate confirmation of its powers for Rusty whisked the towel away to offer undeniable evidence of its efficacy.

'How's that, doll?' cried he and leapt upon the bed and me.

♂

I still reckon it a major mystery. How I got my strength back. But I did. Oh, yeah. After three or four days the mullygrubs just went and I was me again. Maybe more so. Like, for instance, Sal says my hair's redder than ever. But I mustn't keep you. I gotta go see a man and thump him. Be good. And if you can't weave, duck. Ta-ta.

♀

Rusty's reformation was astonishing to us all. First to him – he could not, would not stop talking of it – and then to me and Enoch. I was so impressed by the effect the potion had wrought I started taking two drops a day myself and slipping it into Enoch's bedtime posset. Soon we too were grown much glossier. Our teeth looked whiter (they even appeared more regular), our flesh was firmer (the suspicion of a pot-belly which had appeared upon Enoch vanished), my hair became yet more golden, his more silver, while Rusty's – why, it was a fire-bomb! Our steps grew brisker, our voices brighter. Indeed the entire *lingua franca* of our corporeal deportment spoke unmistakably of success. We were the New World personified.

Even when Rusty came back one night with his two bodyguards – all of them with black eyes, bruised cheeks and split lips – Rusty's injuries were gone the next day. He'd had, he said, over a hearty breakfast of an almighty beefsteak with six eggs sunnyside up on top and a gallon of coffee (he now abjured small beer of a morning as being small time) yes, he'd had a few verbals concerning our girls and a certain fat Peeping Tom who'd been bothering them, that is with Mr Arnold Jay Stone down at his place on the waterfront. Like he'd told him to stay clear or else. There had been seven of Stone's fellas to the three of them, but nevertheless honour had been satisfied. Stone and Co. had suffered worse damage than they had; Rusty having personally twisted Stone's arm out of its socket so it hung loose as a gelding's pecker on a hot day. He reckoned we wouldn't hear much from that heap of ordure for quite a while, no, sir.

The very next afternoon three of my girls went missing, kidnapped on the way here. The rest of them related, in a horrified babble, a tale of masked men with pistols jumping out upon them from a doorway and of a coach that had appeared from nowhere just as they had turned the corner out of Beaver Street into Pearl Street. They had screamed and struggled and tried to keep all together just as I had instructed them, but they had been ordered at pistol-point to clear off and had run straight to me, only one of them, glancing back, had seen their friends – Lucy, Ruth and Arabella – bundled forcibly into the coach which had then driven off at a breakneck pace. Yes, back up Beaver Street so heaven alone knew where they were got to by now. And, oh, dear, what would their mothers say, let alone their fathers? And as for Madame Souligny, they were sure she would forbid their dancing classes and that would be the end because they just *lived* for their naughty afternoons performing for the nice, generous gentlemen.

At once I sought counsel of Enoch only to find him in altercation with Rusty concerning the cost of two new furnaces Enoch was of a mind to have constructed. I told them to forget such baubles at once and attend to me. They did. And were as concerned as I. But while Enoch pondered the matter, Rusty acted. He was gone in the instant, assuring us that he and his fellas – he now had two more pug-uglies beside Mick and Aguma – would find the girls come whatever.

But as the door slammed behind Rusty, Enoch asked me to fetch him the map of Manna Hatta he had bought only the week before from Meister Guert van Boomgaard the Cartographer beside the slave market.

Said I, mistaking him out of sheer trepidation, 'Surely you don't think they'll sell our girls *there*?'

'No, my dear. They'll be kept close I have no doubt, and disposed of privately. And I think we may also be sure they will not be harmed, since their marriage value lies essentially in their unforced virtues.'

'You really think they're safe?'

'For this moment. But now, I beg you, fetch me the map for I believe we must not lose an instant. I left it beside the coffer in my closet.'

'But what good can a map do? And besides Rusty has already gone to find them.'

'And if he should not? What then? Please, Mrs Sally, get me that map.'

When I returned I found Enoch had attached my wedding band which I had so recently entrusted to him to a fine thread which he dangled between finger and thumb. He bade me spread out the map before him and then repeated the girls' names to himself – Lucy, Ruth, Arabella – while also murmuring in an undertone certain characteristics of them such as: 'Arabella, left foot turns in a little; Ruth, tip-tilt nose; Lucy, full of dimples especially on her bum.'

And now he suspended his right hand above the map, holding my ring on its thread as a pendulum that swung forward and back. Meanwhile with the forefinger of his left hand he slowly and delicately, with infinite care, quartered the map of the town.

'When the pendulum's motion changes from to and fro to round and round,' said he, 'we shall have found them.'

'Is this witchcraft?' I enquired, in some wonder.

'Not to a witch,' was all his answer.

Painstakingly, even caressingly, he fingered all of New York before going beyond the wall into the Boweries. Here he followed the winding Breetweg Trail to its end. His finger then moved up the West River, tracing a route as far as Bear Mountain but never once did the pendulum's motion alter. He returned downriver once more to the island, this time favouring the Eastern side after passing over the Bronx and Harlem settlements. Nothing. And so, at last, he was back where he had begun – with us, upon Pearl Street.

I said, bemused, disconsolate, 'Are they gone?'

'From Manna Hatta, yes.'

But now his hand passed over to Brooklyn where at once the pendulum's movement backwards and forwards changed to a similar motion but askew, or at a diagonal, and then this, in turn, became a circle. My wedding band was going roundabout!

In my relief and joy I cried aloud, again without thinking, 'You're sure you aren't doing it, Enoch?'

'Oh, I'm sure I am. Some internal tremor or force within me has caused the pendulum to vary its action. But that is precisely the mystery. And that is where they are upon the wooded heights above the Brooklyn settlement.'

And his finger was stayed upon a spot which he marked hard with his nail. And such was the pressure he exerted that he scored right through the paper and it was at this that I realised how consummately concerned he was for the girls' safety. This was as a father's love. And I, in my turn, loved him for it.

I said, 'We must go there at once.'

He rose up. 'Agreed,' he answered.

As we were going out Rusty returned. He had discovered nothing. Stone's saloon upon the waterfront was quite shut up. And those few male whores he had chanced upon were keeping their mouths as shut as uncooked clams. No one knew where Stone was to be found. In short, he said he was as a hound that had lost the scent.

'That's hardly astonishing,' said Enoch. 'For they are gone over water.'

'Where?'

'To the woods above Brooklyn.'

'Go on wiv you! How d'you know, professor?'

'I've divined it. As a dowser does a hidden spring.'

'Oh yeah? I'm to believe that, am I?'

'You will. Come along.'

And Enoch, brooking no argument nor delay, hurried us out to the waterside, only requiring of Rusty that he brought with him all his personal musclemen and the house bouncers (ten in all) and, from me, that I gathered up aqua vitae and sal volatile.

Enoch did not wait for the ferry but straightway bribed a merchantman's hack-boat that was just come ashore to take us across. And so it was that four stout West India Company oarsmen got us over to Brooklyn in doublequick time at the prodigious cost of twelve dollars – enough to slake their gullets for a month or more.

Once ashore Enoch asked no directions of anybody but made straight for a trail that wound up the incline behind the shacks and houses. He moved at a pace that was breathtaking, pausing only to consult his pendulum where the path forked. Soon we were deep among trees and he forbade further speech.

Already the sun was setting and the arboreal gloom was pierced by swords of light that seemed to increase the darkness between them. Meantime the birds had fallen as silent as ourselves. The trail was soon nothing more than a deer path. I began to fear we might shortly be lost and become a prey to the Indians, who notwithstanding they had sold their land upon Manna Hatta and Brooklyn to the Dutch, continued to suppose it belonged to them; a way of thinking which puzzled me despite Enoch having twice explained the aboriginal logic of it.

But then Enoch, who had led us all this while, leaving Rusty (somewhat to his discontent) to guard our rear, came to a halt. And pointed.

And there ahead lay an obscure cabin built of logs. It stood beneath towering trees whose tops were lost in the last dazzling rays of the sunset. But even as I watched this illumination was extinguished, all was twilight, and at the same instant two pistols blazed out at us from the cabin. I sank to my knees, a-tremble.

But Rusty, from behind, roared 'Charge!' Which he and his bully boys immediately did. I cannot pretend there was any discretion in their approach. They simply ran straight at the place, kicking in the door and tearing the shutters from the two windows on either side. Such pell-mell temerity has its virtues however. For, despite a couple of further pistol shots, all I then heard was the solid thwack of fists pounding flesh and bone, accompanied by grunts and oaths, followed by the invigorating sight of first one, then another, and another, and yet another alien body hurled headlong from the front door by Rusty, who now seemed possessed of a strength given only to men of mythical status such as one rarely meets save in sweet, revolving dreams. Happily, all four of Rusty's foes were quite senseless and they were succeeded by another two, equally inert. Each and every one looked most repugnant. But none was Arnold Jay Stone.

Enoch and I rushed inside, intent upon offering immediate succour to our girls, whom we imagined cowering in some nook of the cabin. But apart from Rusty and his posse, all recovering their breath, there was no one to be seen. No dimpled Lucy, fair Arabella or button-nosed Ruth.

I said, 'Oh, Enoch!'

He said, 'This is not possible.'

Rusty said, 'It frigging is, mate.'

Outside, first one then another of our opponents was beginning to recover. Soon all were sitting up and vacantly enquiring of the air what it was had come upon them. Rusty, having twice told Enoch he was a credulous fool, went out with his men in order, as he phrased it, to *quiz* them concerning our girls' whereabouts.

Enoch continued to shake his head, quite abashed by his failure, and I was sure I was at my wits' end, when I noticed that his pendulum remained ever in his hand, quite unregarded. And it was going steadily round and round. And round.

'Look,' I cried. 'Look!'

Enoch stared, just as I continued to do. There was no doubt of it. Our gaze proceeded from the twirling ring to the floor of the cabin. Outside various expostulations and cursings suggested that Rusty's interrogation was got heavily under way. But I also thought I had caught another sound. From beneath my feet. I knelt down, putting my ear to the boards. I had! At once I banged with my fist. And heard what seemed in reply something very like a groan.

By this time Enoch was kneeling beside me, knocking too. More faint groans. At once we sought, with one accord, a means of entry to what lay below. There must surely be a trap door? But where? There seemed to be no such thing.

At which Rusty appeared, leading one of his victims by the ear. He said to him, 'Right, if you wanna live, cherry pie, show us the trick of it.'

'Sure,' says he. 'There ain't a trap door.'

'So how do we get at 'em, sweetheart?'

'We nailed down the boards.'

'Right! Now you can hoick 'em up again. Wiv yer bare hands.'

And Rusty flung the fellow down onto his knees. But the man pointed to an iron chisel by the door which Rusty, relenting, kicked across to him; and with this he began to prise up the boards. Once the first was removed, the others came more easily. Quite soon we had an opportunity to peer within. Except we could see nothing. For while dusklight still lingered somewhat without, within it was quite extinguished by the confines of the cabin.

But if the seeing faculty was denied us, we still had our ears. And now the boards were opened we could hear more clearly than before. And that which we heard were the most dolorous and uneasy moans.

'Can you hear us?' said Enoch.

'Oh, erm, oh,' was the muffled response.

'Have no fear – we are friends.'

'Mm,' was the next reply in which lurked something that might have been an internal giggle.

Meanwhile Rusty had gone out and rubbed two of his prisoners together (or so he said) and produced fire. Or rather he had borrowed a flint out of their pistols and made a torch. By this uncouth lantern we now discerned three swaddled forms, or girlish *pupae* – as Enoch termed them. Even when pitchforked into deeds he remained ever the wordman – a quality I never knew whether to admire or detest in him.

The girls lay side by side on their backs, tightly bound so they could move neither hand nor foot. Their mouths were gagged with strips of cloth and their eyes were open yet they seemed, if not without sight, then dull or lacking any capacity of direct regard.

While Enoch and I gazed upon them Rusty jumped down and had already lifted up the first, Ruth, as if she were a parcel (which indeed she was) and hoisted her aloft to us. Next he heaved up Arabella and then Lucy. Enoch and I tore off their gags thinking they might speak. But no articulate words came forth. Rather they mumbled and groaned more feelingly than before but of sense they could not pronounce one word.

We carried them outside and there released them from their bonds. To my touch they seemed limp, damp, cheerless, cold. I said so to Rusty, declaring they must have immediate heat.

'Right, doll,' was his answer. And the next I knew he had dragged a bale of straw out of the cabin, and put it to the torch in the doorway. Its happy flames gave us a blaze of light and instant waves of warmth.

This while I had been rubbing Lucy's and Arabella's feet and hands most earnestly, what time Enoch was reviving Ruth with a fervour some way beyond the paternalistic – or so I recalled later once the urgencies of that moment were met.

And how handsomely they were. For Rusty's forthright resolution of the girls' need for warmth was soon translated into an inferno. The cabin, built of a most resinous pinewood, burst into hellish flames. So much so we were obliged to remove further off. Mayhap it was this enforced activity that awoke the girls from their torpor, induced, in Enoch's view, by what he called the pastoral reed of Hermes (another favourite phrase of Mr Milton's apparently) but known to more mundane folk as opium or poppy juice. Be that as I dare say it was since Enoch said it, they recovered some measure of their sensibility. A few words might now be comprehended and their legs offered a partial, if wayward, support.

Lucy said, 'Where am I?'

Arabella exclaimed, 'I want to go home.'

And Ruth suspirated, 'Is that you, ma'am?'

Said I, 'It is indeed, child. But speak no more. Just lean upon me. And I will fetch you back.'

By the time we had got them across to Manna Hatta they were able to speak coherently and told us of their being hustled from the coach onto a boat upon the West Side that had come round the point to the East River and thence across to Brooklyn, where they had briefly encountered the fat man with rings on his fingers who had lurked so recently about Pearl Street. He had assured them that they had nothing to fear, that they would be quite unharmed but then he had fed them a reddish brown cordial that would, he had said, promote within them a most happy tranquillity. They had been held like dogs with their mouths open while this substance was poured down their throats. Arabella, however, had managed to bite his finger, at which he had yelped like a dog himself. All had tried to cough back this distasteful liquid but all had had their throats resolutely fingered to ensure that they swallowed it. After this they had fallen into a profound sleep full of uneasy dreams in which they seemed to be borne upwards among trees only to be buried in a wooden vault smelling of mushrooms.

And no, they had not cried out to us. Any sounds we had heard had come from them quite witlessly in their stupor, although Ruth at one time thought she was hearing thunder, which must have been General Mars, Mr Mick and Mr Aguma subduing their bodyguards. And that was all they had known until we released them from their bonds – bonds which they had not even realised restrained them. For until the fat man had administered the cordial they had not been bound, merely gripped threateningly by their captors.

At Pearl Street three distraught, unmasked mothers waited together with their anguished spouses and Lucille. Their relief at the girls' safe return was unconfined while Lucille proclaimed for all to hear that she had told them, had she not, for the last eight hours on end, that General Mars would deliver them safely?

The girls were borne away to be cherished in the bosom of their families, Rusty departed with Lucille, also for cherishment albeit of a different kind, and Enoch and I were left to sup alone. The which we did in great contentment. Yet one thing remained to puzzle me.

I said, 'Your divination with my wedding band directed us to the right place yet when we first entered upon its seeming vacantness, you were quite as much at a check as Rusty and me?'

'True,' said he with his mouth full of blueberry pie. 'And I've been kicking myself for a dolt ever since.'

'Why?'

'To have been so dull of perception. For I should have understood at once that divination upon a map refers not merely to the lateral dimension but also to the vertical. Thus when we got to the exact spot where I fully and rightly expected to find our quarry I had not considered our girls might be concealed below it, or, for that matter, above it. After all, trussed up like that, they could have been hung like game in the trees. In other words, my dear, it is not enough in this life to cogitate merely laterally, one must needs think vertically also.'

'I invariably do,' I replied, ensnaring his eye. For if that night Lucille was enjoying Rusty I was not to be short-changed by Enoch. And thus, as I tweaked our eyebeams taut, he finished his pie as a man in a dream and set down his spoon.

And so to bed.

♂

Lucille swore blind that was the night I begot Hercules. Or *'Ercule* as she pronounced him. Well, like I'd heard that story before, hadn't I? Too many times over. In fact if I'm honest I'd say I can't count the number of paternity suits I've contested (or walked away from) in my time. I mean, back in dear old London town, every mother's son in six has this uncanny Ironside look about him. I tell you no lie, no. It's thanks to me His Majesty King Charles can boast a standing army. And no again, since you ask, dear squiress, I don't get daughters. Ain't in my corpuscles, is it? In yours maybe. But not in mine. Like to give it a go? Just to see?

Anyrate, Lucille had done her sums and she reckoned it was definitely then – the night of the 3rd October '75 – when we celebrated the happy rescue of her girls. And who am I to say her nay? Nor can I say I minded neither. After all, it ain't all that often a lowly lad such as me impregnates a foreign baroness as hoity-toity as her. Oh, and another thing occurred that night, too. Yeah. Lucille let on (whisper it not in Gath) that she'd known all about our virginals for some time. What's more she'd seen 'em perform at Pearl Street! Oh, yeah. The minx had gone there in a mask borrowed off of one of those two mother cronies of hers. No, not the one I'd turned the initial heigh-ho with, no, the other one, who liked the blue boudoir best. Lucille said she'd thought it her duty, being *in loco parentis*, to make sure of her pupils' welfare and she complimented me (and Sal and Enoch) on the good taste, discretion and sheer social charm of their dancing. It was such a pleasure to see the girls so polished, so poised, so 'finished' as it were, without their having been actually despoiled. Indeed, owing to Pearl Street, she believed their marriage prospects was enhanced an hundredfold.

She had also (and here she giggled and begged my indulgence wiv a lot of conciliatory fingers) she had been somewhat, well, you know, stimulated by the show, and had discovered it a little difficult to resist a discreet invitation by a most distinguished and persuasive gentleman (the father of Arabella if the truth were known) to retire above. To the eau-de-nil boudoir. Confessing this peccadill she begged me not to be jealous of her inconstancy since she was sure I understood better than any man how such things might suddenly come upon anyone? Especially a frail woman?

Well, of course, I wasn't jealous at all, was I? As I've said since whenever, the only doll who can provoke *that* in me is Sal. My dear old Sal. Sally the Alley. But, being a gent by nature, if not by procreation, I pretended to take offence whereat we got to the appeasing and then the begetting as the Good Book says – no, not this one, squire, the holy one you really oughta be reading wiv true seriousity if you're past your allotted time span, right? And the best of God's own luck. Given it starts wiv Genesis.

Where was I? Oh, yeah, wiv Lucille and her saying now we're gonna have to get the banns called. We can't have our little *'Ercule* born an almighty bastard, can we?

Which is worrisome. Like when did I aim to be a married man? Oh, Jeez, if only life was as simple as our urges.

☿

During that fall of the leaf I received the reply I had long awaited from Mr Newton: a substantial packet heavily sealed. Upon opening it I discovered another packet within. And a letter in which he thanked me for the researches I had made at New London. He also said that he had observed in my latest notes an inchoate but resurgent enthusiasm for the sacred art and therefore, now I was settled in New York, he was not surprised to learn that I had begun again with a new, improved laboratory. Furthermore, so gratified was he by my return to the fold (for his heart had gone out to me in my sceptic state like a shepherd's unto a lost sheep) that with this letter he was supplying a proposal so momentous that he was bound to enjoin me to a high silence concerning it.

The packet within this packet was also secured with wax but while the first had been impressed with the arms of Trinity College, Cambridge, this other bore the sign of the Pelican, sacred to Hermes Trismegistos. In other words it was, as is said, hermetically sealed.

I cracked it open and gazed upon a most impossible object. Or rather three octavo sheets covered in designs for an impossible object with written instructions which looked at first sight like gobbledegook. But then I realised that here was mirror-writing such as the great Leonardo da Vinci employed as a cloak for his scientifical enquiries. I seized Sally's looking-glass and held it to the sheets and yes, one genius had taken example of another. Once reflected, Mr Newton's Latin was become quite clear.

But not his designs, which showed, I now apprehended, an outsize receptacle set within and upon a mighty bench. And this device was to be heated by a charcoal furnace of a design quite new to me. This strange construction he had demonstrated in elevation, in plan, in cross-section and in perspective. Staring at it like a child its shape at once reminded me of an onion. But an onion nine feet tall and five feet wide! Yet it was not this great object's shape alone that induced the similitude to that bulbous vegetable. Rather it was drawn as if it were translucent. The which indeed it was meant to be. For there, in Mr Newton's mirrored hand, was a note which translated said: 'This vessel to be made of glass to the precise proportions here set forth.' To this he had added a corollary: 'Here in England there is, I believe, no manufactory capable of making such a thing to these measurements but mayhap the New World (which is full of wonders) can supply one? If not then it is conceivable that a model of it, scaled down to one-sixth of these ideal but impracticable proportions, might suffice to prove the experiment in principle if not in fact.'

Here, since you, patient reader, lack the sight I had of Mr Newton's designs for his putative machine, I must advise you it was intended as three glass vessels in one. That is to say the great outer vessel enclosed another which enclosed another. And each had at its neck two curvaceous spouts like unto pigs' tails only longer. And where they ended were stationed glass reservoirs to contain whatever distillations they were designed to supply. Six in all. Needless to say the neck of the first inner (and middle-sized) glass emerged from that of the great outer one, whilst the most interior (and smallest) vessel sprang likewise out of the middle one.

The perspective sketch my mentor gave offered some indication of how this object was to be set within the bench, so that the six spouts (which Mr Isaac's plan – as viewed from above – showed were to be deployed in the formation of a star) might curl down to the six aforementioned reservoirs placed upon it. The stove below was built of bricks to enclose charcoal which was to burn beneath an iron plate kept at a constant temperature such as that required for cooking buttered eggs.

As you may now perhaps be sure, I contemplated Mr Newton's device with a fervid admiration, while remaining as doubtful as he of the possibility of its manufacture. Even at one-sixth of its ideal size. Who could blow one glass vessel inside another? Truly, mankind's progress in the science of nature oft depends upon instruments as yet beyond his constructive powers. A wistful post-script of a familiar sort (how often had I heard him say it) confirmed this. Mr Newton wrote: 'As I say I fear this speculation goes beyond the bounds of present mechanics and thus it is that we enquirers remain as children playing with pretty pebbles upon a sea shore, while all before us lie oceans of knowledge we cannot venture either upon or into for want of appropriate means.'

But what was Mr Newton's triple retort for? What might it distil? I returned again to his notes and learned, as if I were illumined by Great Sol himself, that this triple glass was designed to improve upon an experiment of Mr Rob. Boyle, a fellow seeker of the Philosopher's Stone. Common to both these colossal enquirers was the belief that there existed in nature one universal matter. All creation was made of this catholic substance. Everything that was mineral, vegetable or animal was germane to it. But what really *was* this matter? Mr Boyle believed (for he was a bold atomist) that it was a white, powdery earth made from the distillation of pure rainwater. He has written, *exempli gratia*, that 'this powder, whether it be the elementary earth or not, if it be really produced out of the water itself, may prove of greater consequence than will be presently foreseen, and may make the alchemists' hopes of turning other metals into gold, appear less wild'.

My mentor agreed with Mr Boyle and was to note some years later in his *System of the World* the following: 'The vapours which arise from the sun, the fixed stars, and the tails of the comets, may meet at last with, and fall into, the atmospheres of the planets by their gravity, and there be condensed and turned into water and humid spirits; and from thence, by a slow heat, pass gradually into the form of salts and sulphurs, and tinctures, and mud, and clay, and sand, and stones, and coral, and other terrestrial substances.'

Later he notes, and here I paraphrase (for life is short and the sacerdotal art long) that water can be transformed by fermentation into all manner of natural substances including those metallic. Further he states, along with Mr Rob. Boyle, that the matter of all things is one and the same.

So now perhaps we may discern the drift of Mr Newton's speculation. And his later notes confirmed it. For, if Mr Boyle thought that condensed rainwater once exposed to the air and having given off its vapours would leave behind this catholic matter, then Mr Newton concluded that there must needs be other natural waters introduced into the experiments. Rainwater was not enough. To it, or rather alongside it, must be added seawater and morning dew. In this manner the enquirer could produce three earths whose properties might be compared one with another. And who knew but a scrupulous mixing of all three might produce that essential, pregnant first material of which both he and Mr Rob. Boyle were so convinced?

But Mr Newton being Mr Newton his glass had another quality. And this was that the steam produced in the first glass, which contained the seawater, was employed to heat the second glass, which contained Mr Rob. Boyle's rainwater, which in its turn with its vaporous warmth heated the third glass, which contained the dew. Thus the first water served to evaporate the second and the second the third. And these three contiguous airs were to be distilled into liquid again only when they reached the long, curled and curving spouts that led down to the bowls upon the bench where they were to evaporate anew, yet naturally, within the dry and ever constant atmosphere of the laboratory, and so at last, yield up their precious residues: this philosophical powder; this created earth; this triplicate dirt containing all things.

Do I hear you wonder (modern cog-wheels in the mind a-grinding) about the third water? The morning dew? Could Mr Newton demand, in all seriousness, such a commodity? Seawater and rainwater are both easily obtainable. But morning dew? True in due season it hangs like angels' tears upon a myriad fronds of nature but to collect it is surely a task beyond human wit and patience? And how much was required?

Well may you ask and well can I answer. Your second question first: six gallons for the ideal glass, one gallon for the model of it. Your first question second (since what goes before comes also behind): by the method indicated in the *Mutus Liber*, published '67, where you may see an explicatory picture of great cloths spread out to soak up the dew upon a morning pasture replete with sheep and cows while in the foreground two persons, not unlike Mrs Sally and myself, wring out one of these same cloths into a tub of unspecified substance. For purity's sake I would suggest this receptacle should also be made of glass. By these means, provided the heavens are propitious (that is, they smile upon your birth sign) and the weather clement, you can collect as much or more morning dew as you may require or ever wish for. Truly the subtleties of the *magnum opus* are often sublimely simple.

Although enjoined to silence I decided I must confide in Master Antonio Stella, the glassmaker out of Murano, since he was, in his art, also something of an alchemist, blowing sand, soda and lime into fiery bubbles that, once cooled, seemed created of a pretty nothingness. Thanks to my dealings with him to furnish my laboratory we had already discovered a lively sense of mutual esteem. I was sure I could trust this worthy artificer. And I was right. Besides, if anyone in the New World might give substance to Mr Newton's high and mighty secret, it was he.

But when he regarded the drawings he shook his head and sighed most magisterially. He could not, he opined, make, at this present time, a thing of such extreme amplitude. To blow a glass six feet high by four feet wide was of itself a task almost impossible. Let alone to place within it two others of a lesser yet still considerable proportion.

'But perhaps you might succeed in making the model of it at one-sixth of its size?'

'Sir, I might,' was all his answer. Then, after another solemn exhalation, he added, 'With good fortune a man could possibly blow one bubble inside another with another inside that. Or rather such an artist must needs commence with the smallest vessel, then blow another about that and so on. But even so – what a challenge to even the most experienced and dextrous glassmaker.'

And again he sighed as if in mourning for his metier. Like any true artist he remained ever doubtful of achieving excellence whilst succeeding every day.

Meanwhile I had noted his choice of words as he spoke of the great triple glass. I said, 'You say *at this present time* you could not make Mr Newton's vessel in its grand proportion? That it would be *almost impossible?'*

'I do.'

'Does this mean that at some future date you might hope, and mayhap believe, it could be made in its ideal dimension?'

He sighed for the fourth time, but this latest expulsion of breath seemed rather more hopeful than his earlier sighings which had smacked of a melancholy acceptance of what he thought might be done.

I said, 'Could it be that when might become now?'

He said, 'It is a question of the metal, sir.'

'Metal? We speak of glass, do we not?'

He grinned at my layman's question. 'In our art, sir, glass in its molten state is ever known as metal.'

'Forgive me. I did not know that,' I lied.

'Few do. But now you are adverted, perhaps?'

I bowed, happy to seem ignorant before him since it is ever my nature to dissemble, and further I have discovered that you can learn much from others if you pretend to know less than they. I said, 'I am your devoted pupil, Master Stella.'

It was his turn to bow. For we stood upon a certain ceremony – it being the custom of New York to exaggerate the courtesies native to those countries its inhabitants have abandoned.

'Know then, sir,' said he, 'that the metal I work with is of the

Venetian kind. When it cools it produces a glass as light as can be and more brittle than a wafer. It will, even so, endure, if it is handled with due care but, as I dare say you know already from those vessels I have made for you, it is ill-suited to rough usage or too sudden a change of temperature. Nor can it be blown to any proportion beyond that of a two-quart jug or apothecary's bottle.'

Said I, apprehending the course his mind seemed set upon, 'You are saying we require another kind of metal?'

'That is so. And such a one may, I believe, be made.'

'How?'

'At large expense, sir.'

'Never mind the expense, man,' I cried in extreme excitement. For I have never yet counted the cost of anything that stood between me and the pursuit of the great work. 'Just tell me what you know and the means you require.'

Whereupon I heard, to my pleasure and surprise, that Stella had travelled from Venice to New York by way of London where he had met a Mr Ravenscroft at his glasshouse at Lambeth. And this great English glassman (whom I had never heard of – small worlds are often larger than we think) had been occupied at that time, back in '72, with the composing of another kind of glass containing lead that would, if his experiments proved successful, show itself to be stronger, heavier and more brilliant than any hitherto known to humankind.

'And you have the receipt to make this novelty?'

'No, sir.'

'Ah.'

'But I know its constituent parts.'

'Though not the quantities?'

'No.'

'Can you guess at them?'

'I dare say I might. You require first an acid element such as sand, let us say 100 parts, next a potash that is alkaline, 50 parts, and then red lead, perhaps also some 50 parts.'

'You shall have them. We shall order them in bulk.'

'A new furnace will also be required, sir, to fuse them together. Mr Ravenscroft said that this new metal may not come in contact with a naked flame.'

'Why not?'

'Because any sulphur in the flame would discolour it once it was cooled.'

'Of course! Sulphur has affinity with lead. How wise your mentor is, Master Stella – almost as percipient as mine.'

We laughed and next shook hands upon my agreeing to supply him as speedily as I might with the funds necessary not only to make trial of this new amalgam which could result in what he called a crystal glass, but also to start at once upon the building of a large, adjacent workshop in which the great machine might be blown in its full dimension. I also undertook to pay the keep and wages of two new apprentices, because he reckoned it would require at least four skilled men to work Mr Ravenscroft's metal in such abundance. And at that time he had only a single assistant, apt enough but not overtly muscular.

In the interim he would attempt the making of the scaled-down model but in his usual Venetian glass. He made no promises but thought this toy might be done within a fortnight. Meanwhile I, upon my side, would provide him with a thousand silver dollars to be paid in four equal parts, towards the realisation of the greater work.

These matters concluded I took my leave with a singular satisfaction and sped back to Pearl Street as if my boots had grown wings. All that now remained was to convince Sally that this projected expense was justified – for as ever she held the purse. But when I was got there she was gone to her dressmaker on Beaver Street on account of an invitation that she had but that day received, inviting all three of us, Professor Mercurius, Madam Venus and General Mars, to a grand reception given by Councillor and Mrs Septimus Ambrose some four weeks hence. Upon the 11th of November at the Feast of St Martin, the stingiest saint in the calendar, if the truth is to be spoken. It was to be hoped, I reflected, that our hosts would not be of his persuasion, that a grand reception meant just that, otherwise Sally's outlay on silks and ribbons, lace and lawn, would be a ridiculous waste of our present wealth. Since it was a fact that by this season we were making a pretty penny.

Even so, Sally took some persuading to promise this latest funding of my researches. A thousand dollars no less! And probably more! Had not the costs of establishing my laboratory already quadrupled upon my original costing of it? Now this! Oh, no. Enoch my dear, I love you dearly, but no, no, no, etcetera. No. No. And you won't persuade me this way neither.

So said she. And meant it. Her vehemence caused me to reflect that her unfortunate experiences with Lord Spark of Oxford and London (that young dissolute who had appeared so charmingly and transparently honest and yet was not) had to some degree curdled the sweet milk of Sally's native generosity. And thus it is that great natures are diminished by smaller ones, whether they would or no.

But I could not afford to allow this melancholy reflection to discourage me. Instead I redoubled my efforts of persuasion, employing every means at my disposal: spiritual, physical, politic, until by dawn (for most of this negotiation was, you should understand, conducted in bed) I had won her acceptance of this new outlay. But upon one salient and portentous condition. To which I agreed with an instant celerity since it was the very same proviso I had formerly suggested when proposing my new laboratory. But then, at that time, she had overruled me.

Sally murmured, as I ran my fingers through her tumbled hair (how it shone in the ascendant sun prying at our window, and it was no wonder Great Sol had become a peeping Tom, for Sally discovered, uncovered, at morning, was as bright and golden as her heavenly self when glimpsed low upon the horizon what time lesser stars depart before the approaching day), she said, 'You're a despicable, calculating, conscienceless Welsh wizard.' I agreed. She continued, 'You flatter, you lie, you tease, but since you're you and I'm me, we must concur, mustn't we?'

'I think so,' said I, with a certain care, biding her conclusion, and meanwhile marvelling at the exquisite curve of her left eyebrow. I did not have long to wait.

She said, 'If the great work's advancement requires an expenditure of a further thousand dollars – '

'It does, Mrs Sally. Or else our greatest philosopher lies neglected. By whom I mean dear Mr Newton. For so I now think of him. As greatly dear to me – given his faith in such a wretched yet persevering impostor as I have been. And granted this gift from him also. His sublime designs for this masterpiece of intuitive experimentation – this his mighty triple glass.'

'You've told me all this already, Enoch. Eight times over.'

'Forgive me, but my devotion to the great work – '

Her finger pressed upon my lips. 'Shush,' she said. 'Do you wish to hear me out or don't you?' Silenced so, I nodded. She continued. 'We will do it. You shall have the means to build this prodigious thing your Mr Newton has proposed but – listen, Enoch, listen – but, of this new and large expense, Rusty must know nothing. Not a word. It is perforce our secret since if he were to know of it he would at once forbid it. I shall keep the accounts and be sure to mislay these dollars to your scheme's advantage. Is that plain, my dear?'

'As the daylight at our window, Sally. But why are you so sure Rusty would be opposed to this expense? Has he confided other ventures for the employment of our money to you?'

'Dozens. And none of them include the great work. But he wants most to invest yet more in waste disposal. It is, he believes, a greater money-spinner than harlotry, pig-racing, cock-fighting, and alchemy all put together. His latest motto is: If it ain't shit it ain't shit.'

I cannot say I had heard this particular New World locution before but its meaning was as clear as its rudeness. I thanked Sally for her complicity in the work and we sealed our covert bargain with a conjunction as pretty as any in the zodiac.

♀

I had ordered a peach-coloured gown for the Ambrose Ball with a décolletage Peter Lely and any of the King's mistresses would have been proud of. For upon this score I knew I could not be challenged by Mrs Ambrose, since according to Rusty, she was none other than Abednego. A pretty toy he might be but when it comes to a proper chest boys remain mere boys, do they not?

It was going to cost almost as much as Enoch needed for his latest alchemical device but naturally I didn't tell him so. Nine hundred dollars for a mere habiliment and its accessories – shoes, muff, petticoats, fan, gloves, seed pearls on gold wire for my ringlets, great pearls at my throat? Had he known of all of this he would have asked double for his old science, upon the presumption that we were far wealthier than I was pretending. We were, but while frills and furbelows are regarded as, well, frills and furbelows, nevertheless with them at least you see more for your money than is the case with the great work where, for the most part, all you get are vile stinks, hopes dashed, and an adept in a filthy temper. For if the truth must be said (and while it's probably best that it isn't, still it needs saying) I had begun rather to lose faith in Enoch Powys, the Welsh wizard. Not as essential co-mate, I hasten to add, but as chemist or alchemist or what you will. The fact was I had much preferred him when he was sceptical and teaching the girls to dance. Then it seemed to me he was himself and of himself – clever, fun, mercurial, difficult, yes – but not that tedious thing, a disciple. Jesus preserve us from such as those! With all that devotional canting about his genial mentor, the mighty Mr Newton with his measureless mind, his old master and ineffable guide in the sacred art at Cambridge, yawn, oh, yawn. Because when Enoch talked like that, it was invariably the case that he could not bring his parts to their task. Could not as we harlots say: get it up. The times I've had to lie there waiting for him to stop worshipping

Mr Newton and start on me. Truly science is the enemy of love. I may tell you the advancement of knowledge and the Schools of Cambridge have much to answer for: Mr Newton and Mr Milton (another of Enoch's master spirits as he termed him) in especial. I swear to you he was a much better bedfellow when he forgot the lot.

So thus was our bargain struck – with ignorance knowingly employed on both sides: Rusty being unaware of Enoch's expenditures and Enoch knowing nothing of mine – at least in their true extent. To say I was looking forward to the ball is to understate. I was in a tizzy of high anticipation like a child before a feast. Nor was I alone. All our ladies and their daughters at Pearl Street were agog at the thought of it. Rumour had it a whole shipload of eligible young gentlemen were to come from England (not one of them less than a baronet and some a good deal nobler). It was even said that this dreamboat was already at sea and making fair weather of the voyage. Invitations had been sent as far north as Boston and as far south as Louisiana whence several French chevaliers were expected – especially by Lucille, whom I now knew to be no better than she ought to have been. I warned Rusty he would be best to keep his eye upon her at the ball whereat he laughed and said something to the effect that the die was already cast. At the time I did not take his meaning but later I did. Not by the noticing of any thickening at Lucille's waist but by the look in her eye. As with my girls, it's always the eyes tell the story – long before their bellies do.

All the older gentlemen at Pearl Street (every one a town councillor) grumbled mightily, maintaining, even as they drank and gambled small fortunes away, that the expense Ambrose was bringing them to had been calculated to ruin them. It was not merely the tailors' and dressmakers' bills but the carriage-builders and the hackney stables were doubling, nay quadrupling, their prices. The sober city of New York had known nothing like this before and all to satisfy Ambrose's over-weening ambition to be mayor. Fat chance of *that* was their opinion. The man was not only newly rich but a vulgar jackass. And among themselves they connived most heartily to enjoy his hospitality while plotting to outvote him when the election was eventually convened. It was true Ambrose could boast of a most gracious-looking wife but even upon that score odd whispers were going about to the effect that she was not quite what she appeared to be. Further if New York were to elect a new mayor next year surely the town might do worse than to look in General Rodney Mars's direction? Now there was a real man's mayor, don't you agree, Madam Venus?

When I said I did, I was advised to advise Rusty to have a quiet word with them one convenient evening. The which I did and the next thing I knew he too was a member of the town's council. Apparently one of their number had been persuaded to stand down in Rusty's favour – he being the old gentleman who ever favoured the blue boudoir and Lucy's mother. Indeed he was that lady's father-in-law as she knew full well, though whether he did I shall never know, nor shall I ask – for some things are better left unenquired into.

I said to Rusty, 'So now I suppose, you're well placed to become mayor? If you choose?'

'Shush, doll,' answered he. 'I don't trust none of 'em. They've only done it so they can say *adios, amigo* to Ambrose. And besides what of Arnold Jay Stone?'

'But he's not on the council?'

'Maybe not. But he's back in town, I hear. And looking for trouble.'

'But aren't you above all that now?'

'No. Nor never will be. The higher you climb the lower it gets, Sal.'

'But that's contrary to mother nature.'

'What's she gotta do wiv it? We're talking privilege, position, power, and silver frigging dollars.'

But I'll say one thing, whatever the pros and cons of Rusty's newest promotion, it meant I had no trouble getting him to the tailor's for a new velvet supper suit and to the wig-maker for an extra set of evening curls. And when the periwig was delivered, oh, dear heaven, I'm still laughing, he looked like a giant red setter from Hades. So fiery handsome was this hairpiece I had to keep running my fingers through it, just for the feel of it, till he slapped me down saying I was mussing it all about. Whereat we argued – but only so we could make up later. Rusty and me in those days – it was as if we were immutable.

Apart from preparing for the approaching festivity, concealing the costs of Enoch's secret machine, and enjoying Rusty's ever increasing wealth and power (he now had twenty more dirt-waggons and had staked out yet another landfill site), I had little to occupy me. Pearl Street almost ran itself. Consequently while I could certainly call myself a lady of pleasure I was also one of leisure.

So much so that I resumed cooking. You may recall that as Mrs Jeremy Bancroft née Smith in Somerset I had rather prided myself upon my craft in the kitchen having learnt a good deal of the art from a young Frenchman my dear husband had seen fit to employ. Now again I was bitten by the bug and had established a kitchen at the back of Pearl Street where I might amuse myself in preparing various messes. Sometimes for myself, Enoch and Rusty; at others for our more valued clients who required sustenance after gaming or daming.

This kitchen was so placed that while Enoch was engaged upon the great work in his laboratory below I could divert myself by creating small edible ones above; and it was soon evident that although adepts are said to be unworldly they are as partial to the occasional titbit as any respectable business man. And so it was that by that winter of '75 I had acquired a reputation as a cook in New York which quite equalled, if not surpassed, my original renown as a whore in London.

Enoch, who had a word for everything and an explication of it too, said my cookery was just as alchemical as his experiments. Did I not transmute primary material – a raw leek, for instance – into the equivalent of edible gold, once it was steamed to melting point, cooled, and subtly dressed for a salad? And was not my clam and codfish stew the great Atlantic ocean itself, conjured in a casserole, and brought to boiling point? Upon a windy November night it might fairly be described as the elixir of life. And as for my curds and syllabubs, why, they were akin to the philosopher's stone – the possession of which afforded visions of the Universal Design of God. Such eloquence meant he wanted another helping, of course. Rusty, for his part, merely stuck out his plate again, belched and said, 'Tasty, doll, very. But what I'd give for a kipper.'

Well, there was I in my kitchen with the first snow of the season falling outside with such steady purpose that I had determined to start an ice-chest and prepare a *fromage glacé* such as Philippe of La Rochelle (and Somerset) used to make when winter allowed it. For it is a sorry paradox that only when the weather's cold enough can we make such puddings – if only Enoch (or Mr Newton for that matter) would address his mind to inventing a machine that might produce ice in midsummer! Then we might enjoy some present alchemy, instead of the historical variety.

However, there I was, with my tin-lined coffer packed with snow set safely outside to freeze on the back stoop, and me gently stirring my sugared milk and cream with the peel of two lemons, sliced as thin as the fruit's flower petals, in a skillet upon a gentle heat by the glowing fire, and the entire concoction just at the point of thickening when Lord Spark, yes, he, no other, burst in through the door with a gun.

I will not pretend I recognised him. I did not. No one would have.

Not then. Not even an intimate such as I had been before getting cheated so viciously. He was half-dressed in a shirt of unspeakable filthiness, no breeches so that he was bollock-naked, with bare calloused feet, blue-white with cold. The only aspect of this desperate creature which might have offered him some protection from the winter's blast was the abundance of his hair and beard. Both were tousled, matted, elf-locked. And if washed and combed they would have reached his belt − except he had no belt.

To me he seemed a lunatic intruder I must expel at once except there was no time since he was pointing his fire-piece at me with an impressively steady pair of hands − the barrel of it thrust at me with deadly purpose.

His eyes burned. He said, 'Save me, madam.'

'How?' said I, at a loss. For it seemed to me that it was I who needed saving.

'Hide me.'

'Who are you?'

'Quick! Or I'm lost! Quick!'

And he advanced upon me. Beside the red glint in his eyes (which was naught but the reflection of the fire) I now noted that they could roll most hideously. It was all too evident this man was in an impassioned world of his own making, not of mine. But his gun was real enough, primed and cocked.

Quickly I opened the pantry door and even before I could indicate that he might enter he had hurled himself forward and was installed within, pulling the door so violently closed that its handle was wrested out of my hand.

From inside he cried, 'You have not seen me! If you say you have you'll die! I'll shoot you dead!'

Feebly, out of shock, I answered, 'That sounds ungracious.'

'I mean it,' was his furious reply.

On hearing this I wondered to what kind of madman I had given asylum? And whether I should live to regret it rather more than I did already? Though what else I might have done, with a pistol pointed at me point-blank, I did not know.

These thoughts, however, were arrested by the entrance of another man, followed by two more.

The first announced himself as a constable of the Court House, the second as the first's superior, a sergeant, and the third, who was perhaps all of fifteen, pink of cheek and close to tears, as a midshipman of the good ship *Aphrodite* − a frigate in the service of His Majesty King Charles.

The first had said upon the threshold, 'Where is he?' I had answered, 'Who?' But it was only upon the contiguous appearance of the others that a dialogue (of sorts) was achieved.

The second said, saluting me, 'Sergeant Culiver, at your service, ma'am.'

I said, my wits now a little recovered, 'And I at yours, sergeant.'

The boy said, 'Is he here? Pray God he is!'

Again I feigned ignorance. I said, 'Of whom do you speak?'

Sergeant Culiver said dourly, 'We're after a murderer, ma'am. Nay, worse. A patricide. And lunatic to boot.'

'He's escaped our ship and I was on duty,' said the pretty midshipman. 'And if we don't retrieve him I shall be flogged. Mayhap I will be anyway.'

'And me demoted I shouldn't wonder,' added the sergeant gloomily.

'I swear he ran in here,' said the constable. 'I was nearest to him. He'd quite outrun you, sergeant.'

'What do you say to that, ma'am?' demanded Culiver of me.

I drew breath, allowing my bosom to swell somewhat – for it remains an eternal delight to me that an artful inflation of the female lungs can do much to divert a male officer from his office. I said demurely, 'I sincerely believe your constable is mistaken, sergeant. No one has come in here.'

'You couldn't miss him, ma'am,' exclaimed the midshipman. 'He's a wild man, a woolly man. And no boots nor breeches neither.'

'Name of Wavenhoe,' said the constable.

Not to be outdone by a subordinate Sergeant Culiver said most portentously, 'The Right Honourable the Earl of Wavenhoe, ma'am. Percival John Thomas William Richard Hampton Spark.'

A tremor ran right through me. Never mind the forenames – here were two surnames most horribly familiar to me: Spark *and* Wavenhoe! Had not Lord Spark's mother been the Countess of Wavenhoe and was not she supposed to have conspired with her son, Lord Spark, so that he might inherit the earldom rather sooner than was natural? And now here, before me, at New York, was an officer of the Law declaring Spark to be both earl and patricide, thus confirming at a stroke these suppositions, not to mention the dark hintings of that gross caretaker I had so abused at Westminster, and the rumours which had reached the delicate ears of my dear, departed Jeremy at Tunbridge Wells? Lord Spark my Oxford lover, London cheat and unnatural murderer was here in my pantry!

I said, keeping my voice low, which is held by poets to be an excellent thing in women, but only so we do not interrupt them, I said, 'I'm sorry, sergeant, but I've seen no one. And no one of that sort. But if I do encounter such a man – though heaven forfend I do – then I shall report him at once to the Court House since from your description of him he would appear highly undesirable upon several counts.'

This show of gentle duplicity achieved its purpose: their departure. I watched them go. Then waited a little longer – a trick I'd learned of Rusty – to be sure they had really gone and would not suddenly return upon a false pretext or a true suspicion. For the Law has its sleights of hand that are quite as dextrous as any card sharp's.

Once sure we were safe I went, not without a certain trepidation, to the pantry door.

As I opened it I was confronted by Lord Spark with a well-chewed ham-bone in one hand and six pickled gherkins in the other. His beard was thick with custard and studded with prune stones.

'By God, I was hungry,' he said. Then he burped most eructively and gnawed greasily upon the ham-bone. And all the while he smirked as one distracted, rolling his eyes all about as if they were quite loose in their sockets.

I said, 'They say you are the Earl of Wavenhoe? Are you?'

'I was, madam, I was!' declaimed he. 'But now – now I'm mere flotsam, jetsam, human driftwood.'

Ignoring this blabber I said, 'Have you lost your wits?'

'Not irrecoverably, no. But they do wander on occasion. Only to return like lost sheep.'

Saying this he smiled like Dan Cupid. And now I had no doubt. Here, beneath the grease and filth, was, without further doubt, my former lover, Percival Spark.

I said, 'You owe me two hundred thousand pounds at five years' compounded interest.' At this he giggled like an infant. I added, with increased resolve, 'You do know me, don't you? Indeed I dare you to deny it. Look at me, Percy. Just you look.'

This time his errant eyeballs seemed to rest upon me rather less waywardly and their pupils appeared more directed to their purpose. Perhaps the food in my pantry had sharpened his perceptions? If so I forgave him the mess his hunger had made of it and of himself. At least with his wits restored the man might be induced to admit his crime against me. And who knew make reparation? For earls, after all, are earls.

He said, 'Madam, I believe I was enamoured of a fair lady like unto you upon a past occasion but that was in another country and besides this cruel wench disdained me – '

212

'Piffle!' I interjected. 'You can't fool me with such play-acting! That wench was me! Your Oxford whore and City mistress! And you preyed upon me with a cunning any Chancery broker would be proud to brag of! You stole our takings at Pudding Wharf! Swore they were placed to my advantage! Upon deposit at three banks! Whereof you were director! Yet when I went to claim this money they denied me! And you! You were quite unknown to them and the papers I had had of you were false! And when, straight after, I called upon you at Westminster I found the house shut fast and you entirely absent! I followed you – as I thought – to Tunbridge Wells where, in place of you I found, God help me, your mother, the Countess of Wavenhoe! From her I learned that you had set forth to circumnavigate the globe upon my money! Except she didn't say that because she didn't know what intelligence I had received of your caretaker at Westminster! Which was, that although you and she had plotted most villainously and successfully against your father, when your unnatural crime was done, you had discovered, to your horror, that your labour had been in vain! There was no inheritance to enjoy so prematurely! Contrary to expectation your father's estate was mortgaged unto seven times seven! Every blade of grass was pledged, every stick of furniture entailed, every unhatched egg already counted and under lien! Whereupon you proceeded to rob me to make good the difference! I dare you to deny it!'

Here I drew breath. The which, given so many exclamations, I sorely needed. Meantime he had said not a word, merely gazing at me as if he were become a pet rabbit and I a vixen.

I continued, rather more measuredly, 'Therefore it follows that whatever living you have enjoyed these last five years has been at my expense. So now I command you to admit I am who I am and that you owe me a most substantial fortune.'

He mumbled aggrievedly, 'Enjoyed? You suppose I have enjoyed these last six years? My voyage round the world?'

I said without relent, 'Answer my question, Percy.'

He nodded, spoke, 'Yes – oh yes, you are to be sure that Mrs Sally. But to tell truth I did not recognise you at first.'

'Nor I you.'

Here we came to a stop. Once again he seemed bereft of all sense while I regarded him with a contemptuous compassion.

He hung his head. 'Enjoyed,' he repeated with a depth of bitterness scarcely to be fathomed. And then, to my disgust, he began to sing in a voice as of an aged man come into his second childhood. 'All alone, that's me, by the coconut tree with naught but the parrots for company, for company.'

This piping doggerel was too much to be borne. 'Stop that,' said I. 'Or I shall harbour you no longer. I'll go straight to the Court House for the sergeant.' These strict words made some impression upon him. He ceased his silly singing and resorted to a sort of humming. 'Now,' I added, 'if you wish to remain here a little you'd best tell me where you're come from and why? But do not imagine that any past affection lingers in my breast, Percy. For it doesn't. I do this merely out of common humanity.'

'Oh, Mrs Sally,' he replied. And quicksilver tears turned to gold by the firelight coursed down his narrow cheeks.

Tears from Lord Spark were the last straw. I turned towards the door, determined to fetch help to throw him out, but who should stand there but Enoch just that instant come up from the laboratory.

'Have you such a thing as a tin ladle?' he enquired but then saw Percy. At which his errand was quite forgot. 'I know that face,' said Enoch. 'By Jupiter, I do.'

'Well, that's more than I did when he first rushed in upon me.'

'Lord Spark is it not?' He strode fiercely to within six inches of Percy. 'Are you not that rogue who stole our monies at Pudding Wharf?'

'I've been into that,' I said. 'He is. But now he's lunatic. And scarcely answerable for his actions.'

'He was before,' roared Enoch. 'Didn't you tell me he fitted out a ship at our expense purposing to sail around the globe?'

'I got as far as the isle of San Isidro,' said Percy.

'Where's that?'

'A hundred miles off the coast of a land called Chile.'

'Why did you stop there?'

'Because my ship sailed on without me.'

'You mean you were marooned there?'

'For two years and three score days.'

'You counted them?'

'Upon the trunk of a tree. Seven hundred and ninety notches I made.'

'You don't sound lunatic to me.'

'Oh, but I am, sir. Mrs Sally is quite right.'

'His idiocy is wayward,' said I.

'And why were you marooned, sir?'

'The crew mutinied against the captain and me. The captain they killed but they spared me my life putting me ashore at San Isidro. But I've talked enough sense now.'

And here he began to sing again – that same childish ditty I had heard before. But now at least I could suppose he had invented it upon that desert island. Perhaps in a vain attempt to keep his wits about him?

Enoch said to me, 'How came he here?'

'In desperate haste. He's on the run from a frigate of the King's Navy. He's wanted for murder.'

'Of whom?'

'Oh, Enoch! I told you long ago.'

'Then that's why I've forgotten.'

'He killed his father. Earl Wavenhoe.'

'Ah, yes. So he did. Now it comes back to me. Yes. A noble patricide no less. Interesting. Excellent. No wonder he's lost his wits. You'll tell me next he married his mother, I hope?'

'No, he didn't!'

'Well, I dare say he wanted to. Such characters usually do,' he said equably.

'But what are we to do with him, Enoch? On the one hand he owes us a fortune, on the other he's wanted by the Law.'

'Quite so. And the Law will assuredly hang him. But where's the benefit in that for us?'

'Exactly. Yet meanwhile we're harbouring a murderer. For which *we* could get hanged.'

'Then we must keep him close. And as a disguise clean him up. Without that beard – is that custard in it? – and with breeches on he'll look quite another man.'

'You'll succour a patricide?'

'Why not? They rarely do it twice. And I need another pair of hands in the laboratory. This way he can pay off some of his indebtedness to us rather than to society at large who would never notice anyway. Besides he seems an interesting case. It's not every day you find a man who's done such unspeakable things. And yet the ancients record many instances of such inner compulsions made manifest. Most notably in that King of Thebes whose name for the moment escapes me – '

'Oedipus Rex,' said Lord Spark. 'We're related – on the distaff side.' And he began to sing again.

'Come along, sir,' said Enoch, with a fine show of decisiveness that truly heartened me. 'You're to be my dogsbody, do you hear? My general factotum. You will go for everything I need. And count yourself lucky in my service. This way, sir. And who knows, between us, we may yet clarify your disordered mind.'

Lord Spark meekly allowed Enoch to conduct him thence and I

breathed a sigh of relief. I was glad to have him out of my kitchen. Enoch was welcome to the poor soul. Though whether he could make good his intent to cure him seemed doubtful to me. Enoch might be expert with chemicals, toads and horse manure but surely he was no physician? Let alone an adept of the mind?

I did not encounter either of them for three days and as many nights. For now Enoch was become as he ever was. That is entirely engrossed by the great work, and, as I had foreseen, he had no time to spare for sleep – or me. I cannot say I minded over much. To sleep alone upon occasion can be a luxury – provided this state may be altered whenever one chooses. On the third night I chose Rusty and after told myself, truly and justly, that I had got the best of two worlds, if not three.

Rusty, however, was less than pleased to hear of Lord Spark's return. And doubtful of Enoch's succour of him. In fact I had to use all my womanly cunning to persuade him to leave well alone: Rusty's choleric impulse being to go down directly to the laboratory (never mind it was three in the morning) and give that thieving aristo a right kicking and then chuck him in the river.

Fortunately by the above-mentioned stratagem, together with some well-whispered flattery, I managed to divert him from this peremptory course; my most effective argument being not the teaching of his fingers to play hopscotch upon my belly but the matronly insinuation that he must perforce maintain his new reputation as the town's most successful man of business and likely new mayor. Throwing lunatic lords into the East River was not the way to promote this new respectable version of himself – rather it was a regression to his old rough ways as an uncouth suburb captain. He laughed, agreed, complied.

But after he said, 'I still reckon them was the days, doll.' At which we both shared a pang or two of home-sickness for Wrestler's Court and Pudding Wharf with him half-laughing and me half-crying. However it was thanks to this final sour-sweet moment that I was able to get at last his promise that he would leave Lord Spark entirely to Enoch's charge since, after all, as that Welsh sorcerer's apprentice, he was, as it were, making some amends for his past misdeeds.

Meanwhile what news was there of Arnold Jay Stone? I wondered aloud. None really, was his answer. Stone had returned to New York only to depart again – upcountry, it was said, to his beaver business at Fort Orange. His bullies still patrolled the waterfront monitoring his rentable beef-cakes but whenever Rusty appeared they doffed their caps, bowed and were markedly civil, even servile. Mayhap the thorough pasting they had received at Brooklyn accounted for this present reverence but still Rusty mused upon Stone and his machinations. Was the bastard planning some new stroke against us?

I said, 'What if he comes to the ball? In fact he's bound to, isn't he? Councillor Ambrose cannot but invite him.'

'In which case, doll, I'll invite him – outside.'

'Oh, no, Rusty.'

'Got no choice. Honour is honour, darlin'.'

'Blow honour! You could end up dead.'

'Not if it's just him 'n' me, Sal.'

'But as with Lord Spark – what about your reputation?'

'Oh, no. No, doll, no. This is quite different. Like if I make a jam-roll of A.J.S. for all to see, every gent in town will cheer. I'll be the hero of the hour and more. There's nothing your New Yorker likes better than a show of strength – never mind the morality, just feel the muscle. Anyrate like I said, it's me *amour propre*, doll.'

'You've got that idea from Lucille.'

'Jealous, are we? Is that it?'

Was I? It was a nice question answerable twice over. Yes, I was. No, I wasn't. As simple Sally Greensmith I could cordially detest Madame Souligny; but as Madam Venus I knew she could never be my rival. Therefore I said, 'Yes and no.'

But would you believe it the only answer I got was a snore? My delectable, detestable bully boy was fast asleep! I kicked him hard. He grunted like one of his own racing pigs and fell silent. And so to sleep. The pair of us. And I dreamt we were caught in a net of gold thrown over us by Enoch.

The next morning Rusty was gone about his garbage business, and I went down to the laboratory to see what Enoch was making of his. I found him hollow-eyed from overwatching of his experiments and Lord Spark. Although *he* was quite transformed. His beard was gone, his hair cropped to a pleasing fuzz all over and furthermore he was wearing breeches. He was, however, besmudged from tending of the furnaces, but it was plain that this soilment overlay an essential cleanliness. To all intents and purposes he appeared an honest apprentice. Also he saluted me most politely even gravely as Madam Venus.

Said I, 'Who's instructed you to call me that?'

'Why, Professor Mercurius, ma'am.'

'Percy likes the work,' said Enoch with an easy smile. 'Given experience he may yet do as well as any. Meanwhile furnace number 3 needs a rollicking rake out, lad.'

As his lordship went meekly to his lowly task I asked Enoch (in a quiet word aside) if Spark's foolishness was at all dissipated, or had I appeared at one of his more lucid moments?

'Not yet,' said he without any diminution of his voice.

'Hush, he'll hear you,' exclaimed I.

'It's no matter. We may say what we like before him. His condition is such that what goes in one ear comes out at the other. However, I have hope of a cure thanks to simple chemistry. At present he is taking five droplets of mercury with warm milk twice a day.'

'But that's a cure for the pox!'

'No, you're thinking of common quicksilver, my dear, whereas I speak of the sublimed mercury and that is quite another thing. It is the universal agent and acts just as efficaciously upon the immaterial as the material. And in particular it finds out those anatomies of the brain where guilty memories hold their state, and eases them.'

'You'd have him forget his wickedness?'

'No, I'd have him speak out loud of it and so come to forgive himself.'

'But he can't! That's God's job!'

'No, Mrs Sally, no. It is science's. Already he's beginning to recall those shameful souvenirs he has hidden from his own cognisance at such great cost.'

'But, Enoch love, when were you ever a physician?'

'I'm not.'

'Then how is it you speak and act like one?'

'By imitation, of course.'

'But that means you must be a false doctor?'

'Entirely. That goes without saying, surely? For when have you ever met one that wasn't? After all, it is practice only that makes the physician. That and a certain even-handedness upon the part of providence to ensure that for every patient who dies at his hands there is another who will live despite his attentions. Besides, it diverts my mind to attempt this cure of Lord Spark. While I await delivery of that model of Mr Newton's triple glass. Oh, Sally, I cannot wait to see it! And meanwhile, between ourselves, the great work hangs fire a little until it arrives. Thus I have time to spare for Percy's predicament.'

There seemed to me something too coolly fish-like in this calculated argument. It smacked of that scientifical apartness from the common ruck of warm flesh and blood which was the least likeable aspect of Enoch's admittedly slippery character.

I said, 'Although Percy has used us badly, and others worse, I would not have him experimented upon.'

'Why not? My treatment may cure his affliction. If it does, that will be good. And if it doesn't, well, he'll be no worse off than he is now. Already he has the satisfaction of knowing that a remedy is at least being attempted, and that the world has not remained indifferent to his plight, which is perhaps the worst case for anyone. Ask him, if you doubt me. Enquire after his enforced and solitary exile in the Tropic of Capricorn upon the savage island of San Isidro where he considered himself abandoned by man and God.'

I didn't. The last thing I wished to hear was a sorry tale of life on a desert island. Rather my concern was with Enoch because it seemed to me that something of Lord Spark's daftness was now crossed over into him.

I said, 'Enoch, my dear, since by your own admission the great work stays somewhat in abeyance for the moment, can you not promise me you'll come to bed and sleep tonight? It may do you good.'

He hummed and ha-ed but eventually agreed that he might venture to leave Percy in charge of the laboratory that night, since, like all idiots, he had a great feeling for the sacred art. Yes, he would come.

With this assurance I quitted the laboratory and spent my time cooking a suckling pig in my kitchen and the accounts in my closet, so that Rusty would not notice the diversion of our whorehouse earnings into scientifical research. Pearl Street might, and did, appear to be a high-class private hotel but, at bottom, it was no better than Pudding Wharf – though far more profitable. The gaming tables alone outdid our Old World earnings.

Enoch was as good as his word, which was not always to be relied upon in one so humourous. He came promptly to supper and enjoyed my suckling pig – especially when he discovered among the potatoes (crisped to purest gold) roast apples cut in quarters – a trick I learned of Philippe. Attempt it, good reader, get it right, and I assure you that you will have achieved a *parvum opus* in your kitchen.

In bed I nursed him like a child and he fell asleep on my bosom and I was glad to see him slumber, because to be frank I feared for the wholeness of his mind. To state it plain, I did not care for his appointing of my sometime Lord Spark as his apprentice. Treat with lunacy and you yourself may become lunatic was my apprehension. Beyond that sentiment, of course, lay a wholesome disgust with Percival Wavenhoe, as we now should properly call him, given that he killed his father for the sole purpose of being known as such. No more *Lord Spark* was my motto. The pretty gallant of that title was quite dead to me.

Such were my wakeful thoughts as Enoch slept so peaceably upon me. Nor did I know how to resolve them and doubted if love at dawn would suffice to assuage them. It didn't. Enoch, however, begged me to forgive Percy, saying his crime against us was as nothing compared with his other misdemeanours. And beside the man was anxious to make amends. I answered that I was not so pliant by nature as he, but, as a Christian, I would try. At this he laughed (don't ask me why) and slipped downstairs to his laboratory, leaving me once more to my reflections. But these being of too sober a kind to endure for long I decided to banish them by sending for Rusty, only he was not to be found, having gone off upon a business errand. So, for lack of him, I was obliged to make do with a warm bath, a brisk towelling, unguents for my skin and teaching my new maid, a pretty blackamoor from Jamaica, how to dress my hair.

♂

Know what, squire? I've just bought the house next door. Well, last Friday week I did. Yeah, on Pearl Street. And, Jeez, did it cost me. I tell yer, property's booming down this end of the island. Like Manna Hatta's on the up and up. Arms 'n' legs ain't in it.

In two days I'd got it strengthened – the house I mean – like I slammed in these dirty big bars at the windows and hung iron doors back and front. Talk about a strong box – it's impregnable. And for why? Use yer head, squiress, 'cos it's gonna be a bank, innit? A lovely beautiful bank. My bank. Yeah. Like there's nothing like founding a bank, is there? Not for pure daylight robbery wivout fear of the Law. Nicely, as the high-class virgin said to the highwayman as he removed her most precious jewel.

Enoch was all for it but Sal's still against. She's got this old-fashioned idea charging interest is a sin. Dear old Sal, bits of her are so honest you could cry – when you ain't laughing. Though I reckon her objection really harks back to that diddling aristo what Enoch's got doing bird down in his lab. He says the bastard's repenting fast. He better be, otherwise it's the canvas sack, wiv him and a loada stones in it, over the side, right? Guggle, guggle. Like I've told Enoch this pot-herb's here only upon sufferance, and he's frigging answerable for the bastard's good behaviour because, between you and me, his showing up here has upset Sally. I don't think she likes us harbouring a patricide – especially one she once had a certain fancy for who yet cheated her (and us) rigid. Anyrate I've made up my mind if this Percy steps just once (just once!) outta line that'll be it, Enoch the Mind Bender notwithstanding, his lordship will join them other cadavers you occasionally clock at low tide.

But back to charm, *politesse* and money, or, to coin a phrase, this private bank next door to us in our very own knocking shop here upon Pearl Street. Enoch had the name for this new venture straight off. And it's struck just the right note – giving the customer confidence and fair warning at one and the same time. Yeah, we've just opened for business as the New World Bank of the Golden Fleece. And the town's flocking to us. The citizenry can't wait to leave their money in our care. Talk about trust. But then talk about the tempting terms we offer: total security, total anonymity, total profit (a rising scale of interest – the more you deposit the more it earns) and no questions asked. And guess who was our first customer? Councillor Ambrose no less. I twitted him, said, 'We can't wait for the ball, councillor. And why don't you tell your mate Arnold Jay Stone to bank wiv us? He won't get better terms nowhere.'

I can't say the shortarse laughed out loud at this jest but he smiled sorta sideways and said my bank better be as secure as I promised or else he'd have me run out of town.

My turn also to smile kinda slantwise, and I said, 'You can't go wrong at the Golden Fleece, matey. We're copper-bottomed. And how's Mrs Ambrose, still as lissom as a boy, is she?'

He didn't relish this remark neither, but he didn't withdraw his money, just himself. Our interest rates are far too interesting to be ignored, right? Like if I've said it once I've said it a hundred times: there's only one thing constant in this world – human greed. You can forget love. Beardless Cupid's got fuck all on hirsute cupidity.

So here we are, the proud owners of 13 *and* 14 Pearl Street, making yet more malooka. If I wasn't me I'd be embarrassed but as I am, I reckon I'm the real alchemist now. Yes, sir! Like I'd only have to pinch your bum, gorgeous readeress, for it to turn to solid gold. You wouldn't feel a thing, I promise. Though it could prove a mixed blessing. Yeah. Point taken. I'll refrain. But while we're at it you can put Enoch the So-Called Adept from your mind – like for good 'n' all. As the great worker he's got left standing at the post, right? Like he's history now. I mean you don't need art (sacred or otherwise) not when you've got craft, two cat-houses, a casino, thirty-six garbage waggons working round the clock, a race-course, betting shop and your very own bank full of other people's gelt. Not to mench a company of bodyguards meaner than any other bugger else's in town. Yeah. I do mean Arnold Jay's.

The which established, do not fail to recall that as and when we meet, I want respect, right? Mixed as ever wiv awe and plenty of it. Message received? Good. You can stop curtsying now, lady, and you, mister, you can let go of your forelock, General Rodney Mars, the four-star war hero and celebrated financier, is on his way. Keep crawling. Keep smiling. And – who knows? – you may yet qualify for a truly extortionate loan from the New World Bank of the Golden Fleece. Of course your life could be at risk if you fail to keep up your repayments. But I know you, don't I? An honest sucker and, like as wiv readers, there's one born every minute, correct? And you being you, you'll keep on paying up till you're bled to death, won't ya? And meanwhile, if she's at all presentable, I could well be shafting your missus, right? How it goes in this naughty world. Here's to iron in your soul, squire. See ya.

☿

Master Stella brought the scale model of my revered mentor's triple glass to my laboratory himself, bearing it in his own two hands. He said he had not dared entrust its complex, compounded fragility to another. Further he sincerely doubted if the piece might be employed as anything except an example of what might eventually be made. To test it could well be to break it.

Gazing upon the glass, once unpacked from its woodshavings, I tried to imagine it at its ideal size – at six times this extent and volume. It would be enormous. A giant thing. At least three times the size of that pretty bauble I'd invented at Pudding Wharf in the shape of *spiritus mercurialis* for the mere show of alchemy. Here was the model of a great machine with a mighty purpose – none less than the creation of the vital stuff of the universe according to alchemical principles. And Mr Newton's.

It looked quite pretty. Stella had made it of three hues of glass. The innermost vessel was yellow, the middle one, green and the outer, red. The glass employed was not, you may conceive, densely coloured – simply of a tinted translucency. For this glass was made with the manner of metal used commonly at Venice for the manufacture of wine goblets, flower vases and chandeliers.

Percy was struck with admiration. He walked round and round

about the bench on which the engine was placed exclaiming like a child at its form, its intricate construction – one glass inside another, how could that be? – and its beauty. Since, as so often happens, something made with purely scientifical intention can possess a certain grace.

He said, 'And all the glass so fine – it's like an onion made of ether. No, a triple bubble. Mayhap it could float upon the air?'

Stella and I laughed at his gentle idiocy. But fools and children (Percy was become both) often speak more expansive, even prophetical, truths than we are ready to admit. So it was with Percy, though none of us knew this at that time.

I said to my master Venetian, 'Do you think the glass of the outer vessel would accept a heat? And if so of what kind?'

'Of a most moderate kind. Possibly. But it must be most carefully supplied and achieve, let us say, no more intensity than that of a bed of charcoal glowing no brighter than a freshly caught red mullet.'

Now that's the trouble with Venetian masters of the blow glass trade – they will talk like adepts out of the time of Cornelius Agrippa or even that medieval Majorcan, Raymund Lull.

I made answer as a modern one. I said, 'A pretty figure of speech, Master Stella, but what heat is that exactly? Enough to vaporise those three waters within: the morning dew, the rainwater, the sea brine?'

'That, sir, I must leave you to discover but I believe it may. If you wish for another expression of the heat the vessel will endure, I would say it would fare best if placed upon heated sand. You have a sand furnace here, I dare say?'

'Two and a hay box – but that's only fit for coddling eggs or keeping a menstrue warm.'

We proceeded to inspect the sand furnaces behind which dwelt my pet snake – a rattler from the south. For snakes love ever to co-exist with the great work – some say they can smell gold in the making. Mine was a present from one of Sally's clients above. He swore it was harmless and I had had no cause to doubt him. Certainly Percy and the rattler got along most amicably together. Percy caught mice and cockroaches for him, and swore his name was Montezuma.

Montezuma was coiled about the second, more moderate furnace and then, when Stella had recovered his usual easiness after his sudden viewing of such a creature here at the very heart of New York, it was this furnace that he advised me to employ. I agreed gladly, since Montezuma's presence so close seemed to me in the nature of a happy augury for this first trial of Mr Newton's model glass.

I said, 'Will you not stay to observe the commencement of this experience?'

'I may not, sir. For I am obliged to wait upon Mrs Ambrose. She has ordered a further three dozen candlesticks and yet more wine glasses for the grand reception she is giving upon St Martin's day. If they are to be made in time we must settle all particulars this afternoon. The which reminds me, sir, may I present my bill for this toy? And also I must ask you for a further payment towards the building of the new workshop in which we are to construct the full-scale glass – God willing.' Here Stella crossed himself – but whether on account of this remark or the next he was to make I could not tell. But be that as it was he added, 'The masons, as honest a bunch of fellows as they are expert, are demanding another three hundred silver dollars, for that extra time they have expended beyond our first estimate, in the digging of the pits where we are to blow the new metal that will make up the almighty glass.'

I said, 'What extra time? And how has this come about?' But even while I expostulated I knew I should get back a plausible answer. With masons, worthy or otherwise, you invariably do.

Said Stella, just as I expected, 'The proposed ground proved full of rock that had to be split and pulverised in order to achieve the necessary depth. For you must know Manna Hatta is founded upon a sort of glistering schist – '

I intervened. 'I know that! And surely this was understood when the work was first surveyed and quantified?'

'It was, sir. But a clause was included in the contract to provide for such additional funding, as is now demanded, should the geological nature of the site tell against the original estimate of men's labour required to complete the excavations.'

I groaned. 'It seems you have learned this contract by rote, Master Stella?'

'It has been repeated to me many times by the chief mason, sir. Also I regret to say that my own researches into the firing of the new metal to make the giant glass have revealed that a more durable sort of brick will be required to – '

'Stop!' I cried. 'I've been here before at London when supervising the building of furnaces to make cannon balls! Dear God, it's ever thus when science and building enterprise go hand in hand. Now. Let us be clear. You say three hundred dollars is even this moment required, together with whatever these new bricks may cost – and at London the price was ruinous – but what I wish to know is will there be any more excesses – after these?'

'I fear there may, professor. Since we are ventured into *terra incognita*.'

'Yet I thought we were agreed a thousand dollars was a sum not merely sufficient but munificent?'

'So it was, sir, before we were started upon the project.'

I sighed, while knowing I had no choice but to pay. Even so I still protested like a Scotchman, telling Stella our masons were doubtless taking us for a ride in a coach and four – as Rusty might say. He agreed dolefully, and even as we complained together (for our argument was now become a mutual acquiescence with the inevitable) I was calculating how I might meet these extra costs.

I knew I could not hope to persuade Sally to any further expense since that guarantee of one thousand dollars had been hard enough to obtain in all conscience (and without it) and only upon condition that our cheating was concealed from Rusty. To ask her to do more so clandestinely would be too much. These further monies would therefore have to be got solely by me, and this implied, not to mince the matter, stealing them. But whence?

As I dwelt within this perplexity I discovered my eyes had fixed, as it were unseeingly yet apprehensively, upon that wall of the laboratory which lay adjacent to the house next door, which was just become the Bank of the Golden Fleece. Had not Rusty, I whispered inwardly to my inmost, mutable self, converted its lowest floor into the vaults wherein was kept a goodly proportion of New York's money, locked behind a door of steel?

Filled with this thought I found I had no need of further speculation. Instead I looked across at Percy who was still gazing with wonder at the glass. How strong and healthy he looked. His mind might not yet be of the best but his physical frame was quite recovered from its privations. His muscles, I surmised, could have been new-made for the job.

I said, 'Master Stella, you can tell the chief mason to continue with the works. He shall have the extra money by the end of this week at the latest. And that upon the word of a Welshman, a gentleman and an adept.'

With this triple assurance Stella departed, and I at once propelled Percy out upon an urgent errand to purchase a new hammer, four chisels, two sacks, a peck of lime and a bucket. I did not, however, divulge my purpose to him, nor did he ask it. His trust in me was become as profound as it was necessary. But this did not mean he might not blab, like a child, to others.

When he was gone I was at last at liberty to admire Mr Newton's model glass for myself. Like Percy I too was entranced. It possessed such an air. Perhaps the fact that it was a miniature of my master's ultimate machine gave it this peculiar charm? For all things large – or projected to be so – seem to win unto themselves an especial piquancy when reproduced in little. I had seen at Pisa in Italy certain wooden models of an architect for the great dome of the baptistry there and been beguiled by the comparison of small with great. And my former instructor in the martial art of judo (that sage of Nippon at Cambridge) had a sort of oak tree of great age – two hundred years or more, he avowed – that was gnarled, stag-headed, beautiful and grew out of a dish not two inches deep. It had attained a height of a mere thirteen inches and a spread of ten. Even its leaves by some oriental miracle seemed in proportion with its ancient trunk and knuckled roots. It was a tiny wonder. I had often stood in admiration of it before going to the mat to be thrown yet again over his shoulder.

Even so did I now gaze upon this present object. But after a while philosophical curiosity overcame aesthetical gaping and I determined to test it upon that moderate sand furnace embraced about by Montezuma. But first I had to introduce the three separate waters into it. They were to hand, kept ready in sealed jars for just this moment. The morning dew I had collected in the manner described in the *Mutus Liber* some weeks before the first snow of winter fell, the rainwater came from the waterbutt and I had made an expedition to Nut Island to be sure of seawater free from any unwelcome effluent peculiar to Manna Hatta.

The induction of these waters required a certain dexterity since the three vessels were hermetically sealed save for the six spouts. However with patience, care and the use of an ink horn made into a funnel (thoroughly boiled clean of all impurities and with its tip sawn off) I was enabled to prepare the machine for the experiment.

I carried it across and in a fit of superstition I begged leave of Montezuma to place it upon the sand. He didn't shake a rattle, allowing me to place the glass entirely as I wished. He did, however, yawn most elastically. Naught else occurred either without or within the glass for an hour or so when I perceived a pretty internal misting within each vessel so that the colours of them were rendered somewhat opalesque. Distillation was begun and in due course the glass bowls placed below the six spouts might expect to receive the first droplets of what could conceivably become that essence out of which all earthly things were first made. We would see.

I say we because Percy was now returned with his purchases and thus I had got all things necessary for my next business. But first I had to gain his attention. It wasn't easy. All he wished to do was to sit before Mr Newton's glass and wait for it to bubble. I told him he might sit there all night before that happened and in the interim he was to be employed elsewhere. On the other side of the laboratory. He would, however, be allowed to return at intervals to rest before the glass.

Inveigled thus I got him across to the opposite wall where I was now obliged to open my secret intention to him.

I said, 'Percy, sit down upon that bucket I sent you out for and listen. You may turn it upside down if you prefer.'

He said, 'Yes, professor,' but I saw his eyes swivel sideways.

'Now listen with care and you may view the glass again in half an hour. For the moment there's nothing to be seen in it.'

'Very good, professor. I'm all ears really.'

'I hope so. For I require no singing whilst I speak, no breaking of wind, no rolling of the eye, no biting of the nails, and no rotation of the backside on that bucket.'

'Yes, professor. But I haven't sung all day, have I? Nor farted save once.'

'You have hummed. And you have belched. But to the purpose which shall, I hope, incline your mind to mine – for I intend to speak of the pretty glass you so admire and also of another.'

'Another?' he exclaimed and it was as if his whole being was suffused with light.

Now had I won his true attention. I said, 'Oh, yes, Percy, there is another glass yet to be made. This toy we make trial of today is but a model of an ultimate engine.'

'What's that?' said he.

'The same only bigger.'

'How big?'

'Six times.'

'In every part?'

'In every part. Or to scale as we should say.'

'But that'll make a glass taller than me – for I'm six feet save for half an inch. And much wider. For while I'm broad of shoulder I am slim bellied, whereas the glass is of its nature round as a ball or Spanish onion or a lady quick with child.'

'The device will appear yet greater and more gravid when set upon a bench.'

'Can such a mighty thing be made, professor?'

'Master Stella is determined to attempt the work. And so am I. But to do this I require your help, Percy.'

227

'Mine? How can I, a poor castaway, help? "All alone that's me by the coconut tree— ".'

Despite my admonition he had broken once again into song. I said sternly, 'Percy, desist! You can help by remembering what I said: no singing. And also by swearing to keep secret what I'm about to tell you. What d'you hold most sacred, Percy? For it's upon that you must swear.'

He fidgeted, sighed, looked up, looked down but not round – he had learnt that lesson – and spoke. He said, 'I dare not say, professor.'

'Why not? We have each other's confidence, have we not? I shall keep yours if you swear to keep mine.'

Still he hesitated, looking boyishly abashed. He even blushed and for an instant I feared his eyes might roll again but he or they remembered themselves in time. Finally, when he answered his voice was all a-tremble. 'There's only one thing I value more than all the world, professor, more than myself, more than life. Though she is not a thing at all, but a warm and sentient being, and I have lost her for ever.' He bowed his head and wept. I let him weep, considering such tears a powerful physic for his condition. After a moment he looked up, blew his nose neatly between finger and thumb (a knack he had perfected for want of handkerchiefs upon San Isidro) and said in one whole breath, 'I will swear upon her name although I fear to pronounce it lest I incur your wrath and I would not have you angry with me because it is thanks to you that I am almost as I was long since before fate and my mother enticed me into evil.'

'Percy,' said I gently. 'I promise you I shall not be wrath with you whomsoever you name.'

'You are sure, professor? For I know you also hold her dear.'

'I swear to you by every toad in this laboratory. I cannot say fairer than that, Percy. For they are as sacred to me as that she you're about to name.'

'You know who it is?'

At this I was tempted to say 'don't be silly' but as he was I didn't. It would have been, as we modern adepts say, neither constructive nor productive. Instead I glanced across at my family of *Bufonidae*, now grown to seven in all. They dwelt in a sodden half-barrel kept moist with a mix of earth and horse dung out of which the occasional fungus sprouted to serve my toads in that very manner which afforded the thing its name.

I said, 'Come along, sir. Swear. I have, so now you may.'

He gulped once, twice and blushed anew. 'I swear,' he whispered in a voice the like of which Lazarus might have employed upon being raised from the dead. 'I swear by Mrs Sally, my dearest Mrs Sally, that I shall keep your secret, professor. What is it?'

To put a plain question directly is ever the prerogative of the wise, of course. It will more often than not flummox the foolish. But here was a fool confounding the wise *viz*. me. For while I was obliged to reveal my purpose to him I was nevertheless sensible that Percy, however sacred an oath he had sworn, might yet, without meaning to, betray it. Was he truly recovered? Could he not relapse at any time? Might I not have flattered myself, thinking to have achieved more than I had? This last doubt was the worst because it is also frequently thus with the sacred art. I hate to say it but we enquirers all too often deceive ourselves. Had I not, in my years of disillusion, perceived, in almost every text I had read for Mr Newton, evidence of this? Claim after claim to successful projection had been made across time and the world, but each and every one was invariably cloaked in the fanciful language of the self-deceived. *Ergo*, might it not be equally so with Percy?

Yet this admitted I was bound to risk it. I thanked him for having given his solemn word and assured him that since Mrs Sally meant so much to both of us this made our compact the more binding, awful and dreadful. He nodded, tremblingly.

I continued thus, 'Why do you suppose I sent you out to buy these utensils, Percy?'

'I don't know, professor. All I could think of was not to lose the list nor the money you gave me.'

'And now? Seeing them placed here?' I looked from the hammer and chisels to the wall in front of us. Percy followed my gaze but it was clear his mind could discern no connective principle between them. Instead he rose, rubbing his buttocks. I said rather more sharply, 'Think, man! Or has all your cognisance descended to your bum?'

Percy thought. Then he smiled. He said, 'You mean to build a wall without bricks, professor.'

I did not know whether to laugh or cry. Instead I answered that he was almost right, that the wall before us was to be breached by the judicious use of the chisels this very night, the bricks being preserved with care so they might be put back in place, secured by a mortar made from the lime he had bought and the sand I already possessed. And the entire labour was to be completed by dawn. Indeed we should make a start at once since I had only now falsely advised all at Pearl Street that the great work had reached a crucial stage and that no one might visit the laboratory for the next twelve hours upon any pretext whatsoever. Had he not noticed me bolt and bar the door?

Percy said, 'But why must we breach the wall?'

'To reach the other side, sir. For within the space beyond lies that which I have need of, if the great glass I mentioned just now is to be made.'

'But what's that you need, professor?'

'Money, Percy, money.'

'We're to break open the wall and take money?'

'Exactly.'

Here occurred a mighty hiatus between us. A chasm or vast such as Mr Milton's Satan was tumbled into never to hope again. Well, haply I overstate a little but it was certainly a momentous pause.

I broke it, saying, 'What's the matter, sir?'

Percy was shaking. Was this the very crisis I had feared? Would I soon be wishing he had never been rescued from that desert island?

He said, 'I cannot touch money, professor.'

'You needn't. I shall remove the money. I merely require your help in making a hole in the wall and then bricking it up again.'

'Nor can I be a party to theft.'

'Nonsense,' cried I. 'Look what you stole from us at Pudding Wharf!'

'But I've repented, professor. And I've sworn to myself, also in Mrs Sally's name, that I shall never steal anything ever again. My mind may still be deranged here and there but upon this resolution it is firm. In this regard at least I am reformed.'

'Oh, dear,' said I. 'I thought you were the perfect criminal for the job. What shall we do?'

'I am truly sorry, professor, but I hope you will respect this my newly recovered honesty?'

'Of course, of course, man,' said I, with a certain testiness. How inconvenient virtue can be! 'You'll be telling me next you want to join the Brethren of Old Amsterdam. They have a ministry here, I fear.'

'I have considered it, professor, when especially in the dumps.'

'I have it!' I exclaimed, stopping him before he became any more scrupulous. 'You cannot and you shall not be party to a crime, Percy. I will not allow it.'

'Thank you, professor.'

'And yet you can help me in the work.'

'How?'

'By doing what I've just said, of course.'

'But, professor – '

'But me no buts. My mind is also firm upon this matter. You can and shall remain honest because here is no crime at all. The wall belongs to me and so does that money we are going to borrow, as it were. After all, it is deposited in a bank of which I am incorporated director – unlike you when at London you merely made pretence of being such a responsible person three times over.'

'But if it's not a crime, professor, why can't you borrow it openly, counted out upon the table?'

I sighed. The man was becoming more lucid by the minute. 'Because, Percy, I do not require my fellow director, Captain Steele now promoted General, to know of it.'

'And Mrs Sally? Does she know?'

Here was no moment for indecision. In the instant I lied forcibly. 'Oh, yes, Percy. She is party to the plan, approves it heartily, and has asked particularly that you play your part in it. She believes the exercise will improve your condition.'

This last invention did it. Percy smiled. The man was won over. He said, 'Mrs Sally asked especially for me?'

'She named you by name. And if I'm any judge I believe her heart has softened a little towards you.'

'You think so?' His eyes shone with satisfaction.

'Just a little. And the more conscientiously you help me in this delicate task tonight the more I shall be able to inform her tomorrow how right she was and how much you are improved. Who knows I may even be able to say you are become as your old self again when you were a careless gallant at Oxford?'

'Give me the chisels,' shouted Percy. But before I could do this he had already seized them and was attacking the wall with enormous strength in the wrong place. I directed him to the correct one – three courses up from ground-level beside the main bastion or pier which supported the middle weight of these adjoined buildings. I further instructed him to work circumspectly so no reverberation would be heard above. After ten minutes or so he had got the method of it, had chipped out the mortar all around the first brick which came loose with comparative ease, thus making the removal of the next yet more convenient and so on.

I kept after him with dustpan and brush, tipping the old mortar into one of the sacks, and continually advising him that we must proceed as busily yet as discreetly as moles and that this was not the time for singing while we worked, even if the song he now kept breaking into was the 'Silver Swan' by Mr O. Gibbons and not his usual doggerel chant. I also adverted him that when the sack was filled he would be required to take it to one of Rusty's many garbage cribs on the sea-shore since it was essential that we rid ourselves of all evidence of this enterprise as soon as we possibly could.

At three o'clock by the watch (how their rattles clattered) we had broken through, all the bricks were cleaned and preserved for replacement without the breaking of a single one, and the sack was full of old mortar. We also had a neat passage through to the vault of the Bank of the Golden Fleece which my gold-mining father would have been proud of. It was just of a proportion to admit a supple person – to wit, me.

Having sent Percy off with the sack of mortar I took a candle and proceeded through our aperture. Or rather, to speak more accurately and less generally I wormed, wriggled, and shifted my way through it. This manoeuvre achieved I rose to my feet and surveyed the vault.

It was stacked high with coffers, chests, trunks, and several small casks. These last I supposed had been deposited by the town's Chinese traders (of whom there was a handful) and doubtless contained either opium or tea, both commodities being almost as valuable as gold.

I selected three coffers that were of a size that would pass through to my laboratory, together with a pretty travelling chest. The trunks were too large and, besides, their absence would have been immediately evident. I preferred to order my haul so that to the unsuspicious eye nothing whatsoever would seem to have been removed.

I pulled them through to the laboratory – no easy task and as I performed it I regretted the loss of Percy's help. But I had sent him out at that time most deliberately, calculating that, faced too closely with the stacks of money boxes, he might well suffer another attack of the scruples. True, his shoulders might not have passed the hole anyway, but he could have seen through well enough, and my candle would have haply illuminated other people's property rather too well; thus bringing about the aforesaid contrition I had no need of at all.

Once I had recovered my breath and dusted myself down I took a chisel to the coffers and soon had their hasps prized out of their housings. I felt like a vulgar burglar which, of course, despite my representations to Percy, I was. Yet I felt no shame. Did not my end, the furtherance of science, justify my means? I know there are many who will object to this argument, but they are mere Christians, while at that moment I was all pagan. As urgent as an ancient god, which to some degree, I was. And still am.

I gazed on gold and silver – mostly Spanish and Portuguese coin but intermingled with pieces from England, France, Holland, Belgium, Sweden. For you must know that this eastern coast of the New World was, by this time, increasingly populous with bold adventurers from these five nations, while Spain and Portugal still invested the south with their substantive powers, albeit by now eroding. Already we had got Jamaica off Don Diego, first by force, then by treaty.

Here were funds enough to build Master Stella's workshop ten times over, but this did not prevent me broaching the other smaller chest. My guess of it was correct – it was undeniably a lady's jewel case. And I regarded its contents with far more surmise than I had looked upon the money. Money, after all, is merely a means for change. While here was a heap of miracles! Here was a wonder. An equal to the intricacy of Mr Newton's glass. Nay more so, for in this pretty box, cushioned in velvet, lay nature's rarest stones: emeralds, sapphires, rubies, diamonds (though the pure carbons were much outnumbered by the crystalline aluminae and the green beryls). Here also were huge amethysts – said to be a proof against intoxication. Not to mention great strings and bands of pearls. And all these were made up in necklaces, pendants, collars, brooches, bracelets, finger-rings, ear-rings, toe-rings, studs and buckles. Nor was there one stone of any pretension not set in gold or silver, or both, so curiously wrought and so cunningly worked that you might say the history of this jackdaw world in all its acquisitive richness was presented here.

Holding a great emerald to the candle's light I told myself even Master Stella's manufactures could never match this thing for intensity of colour married to translucence. The same went for the rubies that ranged from palest rose to a crimson close to purple; while the sapphires and diamonds were as blazing stars and might scarcely be compared with glass at all; they were as from another sphere of knowing.

So lost was I in contemplation of this precious hoard that I did not at first hear the knock upon the door. But I did hear my apprentice's voice as next he called most urgently.

'Oh, please, professor, it's Percy! Please let me in!'

Hurriedly I shut the jewel case (for I had no wish for him to see it) and pushed it out of sight. Only then did I unbar the door.

Percy tumbled in upon me, shaking and shivering – half in tears, half in laughter. In a word, hysterical. 'Oh, professor,' he babbled. 'Oh, professor, I've seen a vision. I'm one of the blessed! You must believe me. Oh, such a vision!'

I barred the door again. And said, as scientifically as I possibly could, 'A vision of what?'

'Of her! Of Mrs Sally. Oh.'

He sat himself down, hugging his knees to his chest like a child or greenhorn.

233

'Where?'

'She was descending the main stair.'

'At this time in the morning?'

'She was in a rare nightgown. It floated about her like a cloud.'

'Did she see you?'

'Oh, no, professor. I stood behind the great cupboard in the hall. At first I did not recognise her. To tell true I thought she was an angel or at the very least the Virgin Mary.'

'Our Sally the Virgin Mary? Are you a Papist, Percy?'

He nodded. 'But a sadly lapsed one, professor.'

'Then how could you even consider turning Anabaptist?'

'By lapsing further.'

I had had enough of this foolishness. I said curtly, 'Well, thank heaven you had the sense to conceal yourself.'

'To see her again,' he continued all a-wash with satisfaction. 'And in such a guise – just risen from her bed, in such a sweet disorder. I tell you, professor, her golden hair was all undone, and the stuff of her gown was so fine I could see –'

'Enough, Percy!' cried I in something close to rage, and a furious jealous rage at that. 'I have no need of any lewd observations. Come, sir, there's still much work to be done and you must start upon it now! This very instant!'

Such peremptoriness recalled him to his more everyday senses which, while yet imperfect, had not, until now, so far as I knew, been imbued with libidinous fancies or lascivious yearnings. Evidently my cure of Percy was proving all too effective if he was now, once more, become a prey to lust. Well, there was a remedy for that. Hard labour. And plenty of it. I would, I determined, transmute his animal spirits into copious, honest sweat.

Consumed thus with a righteous indignation instigated by a primitive jealousy (how dare he leer at my Sally, let alone presume to describe her charms) I hectored and bullied poor Percy into mixing the mortar and laying the bricks. In this he also needed instruction since, being brought up a lordling, he had no practical skills. He had not been obliged as I had in my earlier days to eke out a living as a poor sizar by turning builder's mate in the vacations. Nor serve as a waiting man in some greasy eating-house, nor even, all one summer, labour in the fields cutting corn – an occupation that may look idyllic to the passers-by in their carriages, but is as ticklish a business and quite as tedious and sweatful as working a treadmill, another trade I experienced when naught else stood between me and famine.

But enough of history, which stinks as surely as mankind's

234

unredeemed condition, and let us return to the present which at least has the merit of presupposing a future, never mind what.

No sooner had I got Percy fully instructed in his task, and bent to it, than there was another knock at the door. And whereas before I had expected someone, *videlicet* Percy, returned from his second errand, now I had no advisement of anyone, and was therefore the more constrained or, as some would say, embarrassed. Who might it be? Not Rusty I hoped.

I called out, 'Yes? What would you?'

'It's me, Sally.'

'But I gave you fair warning. The great work may not be interrupted.'

'I know you did, my dear. But I couldn't sleep – the moon being at full – so I came down to prepare you and Percival a refreshment. A hot toddy of rum, sugar and cinnamon. I thought even an adept and his assistant might be in need of such a sustenance at this hour of the morning, after a night of watching over your furnaces and glasses.'

To say my heart went out to Sally for her solicitude would be to blow too cold. Excepting Percy and my subterfuge I would have pulled open the door at once, seized the toddy, swallowed it in one gulp, and embraced her forthwith. What a woman. Goddess, lover, mother. Could any philosopher ask for more?

But within the stricture or bind of this present circumstance what was I to do? Quick thinking, charm, and duplicity were now in instant demand. I had need of all three. And suddenly.

I said, 'My dear, so evanescent, so delicate, so complex is this process I dare do no more than pull the door ajar for a second so you may pass me the toddy. And I must needs shut it again since the slightest draught could well alter the ambient atmosphere and put all my scientifical art at hazard.'

'Then stop blathering, Enoch, and do it! The drink is growing cold and so am I!'

Trust Sally to have a stout reply. I did as I had proposed, taking care to block any view Percy might have of her, and took the toddy. But, by God, she was the vision he had remarked so profoundly, and it was with the utmost effort of will, such as only pure scientists may command, that I kept my word and shut the door in her face, by the expedient of turning swiftly yet smoothly, so as not to spill the drink, and pushing it to with my backside. Not a gallant nor an orthodox proceeding, I agree, but with my hands full what else could I do? And all the while I thanked her profusely with my rump as doorstop, bolt and bar.

Said she, through the door, 'What are all those bricks? And I smelt mortar already mixed. What work is this? For it's surely not alchemy, is it?'

As I placed the toddy upon a convenient surface (that of a hogshead full of bat dung), I invented yet another falsehood to amalgamate with my initial mendacities. Since, as my mother always said – and she, you may recall, was the third-wisest woman in Merionydd – she used to say: A proper lie needs many legs to stand upon.

I said, with my hands now free to bar the door, and in my severest, grandest, professorial tones, 'My dear Sally, the bricks are placed in readiness, with the mortar mixed, so that at the moment of projection, when the Doves of Venus descend and the Green Lion roars at the Black Eagle while the Great Snake Uroborus eats his own tail, my apprentice – none other than the Earl of Wavenhoe, a repentant patricide – and I can stop up the flue of Mighty Athanor, our fiercest furnace, so that the fire within may also, with an infinite desuetude and an ineffable gentleness, consume itself. Only by these means may we produce projection.'

'Is that the truth, Enoch? For I know you. You'll say anything, bespeak any name, to get your own way.'

'I promise you, my dear.'

'Very well, Enoch. I suppose I must believe you but I don't really. I think you're up to something. You always are when you speak runically.'

Hearing this, it was as plain as the day that was already suffusing the laboratory with its snow-refracted light that I must stand yet more firmly upon the sacred nature of my calling. I said in a voice stuffed full of fruit as a college plum duff, 'Madam, the *magnum opus* calls me. I wish you good morrow.'

'Then don't ask for breakfast. There won't be any,' was Sally's short answer, and I heard her sob as she fled upstairs. I sighed. How hateful it is to misinform one's soulmate. But I had had no choice. The great glass required funding and that was that. I turned to see how Percy was proceeding. He wasn't. He lay as one dead.

Hurrying to him and slapping his cheeks with furious resolution it was soon apparent that he had merely fainted. At my repeated pummelling his eyes opened, his lips reverberated and a burble of ridiculous words emerged to the effect that to hear his angel speak even to another had been such bliss that his soul had fled away etcetera to that empyrean where love was infinite and he and Mrs Sally blah blah could dwell in perpetual harmony with the spheres and so on.

236

Detesting such sentiment I said, 'Drink this.' And handed him the toddy. It worked wonders. For him and then for me. In a trice we were revived completely. The long night and its labours seemed as nothing and those that remained mere trifles. I blessed Sally inwardly and straightway urged poor Percy onward like a slave driver and by eight o'clock the work was done. The wall was as it was.

I cannot call our endeavour a great work but it certainly provided gold. Not to mention silver and a hoard of jewels beyond price, which I vowed I would bestow upon Sally at some ripe moment in the future. Rusty's bank had produced the goods. I had got the means. Now all that remained was the end.

♀

We went in two by two. You'd have thought Councillor Ambrose's residence (ablaze with light) was the mighty ark itself and us the simple animals. Me on Rusty's arm, Lucille on Enoch's. Other guests before and behind. Oh, the pretensions of Councillor, would-be Mayor, Septimus Ambrose – yes, that was his first name, and the man certainly lived up to it, being quite evidently, despite his display, the runt of the family litter. Rusty had told me he was a shortarse and Rusty was right. As for Abednego, well, I still cannot bring myself to call him Mrs Marigold, which was how the boy now wished, in his elevation, to be addressed. Such things go against nature, don't they? Well, with me they do.

Once we were got into the house (the grandest upon the canal) we were obliged to wait in a line to be welcomed by our hosts. What a crush of people. *Le tout New York* as Lucille said. And all of us in our best. I doubt the palace of St James ever saw such show. My peach-silk dress was at the very height of fashion. For all its expense I wore it negligently, especially at the bosom, where it was quite unlaced. I looked as if I had just been surprised at my *toilette*, when in fact my preparations had been completed two hours before. But the manners of the time demanded this indecency, as of a nymph surprised, which suited my charms to perfection, since I have ever been happy to parade them and never more so than on that night when I had determined to bedazzle all the world, but most particularly Mrs Abednego Ambrose, whose chest was as false as his fanny – to coin a similitude worthy of Rusty, or indeed my parents, who, you may call to mind, were as rustic as he and I are now cosmopolitan.

But I must confess I had a hard time outshining our girls. What a

237

cloud of loveliness they were. Any one of them was fit to bemuse a chapel full of Baptists; let alone a regiment. The which they did that night. For although the rumoured boat of bachelor rakehells from England never arrived (reality having a cruel knack of qualifying imagination) nevertheless a company of the Duke of St Albans's Fusiliers, a newly raised regiment, already known as Nell Gwyn's bastards, had that very morning disembarked at the East Side so they might garrison the fort and safeguard the town in the name of Old Rowley, St Albans's natural father.

Thus it was that these military gentlemen, who had never yet been tried in action nor suffered any fire worse than a shuttlecock, were on hand to make as fine a show in their way as my girls (how possessive I am become) did in theirs. And to debauch them if they could. Which, I regret to say, they did. But that is the Somerset widow and Virginia matron in me speaking rather than my inmost self – the cheerful country slut newcome to town. Let it merely be said my girls had a wonderful time and New York was left recklessly undefended while its population was vigorously augmented. Seven of my sweetest and prettiest were got with child – the rest being luckier than they deserved. The poor lambs had in due course to be returned in tears to their dismayed families and I was obliged to train replacements for them. What burdens Dame Nature can supply.

Rusty was resplendent in black velvet and foaming lace. Never had I seen him look so commanding. We were announced as General Mars and Mrs Bancroft – my widow's title which was as correct as Rusty's rank and style were not. And stepped forward to be welcomed by our hosts. Septimus Ambrose looked like a fighting bantam cock while you will not expect me to describe Abednego with any degree of impartiality. Yet even so I shall try to speak fair. What artifice could do had been done. The boy, in ruffled rose pink, looked perfectly delicious, no question of it, but not precisely as a woman might. There is a subtle difference in travesty, is there not? A faint air of derision. Of the fair sex (or rather the imitation of us) as a closet joke rather than a natural delight. A sort of titillating parody. Venery as foppish giggle. But Abednego, while unavoidably displaying some traces of these obliquities, nevertheless in candlelight looked almost entirely a woman, even to me. Perhaps he owed this near perfection to his years of practice when in disguise with Enoch? And at this thought I could not quell a shiver of repugnance. You may call me old fashioned but if the goddess in me may not be, who can?

Following the manners of the guests ahead I curtsyed to my hosts. But I held Abednego's eye and let mine fall to where his breast, well covered with lace, swelled proudly enough. But he knew what my look signified.

He blushed and said, looking deep into my *décolletage*, 'Why, madam, do you not fear to catch cold?'

'No, Mrs Ambrose,' answered I, laughing and tossing my ringlets so my best ear-rings chattered like magpies. 'No, I ever bask in the admiration of real men.'

A whore's riposte, I know, but then a residue of jealousy of the boy lingered in my heart, and I was only too aware that Enoch was behind me with Lucille, for whom he did not care one jot. To say I feared that upon their reacquaintance old Egyptian embers might be rekindled into new flames would be to exaggerate, but even so the thought was present deep within me. Rusty often tells me, in his tactless but heartfelt way, that I am the only one of his molls he has ever felt jealous of. It is much the same for me with Enoch.

And all this while Councillor Ambrose and Rusty were laughing and joking as if they were honest friends rather than scheming rivals for power in the town. To observe and hear them you might have supposed they were the best and closest of old pals and that neither would be anything but immoderately loyal to the other. To witness this was, for me, to be reminded of how Rusty and Monty Cruikshank had conversed together before their true interests were discovered to be in a most violent opposition.

After this necessary encounter with our host we were free to admire the house and enjoy the supper laid out upon buffets in the great apartment while beyond, in the ballroom, a band was already at work providing a harmonious but indifferent music.

All about us voices and laughter rose as the wine flowed (not to mention the beer and the whiskey – this being the New World) and very soon it was impossible further to hear the announcement of names in the hall without, albeit the major-domo shouted them at the air with a town crier's robustness. And so it was that neither Rusty nor I, let alone Enoch, heard the introduction of several persons of some pertinence to our enjoyment of the ball which Rusty afterwards accounted a great success while Enoch and I both considered it had been a rather more mixed affair.

But here we were, at least to start with, making small talk between bows and curtsies to our fellow guests – almost all of whom were known to all of us. My talk with Lucille was as always double-edged, since we had not only Rusty in common, but the girls as well. And while, at the academy, Lucille was responsible for their mind's exercise, I, at Pearl Street, cared for their bodies' deportment. Nor would it be a vain boast to say that thanks to their dancing lessons they were become swans rather than geese. Already they were receiving compliments from the Colonel of the Fusiliers and his fellow officers, who were no way behind their commander in preening their moustaches and uttering acceptable obscenities to well-bred young ladies. And they in their turn were responding with speaking eyes and pert mouthings as if they had got the art of it from my Lady Castlemaine herself – the trollop.

Supper was taken standing which led inevitably to an increase in the consumption of liquor, especially among the men. For it is a commonplace that at a seated supper rather more is eaten than drunk whereas at a stand-up revel the opposite is the case. Also the company becomes as moveable as the feast. So it was that night, and pretty soon Rusty had moved off to confer with various bigwigs (though his outdid them all) while Lucille had found several cronies to gossip with, leaving me with an old gallant who could talk of nothing but the activities of the perfidious Dutch in the South Seas – wherever they were. Enoch was by this time also departed, having slipped away to talk business with his glassmaker.

Consequently I was at leisure to adjudicate upon the board itself. And for all its show and profusion I am bound to report, speaking as a cook, that it was less than perfectly executed. The six potted meats were indistinguishable one from another; the twelve *hors d'oeuvres* insipid; the five broths neither hot nor cold; the eight roasts and fourteen different vegetables good – here was honest cooking with little or no pretension; the fish and salads decent but their sauces and dressings coarse; and as for the twenty-five various pastries – oh, dear. While the hired cooks' *fromages glacés*, or what are now commonly called iced creams, were, let me be charitable, little more than tepid curds and whey by the time they reached the tables, not frozen at all, despite the winter weather and enough snow falling to pack a hundred ice chests.

But the wines, my aged companion informed me, were excellent, whereat he hiccoughed until his eyes watered and someone pinched my bottom.

I turned. Who was this? And how dare he? Did he take me for some tuppenny ha'penny whore? Or what?

The man was laughing. And what a man. He looked like the master of a privateer. His left leg below the knee was of solid oak shod with steel, his left eye covered by a purple patch and his left hand whole, but the skin of it seared to polished leather. His periwig was jet-black, his coat of blood-red silk velvet cut in the Persian fashion, all his lace at collar and cuffs as white and crisp as snow new fallen and he stood with an elegant negligence supported by his sword in its sheath for a walking stick.

The next instant the twist of his smile and the set of his nose proclaimed him to me. I cried out in amaze, 'Monty Cruikshank!'

'The same, Mrs Sally.' And he bowed and kissed my hand.

But then I knew not what to say. My initial astonishment had quite overwhelmed any other emotion but now it was gone I was at a stop. What ought I to feel towards this spectre from the past? So different, so handsome and yet so clearly still himself? Monty Cruikshank, Sheriff of Pudding Ward, Rusty's old friend and enemy, my occasional lover – mostly for reasons of business since our enterprise was upon Monty's ground but I must confess I never had any deep distaste for him, he was ever a persuasive fellow. But now he looked if anything even better, despite these injuries he wore so carelessly. Here was a most vital cripple – a distinguished veteran of that battle Rusty had told me of once we were reunited in Virginia. Monty seemed to me to have something about him of Mr Betterton playing Richard Crookback. And we all know what happened to his paramour, Lady Anne. And across the corpse of her husband, too. No wonder I felt of a sudden weak at the knees.

I said, drawing careful breath, 'What brings you here, Monty?'

'Business, dear Sally, business.' And he winked his good eye.

'Have you seen Rusty?'

He guffawed heartily. 'Not yet. But I hear he's among us and terms himself General Rodney Mars. Quite a promotion from Captain Steele. What a fraudster. I can't wait to see his face when he sees me. Yours was a picture, Sally. How is the old bastard?'

'Oh, very well. Full of Boston beans and New York bounce. But I must warn you he speaks nothing but ill of you. He may be thick as a barn door but his memory's that of an elephant.'

My advertisement had no effect at all. Monty simply grinned. 'Oh, I'm sure he calls me every name under the sun. He would. And I've called him a few in my time, too. Especially when they had to have my leg off. It was his *grenado's* doing, you know? And the eye. Ever tell you of it, did he?'

I demurred, as we say. 'He has mentioned something of that affair but then again I'm ever inclined to think all's fair in love and war.'

'Me too, my dear. My very own way of thinking. And that was why, as Sheriff of Pudding Ward, I refrained from pursuing Rusty to the scaffold though I could have done so on many counts. And no question he'd have swung.'

'So I have believed.'

'But I didn't because as you say, all's fair. With Rusty, yes, it was war, but with you, dear Sally, it was love.' And he smiled his naughtiest smile.

Now was my chance to laugh. 'Never love, Monty, not with you. Just appetite. A lawman's love of a free fumble in the course of duty. Admit it.'

'Very well, if you say so, Sally. But I know otherwise. You were ever good value and if I'd been Rusty I'd have done to me just what he did. Given what I'd done to him. Besides his business down on the Isle of Dogs – oh, what a choice one! What a depot. I won't say a gold mine, but I will say a silver mine. Oh, yes. Yes, Sally, yes. Especially the cannon balls. The whole enterprise has made me a mint, I can tell you. Still does. And that's why I'm here. I've got to use the money, employ it, spread it about, get into other commodities such as furs, sotweed, ambergris. I mean this is the New World, right? And we all want a piece of it – correct?'

I couldn't help smiling. I hadn't heard another man sound so like Rusty (only a trifle superior) since I'd left London five long years before. No wonder he and Monty had been such mates. They were both London born and bred in the bone of the place. The Bow Bells variety, and to me, oh, quite delicious. Talk Cockney to me and I'm vaporised, as Enoch would say. I'm at your feet. A-wobble. Like I said – the country cunny just come to Town in '68 and wanting all of it.

Monty added, 'I bet I can still out-piss Rusty. What do you think, Sally?'

I laughed but now I had sobered a little. Recalling the past is all very well but the present is what we've got and upon reflection at that particular moment I rather doubted if Rusty would be as full of loving forgiveness as Monty appeared to be.

I said, 'Rusty may have escaped the rope but he was still transported to Virginia, Monty. But for me he'd still be there, working in the tobacco fields. Yet now he's chief banker to the town. And you must come to my house on Pearl Street – my girls are most distinguished. Also accomplished. Many are here tonight.'

Even as I said this my glance fell upon Arabella giggling immoderately as a fusilier lieutenant tipped a glass of Canary into her open mouth. Much of it spilled upon her chin, neck and bosom and had to be mopped up most tenderly by the lieutenant's lace handkerchief.

Monty said, 'She one of yours?' I nodded. 'Still the same old Sally?'

I nodded again. 'Seeing you, Monty, has confirmed it.'

He laughed, kissed my hand and then the inside of my wrist, quite unnecessarily. 'And I'm still the same old Monty,' he said. 'Nothing like old times, old – '

I cut him short. 'That's enough of the *old*,' said I. 'I am still but five and twenty.'

'And the grandest madam in New York, I hear?'

'The only madam, sir. The rest are mere bawds and strumpets fit for nothing but the pox-doctor.'

'I may believe it. For you ever kept a neat house, Sally. Your nuns were clean as whistles. And that reminds me, our host tells me you still have that other fellow about you? The Welshman who swore he could make gold?'

'He did make gold. But it was only a little bit, no bigger than a pea.'

And now I had a most unwelcome thought prompted by this enquiry after Enoch. What if Monty's *business* in New York was naught but a cloak for his duties as a sheriff? Suppose he had come from London upon some intelligence of our whereabouts in order to haul us home to justice? Could his charm to me, his forgiveness of Rusty, be mere policy? A trick to catch us all?

I said, heart in mouth, 'Are you still a sheriff, Monty?'

He laughed, having guessed at my trepidation. 'No. Have no fear, Mrs Sally. I'm not come overseas to arrest you. My words are true ones. I resigned that office two years ago. I'd grown so rich I no longer needed the Law's protection. Lord Mayors now owe me money, not to mention the Duke of York. Both City and Court come to me for funds. So you may rest secure upon that score.'

I said I hoped I could believe him – he swore yet again I could and we laughed, with me exclaiming even as he kissed me on both cheeks, 'Then it is truly good to see you, Monty, but you may take your hand out of my skirts.'

At this moment the band broke out of a stately *passe-pied* into a *volte* – a joyous, whoopsadaisy dance of almighty energy in which the fair sex are literally whisked off their feet with great bouncings.

Monty said, 'Will you dance, Mrs Sally?'

Said I, without thought, 'Can you? With that leg?'

He took no offence. He said, 'I can hop, madam. You'll see.' And he laid down his sword and led me into the dance. Clearly he had no need of continual support. He could walk well enough without aid, but with a powerful stamp of his steel-shod leg upon the floor. It banged upon the boards with a most commanding thump. Then as he took me in his arms and found the beat, how he hopped. As for his arms, well, even Rusty would have been hard put to match them for strength and flexibility. I could not have believed a crippled man could have so transported me but he did and as the *volte* ended I clung to him breathless as any of my girls who had likewise flown through the air in the arms of their beaux.

But as I broke from Monty's embrace there was Rusty with Lucille and Lucille was saying, 'I have always maintained that the *volte* is almost too lively a dance for polite society.'

'Who's this, doll?' said Rusty. Then he realised. And his face was just the picture Monty had said it would be. 'Jeez! It's frigging Monty Cruickshank! God help us! You of all people. Fockle-ella – as the bogtrotter said to Father Paddy's housekeeper, getting his end in. Where've you sprung from?'

'I'm here on business, Rusty. Sally'll tell you.'

'Oh, yeah?'

They were eyeing each other like fighting cocks. I couldn't tell how this encounter might turn out. What sentiment would prevail? Rusty's despite of Monty? Or Monty's fount of human kindness now he'd grown rich out of the Isle of Dogs, albeit as a victim of Rusty's embattled fury?

Said Rusty, now dead of eye and equally unlively of voice, 'Looks like you was in the wars at some time, mate?'

'True. Pudding Wharf. Remember?'

'Should I?'

I said, hoping to ease this converse, 'It's all right, dear Monty isn't a sheriff any more.'

'What if he was, doll? He's still out of his ground. And like if he was to try anything he'd be dead. In fact last time I saw you I thought you was, Monty.'

'So did I.'

'You was all of a heap on Enoch's floor. In his laboratory. Alongside that Judge who had you in his pocket only by then he was looking even worse'n you. Like he'd really caught it.'

'He had. It was those hand-bombs you slung at us.'

'I didn't reckon they was gonna blow. Only then they did.'

'How it goes.'

And this entire intercourse was conducted in tones so low and so even, with faces so guarded, so alike in revealing nothing, that you might have thought they were a pair of privy councillors or else two pot-house card sharps, each determined to deceive the other.

Lucille said, taking me aside, 'What *are* they talking about?'

'Old times. They've known each other for years and years.'

'So I thought. But are they friends?'

'They were. But they fell out. Very badly.'

'Over a woman?'

I laughed. 'No, Lucille – these are Englishmen. Their quarrel concerned power, influence, money.'

'That sounds quite French to me.'

Meantime Monty had burst out laughing. 'Oh, Rusty, I promise you it's true! As I told Sally if I'd been you I'd have done the same.'

'Maybe. But I reckon you still owe me, mate. That was a nice little depot you took off of me.'

'So was the leg you got from me. And this eye.'

'You saying we're quits, Monty?'

'I am, mate! Like I could've got you a rope necklace.'

'Why didn't you?'

'I said, I let bygones be bygones.'

'I know but can I believe you?'

'Ask Sally.'

Rusty turned to me. 'What do you say, doll? Am I to believe this lying bastard?'

I laughed. 'I'm to be the peacemaker, am I?'

'No, judge and jury – whaddya reckon?'

'Well, he always was plausible, wasn't he? But seeing it's a long time ago and nearly Christmas and you're cock of the walk and king of the midden over here, why not? You can always chop off his other leg if you're less than satisfied – right?'

That did it. Rusty laughed. 'True, doll! You've hit it. Yeah!'

And he turned to Monty grinning so wide he could've swallowed the cat swallowing the cream in one gulp. He roared, slapping Monty's back, 'Right, you rotten, conniving, lousy bastard, I believe you though thousands wouldn't!'

And Monty was slapping him back. 'I should bleeding well hope so, you incredulous, leery, doubting sodomite!'

Hearing these mutual insults repeated with many variations and punctuated by broadsides of laughter and further backslaps and punches to the chest upon both sides, Lucille said, 'If this is friendship restored what was their enmity like?'

I said, 'From what I've heard – explosive.'

And now, as if sensing the fittingness of the moment, the Master of Ceremonies, an upstanding blackamoor of professional charm and parts, called out for us to stand forth for what he called a good old English brawl. This was in fact a circular dance known to the French as a *branle* while to the Italians it is a *brando*. From which we may deduce that frolicking is universal – for it becomes a lively measure once the evening is advanced.

Lucille was as eager to take part as I. So were Rusty and Monty – never have I known a game leg more game for sport. Onto the floor we went. And as we danced Monty confided to me that upon losing the best half of his left leg he had so exercised his right one that it could now perform the work of two and therefore he had got – to all intents and purposes – half a leg's advantage over any other man. He had achieved this miracle by chanting that silly rhyme: 'Jack be nimble, Jack be quick, Jack jump over the thimble stick' and suiting action to the words, although for want of a thimble stick he had substituted a candle stick. By the time he was fitted with his peg-leg he could – from a standing start – clear a lighted candle that stood at two feet six inches. While given a hopping run and a sideways leap at it he could manage three feet and a half-inch. Hearing this tale I was not surprised by his dancing skills. The man was a marvel. Though I fear the floor was marked for ever by the pounding it received from that false leg. I told him he should have a ferrule made for it in the shape of a cloven hoof – for surely we women needed fair warning of the old devil in him.

As we cavorted thus at a high rate Arnold Jay Stone appeared in the room. Rusty saw him at once. As if with second sight. He was dancing to me at the time and he stopped in mid-figure.

'Well,' he said. 'Look what the cat's brought in.'

I did and saw the corpulent shape of Rusty's arch rival eyeing the dance as Rusty broke from me and marched straight to him, striding forward like one possessed, his fists already bunched. In a trice he was lost to sight as the mêlée of dancers closed together again after his passing. I was left partnerless but only for an instant because Monty was at once jumping and jigging before me saying, 'What's the news, Sally? Our Rusty took off like a blue-arsed fly.'

I said, 'He's just seen Arnold Jay Stone.'

'Who's he?'

'The most important person in town – at least in his own estimation.'

'But Rusty disagrees?'

'Most implacably and violently. So do I.'

'I suppose they have opposing interests?'

'Everywhere. And in everything. Be it whorehouses, racing, gambling, garbage disposal, market protection – you think of it they're fighting each other for it. Why, he even tried to abduct three of my best girls.'

246

'For his own use?'

'Oh, no. He's a sodomite.'

'Then why?'

'Oh, Monty, you're no colonial yet, are you? To sell, of course. To farmers upcountry. For wives.'

'Like slaves?'

'Only white.'

Monty looked disgusted. As well he might. He said, 'Now that's a game I would call dirty. Right, reckon I'll go and see how Rusty's going on. Maybe he could need a hand? See you shortly, Mrs S.'

And away he stamped, picking up his sword as he went. I was partnerless again but by this time the *branle* was come to its close – the dancers dispersed or rather re-forming in other groups and pairings. Oh, Lord, there was little Pamela, not yet sixteen, most vivaciously embracing that coxcomb of a captain – where would it all end? Not in marriage, I felt sure, knowing the soldiery. Nor with money. Rather I could hear unwanted babes a-bawling. Would there be time to establish a fund for a laying-in hospital? Since, at this rate, New York was going to need one sorely.

All these thoughts raced through my head as I followed Monty through the crowd. All were putting themselves to rights (or wrongs) after the exertion of the dance. So much so that hardly anyone seemed, as yet, to have noticed the event that was coming to a pretty pass at the entrance to the ballroom.

I reached it as the first punch was thrown. Not by Rusty, already wigless ready for the fray, nor by Stone, still with his hair on, nor by Monty, likewise, but by one of two Atlantean bodyguards who arrived upon the scene even as I did. Big powerful brutes. Human mastiffs in brown serge. Owner? A.J.S.

The first was interposed between Rusty and his master but his initial blow went nowhere as Rusty, who had seen it coming, cocked his chin barely an inch to one side so that this knuckle pie (as Cockneys call them) lost its thrust in air. In the same instant – for all was coincident even if in the telling of it I am bound to space it out as a sequence of occurrences – Rusty had grabbed the man by both shoulders, butted his head straight into his opponent's nose (we all heard the gristle squeak and the bone crack) while in the same lightning moment Rusty's knee had struck the man in the cods. And he was gone! Was naught but a sack of offal to be dumped outside. How we bystanders sighed. In the meantime his fellow bruiser had tried to come to his aid but Monty's sword (still sheathed) had suddenly slid most inadvertently it seemed between the man's ankles and he fell forward, face down, prostrate in front of Rusty who kicked him in the head after which he was as inert as his hired companion.

By now Councillor Ambrose had arrived spitting and crackling like pork upon a spit. 'Gentlemen, if you please!' he cried. 'If you have differences to discuss kindly take yourselves outside or agree to meet tomorrow at dawn at a place convenient to you both. But do not dispute here I beg you – think of the ladies.'

At this one lady squealed, 'Oh, but we adore it, Septimus. I've already got thirty dollars on General Mars. He fights so dirty!'

The General himself said, 'Hear that, Mr Stone? Our host requests us to go outside. I agree. Let's go. I can't wait to bust your face.'

But already more mighty bodyguards were appearing. I decided the time had come to find Enoch. Surely he, by some Welsh wizardry, could save this situation before we were all three disgraced? After all, Rusty, he and I were too well known in the town to participate in common riot and affray – especially upon the grandest occasion New York had yet known. Its first and finest reception. What would people say? We should have lost our reputation, our *bon ton*. Already I could hear Lucille sneering. And now people were quite ignoring the Master of Ceremonies' call to a *courante*. The band was playing yet all were flocking to witness this scandalous contention. Why, these so-called gentlemen were revealed as little more than back-alley ruffians.

But where was Enoch? Not in the ball nor in the hall where to make things worse – surely the dream was turning to nightmare – I met Percy at the foot of the main stair. He looked as melancholy as a dog with worms and he was quite undressed for an evening such as this, being in his working clothes.

I said, 'Percy, you shouldn't be here! Or is there some mishap at the laboratory?'

'I must be here,' answered he. 'In obedience to Lord Cupid's call.'

'Oh, don't be daft, boy. Have you seen Enoch?'

'Only now, Mrs Sally. Well, five minutes ago. Going up these very stairs.'

'Alone?'

'Oh, no. He had with him a lady.'

'Really?' Then, pierced by an hideous insight, I added, 'What kind of lady?'

'A pink one. I mean she was dressed all in pink. And so beautiful but not to equal you, Mrs Sally.' He was panting, his eyes were full of longing. 'Don't disdain me. I could not rest quiet by the furnaces knowing you were here with the professor – '

'Hush!' said I. 'Go through to the servants' hall. They're most of them pie-eyed already. They'll be bound to offer you food and drink and you look as if you need both. Go along.'

And I left him standing, running up the stairs with my skirts hitched up to my knees. Enoch with a pink lady? What lady?

☿

What should one most happily say when discovered by one lover *in flagrante delicto* with another? And that other one's former catamite?

I said, 'Ho there, Sally. Is that you I see before me?'

Answered she, 'Is that who I suppose it is?' Which was in the way of being a fair question, given that Abednego's skirts were above his head, his bum in all its golden perfection warming the air, and me with my breeches about my ankles.

'I admit it, dear Sally.'

'Oh, Enoch, how could you?'

Another apt question if banal. I said, with a sensibility equal to hers (for we are both tender creatures), I said, 'We were close, my dear, Abednego and I, for three whole years. When you were quite gone from my life – had even married another.'

I saw my reply had struck the mark. Sally was about to admit the justice in it when Abednego thrust down his skirts and, seeing who it was, exclaimed, 'Oh, no, not her!'

And I must confess the boy sounded as debauched and petulant as any of Arnold Jay Stone's manful sluts parading the East Side on a moonlit night. Thus it is that Eastern innocence is forever corrupted by Western expediency.

Sally said, without regard for Abednego, who was to her anathema, 'Enoch, you've got to help! Rusty and Arnold Jay Stone are at fisticuffs! We have a riot down below. The evening is in ruins.'

'Oh, no!' yelled Abednego, remembering he was Mrs Ambrose after all. 'I must go! Septimus will need me!' And with that he rushed from the room.

I said, some of my breath now returned to me, 'But Rusty's more than a match for that puff-ball?'

'That's not the point, you idiot!' shouted Sally. Rarely had I seen her so enraged. 'This is a public affray! Stone has got his rough men with him and Rusty has already nearly killed two of them! I tell you it's murder! Any more of it and our name will be mud. Our house will close, the bank will fail – '

I cut her short, 'Enough, my dear! The argument is made. I am with you. Forget what you have seen – it was but a past sentiment passing by and it is gone. So am I.'

And I was. I could not wait to vacate that unhappy scene. I bounded down the stair glad to have my breeches about me again and due distance between myself and my dearly beloved but dearly indignant Mrs Sally.

♂

Could I get Stone to come outside like a man? Answer – can a eunuch frig? No, he stayed where he was like that's where he reckoned he was safest. At the nub of the social scene wiv his myrmidons all gathered round. That was Enoch's word for Stone's pug-uglies. Apparently some ancient Greek warrior always had a load of these hardballs to protect him, just in case he didn't turn out to be quite so heroic as the poets kept on saying he was. Like there's nothing like owning a private army, is there, if you reckon, deep down, you ain't quite what you're cracked up to be?

By this time there was twelve of these bastards all lined up. Looking assertive. And every mother's son of 'em sporting muscles where most people make do wiv arms, chests and legs.

Next thing we know – by which I mean me and Monty (thank Christ he walked in when he did) – we was surrounded by these characters. Wiv A.J.S., outside the ring, smirking. And, beyond him and his fellas, the entire frigging *soirée*, as Lucille put it later, crowded all about, like they was at a bull-ring, to view the sport. And I tell you I could hear some clever dick taking bets, and like Monty and me we was at six to one shading to eleven to two.

So like it had to be like it was. Rough. Wiv me sparking the activity. How? Oh, very traditional. The usual way. By gobbing a load of phlegm at the feet of the biggest bully. That always agitates 'em. And it did. Merry hell was here again. And I was, I will confess, in my element. So was Monty. His fists! Magic! And that wooden leg! Diabolic! He caught two in the cods wiv it and as they went down they was calling for their mothers. Big boys with small voices. And I wasn't doing so bad neither. I'd flattened a couple on me own account but that still left eight to come.

But they didn't. No. They just stayed on the periphical, while one of 'em, a touch smaller, certainly sharper, maybe more evil, pulled a knife.

250

You could hear the world draw breath. And hold it. Like now it was serious. Sorta grave. Wiv naughty angels hovering overhead.

The knife man advanced. Somebody said – yeah, it was Stone – he said, 'Take him, Chico.'

I might've known. Here was yer dago. And from the look of him a Romany to boot. And like he knew what he was about wiv a cutter. I came straight at him. You don't never hang back wiv his sort. Like if they reckon you quail you're dead. But I had no knife. Since it was a rule of the house gents left their weapons at the door. Monty's sword only excepted since he used it for a walking stick. So like this particular derring-do was out of all manner, right?

But that didn't mean it wasn't happening. Oh, no. Here we was going round the mulberry bush, me 'n' this Chico, weighing each other up. Looking for an opening. Like he was light on his feet and though I didn't show it he was earning my respect. He handled himself clever. He was of the kind that takes pride in their work. And can leave you wiv the scars to prove it.

He lunged for me, his knife low. Classic. Go for the belly. A coupla ladies screamed. I side-stepped, stuck out a foot and he almost fell for it, I nearly had him tripped. But, no, he was too smart for that. He pulled back, danced about a bit, said something rude under his breath, but whether to me or himself I couldn't tell, then in he came again. Fast 'n' flashy. I went for his knife wrist. Caught it. Twisted it wiv both hands. He was kicking now. More ladies screamed. And the gents was murmuring too – a nice, low manly rumble of: 'Kill him, general. Whip his ass.' Which was a kind thought but I hadn't got to there yet, had I? Not wiv him hanging on to that knife of his and trying to back-kick me on the shins. But now my steel grip was telling on him – or was he faking? – to be certain I gave it all I'd got. He yelled and the knife fell free. And stuck in the floor. At once Monty grabbed it and shouted: 'Take him, Rusty, he's all yours.'

Well, I didn't need no encouragement, did I? My blood was up. I grabbed that prancing Chico by the throat and was gonna throttle him for all to see when his mates moved in – all seven of 'em. Oh, dear. So now we've got this free-for-all and it's like Saturday night down Ram Alley. Only the setting has made it more piquant, I mean there's nothing like lotsa gentility urging on a loada scurrility, is there? Like both sides love it, really.

So here was anything going: fists, boots, chairs, vases, coffee pots, urns, bottles – when one of the seven suddenly soars upwards, hits a flaming chandelier and falls down to flatten another by the sheer dynamic of his descent. Who's done this? I wonder. And then I see that silver streak of Welsh wizardry, our home-grown adept himself, Enoch Powys, making wiv his oriental arts. And he's so deft it's beautiful. The battle's transformed. Where before it was just me and Monty outnumbered but slugging solid, now it's the three of us and the action's sorta fluid, kinda artistic and the odds are almost even: we're three to five now. Wiv Arnold Jay Stone starting, I note, to sneak away, the cunning cunny.

I shout, 'Hold on, mister. I wanna word wiv you!' But hearing this he makes a break for it. Whereat his bodyguards what are still standing reckon their place is wiv him and shog off likewise. But quick. I shout again, but this time to Monty and Enoch, 'Right! Let's go get 'em, shall we?' And away we go, tally ho, the three of us, nothing loath, just bent on real war. I grab my sword from the porter and there on the steps are Mick the Mick and Aguma M'Kubwa yelling and pointing at the fleeing figures of Stone and his musclemen.

Together they bawl, 'They went thataway!' So we do, too. And now we're a true posse with the odds dead even at last if you discount Arnold Yellow-Belly Stone. I reckon we can.

We race down the quay beside the canal and on West Side we've caught 'em. The boys have stopped to protect their lord and master who's got the stitch and is doubled-up moaning like a kid wiv the croup.

We advance implacably, our boots crunching on the frozen snow. Like this has gotta be the crunch. Crunch, crunch.

♀

With Enoch fled I sat down upon the couch where I had discovered him with Abednego and wept. This reception I had so looked forward to was now become a mere rough house, a virtual shambles. And we would be seen to be to blame, however much the town might assure us that this was not so. After all, we were the newcomers and Rusty's vigour and enterprise (not to mention mine and Enoch's) had challenged the old ordering of things by Arnold Jay Stone and our host, Councillor Ambrose. Rusty's appointment to the council had been merely a convenient device to obstruct Ambrose's rise to power, but might nevertheless (such being the way of politics) have led to higher things for him. But now? Who would want a bawling, foul-mouthed ruffian for Mayor of New York? Surely Rusty's fellow councillors would now despise him as much as already they did

Ambrose? Rumours would soon abound that he was no true general but a self-appointed one. Second thoughts could well be had about the security of his bank. The confidential nature of our house upon Pearl Street might be questioned – particularly if this disapproval I feared turned to old-fashioned distaste for corporeal fun and fleshly games. The probity of our dice and card tables might also come under suspicion.

Yet all these fears – some of which I had voiced to Enoch, but in spite of this still they churned about in my head – seemed to me less dreadful than his relapse into his former Egyptian ways. How could he cheat me so? Meanwhile I had hardly danced at all and my dear girls were all debauched or about to be. And even if, by some miracle, the evening recovered its gaiety after this disaster, I doubted I should have much heart left for it. I might, I concluded, just as well go home to Pearl Street. Whereupon I buried my head in my hands and howled.

What was this? A hand on my hair. Whose? And at the back of my neck. A gentle hand. And a gentler voice that said, 'Don't cry.'

I raised my head. And saw Lord Spark looking like himself as he was before his fall. But now he seemed set about with half a dozen tiny rainbows which were, I dare say, a complicity of teardrops and candlelight. Here was my Oxford beau revived, my London lover, my would-be bridegroom, nay, more – for now I perceived how he was tempered by time and experience. The mooncalf I had but now encountered at the foot of the stair was quite gone out of him.

Said I, 'Oh, Percival. You look so much enheartened? Did you go into the servants' hall?'

'No, madam. I waited where I was. And first the pink lady came flying down the stairs like one worse possessed than I ever was, and next, in no time at all, Professor Mercurius, equally precipitate. While within the ballroom it seemed Pandemonium was come up to earth to found a new colony of hell among us.'

'Why, Percival, you sound just like Mr Milton.'

'The professor ever recites him to me. He says his writings will so exercise my mind I shall find myself made good. They're still at it. Did you ever hear such uproar?'

I rose up. I heard gross shouts, the thunder of boots, prodigious cursings.

'Oh, I can't bear it!' I exclaimed and without heed of anything save comfort I buried my face against his breast. In the instant his arms were about me, and in the next we were embraced. And that, knowing me of old and him restored, was that.

Come the crunch they made another break for it and we ended up in my best garbage crib on West Side. At least the cold made it wholesome, but like it really was a showdown on thin ice. I mean, you ever seen an in-fill site on Manna Hatta's shoreline? Well, let me tell you, squiress, it makes a farmyard midden look like the sweet lawns of St James's Park where the King keeps his cattle to trim the grass. And his courtiers to lick his arse.

First off there's this greasy palisade of mighty timbers or piles (pardon me) to keep the tide out. Here, within this stout marine corral, is where you tip your shit, right? Of course it subsides, dunnit? So you shove in another load. And another. In fact you keep on tipping until the muck has not only settled but reached its true level wiv the street. Upon this you spread a topping of clean earth and there you have it. Another slice of prime land to sell for honest shekels.

But this crib was nowhere near this point of composition nor exploitation. Oh, no. For a start it was only half-full, for another it was all tumpy, and in between was these pools of ugly unguent frozen over, I agree, and coated wiv snow, but still there, lying low. In other words a poxy sorta dump very like the one where I was born at London, full of obnoxiousness shovelled out from privies, kitchens, chicken runs. Also rubble, broken bricks, rotten wood, dead cats and old unwanted tosspots. So you could say like I'd reverted to my origins only at a profit. And what's more I was hoping Sally would, too, because just recently she'd come on a touch too grand for my taste. Like I love a lady, right? But if she's come up from nowhere I do expect her to admit it. Like Sal's double. That brunette does. Know who I mean? Nelly – the King's crumpet. After all, Sal started where I did in the shit – only hers was country, mine town.

But where am I getting to? Not into a contemplation upon human manners, I trust? That's not my game, so put a sock in it, Rusty, and stick to what you know – pure violence.

Yeah, there we was. Us standing on top of the palisade wiv them cowering below. And like I just hope we looked to them as menacing as we felt. Dark shapes against the moon and stars. Fell as death etcetera. And know what? Here's the sublime of it. Mick the Mick and Aguma M'Kubwa pull out from their boots these pistols. One for each of us. And they've got a powder horn and these lovely little balls or bullets as they are known. Of a snugly suitable calibre. We load, we prime, we cock.

I shout, 'Stone! The die is cast, the shooters loaded. So you better come up nicely. No tricks. That way we can keep it neat 'n' clean.'

'Sure, you wouldn't shoot us down like turkeys, general?'

'Wanna bet?'

Stone doesn't. He nods. Kinda more to himself than to us. But no, oh no, I'm wrong, it's a signal to that dago who's got himself another cutter off of one of his mates. It flashes in the moonlight. And it's got me – me, Rusty Ironside, your one and only warman, right through me left bicep! It's stuck there like a skewer through a lumpa beef. Well, that is that. I mean Lucille's got a phrase for it: Lez Majestic or somesuch (sounds like some fella you wouldn't wanna know, dunnit?). Any road I go seriously baleful and shoot that stinking Chico right through the heart, which is the signal for Enoch, Monty, Mick the Mick, and Aguma M'Kubwa to blaze away as well and for Stone's remaining myrmidons to scarper yet again, tripping, falling, climbing over each other, like rats in a trap. Two get winged but they all finally make their exit, up and over the palisade, leaving Stone all by himself save for the inertness of Lez Majestic, as I'd now dubbed that impertinent corpse. I've left his knife where it's stuck – like I'd like a physician standing by wiv bowl and bandages when I pull it out.

Stone's shouting something up at us. His voice sounds sorta tinny. He says, 'Hold it, general. Let's talk. I can be reasonable. I appreciate the force of your argument. It has been well made. What kind of deal are you looking for? Name it and maybe we could cut it.'

Well, I laugh, don't I? And say, 'No, sir, it ain't like that no more.'

'But you'll spare me my life?'

'Why should I?'

'Well, because, general, I'm prepared to sell off various interests – in exchange for it. Whaddya say to my boy bordellos? For a start?'

'No deal.'

'My insurance company for market traders? Established way back. In '65?'

'Don't need it. Got my own. And most of the market prefers my protection rates to yours, Mr Stone.'

'Very well, my racing stable with my stud pigs thrown in as a sweetmeat between men of the world?'

I pause for reflection. I won't say I ain't tempted by his hogs. But then, by chance, I move my left arm and the feel of that knife in it, puts, as it were, iron up my jaxie.

I say, wiv a wince, but spacing out the menace, 'You got the time it takes us to reload our pistols, Mr Stone, to shog off. And to stay clear of New York. Like in perpetuity, right?'

'But, general, this town's surely big enough for both of us?'

To which I say, 'You coulda fooled me.'

At this I see the hope drain out of him, like horsepiss down the gutter on Ludgate Hill. Jeez, I can be evil when I choose.

He says, 'Give a guy a chance, general.'

'I am.'

And I nod to Monty and Co. who reload and prime. I don't on account of my dexterity being temporarily restricted. Instead I kept my beadies on Arnold Jay Stone. And unless it's a trick of the moonlight I reckon he's gone kinda somewhere between green and orange. Like yellow as a very nervous buttercup.

I say, merely to keep the drama of it on the bubble, 'Just gimme the word, lads, when you're ready.'

Says Stone, 'Very well, general. Since you insist I'm going now.'

'Yeah, you better.'

And he backs off, turns and starts on his way over the tumps and slumps of snow-clad garbage. Monty the while announces he and the lads are ready. And I'm about to ask 'em to give Stone the odd, encouraging ballistic up his breeches when there's this sharp and ominous cracking sound. Yeah, you've guessed it, adventure lover, here's the ice giving way under Mr Stone.

The bugger's stopped, he's doing a sorta pirouette, looking down and can't believe what he's seeing – these great star-like splinters of ice poking up at him and his feet sinking into a black hole of the most unfresh liquid. He shouts something but the next instant he's gone just like that, swallowed up, gloop, by this pit of cess, know what I mean? We hold our breaths. Will he come up again? No. That ain't how it's gonna be for him. Detritus has claimed its own and is sticking wiv him. Enoch reckons it's poetic justice but I don't see that. Since when was a garbage crib something to rhyme about? I get the justice side of it, though. Like it's like to like, right?

So back we go. And I must say I couldn't wait to get that skewer outta my bicep. Fortunately there was a coupla quacks present at the ball and though they was both well wined they nevertheless managed between 'em to remove the aforesaid blade and bind up the muscle so as I only lost a quart of blood and Lucille only fainted once. Women! Which reminds me – Sally wasn't nowhere to be seen when we got back but half an hour later there she was all smiles and solicitude, by which time Lucille had persuaded me a pint of red Bordeaux wine chased down with brandy was what we both needed and so I never noticed just how happy Sal looked nor how she never spoke a word to Enoch. To put it briefly I was in a sorta jolly, arm-aching daze through which I was mistily aware that loadsa folk kept coming up to me to drink my health, shake my good hand, and generally opine that I had done the town a service in confronting and demolishing Arnold Jay Stone, who had been a major rascal, sir, nay, a parasite, and a bloodsucker upon the body politic of New York for too long. Even Stone's erstwhile mate, our host, Septimus Ambrose said it, sensing what has since been termed by Enoch (what a verbaliser that moosch is) a power shift.

Make no mistake that was the night I got to be king of the castle on Manna Hatta. I was like the real guv'nor. The place might have a titular one, and even a mayor to boot, but from then on when anybody needed anything done he knew where he'd gotta come. To me. Ditto, if he wanted a favour or a loan. Indeed permission to breathe. You could say my cup was full. As was my bladder.

And there was Monty saying, most conveniently, that he and my mate, Enoch the Adept (who's looking fairly far gone and ethereal even for a philosopher), have got this wager upon a contest of guess what? Well, hearing this, I'm their man, right? Out we go, a very merry threesome, to piss up the wall of our host, Councillor Ambrose.

♀

My fears concerning Rusty's violent rivalry with Arnold Jay Stone were proved quite wrong. Mayhap because they were built upon the sands of my fury at Enoch? He was hailed by all as a hero – especially when it was discovered he was wounded bloodily yet superficially. Everyone wished to shake his hand (if male) and rather more (if female). The same went for Monty and Enoch. And while I no longer cared who made eyes at the latter I must admit I felt a trifle proprietorial of Monty. Though not much, having so recently enjoyed dear Percival.

Oh, yes, my opinion of him had also been turned about. And topsy-turvy. I had made no misjudgement of him at all. He *was* become his old self, only better. But afterwards I had packed him off home to the laboratory (of which he was, after all, the guardian) with the assurance that our liaison now resumed would continue whenever it was convenient, but he would be advised to give no hint of it to Enoch. It was our secret, was it not? At this he vowed undying devotion between further caresses so prettily placed that we were

257

obliged to celebrate our initial conjunction again. So it was no wonder I was not below when Rusty returned in triumph.

Now I danced with Monty as Rusty rested upon a couch with Lucille in so close attendance it was scarcely decent. Meantime Enoch tripped lightly upon the toe before various adoring matrons while making eyes at me to forgive him. I pretended I had not perceived these expressive glances but when at last the reception was drawing to a close at around four o'clock in the morning Enoch came directly to me and requested, or rather begged, a discreet audience with she that was, he said, beyond dispute the belle of the ball, *viz.* me. His Taffy's tongue! However, I must admit my congress with Percy had restored my spirits. And my colour. Nor shall I pretend I did not relish Enoch's flattery of me, since he was plainly deploying it, like honey, to disguise his shame.

We proceeded to a convenient alcove which was at that very moment being vacated by a gasping nymph and her puffing swain for somewhere yet more convenient. For my part I pretended not to recognise dimpled Lucy, who had survived a number of vicissitudes at the hands of Arnold Jay Stone's henchmen and who was now, only too evidently, determined not to survive one or two more of her own devising, upstairs, with a vigorously mustachioed subaltern.

Once they were departed, and we were face to face, Enoch said, like one truly perturbed, 'Never, Sally, never have I known us so at odds.'

'Nor me, Enoch,' was all my reply. And this superfluous pronouncement of our names each to the other seemed more to do with our making ready for a quarrel than for any sort of conciliation.

And yet the next thing he said, calculating only too well that my heart would soften as I heard it, was: 'We met under a haycock when you were a green girl and I a fancy-free scholar and we knew at once the heavens had made us for each other. Remember?'

Remember? Of course I did. But this appeal to old affections was not quite as he had said it was. Nor was I prepared to be too readily disarmed by mere reminiscence.

I said, 'I wasn't that green, Enoch, and you were not so much fancy free as starving, having been turned out of your college for thievery.'

'In the pursuit of knowledge, Sally.'

'Nor did we meet under a haycock but on the road beside a circle of old stones.'

However saying this went some way to undermining my resolve to bear hardly upon Enoch. For I had loved that ancient place ever since I was a child and the apprehension of it was even yet lodged somewhere in my inmost being. It had sprung at once into my mind's eye.

'You were dressed as a boy,' he said.

'No wonder you thought heaven had made me for you.'

At this riposte he blinked. Then countered with, 'But you stepped out like a girl.'

'As for that haycock. It was I discovered it for us after I had shared my supper with you.'

'It sheltered us most sweetly.'

I smiled, remembering how I had wondered if that vagrant stranger would offer me indecencies that night? And how, when he hadn't, I'd been unsure whether to feel thankful or regretful. I said, 'We slept like babies.'

'I fetched milk in the morning.'

'Stolen again.'

'We needed to break our fast, Sally. You were so beautiful.'

Now he spoke so simply I found I was quite won again. I said, 'Do you remember our bathing in the river?'

'But for you I should've drowned!'

'And the old woman who found us on the bank stark naked? And chased us away?'

Now we were both laughing. Enoch said, 'Adam and Eve driven out of Eden by an ancient rheumaticky angel.'

'Not out of Eden, my dear. For Oxford proved a paradise for me.'

And with this the wheel had turned full circle since now I was come to Lord Spark and in consideration of what had so very recently passed between him and me how could I continue to bear resentment of Enoch whose cheating of me had not even been completed? Further it was more than probable I should continue to deceive Enoch and Rusty with Percy (indeed I had promised him as much) whereas I doubted Enoch would ever dare to revive his liaison with Abednego. For Septimus Ambrose was as jealous of his property as any sheepdog. It therefore behoved me to show a certain compassion to both my usual lovers while enjoying a secret libertine.

As I was reflecting thus wickedly, Enoch said, 'I recall best our walking to London. That to me was a waking dream – the marriage of true hearts, true minds.'

'And flesh, Enoch. Don't forget the flesh that is ever truest of all.'

'Thus speaks my perfect Sally who can do no wrong.'

And he went on to say how he often dreamed of what he still thought of as 'my old stones'.

He said, 'We lie together there under the heavens. We see the new moon rise, then below her Venus shines in golden glory and next Mercury appears a perfect silver while far above Mars glowers red as blood. And under us the earth turns.'

'We feel its movement, do we?' said I, laughing. For that is a sensation I ever crave, often achieve, and yet upon occasion have been obliged to pretend to.

'Most certainly,' he answered not comprehending me. For as I have ever advised my girls, most of the unfair sex is nasty, brutish, and short where it matters. And yet we women are ever commanded to assure them of the opposite: that they are nice, civil and of a length. Nothing is further from the truth, of course. In my not untried experience, the only man who answered to *that* ideal description was my departed cavalier, my husband Jeremy. While for your prurient intelligence, dear reader of either sex, I may tell you that Rusty in congress is ever hugely hasty, demanding and thick, whereas Enoch is subtle, often too dainty and rather slight. But then we can't have it all ways, can we? Although I will admit Percy (despite his deplorable history) comes, when put to the breach, nearest to Jeremy.

Enoch continued, 'When we wake – '

'Oh? We fall asleep in this dream of yours, do we?'

'After love's labours.'

'It's a love dream?'

'Of course.'

'Tell it to me. And omit not one iota of its elements.'

'Later. Not here. For we must rejoin the company. I'll tell it to you and our pillows.'

'You suppose I shall admit you to my bed?'

'It would be a sign of forgiveness – and sweet womanly compassion, Sally.'

'We'll see,' said I, teasing slut that I can be. Since there was Monty arrived to convoke Enoch's participation in a pissing contest with Rusty. Off they went to their wager and I returned to the ballroom which by this hour resembled naught so much as the forgetful banks of Lethe peopled with the ghosts of humankind.

Given the dictates of civility – I confess my heart twinged a little to shake Abednego's hand as if he had merely been my admired hostess – Sally and I did not reach our couch until Aurora with her rosy fingers (or rather Dawn with chilblains) was already turning the snow-clad town into a place of faerie.

We embraced for warmth and comfort's sake rather than concupiscence, murmuring of my dream and our early times together. And this conversation of word and flesh was somehow quite as sweet as our more usual expressions of regard each for the other. As the clocks struck nine, and Great Sol himself was risen, we fell asleep, so closely embraced it was as if we were one. And did not wake till Luna the Huntress appeared, slender as her own bow, late that winter afternoon.

♂

Lucille (Gawd bless her) provided Monty wiv a bed full of her best friend Margery (that lusty matron on whose account we was obliged to strengthen the bedsteads at Pearl Street) and we all met for a dirty great breakfast at dinner-time. Like upon the prick of noon, as has been said.

After, Monty and me left the girls to compare notes while we took a walk around town. *My* town as I was beginning to realise it now was. Like my triumph over Arnold Jay Stone was really beginning to dawn upon me, especially as my left bicep was still a touch tender from that knife thrown by that Chico bastard. And where should we end up but at my other whorehouse (the lowdown one after the old fashion on East Side) where the girls gave us hot punch and a lotta lip that was nice 'n' naughty but *nada mas*, as my old mate at the Admiralty used to say when reporting one of his frolics to me over a jar in Seething Lane.

In this wise Monty 'n' me was able to talk serious business and I was pleased to offer him a slice of Stone's fur-trading. Like I'd send the skins to London at Monty's cost where he'd sell 'em on a sixty per cent, forty per cent basis in his favour wiv my percentage invested for me by him in the East India Company at the best market rate available. For by now I was bent on going global. The New World and the Old World wasn't big enough for me, no, sir! I wanted a slice of the gorgeous East as well. Yum-yum.

Just in case it's crossed your worldly mind, squire, to enquire, in due solicitude, if I could truly afford to trust Monty in this manner (given our past differences) let me say that the Battle of West Side Crib had quite assuaged the ill-feeling of Pudding Wharf. Our reunion and that piece of merry riot had healed the rift between us as if it had never been, not to mention our aforementioned pissing match after – wiv me, for the first time ever, beating Monty by half an inch and Enoch by a good foot. And what's more our urinations formed instant icicles to hang by the wall in a golden filigree sparkling in the torchlight. Talk about prettiness and all's well wiv the world.

☿

Master Stella's toy burst. Or rather I should say that after a month or so, Mr Newton's model of his great triple glass could no longer endure the constant heat of my second sand furnace which, until then, had been favoured by Montezuma who rattled indignantly at the explosion and then retired deep behind the hay box. But such are the mishaps of a quest wherein the animal, vegetable and mineral worlds perforce co-mingle.

When the outer glass cracked, the two interior vessels descended sharply and also broke with a surprising force. In my vexation I blamed Percy for blowing too hard with the bellows upon the charcoal that warmed the sand but when he demonstrated most cogently (for him) that this had not been so I forgave the boy and blamed myself for being too hopeful of this trial machine. Stella, upon viewing the pieces, blamed the composition of the glass he had been obliged to employ. Had he not warned me that this might occur? I was bound to admit he had, yet I remained disappointed.

However this failed experiment did yield two sorts of result. Or to be more nice, six earths – albeit in scarcely quantifiable amounts. Within the burst vessels there remained, among the shards, three meagre deposits left from the vaporisation of the waters inside them, whilst within the shattered cups that had received the condensations therefrom there was to be discovered three further sorts of earth. In plainer words I could yet recover (with patience) scraps and scrapings of three earths provided by the boiling away of my different waters (sea, rain, dew) and another three, perhaps of a rarer kind, produced by the vaporising in God's own air of those same waters purified by distillation.

I shall not weary you, or these pages, with an inventory of the investigations I put these scant deposits to. Suffice it to say I owed it to science, and Mr Newton, to labour night and day to discover if these several substances (however corrupted by circumstance) might make up an universal matter of the kind he and Mr Rob. Boyle had prognosticated. The first question being: Of what did what I had got consist?

In sum the answer was that the seawater yielded traces of salt, chalk, iron, mother of pearl and glass; the rainwater offered copper, sulphur, lead, nitre, magnesia and glass; the morning dew sal ammoniac, lime, glass again, and a vestige of a substance I could not honestly identify as anything at all. This last, mysterious ingredient I designated in my notes merely with an X.

These observations I set down in a report for Mr Newton that I composed over the twelve days of Christmas, or Christ-tide as my sweet Tabby was wont to say. And curiously, even coincidingly, just before that season overtook us, I had found myself recalling, ever more frequently, her pretty carnalities – not least when I was at work in the laboratory. Mind you, it has been conceded, by both the ancients and the moderns, that any robust male will call to mind things lascivious at least twenty or forty times a day – a rule from which not even natural philosophers are exempt, although few speak of it. Moreover I was now left alone rather more than formerly because Sally had recently insisted with great vehemence that she must, must have Percy as her kitchen boy. Don't ask me why. Not long after she proudly announced, all a-glow, that she had already made him a dab hand at kneading dough and puffing pastry and therefore and thereafter he was indispensable to her since at that time of year there was so much to be got up for so many frolics, routs and debauches.

Looking back I believe I should have paid more attention to these words but life and science being what they are, *viz.* contrariwise, I did not. Rather I was entirely, nay, overmuch concerned with my research into that exploded model glass as well as with the building and delving at Master Stella's new workshop. Already the roof was on and the first blowing pit almost completed. Given no further snags and an unceasing flow of cash he saw no reason why he should not make his first attempt at the creation of the true, great glass after Epiphany.

And so it was that I was often upon my own (save for my toads and Montezuma) and thus would Tabby slip unbidden into my mind just as she had into my laboratory at Pudding Wharf where she had shown such aptness for the sacred art. Nor were these sugared fancies idle. In fact they were soon proved prescient.

One early morning as I was passing the Blue Dove to take the air after a wearisome night spent decocting a possible sal alkali whom should I see but Tabby? Or another so like as to be her twin sister had she ever had one which I knew she had not. She was deep in converse with a man who sounded most emphatically Irish. The two of them were surrounded by sea-going trunks and other baggage and it was evident they were debating what next to do because the Dove was, as always, packed full to bursting.

On my approach Tabby turned, thinking I was a stranger to her and said, 'Oh, forgive me for troubling you, sir, but can you – ?' But here she stopped. Her mouth fell agape and she cried out in breath-taken incredulity, 'Eek! Enoch Powys! It can't be you!'

Relishing her astonishment I lifted my hat with a civil composure. Said I, 'At your service, Mrs Tabitha. But by what happy conjunction of the stars are you brought here? For surely this meeting is more than mere accident? Nor will I say I am entirely surprised at it since you have been often in my thoughts of late. But this – this is better than thought. How are you?'

We embraced warmly with Tabby saying simultaneously that they were just that minute come off the ship from England, that they could find nowhere to lodge, that she was now married and this was her husband, Mr Brendan O'Bryne.

He and I shook hands while I wondered at his name. Had I not heard it before? But if so when and where?

Tabby illuminated me. 'Brendan was a great friend of Mr Rusty as was. Our protector at Pudding Wharf. Did you ever hear tell of him, Enoch? They say he was transported.'

I laughed and answered, 'Oh, Tabby, we have much to talk on. But tell me first – are you come to the New World to live or upon a visit?'

Brendan spoke for her. 'It is a reconnoitre, sir. I thought we might take the measure of this place my ancestors discovered. For it was known as St Brendan's Land or New Ireland long before the canting Britishers got here, not to mention the greedy Dutch.'

Said Tabby hastily as if she feared her husband's Celtic convictions might sour our reunion, 'Brendan thinks his country deserves more credit in the world. He writes songs about it.'

Now all was clearer still. I said, 'As a friend of Mr Ironside did you compose "The Ballad of Pudding Wharf" by any chance?'

Brendan laughed. 'You know it, sir?'

I laughed too. 'I saw it printed in a broadsheet.'

'Sure, it was a grand uprising. And a famous pome.'

'I helped you escape it, Enoch,' said Tabby.

'How could I forget?' Our eyes met dangerously. I added quickly, 'But you must come and meet Mrs Sally again.'

'She's here? Oh, this is wonderful.'

'As is Rusty.'

'Oh, no! D'you hear that, Brendan?'

264

'I do, Tabs, I do. And I pray you, sir, lead us to him. And Mrs Sally herself also. One of the finer women of the world.'

'Follow me,' I said.

Needless to say Sally welcomed Tabby like a long-lost daughter and soon had her and Brendan lodged in the green suite for the duration of their sojourn in New York. At dinner-time Rusty appeared. His face upon seeing Brendan O'Bryne was as of a lion amazed and then there was this almighty embrace that was more like a clash of Titans than a human greeting. Never have I seen such a backslapping nor heard such baloney (both Irish and Cockney) among so many fierce bellowings of joviality and then in the next minute they were gone to slake their almighty thirsts (sharp as cross-cut saws) in a little snug Rusty said he'd just opened up against the wall. The beauty of this house being there was a covert hatch at the back to which the Algonquin could repair at dusk when in need of naughty firewater. Strictly illegal of course, but warming for them on a winter's night and for Rusty, too. And of course he had taught them to pay with skins – so now he was rich in beaver, raccoon and musquash. And could, at a pinch, also offer the odd virgin squaw under cover if required. In other words, happy little diddly-does were there for the taking if a fellow was smart enough, right?

After dining with Sally and Tabby I descended to the laboratory again. I retreated out of prudence; Tabby's contiguity having been, as it always was, rather inflammatory for me. Already I had been tempted to allow my hand to stray under the table to her knee, etcetera. And this despite Sally's watchful eye and the respect I had conceived for the violence clearly inherent in Tabitha's Irish husband. However, alongside these conflictions, I did apprehend that, having returned to her parents at Penge, Tabby had discovered herself sadly mistook. She had not been received in charity as a prodigal daughter but instead had been soundly reviled, beaten and then kept a virtual prisoner for a year before being forcibly betrothed to a red-eyed Reverend who announced with lip-licking relish that he was prepared as an act of piety to take soiled goods for a wife and would surely drub her once a week to keep her in the strictest way of righteousness.

At this bitter prospect Tabby had sought the help of the family's latest maidservant (who also wished for a world kinder than that afforded by Puritan Penge) and together they had contrived to escape. They had, of course, walked straight to London where upon enquiring after Mrs Sally, but finding no trace of her, they had fallen in with this Irish man who was singing in a taproom at Cripplegate. He and his fellows gave them food and shelter and later made honest women of them, too.

Master Stella was awaiting me in the laboratory. He brought unwelcome news. His furnace for the new process was built but the smithy that had undertaken to forge the steel doors and other necessary garnitures for it could not now deliver, they said, until the end of January next. All else at the workshop was now completed but the lack of these essential furnishings was a threat to the whole enterprise. Stella had intended to build up the heat of the furnace over the twelve days of Christmas but without doors to enclose it this was impossible. He had already prepared the mixing of the new metal in little, now all that was wanting was the essay of it in a larger amount within the heat of the new, great furnace. Would I accompany him to the smithy to reinforce his protestations at this renegation upon the contract?

I was nothing loath. Indeed I was breathing fire. And spitting blood. There lurks within me something of a Welsh dragon. For the most part he sleeps quietly enough, merely coiling and moiling in his dreams. But now he was awake upon hot coals, incandescent, and urgent to fly forth to lay waste all who dared oppose him.

I said, 'Let's go.'

For a master smith, a caster of iron, and a Dutchman, Master Bol was remarkably small. He wore high heels to his boots to make him appear taller. But his chest was deep and his arms powerful. It was only the nether part of him that reduced his stature. His face bore a close resemblance to a squashed bun that ever expected further pressing if not gobbling up for breakfast.

Seeing us he at once gave me a hundred reasons for the delay. The same he had already given Master Stella. All were of the usual kind: there had been a flood of emergency work – broken plough shares, forced window bars – New Amsterdam was become a lawless city since it was given over to the happy-go-lucky English – coopers' hoops etcetera and his three apprentices were off sick with the clap and the pox and – But here I cut him short with a peremptory impatience worthy of Rusty and that fire-drake within me.

I said, with weight, 'Master Bol, do you wish to continue in business in New York?'

He grew pale and puzzled. 'How please you mean, sir?'

His English was clear enough yet a little disjointed. And this his want of easy fluency provoked in me a yet more busy abruptness.

I said, 'It is within my competence, sir, given my standing in this town, sir, to revoke your licence to trade, sir.'

'What licence?' said he, aghast. 'I have no licence.'

'Worse and worse, Master Bol. No licence? Tut tut. Surely you must be aware that from Michaelmas Day last no person may carry on a business or trade or practice of any kind whatsoever in New York without first obtaining a licence at a cost of one hundred dollars payable annually to the Bank of the Golden Fleece at Pearl Street?' I confess that uttering this falsity *extempore* gave me a certain malign pleasure, since it was evident that such officious-sounding blather could frighten poor Master Bol witless.

'Is this law?'

'It is, sir. Of the city council.'

'I have not heard it.'

'You have now. So harken to me, sir. And let your understanding hang upon my words. You are already in grave default yet I may, if I choose, ameliorate your condition. I will undertake, thanks to my close acquaintance with the governor of the Bank of the Golden Fleece, General Rodney Mars, the distinguished victor of the Battle of Pudding Wharf, to waive this awkward matter of your licence provided you complete the work due to me and Master Stella by the end of this week at a discount of two hundred dollars.'

'But that – that is not possible.'

'Then this forge and foundry will be closed forthwith.'

'Forthwith?'

'This instant. These premises are illegal. And only an extraordinary dispensation from me and General Mars can save you from destitution.'

'But – but – if I could do it – this work – and this *if* is very big, sir, a big if, yes, why must I discount you two hundred dollars, please?'

'One hundred for the licence and one hundred for the cost of issuing it out of season, sir, for you must know any rupture in the smooth process of a bank receiving money puts that bank not only to a loss of interest but to the expense of revising the books.'

'Oh, you will pay it for me?'

'Even so, sir. Provided the work is done on time for that much less.'

'Oh, thank you, sir.' He smiled foolishly, so great was his relief at this supposed mitigation of a spurious terror. 'That is very kind of you. I was so worried for a moment.'

Stella said, 'But you must deliver upon Saturday at the latest.'

Said I, 'Or all is null and void. For you should know, Master Bol, that your work is part of an endeavour vital to scientific enquiry. That these garnitures you have so far failed to supply are essential to the manufacture of an almighty machine the like of which has neither been conceived nor constructed before. A machine that will generate the *prima materia* that is that first matter out of which Creation itself was created. I speak advisedly, sir, of that thing we may term "the secret of the universe". Nothing less than that! Furthermore Master Stella and I are not engaged upon some frippish, idle *ignis fatuus* or folly, but obeying the prescription of two of the greatest intellects the world has ever seen – intelligences whose lightest speculations are like unto philosophical fire storms! To wit Mr Isaac Newton of whom even you and your gross cheese-gobbling countrymen should have heard, and Mr Robert Boyle, no less renowned as an atomist, chemist and Christian. In short, sir, you have to date impeded the onward march of science and are in danger of eternal obloquy. For make no mistake, if you fail this second time, I shall proclaim your dereliction so vigorously that you will become an object of scorn throughout this world and the next. So now, mayhap, you have some measure of my impatience? You, sir, in your petty insolence, have put the great work of the philosophers, the *magnum opus* no less, upon – as it were – upon, sir, an obscure shelf to lie forgotten, neglected, disregarded! Given that enormity you must – if you are to make amends – you must now perform what I commanded six weeks ago and forge at once these doors and furbishments the sacred art requires. Do this by Saturday noon next and you may yet restore your reputation in the annals of alchemy as a dilatory yet well-intentioned toiler in the vineyard whose humble skills contributed to the monumental *experimentia* initiated by such gods among men as Mr Newton, Mr Boyle and me – Enoch Mercurius Powys!'

Phew! How I pummelled the pulpit. Sparing neither Master Bol's now sweatful contriteness nor my own glowing self-regard. Even Stella stood abashed, his brow bedewed at hearing me in my Welsh rhetorical mode or hwyl as we call it.

Bol said in scarce any voice at all, 'I promise to work every hour God sends, sir.'

Even this could not assuage me. I added, 'Do so. Or be reviled among men as he who imperilled the discovering of God's own secret. For you must know, sir, that all procedures in the *magnum opus* are calculated, nay, tabulated to coincide with the forceful motions of the heavens, of the great and lesser stars – the moving and the unmoved. Therefore a contrivance uncontrived, or a substance unprepared, or an essence unrefined or an adept unready by a due date can set all at hazard. And understand further that this our enterprise is aimed at next midsummer's day which means Master Stella here must needs have blown the great triple glass by Lady Day at the latest so that the processes this engine is designed to nurture may maturate by Ascension Day so that I may coct and decoct, define and refine, note and notate all that it issues, which will be naught else but the true components of God's own unknown *prima materia* by the aforesaid immutable date – that is to say the noon of Midsummer in this next year of grace, may Jupiter help us all. So that when at that meridian Great Sol shines forth so shall I likewise blaze out with an illumination no less brilliant. Do I make myself plain?'

Of course I had not. How could I expect an humble smith (and a Butterbox from Rotterdam at that) to comprehend my meaning? But at least the force of my convictions had been made manifest to him and as he bowed Stella and me from out his foundry I had little doubt that he would now honour the commission upon time. I cannot say I felt entirely proud of myself. For the most part I detest bullies and bullyings, but too much was now at stake for me to rest gently upon my usual scruples. Thus it is that the sacred art makes tyrants of us all.

Stella said as we strolled along West Side, 'Never have I beheld a man so blasted. But is it true Bol requires a licence to trade, professor? For if he does, then surely so do I?'

I laughed and slapped him on the back. I said, 'You most certainly will if you fail to make the glass, Master Stella. But no, it was but a bogey or bugbear such as we invent to keep children in remembrance of their duties. But I dare say that should I, of an easeful evening, mention this matter to General Mars then by the week following (if not sooner) the absolute necessity of purchasing licences to trade from nowhere but the Bank of the Golden Fleece will have been entered upon the council statutes and adverted throughout the town.'

'I hear on all sides that General Mars is sure to be made mayor next year?'

'All sides are correct, sir. As I understand it the election is, in effect, already made.'

'Yet people say it is to be by a free vote – as with balls in a box – by all the householders of New York that General Mars will be chosen? How can it then be so certain?'

Again I laughed. 'Master Stella, as a sometime citizen of Venice you must know that every town, city or republic's government is without exception ever – how shall I express it? – a little more, no, rather of a greater complexity than that? Some balls in the ballot box have, as it were, a density more specific than others. And besides, should any decent householder have any doubt about voting for General Mars then you may be sure that certain interested parties – as we say – will be on hand to advise them with some severity upon their future, unhappy prospects.'

'Are you saying the New World is like unto the Old, sir?'

I nodded. And at this we were both silent, suspended in a hiatus of perfect ironical apprehension of the world as it was and ever will be. This was superseded by an almighty gust of laughter from us both in concert. After that there was no need of any further discourse upon government between us and we each returned to our abodes with the greatest good will on both sides. To which I shall append a corollary: if you are an adept in need of a spirit akin to your own (and which of us is not?) go at once to your nearest glassblower.

♂

Is it spooky? It is. I mean no sooner does Monty come on over than we've got Brendan too. And Tabby. Comely as ever. Oh, Jeez, whatta flower to pluck that one was when I first eyed her, way back, when she was all of fifteen, in tears, barefoot, starved for the sake of virtue, outside the New Exchange. And her, in her innocence, newcome to London Town to seek her fortune. The which she found wiv me. Then wiv Sal. And next wiv Enoch, the slippery sod, and now at last and deservedly so – for Tabs is what I call yer cosy, hearthrug cunny – wiv the great roofer, rebel, and renowned songsmith, the O'Bryne himself.

That said I shall say I did have quite a time advising Brendan how Monty Cruickshank was all right now. Like kosher as our mutual mucker Abe Shemozzle would say. We was mates again. Bygones was bygones. Everything was forgiven if not forgotten. But that's the trouble wiv your Celtics, innit? They ain't in the business of forgetting, are they? Never mind forgiving. Like wiv them a grudge is a grudge for ever, right? Besides, Bren had written this ballad, hadn't he? Saying in rhyme what a bastard of a sheriff Monty had been? And, as we all know, once yer Paddy's made a bleeding-heart ballad of it, that's the sacred truth, correct?

However, after many jars, not to say quart tankards, the past got set aside (just) and we all start having a most amicable time and I'm hard at it persuading Brendan to set up in New York as a master builder wiv my blessing. Like on an interest-free loan from the Bank of the Golden Fleece. Which is some benefaction I may tell you in this naughty day and wicked age. Yeah. And I can see Bren's tempted but who then puts up her pennyworth? You've guessed it, squire. Sally. My best and only (save for Lucille, natch) but at this particular instant a right pain in the rectum.

270

Sal says, 'But Bren and Tabby intend a musical career, Rusty.'

'Yer what?' says I, a-gob.

Tabby says, 'At London we're well known. We sing and play at all the taverns from Eastcheap to Cheapside to Holborn.'

'You do?'

'Surely,' says Bren. 'And we're after being known as the Singing Shamrocks. And much called for we are.'

'Oh, Tab's turned Irish, has she?'

'By marriage she is.'

'Is that all it takes?'

'Look here upon this, Rusty,' says Sal, producing a bill printed at Paul's announcing the Shamrocks and their repertoire. Like it reads: 'Hear ye, good people! The Shamrocks sing to their viols and portable organs upon Friday at the Bull and Bush and upon Saturday at the Dolphin. They will please your ears with ballads, catches, duettos, including: On a May Morning, The Warsong of King Brian Boru, The Bells of Hell, Pretty Miss Molly, Touch my Thing (to verses by Mr Pepys), and, by public demand, the ever-verdant Ballad of the Battle of Pudding Wharf in its entirety – 101 quatrains.'

Reading the aforesaid I chuckle and say, 'But is there money to be had by this, Bren old lad?'

'Surely,' answers he. 'But necessarily of a supplementary nature.'

'Ah! So you could be, if you was to choose, both a master builder *and* a ballad master – like?'

'I dare say. For I sing when I work and I work at my singing.'

Whereupon we all guffaw and gargle and dear old Tabs gets out the viols and she (Christ, could I get up that one again!) and Brendan warble away making a tunesome noise, I must say. Like they're really catchy numbers, right? And their voices! Pitched like perfect wiv him a pure tenor and her a bright sopranissimo. Whilst their fingers on the strings get so deft and so neat I'm struck dumb wiv the pleasure of it. Especially when Tabs exchanges her viol for a tin whistle yet makes it sound like a silver flute. Clever nay neat.

So this side of things is nicely and we go along towards the festive season and then beyond on a tide of good will, good beer, good malooka, good living, good friends, good loving and happy humorousness. And it's all so pleasing you could get to wonder – if you was a moody sorta sodomite – if it can last? Well, it did. Yeah. I was on the up and up. Like in the ascendant. After knocking over Arnold Jay Stone I couldn't put a foot wrong. I was the toast of high and low. There wasn't no son of a bitch in New York could do enough for me. Nor for any mate of mine. Consequence? We was asked everywhere

– me, Sal, Lucille, Enoch, Monty, Bren, Tabs. What a party. On and on and on. Like we was all high as kites for weeks – and I don't mean the paper variety, I mean them big, red, greedy birds of prey you get wherever there's some poor so and so's liver and lights to be had. Some are born greedy others needy, right?

All our businesses boomed. Pearl Street was at it like knives night and day as was my other knocking shop down on the waterfront. Also Stone's bawdy house for boys (whatta bonanza!), together wiv all his and my above-board interests: garbage, market protection, furs, harbour dues, betting, racing, widows' mites (investment of) etcetera. My rival had also been into opium but on that subject I consulted Enoch in his wisdom and he was of the view I ought to stay clear of it. Like it's all right for your Easterners but it saps the Westerner's will to win, he said, so I put that little bit of traffic out on a franchise to a Chinaman, name of Mr Ho Ho. A ruthless little fella but your oriental will always play it straight if you do. If not, then he's the same as us, right? Like anything goes, the more evil the better.

As for the bank! Jeez, it was a marvel. So much so I had to buy yet again. The next house next door. So now we'd got these *three* premises all adjoined on Pearl Street – Numbers 13, 14, 15, right? And already it had crossed my mind to demolish the lot and build one dirty great bastiment twice the present height in which to accommodate everything: money, cards and cunny – not to mench dice and dancing girls.

But I put that idea to one side of the fire, in a skillet to keep warm for later maybe, because like then I've got more than enough on my platter just dealing wiv the success I'm enjoying. Especially now everyone's saying it's a foregone conclusion I'll be mayor by next summer. Why, even fellow Councillor Ambrose keeps inviting me out to gents' pow-wows and parleys. Seems he's greasing up for honourable defeat. And while I won't say I like him (his filthy morals, for a start, are fit only for bishops) I will say he's starting to sound like a bloke I could do business wiv. You know, respectful – the *sine qua* whatsit wiv me, remember?

So *tout va bien* as Lucille so often says. And, boy, is she filling out just now! And she's dead set on christening the fruit of our loins 'Ercule which leaves me a shade unhappy. Like it sounds too Frenchified for me. So after rumination I tell her I'll accept 'Ercules the Second, provided it's pronounced in the plain old English way. To which she concurs. I then enquire when is this mighty infant due to burst upon a gobsmacked world exactly? And she says, equally exactly, Midsummer's Day next. At noon. That is the 21st of June so he can be baptised three days later on St John's Day and after that I've gotta lay on an enormous firework display like is traditional on that date back home in France, she says.

But that's enough from me for the moment except I can't wait for Shrove Tuesday to come round because that's when we're all gonna ride the goose, right? Me, Bren, Monty, Enoch. What's that you ask, squiress? What's riding the goose? Well, to be honest I can't tell you just yet what really goes on 'cos I've never done it before neither but from what I hear . . . oh, sorry, darlin', here's Madam Venus come round again. How she shines. It's her turn now.

♀

Truly I do not know what else to say except thank you, Percy. Thank you, thank you. I do allow, of course, that I should also enquire where on earth did you get this ruby necklace, that great opal ring, these sapphire chokers, those emerald bracelets? And as for all these ropes of pearls – why, here they lie carelessly before me like fishermen's tackle left about a harbourside. But given such heaps of brilliance, how can I bear to ask so dull a question? Rather I prefer to call back yesterday when you were pleased to place this almighty yellow adamant in my navel. Oh, Lord, how it tickled! So sharply was it cut. Oh! Such a rock not even Danaë got from Jove. Her best was him as a shower of gold. But Percy, Percy, should you be presenting me with all these sparkling baubles? They must have cost the earth and if I'm honest (the which according to Rusty I can now afford to be) then I'm bound to admit to myself that you as cheat, patricide, castaway, lunatic, adept's apprentice, kitchen boy and cook's lover, haven't got a Boston bean. So what, in perdition's name, is going on?

Such were my conflicting emotions on receipt of Percy's bounty. Though very soon my initial girlish delight was overcome by matronly caution. And so it was one snowbound Saturday, when Percy had been given time off by Enoch, and even I had little or nothing on hand in the kitchen, that we repaired to the pink boudoir and after some pretty toyings and a most exquisite debauch I put the necessary question to him. Whence had he got all this priceless booty? And this time he wasn't to fob me off with tomfool tales of buried chests on desert isles – I wasn't born yesterday, not today, no.

It was in this manner that I came to learn of Enoch's thefts from our bank. How he and Percy had burrowed through the wall into the vault next door and removed two chests of coin and a coffer full of these very jewels in order to fund the creation of his blessed bubble as commanded by his mentor at Cambridge. That man! It's him I blame. Always putting ideas into Enoch's head. Crazy, impossible ideas that forever put us to large expense.

The thousand dollars I'd agreed to hadn't proved sufficient for the enterprise. There had been difficulties with the builders and the building of the new workshop where the great glass was to be made. And now, said Percy, the professor was obsessed by time, too.

'Time?' said I. 'Why?'

'Because the glass must be made by a certain date so the contents may be distilled by another so Professor Mercurius can have discovered the secret of the universe by Midsummer's Day at noon sharp.'

'That's as maybe,' said I. 'But it isn't the point. I'm talking about your joint thievery, Percy. Yours and Enoch's. Suppose those who have left their precious goods with us for safe-keeping return to claim them out of deposit? What then?'

Here Percy was at a loss and tried to distract me with a kiss. But I would have none of it. I said, 'You must take these jewels back, Percy.' And with that I tipped them all into his naked lap at which he giggled like a schoolboy caught with his breeches down. As indeed they were. But, despite this distraction, I told him I was serious and, that much though I loved such beauty and brilliance, I could not be a party to embezzlement of our customers' goods. I now had a reputation to keep up that I would not put at hazard.

He, however, protested he was unable to receive them back again – since to do so would be sure to make him run mad again.

At this I lost all patience. 'Oh, no, you won't, sir!' I cried. 'This is quite different from before. You are as sound in mind, and as crafty, and as wholly a cheat as any of us! And I don't exclude Enoch, Rusty or, for that matter, me!'

'But can't these jewels be our secret, Mrs Sally? As secret as our reawakened affection for each other? For I'm certain the professor has no notion of this our liaison. He thinks I'm just your pastry cook.' And with that he began to knead my buttocks as if they were a pair of cottage loaves to be set by the fire to rise.

Removing his hand (despite his possessing a most exact touch for both pastry and parts) I said – just, 'Of course, our pleasures have to be kept secret, my dear. But the jewels must be put back. Should Rusty discover them gone all chaos would come. It would provoke such a storm as could wreck us all.'

'Provided it washed us up upon a tropic shore I should not

complain, Mrs Sally,' answered he, in a voice as dulcet as his fingers that were now about my left tit.

Nor me, thought I and at once I was obliged to bite my tongue so as not to say it for my lord did have – oh dear – such a way with him. Thus in this wise did commonsense pretty well prevail and after some further converse I did succeed in persuading him to take the jewels down to the laboratory and to place them yet again in the coffer. I also tried to make him swear he would persuade Enoch to return them to the vault, even if it meant breaking open the wall once more. But in this I confess I failed – largely because, at last, out of sheer, revived luxuriousness, I allowed certain other expressions of his to distract me from the very discourse I had instigated. But that's the trouble with me, is it not? The flesh is ever willing while the spirit is ever weak.

Later, upon a snowbound Saturday night, a good while after Epiphany, where should I find myself but enfolded, most sentimentally, in Enoch's arms? Back again with my Welsh wizard. No wonder Dame Fortune is reported to be worse than me. We were both warmed by wine as were Brendan and Tabby, Rusty and Lucille, and Monty with his latest lady – a blonde from Breuklyn. The evening was something of a celebration, it being Tabby's twenty-first birthday, and after supper we had become happily awash with remembrances of our earlier days and the singing of old songs. And whilst all these our vaunting reminiscences proceeded with an easy, hearty, sometimes tearful warmth which pleased us mightily (for once enough wine has passed there are no tunes like the old ones, are there? No jests that aren't the better for their being heard before, and, I dare say, no friends like those tested by time and change) I found myself remembering what Percy had promised me so recently: *viz.* to persuade Enoch to return those jewels to the vault. The thought preyed upon me so much throughout Tabby's rendition of Old Ben's old song, 'Drink to me only', that when the others got up to dance to Brendan upon his bagpipes – oh, yes, he played them, too – I decided to confess my knowledge of their presence in the laboratory and to beg Enoch to return them before their loss was revealed. Suppose, said I, the lady to whom they belong were to claim them? Indeed I am surprised they were not called for during the season just past. Will you promise me, Enoch? I ask for your sake, not mine, since, as I told Lord Spark upon his showing me the coffer one afternoon when you were with Master Stella at his new workshop, I fear that if Rusty – and, shush, let me whisper it close to your ear – I fear Rusty would take it very hard to discover the bank had been cheated. Especially now he's to be elected mayor and is therefore presenting himself as the shrewdest of financiers, the soul of rectitude, and a paragon of honour. What do you say?

☿

Well, for a start, I did not tell Sally I was now become aware of her dallyings with Percy. Nor that I had noted his continual rifling of the jewel case followed by the sudden restoration – last Tuesday – of all that he had stolen.

I admit that after the Ambrose ball and before the ending of the old year I had been so intent upon my pursuit of Mr Newton's secret that I had failed to notice Percy's disaffection with the laboratory. But of late he had made it clear as daylight that he much preferred his labours in Sally's kitchen to any I might require. Whenever he could he would find an excuse to disappear upstairs. And depart with what I may justly describe as an extreme, tumescent impatience only to return soft, pliant, moderated.

As you may imagine it did not require an abundant experience of the world to infer that his reformed lordship had found a mistress. And that she must be none other than his old one – Sally. Half of me was glad of it, half not. The one half told the other we were, after all, but back where we had been before. But that other half was not so sure, nor so sanguine. In a word I was divided within and that being the case I had proceeded to lose myself in my work rather than seek a resolution to the affair. *Quieta non movere* became my motto – let sleeping dogs lie.

But now I was informed by Sally (however disingenuously) of her cognisance of my theft of the jewels, I answered as follows: 'My dear Sally, you are quite right. Rusty would be most put about if they were called for. I shall return them as you request.'

Upon this reassurance she kissed me gratefully and we got up to dance and shortly after the evening dissolved into a succession of joyful retirements among which Sally's and mine were not the least.

But the next day my promise to Sally was quite set aside by Master Stella coming to me, through a blizzard of sleet and snow, to announce that I must go with him at once to observe his first attempt to blow the glass. Master Bol, thanks to my rebuke, had delivered the necessary furbishments and the furnace was at the required heat. Moreover, Stella's new assistants were now appraised of the intended process and as impatient as he to proceed.

I needed no urging but went with him at once. Yet in the event we were disappointed. Such are the constant frustrations adherent unto new science. The elements Master Stella had mixed together in which red lead preponderated were not yet in a just proportion, and in his first attempt to heat this metal in the new furnace and blow it largely within a bronze mould set inside the new-dug pit which was of a capacity to give room to the manufacture of such a mighty ball, I saw him fail. The molten mass fell from the blowing iron with a fiery plop to cool into a lump of glassy jelly at the bottom of the mould.

Stella announced that with this size of gather (for so the embryo glass is termed) at the end of the iron no blower in the world, had he the muscles of Atlas or the lungs of Boreas, could inject enlarging breath into the substance. The weight was too much, exactly as he had feared it might be. Another yet lighter mix must be sought and found and he begged my pardon for the raising of my hopes thus prematurely. He would work upon the formula again and also upon the means of breathing air into it for, as he had likewise suspected, it was clear this present approach to the problem was, unfortunately, false. Apart from a new mix of metal what was equally required was not a single blowing iron but a triple one.

'A triple one?'

'For a triple glass, professor. One tube set inside another with another inside that. For three different potencies of breath.'

I said, 'But how can one man blow three breaths into so much metal at the same time?'

'He can't. But bellows could.'

'Go on,' I said, counting the cost. And Stella proceeded to advise me that this triple iron would not only receive air from these aforesaid bellows but it would also be rotated mechanically by brass cog-wheels. In this wise the iron inserted from above into the furnace would lift out the molten glass revolving all the while and proceed with it, ever turning upon itself, by way of a steel gantry set upon wheels to the mould into which it would be gently lowered while the system of various bellows worked by himself and his assistants would provide three carefully calculated currents of air – a forceful gale for the outer glass, a stiffish breeze for the middle one and the merest zephyr for the inmost vessel.

'You really intend to blow all three glasses simultaneously?' I cried, astonished.

'Oh yes, professor. Just as I did with the model glass. Each within the other.'

'Or do you mean each outside the other?'

And at this we both laughed in unison, recognising at once the paradoxical truth that opposites may become compatibles when looked at another way.

But even as I laughed my heart was sinking for it was clear these new necessities would be excessively expensive. And here I also recalled my promise to Sally that I would return the jewels to the vault. That was now impossible. I should have to sell them covertly and break that promise, deceiving Sally as well as Rusty.

I sighed and told Master Stella I needed to see comprehensive plans and designs to justify such increased expenditure. He produced them at once thus prompting me to suspect that the entire business that day had been a deliberate play or ploy (or plot indeed) to soften me up, as they say. Well, Rusty would.

Here were detailed working drawings for the triple blowing iron; for a swivel arm that would guide it into the furnace; for the cogs to rotate it and for three sets of bellows connected to it by way of flexible tubes made of softest leather which would convey the air to the gather.

And beside these designs (all impeccably drafted) were others for the gantry, presented in plan, elevation and cross-section, that would as aforesaid bring the metal to the mould where, once it had expanded into three vessels in one, it could rest and cool prior to being set upon a bench also to be built expressly for the purpose. Only then might the spouts and collars be attached.

Said I, 'This bench will support the glass here at your workshop, Master Stella? Once it is finished?'

Stella crossed himself, murmured *deo volente* and added with a nod, 'It and the glass will then be placed upon a cart to be brought to your laboratory, professor, where it may also be employed as part of the machine. And that reminds me – it will need to be a strong cart for the transportation. Possibly also built especially for the purpose?'

'No, sir,' I said briskly. 'General Mars has a plethora of mighty garbage carts quite suited to the transport. We may employ one of those. But this moveable gantry or scaffold – who will build *that*?'

'I have already spoken with the builder and Master Bol and they will do it together.'

'On time?'

'Most assuredly. Master Bol lives in fear of you and the builder has a great respect for you now that we have paid him.'

'How much will all these new things cost?'

Here Stella hesitated before naming a sum as prodigious as the groan I emitted upon hearing it.

Expostulated I, 'Six thousand dollars! Why, that's half as much again as I've already expended on the project. And we began with an estimate of a mere thousand!'

Now Stella commiserated. Said he, 'I warned them you would say that. But they insist they cannot do it for less.'

A silence grew between us as we both stared down into the mould where the molten blob was now a solid mass. It looked forlorn. A stillborn nullity at the bottom of a grave. I shut my eyes at it then turned away to gaze up at the workshop's timbered roof where the tiles lay so snug not a drip or drop of the snow that covered it outside had come through since the lighting of the furnace. Truly the builder knew his business and so in the end had Master Bol. They had earned Master Stella's respect so who was I to baulk at this further expense? Was I to prejudice the completion of Mr Newton's alchemical machine for lack of mere money?

I said at last, 'I bow to necessity, Master Stella. Tell them to proceed.'

♂

Come February – wiv brass monkeys still in dire trouble – Shrove Tuesday came around. I mean, if there's one thing you can rely on it's God's own calendar, correct? Some of His holy days may be a bit shifty, but at least you know your major ecclesiasticals are gonna make sure they've been calculated way ahead and then get duly celebrated. Wiv loadsa kneeling, extra long litanies and lotsa moaning, groaning and contriteness from the laity. Like let us pray, 'Sorry, guv, we've done it *again*.' Which is why I've never been that much of a churchgoer. Just don't have the knees for it.

However, that's enough of the theologicals. We gotta ride the goose, right? And that's as wicked a day's sport as any gent could wish for. And maybe a lady, too. If she's of a gamesome humour. You are, bookeress? Jeez! And there was me thinking you'd got your head stuck into this lumpa verbalisation. Right, let's go. Like I know what it's about now.

It proceeds thus. After breaking our fast on Sally's pancakes wiv maple syrup, eggs, bacon, hash, mushrooms, dipped bread, coffee, root beer, real beer and canary wine according to taste we all tool out downtown. You wiv me, doll? I bet you are. And all a-wobble to be close to me, right? Whoops, don't slip on the icy cobbles, darlin', lean on me, good girl.

Now us being high society we make a late entrance upon the scene. Like keep the common people waiting is ever our motto so they know we're of a different kind to them. Not *too* different, of course, because this is the New World, but just enough different for them to know it's us who's really in charge however matey we may make out we are.

So here we are in our finery, bookeress: you, me, Sally, Enoch, Lucille, Bren, Tabby, Monty and his latest, a brunette from the Bronx. Unusual that. Most of 'em settled up there are your typical blonde Hollandesses. And yeah, the whole town's here, ready and waiting. And we get the full New York welcome – hats in the air, thunderous applause, quivering curtsies, big mitts stuck out and cheers from one and all as we make a sorta regal progress down the course.

Now what you're seeing is this: a dead straight run for the horses – say a good three furlongs – wiv salt and gravel put down on the snow to make the going soft for the run-up to the goose. Like you could say it's a sorta race. Get there first and you get first strike, right? Like unimpeded. At the goose. The said bird hangs head down, suspended by its tootsies from the crossbar, hissing like fuck. What? The crossbar? Oh, it's set up on two big posts so as to bestride the course. And it could remind you of a gallows seeing how that's exactly what it is. Yeah, we've borrowed it for the day off of the Court House. It's their spare one what they use when the main waterfront scaffold on East Side gets, you know, overloaded. Like it can only take ten felons at a go to hang there as a fair warning to others, so our justices often have to string up the minor offenders on this other one out the back. I tell you, New York's getting to be quite a merry town, but when I'm mayor I'm gonna have this big clean-up on crime. Like so no-body does it but me, right? Jest, squiress. Just my jest.

Anyrate here's this arse-over-tit goose hanging from the town's spare gallows over the track wiv its neck all greased. Wiv goose grease, natch. Good for the hair, Sal says. And you should see hers. Lustrous. Like spun gold. But the goose's neck shines in the sun more like silver – it being a white goose. Got it? Hope so, 'cos now it's time for the off. And we're taking our privileged positions on this dais right by the goose where the action's gonna be.

Down at the far end they've got six ponies lined up. Wiv six apprentices on top. Like this is the warm-up, right? Our turn comes later. And they're off! Here they come, pell-mell, belting down towards us wiv one lad on a nice little chestnut well out in front. And he's got his cleaver out! Christ, how it flashes in the sun. What, bookeress? I didn't mention cleavers before? No, well, maybe not, but

I thought it was obvious? Each rider at the goose has gotta have his cutter. Stands to reason. I mean, that's the sport. And this lot being apprentices have got the tools of their trade, haven't they? Like cleavers, kitchen knives, choppers, bill-hooks. Of course, us gents, when it comes to our go, we will have swords, natch. And ride one at a time. Sorta after you, squire. But not this lot. No. For this loada youth it's altogether now, rough 'n' raw and Hell's Highness take the hindmost.

For why? You ask for why? For why what? Cutters? Gawd, gimme patience. Let me spell it out, lady. The-lads-have-got-cutters-like-I-said-so-as-to-chop-off-the-head-of-the-goose. Yeah, that's right! The-living-upsidedown-goose-you-stupid-cunny! Like that's the name of the game, girl, the object of the exercise, the reason for the race. Jeez! And I thought you was the brain box round here – Enoch apart.

Yer what? It looks dangerous for the ponies? Well, yeah, yeah it is. They take their chance, too. But that's enough now because . . .

Wow! The lad out front on the chestnut is up in his stirrups swiping at goosey wiv a mighty swipe. Misses. And here come the next three and there ain't a pony's nose between 'em! They're all in a bunch. Their knives are out. One pony goes down. And how that bird twists and turns, beating its dirty great wings and squawking like – Jeez, one of 'em's hit it! Yeah! No, no, I tell a lie the grease has done its job, the knife has slid away and – what? What? Oh, no. You feel funny? Oh, heck, I thought you said you was gamesome, lady? You ain't? You reckon it's cruel. Oh, darlin'. You should see what we do to people out here. And besides the goose gets roasted after. Yeah, we'll all have a roast goose supper wiv . . .

Right! If that's how you feel, shog off. And you better skip the next page, too, while you're about it. After all this is history in the raw, doll. Tradition. Heritage. Frigging folklore. Like this is what Shrove Tuesday is all about on Manna Hatta: chopping heads off of innocent creatures at risk of yer own life and limb so as to eat 'em later.

Well, well, *adios*, *amiga*. Like that's the last time I ever invite anybody to interact on paper wiv me. As from now you get told.

So. Right. Next – at the climax of the merriness, and by popular acclaim, we was urged, ho ho, to ride the goose. By this time the apprentices, the fishmongers, the fish-wives (do any come harder?), the rattle watch, the masons, the chandlers, the mercers and even – wouldya credit it? – the milliners (devilish deft) have all had a go and variously succeeded or not. Like the score was: apprentices nil, fishmongers 2, fish-wives 5, rattle watch nil, the masons 1 (later disqualified – not enough grease on the goose's neck), chandlers 1, mercers 3 (surprise that) and milliners 4. So there you have it: sharp brutality and sharper finickiness have won the day and the fish-wives and milliners will eat hearty tonight.

The which brings me to us mounting our steeds. And like all of New York can't wait to see who, out of me, Enoch, Monty and Bren, will be the first to slice the head off of our particular feathered friend, sherwoomph, and ride clear of the jetting blood and flying head. Because, make no mistake, that is how it goes. Like goose heads, when struck, go every which way. And if you're in the crowd and happen to catch one while it's still squawking, well, I tell you, you'll be lucky for a year.

Moreover, as I said, us being who we are like gentry, we don't race up all together. Oh, no. That's for the common ruck. We go one by one. But for us the goose is strung up that much higher and is a bigger, stronger bird. Like it's a dirty great gander and it fairly glistens wiv grease from beak to crop. Also by this time we're all four kinda warm wiv the brandy Lucille's brought wiv her so one way and another it could be as perilous for us as for the gander.

Bren goes first. Riding like a champ. Such a way wiv horseflesh has Bren. Enoch, me and Monty have to strain our eyes against the sun to make out how he does. We see the sword flash, hear a mighty roar and mightier cheer. The bastard's done it first off and know what, Lucille's caught the head (we hear this later) and is saying to one and all, 'Quelle chance! Quelle bonne chance! C'est pour Ercule!' Talk about the luck of the Irish. And the French. But then they're ever in cahoots, right?

So now there's a wait while they put up the next goose and it's Monty's turn. He don't race up so quick as Bren but even so he sets a fair pace for a one-eyed jock wiv a wooden leg and takes a magnificent swipe at the target but it's no go. The bird eludes him.

Next, it's Enoch. And he's on my favourite mare – Miss Nosegay. Strawberry roan. A lovely little runner. He gets a big cheer. Oh, yeah, by now Enoch's a character, right? Like every jerker in New York knows the mad professor of Pearl Street.

Off he goes, kinda cool, at a briskish trot. Could be he's stretching the rules which are that the rider's gotta pass under the goose at a fair old clip. You don't just walk your nag up to it and take a standing swipe, no, that ain't the name of the game. No. You gotta be at least at a canter, better still a gallop – like that shows you're a real sport. But, of course, if there's one thing we know about Enoch Powys he ain't one of those, is he? Ah! Now he's broken into a canter. At the very last minute so he don't get disqualified. What a calculator. And he's there! He's up in the stirrups! He's making his cut! It's a nice slice. A mate would call it poetry in motion. The New World holds its breath. Has the Welsh wiz dunnit? Like the Irish balladeer? Also at the first attempt? If so it's a triumph for the Celts. But what's this? What is occurring? Oh, no. Oh, dear. Whatta catastrophe. Our wily conniver's sliding off of his mount. Gentle Miss Nosegay. He's falling. I know I shouldn't laugh but really. Oh, dear, oh, dear. He's all of a heap. And my roan trots on snorting like she's laughing, too. Which could well be. Oh, dear. Miss Nosegay and me, we both enjoy a risible.

But Christ! The women! They've all gone barmy! There's Sal, Tabs and Lucille, plus at least six of our so-called virginals, all rushing out onto the track to make sure their pet adept's all right. And, natch, the so-and-so is. He's on his feet shaking his head wiv loadsa rueful charm and leaning all over Tabs, Arabella and Lucille like they was cushions on a daybed. Whatta coxcomb.

How can I tell at this distance, you ask? Well done, squire! Attentive of you. Like if I couldn't see Bren chop off the goose's head, how was it I've come to see our resident sex mechanic goosing the girls? Right? That's your wonder, innit? Right. Answer? The sun's gone in. Behind a cloud. Got it? Good. And now they're helping him off the track and he's still taking advantage – I mean, why does he need Tab's left tit for support? – and it's time for me to mount. Wiv a manly leap into the saddle. The which I perform to general admiration all round. My horse is as handsome as his rider, of course. And as entire. A bay stallion going by the name of Rakehell. Sixteen hands. Mean as hell. And a right charger.

Away we go – Rusty 'n' Rakehell. A real team. Belting straight for it. No poncey hanging about for yours verily. It's like we was shot from a gun. And the sun's still behind that cloud so I can see the target wiv a deadly clarity. And is this bird a biggy! And does it squawk! Rakehell's going like the clappers, the bird's making wiv its flappers and I'm here and I go for it. Whatta cut! Such a flashing arc the like – oh, shit! Missed. I've frigging missed. Me! Like now we've gone past and I'm looking back, right? But no. No, no, hold on. For Chrissake, Rakehell, pull up, will yer? Can't you hear, you stupid nag? Everybody's cheering. We've done it, mate. You 'n' me. That's two outta four. So now it's gotta be a ride off, right? Like a sudden death dispute for the mastery twixt Bren 'n' me. To settle who's the man of the day.

Yeah, we went for it neck 'n' neck like them roaring boys the apprentices did. And like there was nothing between us – three times running. But everybody wiv their hearts in their mouths in case we cut off each other's head instead of the goose's. But we didn't. Like Bren nearly took off my nose and I almost skewered his nag but in the end no harm was done, a loada strenuousity got exerted and the goose survived wiv not a feather touched.

After our third go I decided to make a popular announcement. I said, sitting tall in the saddle, 'Ladies, gents and all. I reckon we've had our sport, don't you?' Yeah! they all shouted. 'And given that – given that – I also reckon' (and here I pointed to the bird still squawking like an oyster wife) 'that goose up there's a good goose, a fine goose, a brave goose, that deserves to roast another day, right?' Right, they all shout back, cheering fit to bust. Right. Well said, Rusty, etcetera.

And that's the finish of it. Away we go wiv me donating the malooka I've made on side bets to charity – in all the tidy little sum of sixty-four dollars which is what some Dutch bastard paid the Indians for Manna Hatta in the first place. And given how the dump's come on since, I'd say it was a snitch.

Oh, and the last goose gets taken down and made a great fuss of. So like it's a fairy tale ending, innit?

♀

Truffled roast goose
Take one 8lb-goose, 8oz of minced pork, the giblets of the goose, 2 black truffles and $2\frac{1}{2}$lbs of potatoes.

First, with a pointed knife, make several incisions in the skin of the bird and slide slices of the first truffle underneath. And here I should explain that after our day of riding the goose Lucille presented me with what she called her last treasure from home. It was a sealed jar in which four wrinkled lumps of something black were preserved. She said these objects were a special sort of subterranean mushroom from France. They were called *truffes* or truffles and were highly prized by *bons viveurs*. They would give a unique savour to the goose if I followed this recipe: *Oie rôtie à la truffe* as she called it. I did and I cannot recommend it highly enough. Follow this receipt and you will find it to be, as Enoch said, food fit for the gods.

Next, prepare a stuffing of the minced pork and the giblets *viz.* the goose liver, gizzard and heart all finely chopped and mixed with a little goose fat. Add the other truffle chopped. Season with salt and pepper and moisten with a small glass of applejack.

Stuff the goose and sew up securely. Place on the spit and roast for 2 hours, basting regularly.

Serve with the potatoes sautéed in a little of the goose drippings. One goose will suffice for 6 to 8 persons provided they are not greedy. However given this dish they will be, so allow for 6. Oh, and another thing: do not admit Rusty or his latter-day co-equal into your kitchen while the goose is roasting or he will be forever dipping pieces of bread into the dripping and groaning appreciatively at you – for the scent and flavour of truffles reduces strong men to grunting pigs.

That night we supped like kings upon two such birds and I cannot describe the taste. Suffice it to say that if mushrooms grow in heaven then they must surely taste like this? And could it be for these that Lucifer went to war?

But that's enough of the cook in me talking, because as we were finishing this feast we heard another discourse – from without. But this was more of a continuous roar or rant. No words could be distinguished but there was no mistaking its vehemence. Someone was plainly convinced of something and wanted all the world to hear.

Rusty rose up with an oath that was also a belch and strode to the window. He pulled back the shutters and stared out through the glass. And started to laugh.

He said, 'Hey, get a view of this!'

Up we all got from the table and crowded to the window to see the figure of a snowman standing upon a beer barrel. And below him, crouched amid tumbling snowflakes, was a single auditor: Percy. Moonlight and lantern light illuminated both as if they were set upon a stage and now there was but a window pane between us we could hear windspun words as well as notice that, beneath his blanket of snow, this lonesome rhetorician was dressed in black.

His words whirled as follows: 'Repent all ye that dwell herein . . . the Lord hath decreed . . . this lewd house shall be broken and every harlot scourged . . . repent . . . thy enormities, thy filthinesses, thy blasphemies . . . repent o Pearl Street for the planet Venus reigns in thy lower parts and shall be cast down, yeah, unto perdition. Repent . . . the end is nigh, nigh is the end, nigh, yeah, nigher than ye think.'

'Right,' said Rusty. 'I reckon that's enough of him, don't you? I'll go and shut his gob.'

'Surely,' said Brendan. 'A brute, intolerant pig of a Protestant.'

'I'm with you,' added Monty.

But I said, and as I said it I heard Enoch join in, too, and Tabs and Lucille even, 'Oh, no, Rusty, leave the poor soul be. He's harmless. Just another tub-thumper.'

'Oh yeah? Never. No. Bad advert for us.'

'But who's to hear? At this time of night? And besides who listens to a fanatic?'

'Well, that horrible Percy for a start. Look at him – drinking in every frigging word.'

'I fear his lordship may have regressed,' said Enoch. 'In which case I think it best, Rusty, to let things be for the moment and review the matter in the light of day tomorrow. For surely the only harm they may do tonight is to themselves, out there in the cold?'

Enoch's words prevailed and we closed the shutters, drawing near to the fire while Brendan and Tabs refreshed our ears with many a sweet song until it was time for us all to retire to bed. And as I slid down beside Enoch I could not help likening the chanting of that pious soul outside to the steady beat of waves upon a beach. And in that there was a kind of comfort – since not a single syllable of his manifold reproaches could be heard. And so it was that vice was lulled to sleep by virtue.

♂

We saw Monty off on the good ship *Vulcan* and it was a moving moment for some of us to think that give or take six or eight weeks he'd be back in dear old London Town. Sally was grieved, I was grieved, and so was Tabs, 'cos Bren 'n' her had decided, thanks to my persuasions, to settle in Manna Hatta after all. But Enoch wasn't much affected, nor Bren. Neither of 'em being of a sentimental tendency. In fact all that interested our chemical genius was some letters of a scientific nature he'd asked Monty to take back to his mate in Cambridge – that Professor Whoever. From the way Enoch went on about 'em you'd have thought they really mattered. But there again, between you 'n' me, I reckon he's now seriously up the flue, right?

On my left I hear Sally stifle a sob (I don't think she put out for Monty, not this time. Though I could be wrong, I dare say – but we won't dwell upon that) while on my right there's this line-up of these other ladies – what a dockload of chestfulness, your regular tit man is Monty – all heaving away as his ship eases out to sea. Talk about the ones you leave behind you. As I've previously said, for a one-eyed jock wiv a wooden leg our ex-sheriff doesn't do too bad, does he? What's more, and this more is, believe you me, squire, a very real more, the hold of the aforesaid *Vulcan* is stuffed full of beaver skins, musk ox hides, raccoon tails plus barrels of Virginia tobacco, bolts of linen and canvas, also good ship's cordage (attention Mr Pepys). In plain terms, Monty is sailing home in true merchant style as my trusted partner in the export/import enterprise that's now him 'n' me. Like we may have been deadly enemies at Pudding Wharf but we was true muckers, fellow pissers at West Side Cribs when we demolished Arnold Jay Stone. And like urine is thicker than water, right?

So that's Monty seen off and back we go – back to the normalities of running this town to our advantage. Why – one old buck told me only the other day he reckoned it was getting to be my private fiefdom. I demurred, of course, full of modesty, but I won't say I wasn't gratified, since the more that sorta word gets about the better for me. It gives confidence. And, as I've ever said, confidence is all.

Bren's business is on the up – like everybody's after him for roof repairs now the winter's on its way out and I've made sure (a word there, a nudge here) that nobody of note goes to any bugger else. And, as you might suppose, Bren's recruited pretty well every Paddy in town for the work, so the roofs of New York are like resounding even now wiv song. Jigs, ballads, laments. You name it Bren's roofers are bawling it – but being imaginative Micks it could be the words are a bit different from what you might expect, given the old familiar tunes.

And Tabby's followed Lucille's example. Yeah, she's in the family way. As are most of our virginals. Sal blames them fusiliers at the Ambrose Ball – Nell Gwyn's lot. But there again the New World's gotta be peopled, correct?

Meanwhile our pussy palace on Pearl Street continues as the most prized house of ill-fame on Manna Hatta wiv Sal running it like – well, words can't do her justice. I mean here we have Madam Venus, no other, and hostesses don't come better'n that. I tell you, squire, Sal sails in upon you like the goddess of love herself. She was born to make fellas feel good. I once had a dream of her (don't laugh – I can have my moments) coming towards me out of the sea. Yeah, I was on the beach doing press-ups. And there she was, my Sal, riding in on this dirty great cockleshell over these bubbly wavelets. Wivout a stitch. Like all she's got on is this unearthly smile and her hair in a golden plait that just about reaches her heavenly bits. And me, her protector and Sunday man as I then was, me I'm gob-smacked. It seems beauty can make gentles of us all. But what am I saying? Any more such talk and you'll take me for a right cod's head.

So all is well, nay, fine and dandy save for Enoch. I can't make him out. Not these days. I mean he's always been a law unto himself – specially in his laboratory – but what was he up to last week when I caught sight of him beside the Gentleman's Canal at well past midnight? Me 'n' Bren was just coming back from duffing up a market man who hadn't paid his dues when there's Enoch nipping along on the other side of the water. All hunched and furtive. He didn't see us but we saw him. Bren wondered if he'd got himself a new doxy but he didn't look to me like a fella on that sorta errand. Unless, and only now does the thought strike me, Jeez, unless he's struck up wiv Abednego again? After all the Ambrose residence is up there, facing the canal. And on the side we saw him. Could it be? If so I don't like it. That boy spells trouble. And wiv me coming up for mayor against Septimus Ambrose I want everything neat 'n' tidy. No dirty tricks or dirty rumours. If I'm seen as pals wiv mollymen there's some in this town are gonna include me out. I better have a word with Sal.

☿

To pay for Master Stella's latest requirements I had little or no choice but to sell the jewels. I had briefly contemplated reopening the hole in the wall and exchanging them for another money chest – stolen coin being, of course, less distinguishable than precious stones. But in the event I could not stomach the job. Once had been enough and to burrow through again would surely tempt providence? Beside, while waiting for Stella to complete the great glass, I had set about a series of experiments that I dared to hope might prove Mr Newton's seven precepts of the *magnum opus*: those very precepts which, thanks to my earlier travels and researchings, he had distilled from the transcripts I had made. These delicate enquiries could not be disrupted by digging through a wall and bricking it up again. And furthermore, Percy, since the coming of Brother The-End-is-Nigh, as we had dubbed him, was changed yet again. From thief and patricide to lunatic castaway and fugitive to reformed apprentice and pastry cook to clandestine lover of Sally he had appended another transmogrification: *viz.* disciple. And so devoted to his new master was he that he scarcely waited upon Sally, let alone me. In truth I rarely saw him save when he sat at the feet of that ranter (who now harangued the air outside our house every night) or took his place upon the tub and added his denouncements of us to his new master's. Oddly the pair of them soon became accepted as part and parcel of the town's diversity

288

while serving as a mighty advertisement for us. Our enterprises thrived yet again with an ever increasing clientele intent upon enjoying all the vices Brother The-End-is-Nigh and his disciple Percy (now self-styled Brother Praise-the-Lord) condemned so assiduously.

In consequence of these remonstrative vigils I was obliged to slip out the back way when upon my covert errands to a certain jeweller who dwelt by the canal. To this Levantine personage, who prefers to trade incognito, I sold all the rubies in that chest, most of the sapphires and emeralds, several of the larger diamonds and whole ropes of giant pearls. I fear he drove a hard bargain, forcing me to sell them for far less than their true worth but I was in no position to argue, let alone prevaricate, because if Stella did not have his gantry, triple blowing iron, bellows and cogs, the glass could not be made upon time and the whole process would be put at hazard. But what is a loss made upon things that have cost you nothing (save a measure of turpitude) when set against the resolving of the enigma of creation? The jewels got me the six thousand dollars and Stella got his necessaries.

By Lady Day, spring was come upon us with such limpidity and playfulness that the severities of the winter were quite forgot. And it was upon this day, precisely as I had commanded, that Master Stella completed the great glass. To say it was a miracle would be to invoke credulity to belittle science. Stella's cunning, labour and craft together, together with all his demands for a workshop and garnitures built to the purpose, were here justified as triumphantly as I hoped Mr Newton's theory would be proved.

But this is not to say that Stella's proceedings had been without their hazards. In an initial trial the swivel arm had refused to swivel sufficiently, and then his assistants had not worked the various bellows as shrewdly as was necessary, with the result that the two inner vessels had in the blowing fused into one. However at the next attempt all went better. The gather out of the furnace was exactly right, the blowing iron rotated sweetly, the swivel arm performed correctly, and the gantry ran to the mould in the pit with oiled precision.

Then, when the triple blowing began I found I could not bear to watch. As the glass expanded my heart was in my mouth and my bowels turned to liquid. I was obliged to retire and to return, tremulously, only when Master Stella, proud as a peacock, came in search of me to announce that the job was done and that none but he, and perchance a certain Master Stern at London, could have done it.

There it was. If in my mentor's drawings it had appeared not unlike a translucent onion now it was made it looked yet more so. Especially if you fancied that the six spiralled pipes sprouting from its topmost parts could be such curling leaves as many an onion kept in a dark place will generate of itself. The huge vessel was securely set within a circular aperture cut in the bench. Below that the slow-burning stove Mr Newton had designated would be placed once the entire glassy device was transported to my laboratory there to perform its part in determining the secret of the world.

♀

I was just come out upon the stoop on my way to my milliner when I saw it. Rusty's biggest garbage cart drawn by his mightiest pair of horses. And upon the cart, set amidst straw and secured by ropes, this shining ball. Behind it came another cart bringing a wooden bench like unto a giant butcher's block, and a machine upon wheeled legs that was very like a moveable scaffold. Ahead of this slow-moving procession walked Enoch with Master Stella, the glassmaker. Beside the carts, and behind, ran the street children of the town, shrieking, laughing, pulling faces. After them came every adult idler of New York.

Thus was the great vessel brought home to us at Pearl Street. As in a carnival. And it seemed also that the day itself was in a mood for frolic. How the breezes danced all about, fluttering the flags above the Court House and the masts of all the ships at anchor in the East River. How the clouds frisked, making the sunlight seem to dance. And when Great Sol's beams struck the triple glass how it blazed, as if set not merely to reflect light but to formulate it of itself. The thing flashed and winked and glowed like a round, complacent land-bomb or engineer's mine secure in the knowledge of its power. For the various reflections caught within its several walls of glass seemed not only to reinforce each other in all the colours of the rainbow but also to shoot out rays like fire darts. Why, the whole world was bedazzled, just as poor Mary must have been upon this her day when Gabriel flew in to inform her that she, in her simplicity, had been chosen to be the Mother of God.

On the vessel's arrival before the house Enoch strode up to me and, with a lordly gesture as of a philosopher justified, he said, 'There! D'you see, Sally? What do you say now? Has not your trust in me been well spent?'

But before I could reply a huge whistling, cheering and lewd capering broke out among the children and other onlookers. Our virginals had crowded to the windows of the dancing room to see what was happened outside, quite forgetting that they wore merely their masks. And if I'm honest their appearance caused just as much of a sensation as Enoch's alchemical machine. Nay, rather more, and of a singularly robust and ribald kind. So much so that I was obliged to run at once indoors and advise them to draw back from public view.

When I was come out again the task of removing the bench and glass from the carts had begun. But this proved a tedious labour and much of the crowd drifted away. The bench was installed first within the laboratory and then the scaffold was so placed that it might hold the great glass in a rope mesh (such as fishermen use to secure buoys that keep their nets afloat) and in this manner the whole contrivance could be, it was earnestly hoped, wheeled safely in. But the business was not easily accomplished and twice it looked as if the glass would fall. Indeed so fretful and abrupt became the comport of all involved in the work that I decided I was not wanted there and proceeded on my errand.

As I walked along to the milliner the apprehensions wrought in me by the taking in of Mr Newton's device (the manufacture thereof being, in my eyes, an imposition placed upon one philosopher by another who should have known better), these aforesaid apprehensions resolved into an earlier concern left over, like gristle upon a plate, from the night before. This was that Rusty had informed me of his glimpsing of Enoch one night, not a week ago, creeping along beside the canal. Whereat it had crossed his mind that Enoch had been upon, what he called, a naughty errand. 'You know, doll,' said he, 'a dodge or diddle-doddle? Like maybe Abednego? Could it be our adept has struck up again wiv that little bugger? What do you think, Sal? He was close to the Ambrose residence. You heard anything?'

To say Rusty's report, supposition and questions pierced me to the heart and soul is to state naught but the truth. My recollections of the ball were still only too lively; Enoch's perfidy with Abednego quite outweighing mine with Percy, naturally. Since then I had supposed, perhaps foolishly, that Enoch had become utterly in thrall to his latest chemical researches and the construction of his mentor's almighty machine. I could not bear even to imagine that he might the while be slinking out at night like an alley cat to visit Mrs Ambrose.

Rusty added, 'Like I don't like it, Sal. In my position I can't afford to be the partner of a sodomite.'

Said I, 'I know nothing of it, Rusty.'

'Yeah. But maybe you could, you know, work on him? Like tease the truth out of him? I mean I need to know, doll, or my chances of getting to be mayor could be down the conduit, right?'

I promised him I would try to inveigle the truth out of Enoch and that very night (this last night, as it happens) I went down to the laboratory only to find the place utterly shut up. No sign of Enoch and only the burble of Percy outside, roundly yet routinely cursing the house for its usual sins (hadn't he only recently delighted in the very best of them?) under a starlit sky. I waited a long time but at the last gave up only to see Enoch hurriedly returned at dawn for breakfast before dashing out once more to Master Stella's workshop.

'For today is Lady Day, dear Sally,' cried he. 'And Mr Newton's will is hereby accomplished. The world can now be quick with truth – not God's truth this time, Sally, but ours! All humankind's!'

And with this high boast he vanished. Said I to myself, 'Mayhap the Lord has yet to pronounce upon the event?' But even as I comforted myself with this pious thought I realised Enoch had allowed me no time at all to ask that question whose answer meant so much to Rusty and to me. What had been the true purpose of his nocturnal excursion along the banks of the Gentleman's Canal? All I can say is that had Enoch stayed and had I asked it our histories might have been other than they were. And are. For the past has a way of lounging like a rascal at a street corner, looking for present and future trouble.

But my new hat rallied my spirits. The above forebodings were quite banished. Looking at myself in the mirror I decided all my doubts were malignant fancies brought about by a long and savage winter. Spring was now come, my head was crowned with plaited straw and dancing feathers, my smile was full of hope, and the past, whatever it was, could go hang.

☿

With the glass got in and put upon the bench our present work was at a most satisfactory stop. Master Stella, his apprentices, and I drank to its safe installation whilst recalling together the last and most perilous moment when the great glass had slipped and would have dashed itself to pieces upon the stones of the street had not our manufactory's master spirit, Master Stella, in his best coat with the badge of his office in his top pocket – a pair of parrot-nosed shears – at once projected himself headlong beneath it. The Venetian was thereby brought close to annihilation but his ample buttocks receiving the fullest brunt had – let me not mince words – conserved the future. This deed we all considered worthy of a ballad such as Brendan O'Bryne might compose. The which he did and Tabby sang it. And surely its chorus was prophetic:

All hail the arse that saved the glass!
All hail the glass that shall prove the past!

There now commenced for me the most prodigious labour of my life. A labour beyond even the making of the glass that had so exercised Stella's wit and my pocket. The careless world had departed rejoicing at the machine's delivery but now the adept was duty-bound to suffer yet further for his art. In solitude and silence. Truly the way of knowledge is long and winding and the life of the philosopher all too short and far too straight. We chemists are but as arrows shot by another hand; our flight so swift, the gold so easily missed.

That said I determined to proceed exactly as I had said I would, and should, to Master Bol. To date, thanks to much shift, expedience and downright compulsion of others the work was upon time. Now what remained was no man's concern but mine. I alone (now I had lost Percy to bigotry) must answer for what might follow. I alone would charge the triple glass with its three waters, set the stove at heat and watch its condensations and distillations night and day.

My first necessity (so the heavens might smile upon the work) was to have distilled the several earths by Ascension Day. For this proceeding I had just seven weeks and four days. That achieved I would then have five further weeks in which to determine the elemental properties of these deposits so that by Midsummer Day at noon, when Great Sol would be at his highest and mightiest, I would be empowered spiritually, physically, and philosophically, to announce to myself, to Mr Newton, and to any in the world who chose to listen, the true and exact composition of creation. To say: The universal matter is in the way of being nothing less than this plus that plus those and these, mixed with a modicum of the other. What was hidden is at last discovered by the light of modern scientifical investigation. We philosophers now comprehend as much as the Prime Mover ever did. And let it be understood that as of twelve o'clock of the 21st of June that what has hitherto been called the philosophical gold is naught but this – Man's absolute apprehension of God's own receipt or recipe for the making of all things.

That was my dream. But there now remained the business of making it come true. And so I set to work.

First I inducted the three essential waters into the three vessels which were as one and yet were not. And whereas before (with the model of this glass) the quantities had been but small now they were more copious: *videlicet* three gallons of seawater, two of rainwater and one of morning dew. And here I would advise you that the gathering of even a pint of dew is no mean labour while the soaking up and wringing out of sufficient cloths (as heretofore described) to get eight pints to make up a gallon is a task fit only for self-chastising saints, lunatics, or adepts wedded to their work. However I had foreseen the necessity of having these waters ready long before the glass was finished and so, as soon as the snows were departed, had spread my cloths upon the grass of Rusty's race track in the Boweries. My hope was that since no meeting had been held there since October the dew would be quite free from human or animal extracts. In other words as much of itself and nothing else as it was possible to be. As were my other waters.

Ergo what I had to distil in Mr Newton's glass was the purest the New World could supply. And herein lay my chiefest hope: that this very newness would of itself provide that native innocency (quite lost to the Old World) which, once distilled, might bequeath (thanks also to the airy spirits that ever play about Manna Hatta) the essential earths that I, quite as earnestly as Mr Boyle and Mr Newton, sought. Nay, I believe I was even more in earnest than my mentor since I had here realised that which he had only projected and believed impossible. To wit this glass that now stood before me, charged with its waters.

As I lit the stove for the first time I offered a prayer to every god I knew (and some I didn't) begging them to aid me in this experiment which I dared hope was as fundamental as Jehovah's making of Adam out of clay. After all, given that we might be mere mud-piemen given breath by God's own puff it surely behoved us to discover the nature of the earth He had formed us from? I rather doubt my prayers were heard. Or rather if they were then Jehovah disagreed. But at that time, of course, I had no means of knowing anything except that road I had set myself upon.

The first weeks of distillation were as unremarkable as they were necessary. All that was required of me was an unceasing watchfulness. I was a mere sentry upon the walls of science. My duty was simply to stay awake, observe and resolve anything untoward. Nothing was. The great glass, misted within, kept at a constant warmth beneath, behaved as benignly as any ordinary retort. I had no fear now of the glass cracking. Master Stella (who would call upon me from time to time) had long since shown me in several trials just how resilient this new lead-based metal of his could be and at no time did my experiment require a heat close to the point of any danger.

To him I had, of course, explained the purpose of the work and he professed great interest in the outcome. He had not, however, got an equal knowledge of the history of the sacred art and this I endeavoured to make good when he had time to sit with me before the glass.

One day Stella said, 'And if this machine uncovers the secret of everything – what then?'

I said, somewhat wary of his question, 'Why, then we shall know it, shall we not?'

'I wonder,' was all his answer.

Wherewith I exclaimed in fury, 'Have faith, man! I've had faith save for one foolish lapse since I know not when so why shouldn't you?' For I must confess that when the art of chemistry is doubted I am upon a fuse so short I am like to explode almost instantly.

At my outburst he merely nodded and said no more.

By Mercury's day before our Lord's Ascension feast I had accumulated divers quantities of different earths deposited after evaporation within the receiving basins and also within the glass itself. Put all together and I had enough to fill a moderate bucket.

The stuff was powdery, flaky, dull. Mostly of a whitish hue but also yellow, brown and grey. I observed it with some disgust. Despite all my knowledge and experience I had, like an eager beginner, expected a substance more impressive than this. Could this ashy residue be the universal matter? Surely a sediment whereof all nature was comprised would not appear to be little more than crushed and powdered egg-shells?

Seeing it and sifting it I became impatient to begin my analyses, my atomisations, my coctions and my decoctions which would lay bare all that these earths contained. But I obliged myself to wait until the day I had appointed for the commencement of this work. From noon of Ascension Day until noon of Midsummer Day the aspects of the heavens were particularly favourable not only to the work but to me. My star would be in the ascendant while Mars and Venus were conjunct in a most benign manner and Jupiter was at his most jovial. You might say, if you were Rusty, that the stars were laughing. And their forces (those sidereal forces which Mr Newton also considered essential to the great work) would all be bent upon me and my laboratory. And as I dare say you know – since who does not? – that in these enquiries the nature and character of the enquirer is as much in question as that which he seeks to discover.

The moment that first noon was struck I began. To say I proceeded with my heart in my mouth is merely to speak plain truth. Was not I, Enoch Powys, self-appointed Doctor of Philosophy, embarked upon a course the end of which not even my mentor, the Lucasian Professor at Cambridge, could foresee? Had I not become his universal agent? With these reflections all my pride was fled away. My spirits seemed condensed into a genuine humility. I was become a questing cypher, a mere chemical question mark, an airy nothingness. My animal qualities were all diminished, dormant, docile. I seemed to have no need of food, of drink, of love. I felt I was becoming as transparent as Master Stella's crystal glass. And yet I did not feel weak or faint. Quite the reverse. As the days grew longer yet, the nights shorter and the world without seemed one whole luminescence, my physical being and mental faculties grew ever stronger. And I said to myself, 'Why, this is the true, invisible star-bread. Philosophy is feeding me.'

♀

By the end of May Lucille was out to here and Tabby wasn't far behind. As for my girls, well, I saw less of them (the fallen ones, I mean) because they'd all been packed off home, the poor souls.

All of this progenitive display did, however, recall to me that fancy I had entertained at the Ambrose Ball and I spoke of it to Rusty.

He seized upon it with an almighty enthusiasm. 'Jeez, doll, you're a marvelosity! A laying-in house! Yeah! Like it's a logical extension to our laying-on houses here and on East Side. I'm forever getting moans and groans from my minxes – "Oh, general, I'm up the spout again, what shall I do? I can't afford the midwife etcetera" – yeah, we'll do it and make it free for the deserving pauperess, yeah. Nicely. Like this way, wiv this gift from me to the city – for that's what I'm calling New York now, Sal, in my campaign to be mayor. This burg ain't a piddling little town no more, oh, no, it's a city, right? Like under me we're on the up – that's the message. Growth, that's the idea. And what comes more growth-like than a loada happy mothers wiv their offspring. See ya!'

And away he sped. And the next thing I knew he'd bought a barn on Beaver Street and Brendan was converting it into a hospital that

296

would be open for deliveries come the 20th of June at the latest, because, as he confided to me, young Hercules the Second (the first having been the well-known demi-god) was due upon the 21st. And like the mayor's mistress had gotta be the first one in and 'Ercule (as she still kept on calling him) the first one out. Right?

I said, 'But that's the very day, the same day that Enoch says he expects to have found the answer to everything.'

Rusty looked blank. 'Yer what, love?'

'Oh, Rusty, I've told you so many times. Midsummer Day is the day Enoch completes the *magnum opus* with Mr Newton's triple glass.'

'You don't still believe in that old bollocks, do you, doll?'

Now here was a true question. Did I? Didn't I? Did Enoch? Did his blessed Mr Newton?

I had no way of telling about them, of course, but for myself all I could think or say was that I was in two minds about it.

Rusty wasn't. He was now adamant upon the matter. Alchemy was for suckers. 'Like even as a bamboozle it's peanuts, doll, compared wiv what we've got rolling now. Here, take a gander at these!'

And he thrust a bundle of printed handbills at me. There was a woodcut likeness of him labelled General Sir Rodney Mars and a text setting out ten good reasons why every householder in New York should vote for him as the next mayor.

Say I, 'Since when were you a knight, Rusty.'

'As of when I went to the printer's.'

'But you aren't!'

'Who's to know that? I'm telling everybody I got dubbed Sir Rodney by good King Charles *in absentia*. For services to the Crown.'

'What services?'

'Oh, don't cart on, Sal. Use yer head. Like mayhap one time I supplied his Navy wiv high-calibre cannon balls dirt cheap, didn't I? And then there was them doxies I used to deliver by the dozen to his backdoor every Friday night. And wasn't he forever coming to me for racing tips. "Rusty old lad," he'd say, "what's good for the three o'clock at Newmarket?" And I'd say – '

'Stop!' I cry. 'I've heard enough. I don't believe you though I dare say the pig-ignorant will. When's election day?'

'Three weeks tomorrer.'

'The 20th? Why, that's the very day our hospital opens.'

'Yeah. Like it all comes together, dunnit? Must be something in our stars, love,' says he with that rogue's grin of his and both hands up my skirts.

Say I, 'Oh, must you, Rusty?'

And of course he must. Therefore so must I. Heigh ho. Such are nature's laws, are they not?

♂

You oughter see this mayoral chain I've got on order. Wiv my new coat of arms on it. Enamel on silver gilt. The chain itself pure gold and heavy wiv it, natch. Not to mention me mace. Oh, yeah, I got this thumping great cudgel (solid steel this time) getting forged by Master Bol – a smith Enoch's recommended. I mean, as mayor, you gotta have a mace so everybody knows who's in charge, right? For my crest I've got two beavers *or* what are *rampant* on a field *argent*. Yer what, bookeress? What's a beaver *or* on a field *argent*? Well, darlin', in matters heraldical, *or* means gold and *argent* means silver, right? And *rampant*? Ask your old man, lady, next time he's feeling fruity. And my motto is what Julius Caesar said upon first landing in Britain wiv not a native to oppose him. He said: *veni, vidi, vici.* Meaning: I came, I saw, I conquered, right? As I have. Here. Sorta classic, really. I mean, old worlds, new worlds, they're always up for grabs, believe you me.

♀

When, upon that fateful midsummer morning, a letter came for Enoch I regret to say my attention was diverted by the sight of Abednego, flanked by two mountainous bodyguards, entering our bank next door.

Rusty was already gone to call upon Lucille at her laying-in before attending his investiture as New York's latest mayor. He had been elected the day before by what he called a landslide: *viz.* five hundred and eleven freeholders had voted for him as against sixty-three for Councillor Ambrose. The rest of the town, consisting of some four and a half-thousand property-less men, and every woman whatever her status, had no say in the matter at all. But, mayhap, they were lucky, for Rusty had already noted those who had not put their balls in the box for him: 'I got 'em pricked down for various unaccountable future misfortunes, doll, don't you worry,' he'd said many times over at our celebration of his victory.

Which Enoch had failed to attend, pleading the exigencies of his work. Indeed none of us had seen him for several weeks now so intent had he become upon his experiments. And I fear my inattentiveness that morning was caused as much by the after-effects of our rout the night before as this unexpected sight of Abednego.

The ship's boy announced that the letter was come from a merchantman just anchored in the river and the sender of it had paid his captain good money to see it safely delivered the moment landfall was made. And would I mark his chit, please, to say it was received?

I heard these words but I regret to say the viewing of Abednego, a-shimmer in green silks and as proudly gracious as any duchess, made me quite deaf to the boy's exhortations. I marked his chit, however, and took the letter, giving him a dollar for his trouble but then, before I could go down to the laboratory to deliver it to Enoch, I heard a most tumultuous commotion next door. Our bank was resounding with high-pitched expostulations of a most distempered sort.

Out shot Abednego, his hat askew and his mouth agape, crying: 'Oh, my jewels! My jewels! I've been robbed! They've lost my jewels! Fetch Mr Ambrose!' And all the while he clung to one of his bodyguards while the other made off towards the Ambrose residence in search of Abednego's so-called spouse. Passers-by and bank clients gathered about the frantic boy, tut-tutting and shaking their heads at this public announcement of our business's negligence and dereliction of duty. What was a bank if not secure? A safe deposit if not safe? How could General Mars allow such a thing? And he just elected mayor to boot?

Three of our clerks appeared, seeking in vain to persuade Abednego back inside while the search for the missing jewels continued. But another came to me, clearly much exercised in his mind, for he was sweating profusely, to advise me – confidentially, madam – that other valuables were also missing from the vault. It was not a matter of Mrs Ambrose's jewel case only but also of several chests of gold and silver and if this news got out there could be a panic, a crisis of confidence among our clients, a general demand to withdraw funds, in a word – a run on the bank! And therefore it was imperative the President be found so he might make a statement to calm the public's disquiet. Not a moment should be lost.

I directed him to the council chamber where Rusty was even then being sworn in as mayor. But as I did so my heart sank. Or rather it was already sunk. For upon hearing Abednego declare his loss, I had apprehended at once that these missing jewels must be those I had refused to accept from Percy. And which I had implored Enoch to return to their proper place. Evidently he hadn't. His promise was broken. What could I do?

I determined to go down that instant to him but as before I was prevented. And again by Abednego. His hysterics were mounting to a crescendo. The boy was pure noise. Someone had need to restrain him. And that someone was me. I dashed to him as he screamed that he would die, that his pearls alone were worth a Queen's ransom, that his great diamond was a gift of the Nabob of Nabobs and he must have redress from such bold cheaters as General Sir Rodney Mars and his harlot, Madam Venus.

At this I smacked his face. 'Cease your outcry, madam,' said I. 'Or I shall proclaim you to all the world for what you really are!' Such was Abednego's surprise he did as he was bid while his guard had so much of him to support he could not repulse me. I continued, 'Your panic is unfounded, your insults slanderous, your comport ridiculous. Nor is this the place to treat of this matter. Come into the bank again, madam, or you and Mr Ambrose will be a laughing-stock. I shall expose you both as common-law mollymen.' And to the guard I said, 'Bring her in. If there's anything worse than female hysterics it's a male travesty of them.'

I had won. Abednego was struck dumb and his guard, grinning now from ear to cauliflower ear, was only too pleased to obey my every word. But at this very moment who should appear but Councillor Ambrose himself, waving his stick and fulminating like a turkey cock done out of his dinner.

He was accompanied by several of his cronies, all smelling blood and variously shouting, 'Send for General Mars! Where's our money? This is daylight robbery!'

At once the idle rabble (at the back of them I noted Percy Praise-the-Lord and The-End-is-Nigh setting up their tub) echoed these expostulations and some started to throw stones at our windows yelling, 'Robbers, whores, cheaters' or whatever other expletive helped them hurl the harder.

Fearing this agitation Ambrose hurried Abednego into the shelter of the bank together with his posse of familiars. So at least his arrival brought about what I had sought to do, even if it also ignited this more than incipient riot.

I dashed down to Enoch. His door was barred. I banged upon it, shouting, 'Open, you fool, open!'

When at length he did he was smiling like a soul above who has just received beatification from below.

He said, transported, 'Sally, oh, Sally, I've this minute laid bare the universal secret. The covert centre of creation. That mystery which has eluded philosophers since time began. Oh, Mrs Sally, you above all must be the first to know it. The secret of the world is – '

Forgive me but yes. Yes, I cut him short. Such was my fluster I refused this piece of unusual intelligence.

I said, 'Enoch, you liar! You didn't give back those jewels, did you? So now they're stoning the bank! We're ruined! And it's all your fault! Listen!'

But he didn't. Instead he asked what it was I held in my hand? And to tell true so tightly was it clutched I had quite forgotten that letter just arrived.

Said I, 'Oh, this has come for you. From England. But so have I come, Enoch Powys! From here. Where are those jewels? We must deliver them up this minute!'

But Enoch paid no heed at all. 'A letter from England?' said he. 'Give it me at once.' And he snatched the missive from me. 'That hand! I know it! It's my master's.'

'Will you listen?' I cried. 'Where are the jewels?'

'What jewels?'

By this I was weeping in my fury. 'Your catamite's jewels! Abednego's! He wants them back. In his character as Mrs Septimus Ambrose!'

But already Enoch had broken the seal and was unfolding the letter as if it were holy writ. Nothing I said was worth his hearing. I turned away to search for them myself and saw at once the chest that had contained them standing empty save for that awful rattlesnake of his. It appeared to be devouring its own tail.

Lost for voice I whispered, 'Oh, Enoch, what have you done?'

This he heard for he replied, 'Much, it seems. For Mr Newton says – '

But as with his chemical secret I did not stay for explication because the hubbub above was now tremendous.

Then I heard Rusty's mighty roar bawling, 'Hold on, ladies and gents, gents and ladies, hold on. Your mayor is here – have no fear.' And there was some foolish laughter and the noise abated.

♂

Yeah, I soon had that mob eating outta my hand. Call it natural authority, the common touch, what you will, there was me mounted on the stoop in my new regalia, mace in hand, and catching the odd half-brick wiv the other. The which I would kiss in jest and toss gently back. That sorta thing ever gets a laugh, dunnit? And calms the jerkers down.

Whereupon I issue a public statement along the lines of: 'Good folk all, take it easy. General Mars has everything in hand. Together we shall go forward in mutual trust towards a prosperous future. The bank is sound, its practices above suspicion, its financial probity wivout parallel. Like it's mine, right? And you know me, I'm the Cockney general you just gotta trust.' Another laugh. I continue wiv the spiel. 'United we stand, right? Divided we fall.' Wise groans of agreement. 'All New Yorkers are equal in the eyes of the Law. A commission of enquiry will be appointed headed by yours truly,' etcetera – blah-blah – rest assured, no avenue unexplored, findings published, grand jury, scapegoats punished, business as usual – you name it I soft-soaped it.

Well, wiv that bollocks unloaded all was calm, especially as, even while I spoke, Mick the Mick and Aguma M'Kubwa together wiv me other lads was subtly taking out the leading troublemakers. My boys have got these little black leather truncheons now. To see one of them laid behind a fella's ear – well, it's like mystical. His noise ceases just like that and he's gone. I don't deal in rough justice no more. No, all is smooth. Kinda civic, now I'm mayor.

Public order restored I make my way into the bank. There to sort out the real trouble. And what do I find? That jackass Ambrose and his muckers wiv Abednego fainted dead away across one of the counting tables and Sally making faces at me as of one wiv intelligence to report. What gives?

Well, Septimus Ambrose for a start. He comes at me at once. Backed up by his mates. So, like wiv the crowd outside, I tell 'em to simmer down but this lot ain't so amenable. They're smelling revenge for Ambrose's election defeat and want trouble. Loadsa trouble heaped on me – the victor. Jeez, to hear 'em! Whatta cacophony.

But I ride it and order the bank to be shut up. Yeah. That minute. Wiv the lot of us all inside. Off dash the clerks to obey my edict and now I invite Ambrose and Co. into my managerial closet, there to confer, I say, like gentlemen. In we go – only once they're all inside, wiv me still outside, I turn the key in the lock, don't I? Nicely. They can stew in there for a bit while I confer wiv Sal.

To say her news confounded me would be to put it mildly. It left me steaming.

Whatta tale of cross and double cross! Me hearing how she'd helped Enoch to help himself to our clients' valuables and all to pay for his stupid triple glass when them same valuables was in the vaults for my use, not his. The conniving conniver! Selling off them jewels, too! That's what he'd been at, she said, down by the Gent's Canal. So we'd got nothing to shut Abednego's gob wiv. So like his accusation stood! And Ambrose and Co. had got us on the hip. No! By the short and curlies. I was seeing red. There was stars all about my head. Me heart was hammering like a hammer. I was lost for similitudes. Me mace was swinging in me hand. Like it wanted action. Like I wanted action. Like I'd give that Welsh wizard a right drubbing.

Say I, 'This is it, doll. This is the last time he fools me.'

And, thrusting Sal aside, through I go, next door, and down to his laboratory of the sacred art. Spitting blood and fire. Like here I come – the complete warman.

♀

For an instant I was stunned though scarcely surprised by Rusty's outrage but then I collected my wits and followed him. My anger at Enoch was as nothing when weighed against Rusty's. What would my one lover do to the other?

I discovered them locked in a furious tussle with Rusty using all his weight and Enoch all his dexterity.

Rusty was emitting various predictable insults of an unforgivable kind while Enoch cried, 'Wait, Rusty, wait! We have discovered the secret of the world!'

'Bugger that!' responded Rusty, stepping back to take a swing with his mace at Enoch. And I swear the steel it was made of glowed red hot.

'Stop,' I shouted.

But neither noticed me. Rusty swung, Enoch ducked, Rusty missed his mark, staggered, recovered his balance and roared, 'Stay still, you thieving cunny!' And he raised his mace again.

'Mind the glass!' I said. And thus our fate was sealed.

'The glass,' said he. 'Yeah, the glass! That's the nub of it. The cause of all our trouble. And all your double-dealing. Jeez! The pair of you in league against me! And for what? For this loada scientifical garniture! Right! It's gotta go. Go, go, go!'

And he leapt upon the bench to stand before the mighty triple glass.

'No,' shouted Enoch, 'Mr Newton says in his letter – '

But it was too late. Again I was destined not to hear what the great philosopher had said. Nor was Rusty. His mace was twirling all about, white hot now. While he himself glowed red as fire. And Enoch, gazing up at him, was as sweating silver. And I, reflected in the glass's belly, appeared as burnished copper and even as we stood there, transfixed, transmuted, Rusty struck the glass. Whereat –

$$☿$$

Great Jupiter!

$$♀$$

Dear heaven above!

$$♂$$

Whaddya know! Jeez! What fucking gives? Oh Shit!

$$☿$$

How prescient of Mr Newton –

$$♀$$

Help!

$$☿$$

– had he not written most earnestly to advise me against any sudden introduction of iron into the work? He feared the conjunction of elements would prove too volatile. Particularly if I had succeeded by Midsummer Day of all days in abstracting that substance his recent speculations had advised him must be present within the universal earth. That previously unknown quantity which I had designated by an X might in my present experiments be proved in violent, elemental fact rather than in tranquil, scientifical inspiration. That very thing I had that day uncovered and which, for want of a better term to describe so new an entity, I shall nominate 'the philosophic saltpetre' or 'royal and sacerdotal gunpowder'.

The forces present within his triple glass (Mr Newton said) would make those malignant barrels, placed under Parliament by Guy Fawkes and his ill-contented friends, seem mere squibs.

But my dear and absent master had, in his sensible concern, presupposed some mere laboratory mishap, not this deliberate violation of everything he and I respected. This almighty assault wherein all the powers of Heaven and Earth, Past and Present, High and Low were equally situate.

After all, Mr Newton had no knowledge of Rusty's essential nature, nor of Sally's, nor of mine, come to that. Or rather come to this: this supreme and fated instant.

Consequently the result was more remarkable than anyone – even one as ingenious as he – could have readily supposed.

As Rusty's mace struck the glass, Time itself drew breath. Then the triple vessel was shattered all about into a myriad translucent scimitars and glinting daggers which seemed at once to rush in upon themselves as if Mr Newton's great machine was, in this enforced destruction, bent upon piercing its own invisible heart. These deadly splinters were become a vortex that would engulf itself.

And the noise! As of a host of tintinnabulant acerbities hurled into a metal drum. Such a savage crashing. So brittle, so shrill, so sharp as to set even a healthy tooth on edge and to make every hair start from its root. But now behind these superficial excruciations there was to be heard a deep resonance, a mighty grumbling bass note, a reverberative roar as of many lions impatient for their prey.

As we gazed, the three of us, quite dumbstruck, there grew at the very depths of that churning vortex a light so fierce we were obliged to shield our eyes. But even through our fingers it burned green and seemed to gather itself into a living, spinning ball as big, nay bigger than the glass that had given it birth. And now as it expanded ever more hugely it turned red and from that – though by now we were all forced back against the walls of the laboratory by its ever-evolving vastness – now it was become gold. Gold as the Sun. Whereupon it burst with a force beyond all measurement.

♂

Like I was blasted to kingdom come, squire. I lost the lot. Every sinew, merry organ, muscle. I mean I was stripped to the bone. Talk about going the way of all flesh, I can tell you which way mine went. Upwards. Yeah, all my parts save my bones what fell, quite unhinged, lacking any thew or tendon, down in a sorta shower, clatter, click, clunk, into my latest garbage pit on West Side. Like I saw them go through my eyeballs that was now quite out of their sockets and rolled up altogether wiv my other corporeals into this frigging great fleshly ball shooting heavenwards. And my grey matter – also out of its usual abode – was busy informing me (Jeez, that part of you never packs up, does it?) that I was in the process of becoming what Enoch the Adept had always said I was really: the planet Mars, no less. And I reckoned this could well be so because I seemed to be mounting ever higher and there was all these other spheres above me rotating against the eternal empyrean. And was it getting cold. Brrrgh!

$$\venus$$

To find yourself ablaze and yet feel nothing must I suppose be a dispensation granted to few persons, and I dare say I ought to feel grateful. But, oh, dear, I don't. Here's me, Madam Venus, burned to a frazzle. What's a heavenly whore with her heart of gold without her pretty parts? Oh, Rusty, what have you done?

$$\mercury$$

Has a vapour vision? Answer: Yes, I had. For at that moment when we were all exploded I knew myself to be dispersed into a mere airy exhalation and yet, conveniently, I could still observe the effects of this almighty occurrence. And from a position of considerable advantage as I, along with Sally and Rusty, flew ever upwards, my soul, or my sensibility, or whatever you choose to call this sense of apprehension that is quite outside our bodily bounds, had a bird's eye view.

What I saw were the houses known as Numbers 13, 14 and 15 Pearl Street, our tripartite emporium of flesh, money and philosophy, together with all those curious New Yorkers who had gathered to observe the collapse of the Bank of the Golden Fleece, I saw all these burst heavenwards as out of that hellmouth which had been my laboratory. Up they all flew beside me: bricks, lintels, floorboards, joists in flame, bedsteads, gaming tables, gamesters, mirrors, virginals (both human and material), cooking pots, coffers full of cash, account books, ledgers, money-scales, a blazing leg of pork, Rusty as a sort of meat ball violently gyrating, Percy on his tub still denouncing our house of iniquity, Brother The-End-is-Nigh streaking like an arrow towards the Pearly Gates shouting, 'What did I tell you? Don't say I didn't warn you! Repent! For now the end is no longer nigh but here! Repent!'

And Sally, oh, my Sally, blazing like the evening star and beside her Abednego tumbling over and over with his pretty bottom twinkling out of his silk skirts (but I digress) while all about them came the roof tiles, nay the very chimney pots. But oh, alas, here's Tabby too, dashed into immortality before her time, or her baby's, but holding to her hand is Brendan (such Celtic devotion) and would you believe it, he's singing the ballad of it already? But I can't hear the words for this terrible caterwauling. Who's this? This giant new-born babe screaming fit to burst. Why, it must be Hercules the Second bouncing up to find his father. What a lusty lad. And he's pissing as he goes. Pissing pure gold.

What is that, you ask? Gold? We thought this was a mere accident? Don't tell us you made gold?

♂

She-aye-it. What's yours truly done? Like I thought I'd seen it all. But no, sir. No, siree. No, like this is getting like a warm-up for the Day of Judgement like. And all because I took a merry swing (in justifiable anger, mark you) at Enoch's precious glass. What an outcome. I mean, this feat of martiality has turned the town upside down. Who'd have thought the very first thing I'd do as Mayor of New York would be to blow the place up? Well, I tell yer I wouldn't have reckoned it. Not me. No. Most untoward.

There's Sal, gone up like a torch. And do I feel bad. And here's Enoch. But hold on, what's he up to? Oh, yeah. Clever. Crafty. Trust him. The bugger's evaporating. Doing the full disappearing act. Like he's fading into nothing. Typical. Always said he was a loada hot air. Gone. It's *adios* to the Welsh wizard.

No sign of Lucille. But this has gotta be our boy. Like he's meaty wiv it and just like his dad – look at them cods! Wait for me, Hercules. Jeez, youth! So eager to get somewhere.

♀

The spheres are singing. And so am I. I'm Venus again. But my earthly parts have been taken to the hospital called Jerusalem. The nurses are swaddling me in softest gauze, they're saying I shall live. I rather wish I wouldn't.

☿

Without doubt it was young Hercules who started it. His innocent piddlings were but part of an action that his father, with an almost equal simplicity, had instigated.

For now as I looked down upon the volcano that had been my laboratory and, even as the debris of that explosion hurtled all about me, so various twinkling droplets from new-born Hercules the Second touched these flying objects. And they, by this coincidence, were turned at once to purest gold. There, in full midsummer daylight, all was changed. All things, whether they were animal, vegetable or mineral; whether chimney pot or chamberpot; Tabby or Brendan; warming pan or frying pan; councillor or fish-wife; carthorse or seagull; Percy become Brother Praise-the-Lord or Brother The-End-is-Nigh; dancing girl or Abednego; cat or dog; corncob or cranberry; brick or lintel. All were transmuted.

And with this elemental change their upward course was checked. At this sudden zenith of their trajectory they tumbled over, were quite topsy-turvy, and began to fall earthwards as precipitately as they had just sped forcibly heavenwards.

But now these objects falling struck those still rising and by their percussions created yet more gold. Yellow metal was now begot by mere collision. Furthermore at these abrupt convergences such sparks were made that the heavens were filled with a million minor stars that shot all about. And as they flew so madly this way, that way, so they cooled, congealed and solidified into the various shapes of gleaming coins or fiery medallions. Thanks to the royal and sacred art the firmament was become Great Sol's royal and majestical mint. The very air was stamping out his golden coin. And each piece was marked upon the obverse with his sign of a point within a circle, and upon the reverse with the figure of the pelican sacred to Hermes. Or if you prefer – me.

How they spun! How they twirled and tossed before they also began to fall in streaming torrents and rushing cataracts as they leapt and vaulted over all else that was still erupting upwards.

And above this glittering commotion what should I see against the everlasting blue but Mr Newton's triple glass miraculously reformed? There it glistened like an almighty bubble just as Percy in his early foolishness had predicted. And within the inmost vessel I thought I discerned the pretty forms of two perfect lovers conjoined but before I could tell who they might be the glass had floated higher yet and was dissolving even as it ascended.

Let me now speak plain. That bubble may well have been a phantasm of my fancy but the effect of our combustion was not. No. The gold thereby created was pure gold, true gold, not that alchemical consolation prize – philosophers' gold. No, this was the triumphant materialisation of every adept's dream since time began. Here was Mr Newton's victory. And mine. And Sally's. And Rusty's. We had, as the vulgar say, made it. Here was the sun as it were solidified, turned into most precious metal, and broken into bits within the airy compass of the world. Here, created by us, out of everything and nothing, was 24-carat gold in quantities far beyond immediate measure.

For now out of the dazzling starbursts of all those new-struck coins and medallions I could see great bars of bullion a yard long emerging to tumble and turn together with – what were these? Why, spinning globes the size of almighty pumpkins! And these? Rough nuggets as huge and as horned as monsters from the deep. And all of this, our creation, was hurtling down in a furious deluge upon Manna Hatta, impelled by those omnipotent gravitical forces that Mr Newton, by his genius, has also identified.

And thus was the town most ambiguously blessed. Since here was more wealth than its citizens had ever dreamed of and yet even in its delivery it struck down the unwary, demolished the Court House, choked the streets, immolated the market, sank three merchantmen at anchor, and even destroyed the roof of St Nicholas's church whilst simultaneously supplying the means to repair the damage umpteen times over.

But these inconveniences admitted it may be said at last, after countless centuries of enquiry, that science, faith, accident, concupiscence and deceit have all conspired to complete the great work.

Now, however, the happy misfortune of New York is too far below me to be observed further in any detail. The New World and the Old have become mere component parts of that pretty ball called earth while I am restored to my eternal orbit about the sun. Ah, there goes Rusty, too. How he glowers. And here's Sally. How brightly she shines.

♀

Take care, Enoch. You too, Rusty.

♂

See ya, doll. Watch it, professor.

☿

Farewell, all.

☉